DEEP BENEATH US

DEEP BENEATH US

Catriona McPherson

SEVERN
HOUSE

First world edition published in Great Britain and the USA in 2024
by Severn House, an imprint of Canongate Books Ltd,
14 High Street, Edinburgh EH1 1TE.

severnhouse.com

British Library Cataloguing-in-Publication Data
A CIP catalogue record for this title is available from the British Library.

ISBN-13: 978-1-4483-1207-8 (cased)
ISBN-13: 978-1-4483-1208-5 (e-book)

All Severn House titles are printed on acid-free paper.

Typeset by Palimpsest Book Production Ltd.,
Falkirk, Stirlingshire, Scotland.
Printed and bound in Great Britain by
TJ Books, Padstow, Cornwall.

Praise for Catriona McPherson

About the author

Born and raised in West Lothian, **Catriona McPherson** left Edinburgh University with a PhD in Linguistics and worked in academia, as well as banking and public libraries, before taking up full-time writing in 2001. For the last fourteen years she has lived in Northern California with frequent visits home. Among numerous prizes, she has won two of Left Coast Crime's coveted Humorous Lefty Awards for the Last Ditch comedies.

www.catrionamcpherson.com

This is for my sister, Audrey Ford, with love.
I could never have been a real nurse in
a real psychiatric hospital (curtsey)
but I hope I've imagined it okay.
I know you'll tell me.

PART ONE

October 2015

ONE

Tabitha

It's been twenty years, half my lifetime, since I sat here and looked up at you, Mr Moon. Since I looked at you and searched for the others, for Mrs Moon, Baby Moon and Moondog. Twenty years since I sat here and wondered if you're a bully. Is that why I can't ever see the rest of them? Is your wife scared of you? Is your baby alone and crying, round on the dark side? Is Moondog chained up and whimpering, a rim of white around his eyes and jitters under his skin?

The moon stares back at me, thick titanium white in the sky and brittle zinc white where it's thrown itself into the water.

The water.

It's been a while since I sat here and looked down at you, Miss Mirror. Looked into you and beyond you and searched for him. Wondered if one day he'll come back, rising and breaking the surface to grin at me. If I'll see weeds and water leaking out at the hinge of a bony jaw, while the long teeth stay clamped together. Is he there? Can he hear me?

The reservoir flirts back at me, a stiff wind whipping it into ivory-black hollows and viridian tips. (I need to stop thinking paint colours.) *Black* hollows and *green* tips.

I keep trying.

I send my thoughts back into the past, out into the air. It's bound to happen if I stop preventing it. I'm too ill to keep my job. I'm too ill to raise my son. So surely I must still be too ill to come back here to live and not get ill again. Bring it on. I'd howl if it would help. Rend my garments. Smear shit. Eat stones.

Only, *this* time, I won't let it go. I'll pack my bag and choose a bed. I'll make my pictures, with the flat thick brush and the flat thick paint: red and yellow, black and blue. When they're dry, I'll discuss them in Group. I'll nod at what the others say. I'll exercise like the physio tells me, munch salad for the dietician, sip my pills from a plastic cup – morning, noon and night – then open wide to let them check I've swallowed.

But I won't get better. I won't give it all up and fight my way back like a good girl. Not again.

I wasted it last time. Of course, it didn't strike me that way while I was doing it. For a start, I was only fifteen and those six months on the ward was the first time I'd been away from home. So it was a lot to deal with. And then I had no reason to doubt the diagnosis: the doctors said I was schizophrenic and I didn't argue. All the signs were there. Auditory hallucinations, visual hallucinations, disorganized thoughts shared in disorganized words. And, whether you think it's genes or the other stuff, there was family history too.

Trouble is, when they told me what pills to swallow, what thoughts to dodge, how to become 'better organized' – like I was a walk-in wardrobe on a make-over show – and I did it . . . it worked. And that pissed them off more than shrieking insanities at them. Because me getting better meant they had to go back over my file with the old Tippex and change 'schizophrenia' to 'spontaneous psychotic break of unknown cause'.

Bad news for the docs. Embarrassing. But, until very recently, I always thought it was good news for me. Not that the hospital was terrible, once I settled in. Me and Elspeth – this other girl on the same ward, pretty much my best friend – made the most of it: invented a psychotic break dance, made up a company that did psychotic mini-breaks, that kind of thing. It was a lark. Sort of. With a few pills to take the edge off anyway. Which means it wouldn't have been the end of the world if I'd *never* got better. Never come back from the ward, never grown up, got married, had Albie. Turns out, if only I could have stayed off my head, I would have been fine. And, like I say, I won't make the same mistake again.

I need to be clear here. This isn't because Scott divorced me. I'm not that pathetic. I'm not some Brontë cliché falling apart for a lost love. I mean, it was rough. We'd been married fifteen years, happy enough in a nice house in an okay town, with a healthy son that we brought up here to visit his granny a normal amount. But then he met 'Cassie' and left. Which is exactly what happened. No 'let's take a break' or 'let's talk it over'; just so long and don't let the door hit you.

But I was fine, like I'm saying. I did my sums and reckoned I could buy him out of the house, keep things more stable for Albie. That's when Scott really turned. I was perplexed, to begin with, until I thought that maybe Cassie fancied the house as much as she fancied him. (To be fair, I'd done a lot of work on that house and pretty much left *him* to his polo shirts.)

Then came the masterstroke: Scott's anonymous tip-off to my work about my mental-health record. Oh the irony, with me a JEDI compliance trainer and all. Justice, equity, diversity and inclusion have their limits apparently.

That's not fair. It wouldn't have touched me, except I had never disclosed it. Which put me in breach of everything I'd ever run a workshop on. And the real genius was that Scott didn't tell them about any 'psychotic break of unknown cause'. Far from it. He sent them a copy of a doctor's letter from when I had the schizophrenia diagnosis. I had kept it, like an idiot. And I hadn't hidden it from my husband, like a bigger one. I got an interview with a pair of very nervous HR who'd come all the way from Hong Kong and the more I said, the worse it got. So they sacked me.

No matter what they called it, and no matter what was in the slap-in-face gift basket they gave me on my last day, they sacked me. And me hanging out of my office window, squirting the gift-basket lotions all down the outside of the building from the executive floor didn't help. It costs a bloody fortune to get those high windows cleaned. It would have been cheaper to have me hosed off the car park like they all thought they were going to have to, for a minute there.

My God, their faces! Elspeth would have cackled like a hen with a crack pipe. But, satisfying as it was in the moment, it pretty much put paid to me getting to keep my corporate mortgage and so, once I lost my job, I couldn't afford the house. And once I lost the house (and Scott told the court that I'd lost my job because of undisclosed mental health problems), that's when the custody mediator got involved.

They're not so rotten that they took him off me. They did something much worse. They left it up to Albie to decide between his house and his school and his pals and his dad on the one hand, or his mum on the other. And he—

This is where I get off. This is why I would never have clawed my way back the first time if I'd known what was waiting for me. He doesn't. He chose. I'm not. Like last time. When I. When he. When they. When all of. But I. It was.

I learned that trick on the ward. You stop the disordered words before they come out and that stops your disordered thoughts from taking root and getting strong. 'Not being funny,' Elspeth used to say, 'but it does make you sound like a total nutter. I mean: it does. You sound. Nut job. See? I can do it too.'

People say pain is like a knife. Not usually people who know what a knife feels like, mind you. The Albie pain is more of an ache, as if I've been flash frozen from my neck to my knees and yet I've still got to move around, banging off hard edges and bruising deep inside, bleeding from freezer burn. I don't actually know what *that* feels like. Those were hallucinations, so they tell me. The pain isn't a hallucination. This pain is real. This pain, I think, as I breathe it in. This pain, I say to myself as I breathe it out again and yet only feel it settle deeper into me.

Something is moving at the edge of my vision and I turn to it like a lover. But it's not a hallucination starting up in the nick of time. It's just a guy on the far side of the loch, out bat-watching or badger-watching; star-gazing, I might have said if the moon wasn't too bright to make it worthwhile. Maybe he's hunting rabbits. If I was in the town I'd worry that he was hunting women, but you'd have to be daft to trudge all the way up here to assault someone. Anyway, there's lights on in Davey's house and it's closer to me than the badger-botherer. Besides, he's not interested in me. He has *seen* me. I clock the flat glint of his glasses as the moonlight bounces off them. He stands there a minute, looking over in my direction, maybe wondering if *I'm* real, but then he puts his head back down and carries on his way, leaving me alone.

I think I'm alone anyway. I glance back at the car I noticed when I came out. It's parked at the water's edge, facing back up the hill towards Davey's house. That's strange, it occurs to me. Who would come to a moonlit loch and turn the car to point the other way? Or maybe it's been here since before it was dark. But then who would come to a *sunlit* loch . . . Or maybe it's been there for days, abandoned after a joyride. Maybe it's got a 'police aware' sticker on it, waiting for the tow guys to come and take it away. Except, now I take a closer look, I could almost believe there's someone sitting in the driver's seat. Am I imagining that the shadow on the one side is bulkier than the shadow on the other? Probably. It's more likely the headrest set at a different height for a tall driver and a short passenger. Like ours used to be for Scott and me.

I'm starting to think this is a bust. If I can't make a creepy guy with flashing glasses into a demon, if I can't make an abandoned car with a lump on one side into a nightmare, maybe I'm wasting my time. I haven't tried thinking about the paintings yet. I might have to.

And that's all it takes. I feel it starting. There's a rumble under the surface, sloshing the calm water up the side of the dam and breaking into the air with a spit of rock and a spray of foam. He must be bigger than he looks in the paintings. He must be enormous! And he's rising. He will clamber out and take me in his jaws, shaking me witless, dropping me limp and sodden back on the ward. As the ripples spread and the echo fades, I sit waiting. The car starts – that lump *was* a driver! – but it's going away, nothing to do with me. In the far distance, I see two tiny spots of light, as that bat-watcher guy turns my way again, briefly. I refuse to consider him. I let him fade like the sound of the car and the lights in Davey's windows, like the cold air in my face and the hard bench under my bum. I push it all away like a croupier shoving chips at the winner. I'm done with reality. I sit back and wait for my mind to wrap me up in a hug of madness, like the thick layer of fat on a Channel swimmer. It won't be long now.

TWO

Gordo

He's come to Kirkconnel Police Station because it's the closest. That, and a bit because he's thinking it's probably shut right now, what with reduced hours and centralization. If it *is* shut, he's been telling himself all the way down, he'll have made an effort. Tick the box and move on.

Absolutely!

All the way down.

It was dark when he started, up there on the open moor, with that thin wind blowing over the tops, guttering his trouser legs against him and whipping a rich stink up out of the hollows where it belonged, sending it scudding over the hills. It smelled like bad food, like coming home from school to cabbage boiling. Really, it was nothing more than dying bracken, rotting mushrooms and sheep shit, but so thick he was nearly sick with it. As if he'd drunk the brew.

He's not scared of the dark, even when it tricks him like it tricked him tonight. Still, when an owl took off from the wigwam top of a stile, close enough that he felt the beat of its wings, there was a leap in his chest and a tingle down his arms as the fright worked through him. He stood staring at where it had gone, then ducked as it wheeled back over him and cut the moonlight. He tried to laugh at himself, but his voice was too loud and too wavery.

It wasn't funny! It was scary!

He stumbled his way first on to the footpath, rough with stones where the beasts had kicked them loose, next the track, pocked and rutted with puddles he could barely see once the moon started setting, then the farm road as the hills darkened and the sky paled, then at dawn the real road and the footbridge over the railway, diesel fumes soaked into the gritty boards, and at last in cold grey daylight he finds himself on the pavement, in the town.

And hell if Kirkconnel manned hours aren't nine till twelve Tuesday and Thursday plus every other Friday afternoon. He can't believe it's still going at all. Not much else is. Pub, of course, and a chippy for after, a chemist kept open for the daily 'done, a hairdresser kept open by the grannies, a brave wee tearoom he hopes someone's using or it won't be here long.

Dougie Downer!

He smiles. He loves hearing her voice, even if it's only in his head. Even if she's taking the piss.

As the chemist, or a woman in a white coat anyway, removes the window grilles and sets out a standy-up sign for cholesterol checks, he lets himself in at a wooden door with an arched stone surround. It's still got a bracket above it for the blue lamp. That mad old bat has probably done a jigsaw of a station like this one used to be. He can see it plain as day: a bobby in shirtsleeves and braces digging spuds in his garden, his helmet hooked over a barrow handle with a wee bird perched on top, baby kicking its legs in a pram, wifie hanging out a line of whites, pegs in her mouth.

What an imagination you've got!

He smiles again, because she's not wrong.

Back in the real world, the high counter and the painted panelling have survived from earlier days, but there's plexiglass above them now and posters about needle exchange, intimate partner violence, cyber safety. The officer leaning against the photocopier looks bored already at just gone nine. He's in his stab vest and shirtsleeves, sipping coffee through a slot in the lid of a cardboard cup.

'Morning,' Gordo says.

The copper gives him a slow, insolent look. Not the first time it's happened. Not the last time it will. Afterwards he'll try to think what he should have said, instead of what he *did* say, and he'll decide there was nothing wrong with it. It's not his fault it comes as a surprise.

'There's been an explosion. At the reservoir.'

Things go downhill fast from there.

'Name?' says the officer, phone in his hand. He's not local; his voice says Glasgow.

'Lyle,' he says. 'Gordon.'

'I've got a Mr Lyle here,' the officer says to someone on the other end.

'No, it's Lyle Gordon. Mr Gordon.'

It's an honest mistake but the copper flushes dark and turns away. 'A witness to the incident at Logan,' he's saying.

'Eh, excuse me?' Gordo says.

'Is someone on to SEPA already?' The copper's barking into the phone. 'Have they worked out if it's Scottish Water or SusDrain or who the hell . . .' Then he stops and his eyes go wide as he listens. He puts his coffee down. 'Seriously?' he says. 'This the first of anyone hearing? Me phoning you? Naeb'dy's been in at Lesmahagow?'

'Excuse me?' Gordo says again. The cop puts a finger in his free ear. 'It's not Logan.'

'God Almighty! Glengavel?' the copper says. Gordo can hear the person on the other end of the line. It sounds like a duck quacking.

'It's Hiskith,' Gordo says. 'Just up the back hill. Hiskith Water.'

He gets sent to sit in an interview room, while the officer cancels the cavalry and explains the mix-up. It takes long enough that his coffee's cold and even *that's* Gordo's fault.

You're too hard on yourself! 'Hiskith Watter's no' a reservoir,' the cop says as he sits down. 'Nae need for all the drama.'

'It is though,' says Gordo.

'Those hills are full of lead,' says the cop. 'Clue in the name.'

Gordo nods. The town of Leadhills is hardly a mile from Hiskith as the crow flies. 'It was never drinking water,' he says. 'It was used to power the mills. Dammed and flooded away back last cent—' He means the century before last and so he's glad to be interrupted.

'Aye, whatever,' says the copper. 'It's no' a reservoir now. It's a fu— It's a puddle in the hills. And you reckon something exploded?'

'I don't reckon,' Gordo says. 'I saw it and I heard it. It was under the water.'

'Eh?' says the copper. 'What's under that water that could explode all of a sudden?'

His voice is scornful but the look on his face doesn't match it. Gordo wonders if they're both thinking the same thing. What *is* under that water exactly? What was left there?

'And the thing is,' Gordo goes on, 'it was near the dam. It

sent up bits of rock. Someone'll need to go down and check the—'

'You saw all this in the dark?'

'It was a full moon,' Gordo says. 'Bright as day.'

'And what were you doing up there? In the full moon?' He doesn't smile but he doesn't need to. His voice does the smirking.

'Walking,' Gordo says.

'Walking to where?'

'No, not walking past,' Gordo says. 'Walking for the sake of it.' The copper frowns. Gordo briefly considers saying he was training for something. Out on manoeuvres. Wild camping. Geocaching. Even more briefly he thinks of saying he was praying, honouring, aching.

'Takes all sorts,' the copper says, breaking the silence. He flicks a glance at where the stud sits under Gordo's lip and Gordo wonders if he's joined the police because his mum wouldn't let him join the army.

It sounds daft when the copper reads it all back: walking at night in the dark in the middle of nowhere. No, he wasn't bat-watching or badger-watching. No, of course he wasn't poaching. He thinks of mentioning Davey, dropping the name as a legitimate link to the place. But if the cop asks for details and he talks about the musketeers – even if he doesn't say 'musketeers', and he wouldn't – he'll sound like a nutter.

You'll sound like an activist. Like someone who gives back instead of just taking. It's a good thing.

But he didn't go anywhere near Davey's house last night, although he saw the lights on. And Davey doesn't need the trouble. He's not been great lately.

The copper asks to have a 'quick squint in your car, sir' and the look on his face when Gordo says he hasn't got one and he's walked here!

'Fae Hiskith?'

'It's not far. I walked up too.' He didn't mean it to come out cheeky. He just can't put a foot right with this one.

But at last it's over. He signs the printed sheet and has to peel it off his sweaty hand after.

'If we need to follow up, Mr Gordon,' the copper says.

'Follow up?' Gordo can't help echoing. 'I've told you every-thing I know.'

'In case we need to double-check for any reason. Once we get up there and speak to the other witnesses.'

'There weren't any.'

'So you didn't go up there to meet anyone?'

Not the way you mean, Gordo thinks. 'No,' he says.

'Did you see anyone?'

'No,' he says, because that woman at the water's edge was surely a trick of the light. Or wishful thinking.

'Did you *hear* anyone?' the cop says, picking up on something.

'There was a car,' Gordo says. 'I heard it, but it could have been anywhere.' Except it couldn't really. One road in and the same road out.

'Exactly,' the copper says. 'Other witnesses. Like I told you. So if we need to follow up, will you be at home?'

'I'll be at work, but I'll keep my mobile on. If the reception's bad, leave a voicemail. I'm not sure where I'll head today.' That's another lie and his voice shrinks away from it before the end.

'And what line of work is this,' the cop's asking, 'where you don't know where you'll be? I wouldn't have thought you'd left yourself many options.' He throws another look at Gordo's neck, at the barbed-wire choker.

Cops are supposed to take all kinds these days, Gordo thinks. Supposed to be trained to it. They're a long shout from a clip round the ear and be glad I'm not telling your da. But they can't help themselves.

'I've got a sanny van,' he says, because he can't help himself either. Sitting up and begging for approval like a biscuit. 'I park it all over, wherever the mood takes me. Thursdays when there's no market on at Dumfries I usually hit the schools at dinnertime.'

The copper's rereading the statement he just signed. 'Says here you don't own a vehicle.'

'Car,' says Gordo. 'I don't own a car. I do own a sanny van. Peace and—'

'That's you?' says the cop, looking up again. 'Peace and Bacon? Cool name.'

He should tell him the truth: that it wasn't his idea; that he'd never have come up with it if she hadn't helped him.

We did it together. We're a team.

But he's been up all night, had a shock, and then the long walk down. If he tries to say her name right now his voice might crack. So instead, he says, 'I sometimes go up Hiskith at the weekend for the walkers and fishermen. I might head up there today. Then you wouldn't need to phone at all and you could get a butty.'

Back out on the step, he blinks hard, still thinking he might cry if he's not careful. Fifteen years on, and he could sit down on this wall and howl like a wean.

You should forget me. You should live your life.

It's only three miles along the road home but there's a long stretch with no footpath and he's tired now, so he's looking up the street for buses when a *pock-pock-pock* startles him. It sounds like a magpie jabbing at a windowpane, or a gull pecking a mussel. He turns and feels a smile break over him. Of course! They only ever see each other up Hiskith. They only ever gather at Davey's house. He totally forgot he had a friend right here.

THREE

Barrett

I f pressed, he would call himself a man's man. He likes a pint, works with his hands, and his pals are all men. To be more accurate, both his pals are men. So when his wife left and took his daughters, he never dreamed of arguing. He missed them quietly, then he bought a house big enough to give them a room each when they visited. He took them to Ikea and stood like a horse asleep on its feet while they chose sheets and rugs and something like long Chinese lanterns for keeping shoes in.

'Daddy! Open your eyes!'

He paid up, packed the car, wielded the Allen key, adjusted castors, left them to the rest of it – the soft things – went downstairs and rang for a Chinese. Those were the days when they'd eat a takeaway.

'Rice, Dad? White boiled rice? Jeez.'

It wasn't until the dog that he cried. A full eight months after the decree absolute, when he'd missed a birthday for each of them, it was the night he lost Bess that his throat formed cracks like old mud in a dry bed and his mouth trembled like the flank of a cow on a flysome day. Water, sharp as spikes, squeezed out of his eyes and he stared at the wet patch on the pad of his thumb as he wiped it away, trying to remember when he had last shed a tear. It might have been when his old dad died, and he was locked in the tiny toilet cubicle of a Co-op funeral home, clearing his throat and thumping his fists on his thighs until he mastered himself.

He hasn't cried for Bess again. He does his job, priding himself on being the most dependable and thorough gardener in the valley, not some cowboy. He transfers cash to his girls, all three of them. He walks the hills in head-to-toe Gortex and good leather boots, dark with dubbin and watertight as ships' hulls. He rinses his flask with baking soda and leaves it airing with the stopper out, re-uses the foil from round his sandwich if it's cheese, throws it away after ham, for hygiene.

'Ever heard of M&S, Dad? Does the word "Greggs" mean anything?'

He doesn't need a dog for the hills. His litter-picker gives him purpose. Sometimes, if no one's watching, the Musketeers hold their pickers high in the air and clack the claws like the legs of giant crickets, like the beaks of metal birds, *snick-snick-snick*, then they lower them to the ground to peck at crisp packets and chocolate wrappers; orange peel and apple cores; bread bags and pack rings; bottles and bottle necks and bottle shards and splinters and crumbs; fag ends the colour of bracken, nearly invisible; Rizla packets a bright, fake green like nothing in nature; can after can after can, stark and new, still rolling in a high wind, or flattened and split, sharp edges digging into the ground.

There must be years' worth *under*ground now, from before the Musketeers began. They could truffle out some of it. They'd need metal detectors to get the rest. But what's invisible is doing no harm. What does it matter if foreign objects lie under the grass and moss, under the mulch of old bracken stalks, under the leaves rotting where they've blown, under the logs mouldering where they fell at the boggy edge of the plantings? What does it matter what's fallen in the loch and sunk, filling with mud and weed? He's not – none of them are – the sort to go poking.

That's the problem eating at him tonight, when he could be happily oiling tools with a podcast on or having a cold bottle of lager in front of *Storage Wars*.

'Da-ad! You'll watch *anything* with "Extreme" in the title!'

He's too worried for soothing chores. They don't live on their phones like a couple of kids, but Davey usually picks up the landline and it's rung out unanswered twice now. So, at bedtime, once Barrett has brushed his teeth and tied the top of the bin-liner ready for the morning, he puts a jerkin on over his sweatshirt, changes his slippers for a pair of rubber clogs and sets off.

If he'd a fourby he could head straight up the hill behind the house, but as it is he takes the main road down to the outskirts of Sanquhar, then peels off on to the two-lane, past the wee pony paddocks with their corrugated iron and tarpaulin shelters. There are letters in the *Standard* sometimes, complaining about the state of these not-quite stables, but it makes Barrett happy to think the Sanquhar weans can have a horse if they want, that folk like him can keep a few sheep or some chickens. He hears all of them as he drives past: whickering, bleating, a soft cluck from inside a huttie as the birds notice a car in the dark then resettle themselves. He passes a cottage or two with their lights on, a farm with the men still busy in the sheds – autumn calving like they all do now – then he takes the Hiskith turn, on to the single-track with the drystane on either side, his headlights picking out the soft green of the lichen at the foot of the dyke, the sharp green of the moss on the lee of the stones, that egg-yolk yellow of the hawthorn leaves that only lasts a week till a wind clears the lot. It's lonely up here but there's no denying it's bonny when the sun shines or on nights like this when the moon's like a great big gong hanging in the sky.

He clicks his headlights off, checking, and right enough the moon's bright enough to drive by, its cold light making the mica glitter in the copestones and turning the stalks of dead grass to silver. Beautiful.

But it's not safe to keep driving like that. Even on this road to nowhere. To Hiskith, which is the same thing nearly. And it's a waste of a journey that's a bugger in the daytime, far better at night when you can see headlights coming miles off, round the blind bends.

Soon enough, Barrett bumps over the cattle grid and the walls fall away at either side of the track, revealing an open moor stretching ahead as far as he can see, with blots of black trees here and there and dabs of white sheep hunkered in about them for shelter.

As he climbs, feeling the wind buffet the chassis, seeing the last farm lights disappear behind him, he thinks again about what to do if Davey comes to the door. Will he accuse his friend of not answering his phone? What business is that of anyone's? He'd sound like one of the girls:

'She's not answering her phone!' Voices hushed and thumbs flying. *U OK GF?*

'What does UOKGF mean when it's at home?' he asks, reading over a shoulder.

'"When it's at home"! What does that even mean, Dad? Are. You. OK. Girl. Friend. Jeez!'

Barrett could say, 'Are you OK, boyfriend?' if Davey answers the door. Through his worry, the thought makes him smile. Maybe he'll just park up and watch the house, see that the lights are on and check they go off at bedtime. Davey heads up at ten o'clock, usually.

He watches the strip of turf up the middle of the track disappearing under his bonnet as the miles unspool behind him. Then, as he breasts the final hill that hides the reservoir, he lifts his foot and slips the car out of gear, keeping it poised on the brow, looking down to where the track passes the old school, goes on again skirting the head's house, and then suddenly stops, nothing but a shining plaque of water with a perfect mirrored moon floating in it and the road emerging again at the far side beyond the dam. Barrett isn't a fanciful man – this expedition is the most he's indulged a feeling since Bess died – but he shivers to see the truth so clearly laid out before him in the moonlight.

They didn't demolish anything before they flooded it. He knows that, but he tries never to think about it. Tonight, though, with the road catching the light that way, it's too easy to imagine a cart trundling down, past the school and the heidie's house, on past cottages and a church, past gardens and middens and byres. A smithy, a shop, a bridge. He can almost see the beak counting the bairns coming up for the bell. Would he have worn a black gown and a board? Barrett shakes himself. 'He' was probably a nice woman that cuddled them when they scraped their knees and took them out brambling. He hopes so. Bairns need a woman.

Only, this nice woman in Barrett's mind is wearing a tweed skirt and a jumper but the village was flooded when women still hid their ankles. It's that daft bat and her tea towels he's thinking of.

'You can't say that, Dad!'

He flicks a glance at the old school, all its windows black at just gone nine o'clock, and thinks, Aye, I can.

Maybe *she's* why he finds himself lifting the brake and coasting down silently, out of gear, passing the gate without looking, passing Davey's too, with its warm light behind drawn curtains. He pulls up with only a crunch of shale chips at the water's edge, turns to face back up the hill, and switches the engine off.

Bess, Bess, Bess. It's only the wind, finding the slits in his hubcaps and whistling through them, but bugger if it doesn't sound exactly like somebody saying her name. And just like that, even though he's up here with a sheet of silver water and the black velvet mass of the hill beyond, what he *sees* is a bright day of scudding clouds and the droplets coming off her coat like diamonds as she clambers out of the loch and shakes herself, then sets off lolloping along the stones, snuffling at nothing with her tail going.

He shouldn't beat himself up for worrying about Davey tonight, he tells himself. He's a good man, a good dad despite everything, and a good friend. He's a failed husband, it's true, and not much of a . . . he's long past thinking 'boyfriend' and he can't say the word 'lover', even in his head.

'Ewwwww!'

But he cared about his ex-wife while he still could, he cares to a fault about his stroppy daughters and of course he cares about his friend. He lifts his head and looks at his eyes in the mirror. *Should* he go and knock on the door? he asks his reflection. What's the worst that could happen? He looks away from his own eyes again and settles down with his hands in his pockets.

Old fool. He's pushing fifty now and he's been outside in the air all day, doing a last mowing at the care home, raking it, bagging it up, hoiking the bags of clippings into the back of the pick-up. His last thought as his eyes close is, if he'd known he was coming here tonight he could have brought some big bags of that sweet grass up the hill road and turned them out over the fence for the ponies.

He jolts awake, bucking against the seatbelt with his heart clattering, catching sight of his own wild face in the mirror and rearing back to get away from it, all this before he remembers where he is. What the hell was that noise? Was it in his dreams? Was it out there in the real night?

As he settles, he sees the churned water on the surface of the reservoir just now fading to ripples, and he can't help a moan escaping him. It must have been a rifle shot, although it sounded deeper and bigger than that. But what else could it be? He rakes his gaze along the dam and the barrier, passing over something that looks like a figure, but surely can't be, and then he's on his way, still rattled.

He's miles down the road, almost on the two lane, before he realizes that Davey's downstairs lights were still shining.

Thank God he hasn't got a job first thing. It took a bath to warm him through again and two whiskies to get him to sleep, so it's nearer nine than eight when he opens his eyes as the duty officer's door slams in the wee car park round the back, right underneath his bedroom window. He swings his legs out of bed, shuffles his feet into his slippers, shrugs into his dressing gown, and heads over the landing, congratulating himself on sleeping through the night still. He's got no need to worry, no need for a check-up. Not yet.

Downstairs, while the kettle boils, he goes to look out the front window on to the street, watching young mums straggle home with their buggies after dropping the bairns off, a trickle of youngsters headed to the chemists for their morning dose, nose-to-tail traffic. No wonder the weans don't get to walk to school on their own. Davey's right there.

It's an old argument, barely worth the name: Davey defending his childhood up there in the back of beyond with nothing but sheep and crows to talk to, and Barrett banging on about swing parks and Scouts and bike sheds to smoke behind. Just as well there's three of them, one to break the tie.

One to share a worry with too, he thinks, still standing at the front window even once the kettle's clicked off. He should text, just briefly. He could say something like: *Heard from D? Hope he's OK.* (UOKGF, he hears again, even as he tells himself texting's a normal thing to do for anyone, any age, either sex.)

'Any gender, Dad!'

Then he hears the door of the station opening and he laughs out loud. It's Gordo! Right there on his doorstep, no need to text now. He leans forward and taps the window with his fingernail. If he believed in signs, he'd be having a really good day.

FOUR

Tabitha

And yet waking up in the morning has none of the blood-curdling brightness from last time. (Maybe going off your head at fifteen and going off your head at forty are never the same.)

'Please don't use that expression,' one of the nurses said.

'I'm talking about myself,' I reminded her.

'Not in a vacuum,' she shot back. 'You're part of a community.'

'OK.'

'So how are you feeling today?' she asked again.

And when I didn't answer, she glared at me and noted down – saying the words as she wrote them – *silent and uncooperative*. Bitch. I probably wasn't allowed to use that word either.

Thank God for the cats who ran the stationery cupboard in the nurses' little kingdom. They weren't real cats. (I wasn't that crazy.) They were cartoons. Garfield was one of them and I didn't know the name of the other one, which used to bug the life out of me. I'd lie in my bed at night and say, 'Felix, Sylvester, Tom, Figaro, Thomas O'Malley, Duchess,' until someone told me to shut up. The worst of it was that I *knew* this other cat. I recognized him. I remembered him from when I was a kid. He wore a hat and he walked on two legs. Only, there was a cloud in my brain where his name should be.

I kept them quiet for six weeks, those enterprising cartoon cats. (Did I say they ran the cupboard as a business, turning a profit right there under the nurses' noses?) I would have kept it quiet a lot longer, only that elusive name was like a miniscule bit of chaff poking through my clothes, denting my skin but hiding from my probing fingers. So I asked the doctor one day. And she, always much less bossy and cold than the bitch nurses, said, 'Macavity, Jellico, Rumpleteazer' in such a lavish, unstoppable, gushing torrent of sounds that I had to go away. I stayed away quite a while that time, as I remember.

So this morning, hours after he rose with a fizz of cold water and a splat of wet rock, I'm more than a bit surprised to open my eyes on to the plainest of plain days, nothing but lamp black and lead white mixed to a cold, dead grey. (I really need to stop with the colours.)

Obviously, I'm going to have to do more than open the door in order to usher the demons back in. I could call in a favour from that bully Mr Moon, ask what *he* could see from all the way up there. I could demand to speak to the rest of his family and threaten to report him if he won't let me. Coercive control is illegal, I'll tell him.

Or I could ask *him* what *he* thinks of an interloper causing trouble in his watery world.

I'm telling myself I've got all these options, but the truth is, right now, I can't get within a *mile* of my old friends. So. Much. Reality. Such as the pillow under my head, which is thin and lumpy, and the pillowcase which, like the sheets, is sharp-smelling from getting folded away still damp. And there's dust on the windowsill and more dust in the folds of the heavy curtains I haven't drawn. I sit up and then let myself drop back. I always forget that the classroom windows are too high to see out of. It was different in a bunkbed.

Zelda's already at work in the old drill hall beyond the coat pegs, what she calls her studio, even though there are lines marked on the floor for ballgames and badminton, still traceable under years of her paint. The door is shut tight and her favoured discordant music is blaring behind it. I skate down the length of the cold corridor to fill the kettle. Then I skate all the way back up the other end to the even colder bathroom. Zelda must have had a bath when she got up. The painted pipes are dripping with condensation and the window still blooms with it. This window is even higher than the classroom ones, more like a skylight, that drops down on a rusting iron arm. You have to mind and shut it quick if the rain comes on, but you have to open it after a bath or the shiny paint bubbles on the walls, and the floor gets so thickly beaded it needs mopping.

I pee, in Zelda's suffocating lily-of-the-valley steam, then leave the room, holding my hands up to remind me I haven't washed them as I skate back to the kitchen sink where there's no mirror above the taps. I don't want to see myself this morning.

I know I'm not really skating, by the way. I'm not that crazy. Only, the floor is so shiny and there's so much of it that, whenever it was too wet to play outside, we used to swish about on our socks and pretend, especially during the winter Olympics. I'd grab Jo's foot and run in a circle like a hammer thrower. At the centre of my mad scampering, she would raise her hands above her head and arch her back, graceful and perfect, until I pulled her sock right off and she stopped.

I elbow on the taps and wait for the water to run warm. This used to be the staffroom when the school was just a school and it's still the best room in the house, with a fireplace, glass-fronted book cupboards and a window low enough to see out of over the deep stone sill. So the teachers could keep an eye on the playground, probably. The living room was the head's study and the window there is marbled for privacy, the same marbled glass on the door that still says WC. The head couldn't use the same loo as the teachers, apparently.

'He could have used the piano stool,' we used to say. 'The pee-in-a stool.' I don't know who first discovered that, under the lift-up velvet seat, there was a chamber pot where the sheet music should have been, but we found it hilarious, my sister and our boy cousins, and me. When I was five and Davey was nine he only had to look at it to crack me up.

So it's not that I was a prude, but I always hated that bog right off our main living room. Johnny was the only one who ever went in there, barely closing the door in case he missed what we were watching. I'd turn the sound up to drown him out but then Zelda would shout through from her studio that she could 'hear the babble of the barbarians' and make me turn it down again. Zelda didn't watch telly. Still doesn't.

Mostly, she works in that 'studio' of hers. It was the drill hall that made her agree to live here; an enormous room with a glass roof for shadowless light and climbing bars to hang her canvases from. It's one of many actual practicalities in this impractical-seeming house. Such as how the girls' entrance makes a perfect front vestibule and the boys' entrance at the other side is our utility and boot room. The two classrooms were ideal bedrooms: one for Zelda and the other for Jo and me. Long before I was born, they had put a bath in the pupils' toilets and taken out all but one of the basins.

But still, the first time Scott came here, he had a good look about himself and said, 'Can't accuse your parents of destroying the ambience, can we?' I looked around too then, with his eyes, but I still couldn't see what he was seeing. It was my home, the only one I'd ever known, a solid little cruciform of red sandstone, its four arms made of the drill hall, the classroom corridors, the boys' entrance and the girls' entrance and its steep slate roof an origami of gables and chimneys.

Scott nodded up at 'GIRLS' carved in stone over the front door and made a joke about strip clubs. He wasn't the first but I was mad about him then, head over heels, and I tittered without trying.

'Well, we always think the way our family does things is the default way, I suppose,' he said next.

Not my family, pal, I wanted to tell him. Hardly. But I was more or less keeping it all quiet at that point. And anyway, Zelda came out of her studio just then, wiping her hands on a rag, wearing one of the ultramarine smocks I should definitely call 'blue', the ones that made her eyes look like cornflowers. Scott was sold.

I saw him studying us both during that first visit, tracing her face in mine or my face in hers. It was months later he found a subtle way of *saying* what a relief it was to find out your fiancée's mother was still good-looking, but it was right then on that first day that he *thought* it.

People are either pigs or foxes, generally. My God, the uproar when I said that in the hospital. 'No, no, no, you've got it wrong!' I insisted. 'I've always . . . This isn't . . . I don't mean . . .' but it was just after I'd told them about the cats, Garfield and the other one, so you couldn't blame them. Anyway, it's true. If you think about the people you know and you have to say 'fox' or 'pig' it's usually dead easy.

My dad and Uncle Roddie were both pigs. Pigs, I should say, aren't necessarily ugly. They're just people with wide faces, short noses and mouths that curve up. Jo's a pig; so's my cousin Johnny. But Auntie Rowan was a fox, with a narrow, pointed chin, a thin nose, and hair that grew in a V on her forehead. My cousin Davey got his looks from her. His hair grows in a V that's deeper every

year and his mouth is so narrow that his teeth looked stacked
for storage.

Scott's a pig. Ha ha ha.

But Albie, my son, is neither a pig *nor* a fox. He got himself
from me, and I got myself from Zelda. We're horses, all three.

Zelda's hair is a mane. It's thick and coarse and it makes one
big wave that either hangs down her back, bouncing as she
moves, or rests over one shoulder. And her profile – she says
this herself – was a pain at art school. There wasn't a single
sculpture specialist who didn't want her to sit and gaze into the
distance while he, usually he, tried to mimic that curve of forehead, the wild nose and long top lip. She drops her eyelids,
remembering, as she tells this story and then you can see what
long thick lashes she's got, putting those eyes – Payne's grey
without the smock – in deep shadow. Albie got the eyes, and
the lashes, and the mane, although his is more like a pelt now
he insists on a buzzcut.

I rake my hands through my own hair while I'm waiting for
my toast to pop up. I dye it a colour that's says 'chestnut' on
the box, but it's more like Nutella. I always said I'd stop when
I was forty, cut it short and let it grow in like hers, pepper and
salt with a streak just off-centre. Now's my chance, I suppose.
Who's going to see me?

'So what's on the agenda today?' Zelda's in the room beside
me suddenly, putting her hands on either side of the kettle to warm
them, leaving streaks of paint behind. I don't know why she doesn't
keep one in the studio. She's got biscuits in there. And whisky.
She smiles at me. Her teeth are horsey too – long and stained from
years of hand-rolled cigarettes while she's working. (She says
smoking helps her concentrate.) Somehow though, those teeth
don't make her less attractive, just even more original.

Still, I run my tongue over my own before I answer. 'Unpacking.
I can do anything around here that might need doing.'

'Such as?' says Zelda, looking round.

She's never been house-proud or even hygienic, finding a
concern for cleanliness far too pedestrian in her artist's life. But
the house is worse than I remember. It doesn't look bohemian
any more. It looks poor. I back away from the idea of Zelda
struggling before it can take hold, but I remind myself not to
assume I can sponge off her.

'Or I could look for a job,' I say. 'Sign on even. Is it still called signing on?'

'Universal credit, as brought to you by Franz Kafka,' Zelda says. Has she tried to get it? Are things that bad? Or is she quoting the *Guardian*? 'If I were you, I'd look for a job.'

I try my breathing, hoping it doesn't sound like a sigh. I've just said that.

'If there was still arts funding worth the name in this benighted country,' Zelda's saying now, 'you could apply for a grant and take the time to find out what you really want to do with your life.'

And breathe in, and breathe out, and imagine a desert. 'I've already worked out what I really wanted to do with my life, Mum,' I say. 'I wanted to build a solid marriage, bring up a happy child, do a worthwhile job. This isn't a "gift from the universe". It's a kick in the teeth.'

Zelda puts her head on one side and twists her mouth up to the other. That's one of the benefits of being a horse; you can pull all kinds of faces and still be striking. Pigs have to smile and keep their chins up or they get a look about them. 'The universe doesn't bestow gifts,' she says. 'It's indifferent.'

I suppose it's a blessing I haven't moved in with someone who'll dribble long ropes of 'mindfulness' and 'gratitude', and I'm used to her deafness when I tell her unwelcome facts but it's still annoying. She never bugged Jo about being an artist. I wonder if it's anything more than me looking like her.

'Or why not toddle down the hill and see Davey?' she says next. 'Have you told him what's going on? Have you even seen him since the summer?'

Oh, she's good. She's subtle. Nothing so mundane as complaining that I didn't visit *her*. Nothing so suburban, nothing so predictable. Not from a woman who talks about Kafka. Have I seen *Davey*, is the question.

'We're in touch,' is the answer. As well as television, Zelda finds modern methods of communication unsatisfactory. I'd love to tell her it makes her look old, not original, but then she *has* let me move back in here to curl in a ball and lick my wounds. I can surely behave the way I would to any other housemate. I don't have to revert to snide remarks and eye-rolling.

'He might know of jobs,' she's saying. 'Word of mouth and all that.'

Since my cousin Davey is a coder and I live on the help line
for six weeks every time I get a new phone, this doesn't seem
all that likely. But I suppose there must be general admin staff
at the places he works.

'I'll wander down and see if he feels like a walk,' I say.

'That's it,' she tries next. 'Fresh air and exercise! I'd be driven
off the Left Bank for saying so, but there is an argument for it,
as and when.' Her head's on the other side now. 'Because . . .
How are you, Tabitha? How *are* you?'

'I'm fine.' It's what she wants to hear. And also, despite my
best efforts, and the loch monster aside, it actually seems to be
true. She winds the string of her teabag firmly round her cup
handle and tucks the label in tight. 'It's good to be home,' I add.
'If I can't be home home, it's good to be here with you. And
Davey. Thanks for the suggestion.'

'Good old Davey,' she says, and so many clouds pass over her
face one after the other it's like a speeded-up film of a stormy
sky. 'But be careful not to get drawn in.'

'In where?' I ask.

'Anywhere. Either side.'

'Of what?' But I must sound too avid and Zelda's hatred of
petty gossip takes over.

'Oh, the latest cause célèbre, you know,' she says, with a wave
of the hand.

It's news to me that Davey had an earlier cause célèbre to turn
a new one into the 'latest'. He codes, he games, he still collects
stamps, for God's sake – just like when he was a wee boy steaming
them off postcards every summer and cozying up to kids at school
with aunties in Canada. Except now he collects franks too.

'I won't get drawn into anything except paid work,' I assure
Zelda. 'Now, you get back to *yours*.' She bestows another smile.
She always appreciates hearing that her painting is a real job.
'I'll make lunch.'

'A crust of bread in the hand not holding the brush.'

'Dinner then,' I say. She clearly wants to stay away from me
and I wouldn't mind a day away from her. Because I know this
is true, I can appreciate what she says next for the act of generosity it is.

'Come in when you get back from your walk. See what I'm
working on.'

'I might just do that,' I lie. 'Is it a . . .' She quells me. Her dark eyes can't flash even if she wants them to; not with those long straight lashes, thick as stick-ons. But did they glint? I'm still asking myself when I'm washed and dressed and on my way down to Davey's house. Did Zelda's eyes really glint with anger, or with malice perhaps? Or did I see something that wasn't there? I hope so. I hope there's really a devil behind Zelda's eyes to match what happened under the water last night.

That's what I'm telling myself. I'm such a fraud. I'm a big-talking coward, me. As I trudge down the side of the road on the short grass, spongy with moss and dotted with sheep purleys, I don't even *look* at the water. King Kong and Godzilla could be floating on their backs, holding hands like otters, and I wouldn't know. Instead of checking, I trace the lines of hills folding in on themselves as they stretch away from me, the clouds unfolding out of themselves as they roll towards me. She never paints these quiet ribbons of land undulating for miles, nor those extravagant skyscapes. No. All this time, all she has ever done is peer down into the deep and use that brush of hers to winkle out nightmares. I lower my eyes at last. The water is a cobalt green-grey this morning. Stop! The water is grey. Wait! Unless courting my old friends Naphthol and Phthalo might help my mind break. But this grey is as dull as a stale fish eye on a slab, not even a ruffle at the edge now the wind's dropped. I turn my head from the point at the far side where the track emerges again and that's when I see that Davey's lights are still on. It's after nine o'clock and the sun has been up for an hour but his kitchen window is lit behind haphazardly-pulled curtains. I speed up and let myself in the gate with a maggot of worry starting to eat me.

The back door is closest and it's usually open. I knock lightly. The thick layers of old paint deaden the sound, so I try the handle but it's fast as a fortress. I creak open the letterbox and put my mouth close. 'Dave? It's Tabby! Are you there?'

There's no answer. He might be out, or not up, or wearing earbuds, or in the bathroom – except the bathroom is right beside the back door and there's no light on. Besides, something about the stillness is undeniable. It's coiling out of the letterbox and starting to steal over me. I step back and make my way round the front. This door's locked too but when I bend to lift the letterbox flap, I can see the table on the other side of the little vestibule. I can see the envelope propped there. I can read what it says: *To whom it may concern.*

FIVE

Tabitha

I breathe in. I breathe out. I think of a forest.

But I'm wasting my time. There's no way I'm going to calm down until I know what's happening. So. I check under the mat, under the flower pots, even down inside the letterbox in case there's a key hanging on a string. Finally I head for the gate again, gearing up to run as fast as I can for the spare keys Zelda must have. Surely. I concentrate on pumping my arms and setting my boots squarely down one in front of the other on the knobbly chips, until the sound of a car approaching the crest of the hill makes me hop on to the verge. Trying not to slip on wet grass, moss and sheep shit takes concentration, so I almost don't look up as the car comes closer.

Maybe it's the brightness that snags my attention. The car is blinding white with acidic manganese and Hansa – stop it! I need my wits to stay about me – with a blue and yellow band running up the sides. And it's huge too. Police cars really were *cars* the last time I was this close to one. I veer back on to the track and wave my arms. It pulls up in front of me.

'I think my cousin's in trouble,' I say, running up to meet the officer (fox) as he steps down. He's blinding too in his hi-vis and I'm glad. I might have grabbed for his arms if he hadn't looked so much like a warning sign and it's probably illegal to touch him. 'His lights are still on. His doors are locked. And there's an envelope propped up as if—'

He's looking over my shoulder at the loch even as he nods. 'Your cousin?' he says.

'Davey. David Muir,' I say, pointing. 'That's his house right there.'

'Oh,' says the cop. 'Muir. Right. Your cousin? And so you would be . . .?'

'Tabitha Muir,' I say. 'Well, Tabitha Lawson. Tabitha Muir.'

Maybe he's smiling at me for not knowing my own name. Except he's not, because the smile is only lifting one side of his mouth, and also he just flicked a glance behind him at the old school. 'The Muirs of Hiskith,' he says. 'I'm Glasgow myself, but my wife's Sanquhar since her granny. And all the men in her family were miners.'

'I think my cousin might need help,' I say, speaking slowly and clearly, to cut through the wittering. Why the hell would I care what his in-laws did for a living? Typical Kirkconnel, this was. 'Can you break the door down and see if he's OK?'

That gets his attention. He climbs back up into the car to drive the few metres to Davey's gate and, while I'm following, it occurs to me to wonder what he's doing here.

'Did someone already call you?' I ask when I catch up. He's at the back door, rapping on it. 'To do a welfare check?'

'A safe and well check,' he says. 'No, no one called. Someone came into the station. Mr Muir?' he shouts. 'You OK in there?'

'There's an envelope,' I tell him again. 'Inside the front vestibule.'

'A note?'

'God, I hope not.'

What he does next chills my blood to slush in my veins and makes goosepimples pop out on my arms inside my coat sleeves. He takes his cap off, bends down at the open letterbox and sniffs.

'If you're going to break in,' I say, 'there's a side way into the kitchen that's half glass.'

But he goes round the wrong way and comes to the front door first, with me at his heels like a wee dog. He bends again and sniffs again and then he goes very still. 'To whom it may concern?' he says softly. 'Aw, man. Right. Right then.'

He's gone a bit pale. I don't think he wants to see what he believes he's going to see.

'I could go and get a spare key from my mum up at the next house,' I say. 'I don't mind checking on him. Unless it's got to be you because, like you said, someone came in.'

'Eh?' he says, as if I'm annoying him. All I'm doing is trying to spare him. 'I'm not here for a safe and well,' he said. 'I'm here because of the explosion.'

He's off again, away round the far side to the door I've told him's got glass in it, and this time I don't follow. The explosion?

My diver eel ten times the size he was painted? How could a copper know about him? No, he must have said something else. I'm here because of the . . . exposure. Because of the symposium. It'll be some cop jargon I've never heard before.

But still. I walk away from the front door, down over the tussocky grass and past the empty vegetable beds to the corner nearest the loch. I strain to look past the surface, see what it's hiding, but I've seen nothing except the greasy, slippery skin of it when I hear cars. I turn and crane to see over the tops of the bushes lining Davey's garden wall. They're too tall but I get a view through the bare stems and see two vehicles trundle straight past the gate and carry on beyond. *Peace and Bacon* is painted on the side of the van, with a CND sign in rainbow colours. *One Man Went To Mow* is painted on the high, open flank of the pick-up, pale green on dark green as if the letters have been cut into sward with a lawnmower. As it passes me I see a cartoon man pushing the lawnmower across the tailgate, making for the other side to write something else.

They pull up in the parking bays by the water's edge and a man steps down from each. (Pig, fox.) I can see them clearly, hard-edged and in full colour. It's a completely realized, complex vision. They're even casting shadows. Their feet make a noise as they hit the ground. The doors make a noise as they slam them. And they get bigger as they come closer.

The only thing that's strange is that, as I watch them approaching, I start to get the impression that they can see me too. That's new.

The fox, who's younger than the other one and younger than me, puts a blue hand up and shades his eyes as if to get a better view. 'Is Davey OK?' he says. 'Why's that police car gone straight to him? And who are you?'

The pig, who's older than the other one and older than me too, says, 'Who are you, hen?'

Which means he can definitely see me, which means that they're both real, them and their unlikely vehicles. And the cop did say 'explosion'. No rising, no visions. I'm stuck here in reality. Funtown is closed for the night. That's what Elspeth used to say as her sleeping tablets kicked in. 'Funtown's closed for the night. Open in the morning.' And that envelope – *To whom it may concern* – means that reality's worse than ever.

'I'm Davey's cousin,' I say, answering the easiest of his three questions. 'Tabitha.'

'Right, Tabitha,' says the young one, nodding. 'You got married and moved to Castle Douglas. But now you're . . . back.'

'But now I'm back,' I say, nodding too. 'Yes, that's me.'

'I'm Barrett, hen,' says the older one, 'and this clueless lump here's Gordo. Never mind him.' He rolls his eyes but he speaks kindly.

'*Is* Davey OK?' the clueless lump asks again. 'What's that copper at?'

'He'll be taking witness statements, lad. Nothing more,' says Barrett. 'Davey's fine.'

'But the thing is I think Davey might be . . . not fine,' I say. 'The doors are locked and the lights are still on from last night and the worst thing of all is there's a note.'

'No,' Gordo says. 'Davey? Never.'

But before the words are out of his mouth, the copper's back in the garden. He doesn't puke but he's got his hand over his mouth and his chest is heaving.

'Is everything OK?' Barrett shouts.

The copper waves a hand. 'Stay out,' he shouts back. 'Stay away.'

He stumbles round the back towards his car and I feel my legs go like noodles. I have to brace against the wall with both hands to stay upright.

Or maybe I don't stay upright because the next thing I know I'm sitting on a folding chair inside the Peace and Bacon van. I deduce this from looking around myself at the fryer and the griddle, at the big plastic boxes of rolls and huge tubs of spreadable butter. There's a thing that looks like a bomb – a high-sided cylinder held tight with clamps. And there's an old-fashioned, covered cake stand in a sort of a nest made of draught excluders. I want to run out of there and find the copper and *make* him tell me. But I can't move. And I don't want to know. But I've got to say something, if only to stop my brain from making the thoughts I can't bear to think.

'What's that?' I say, nodding at the bomb.

'Road-proof soup pot,' the young one says. He sounds grateful. He doesn't want to think things either. To know things. I've forgotten his name and I don't want to ask again.

'Welcome back,' Barrett says. He's standing up looking out of the window in the rear door, doing it like a spy, with just one finger hooking the blind away from the glass. 'You were in a right wee dwam there.'

'What's happening?' I find myself asking him. I didn't decide to.

He shakes his head. 'No sign of l . . .' he begins, then clears his throat. We look at each other, the three of us, wondering if anyone is going to say what we all suspect. And more than suspect. But can't bear.

'So are you friends of Davey?' I ask next. Then tears gather and I can't say any more. Bearing or not makes no difference.

'We're the Three Musketeers,' the young one says, a bit too loud. He's trying to help me. 'We get together every weekend and the light summer nights. We walk the path round the loch here. And the Southern Upland Way. Sometimes other paths, but that's our beat.'

'Beat?' I echo. *Musketeers?* I consider them in turn. The older one, Barrett, looks as if he buys all his clothes at a garden centre: fleece and moleskin, a checked shirt and slip-on shoes that might be waterproof or might just be ugly. But he's neat with it. I'd believe he was ex-army. The young one – Gogsie? – is dressed for the hills too but it's army-surplus, cheap and rough, and tattoos spreading out from his collar and cuffs, snaking up his neck and over his hands. Little silver bolts with bobbles on the end run through his brows and lips. I try to add Davey to make a set out of them. A trio with a 'beat'. I fail.

'Litter-picking,' Barrett says. 'Davey always keeps this bit nice on account of he lives here.' I'm sure he gives the word 'keeps' an extra bit of emphasis. Present tense. I'm sure of it. 'And then Gordo started clearing up after his customers,' Barrett goes on. Gordo! I'll try and remember it this time. 'And I . . . well, I fell into the same game what with one thing and another.'

Gordo nods solemnly, as if there's a story there that's not being told. Then he too makes a stab at cheer. 'You're currently sitting in the cleanest car park in Scotland,' he says.

I clutch the distraction and, thinking back to this morning and last night, right enough there wasn't so much as a chewing-gum wrapper anywhere on the ground. 'And does it *take* three of you?' I say, because if they can make chit-chat for my sake, it's the least I can do for them. 'You'd think the road would put people off. It's not as if there aren't places to leave your litter down in the valley.'

'You're not a fishing enthusiast then?' Gordo says.

Barrett nods. 'Aye, they're not all ramblers,' he says. 'But they're not all anglers either. A fair few of them are pilgrims.'

'Because of the mad old bat and her jigsaws,' says Gordo.

Zelda has often said as much. She regales me with talk of 'hordes of visitors come to be a small part of it any way they can'. I always thought she was bragging. I mean, it's true she sells the rights to reproduce, but they don't even stock them in the newsagents down in Kirkconnel. It's hardly Haworth parsonage.

'Don't forget tea towels,' says Barrett.

'And mouse mats,' says Gordo. 'And novelty condoms for all I know.'

We all know Davey is in serious trouble up there. We know, deep down, that he's in the worst trouble anyone can be in. I've known since the cop came back out with his hand over his mouth. And yet, thinking about Zelda Muir condoms, I feel a laugh bobbing around under my collarbone, tickling me. What the hell is wrong with me?

'She'd faint if she heard you,' I say. 'She doesn't make jigsaws and mouse mats. She paints pictures. She's a serious artist.'

'I don't think we're talking about the same person,' Gordo says. 'The mad old bat paints a kiddy-on vill—'

'Oh we are,' I assure him. 'She paints pictures like a serious artist but then she licenses reproductions. Business decision totally unrelated to her art.'

'You seem to know a lot abou— Shite!' Gordo says. 'Aw, shite! If you're Davey's cousin, that means the mad old bat's your mu— I mean, it's your mum who paints—'

'The novelty condoms,' I say. 'Yes.'

'Shite!' says Gordo.

'Fuck!' says Barrett, and at first I think he's telling Gordo to make even more fuss about his gaffe. Then I notice that he's been peering out the edge of the blind again. He turns towards us and the look on his face is sheer misery. 'More polis,' he says. He swallows. 'And . . .'

'What?' I say.

'And an undertaker. Oh, Christ. Oh, Davey.'

'No,' says Gordo. His voice is soft with wonder, as if he didn't
know. Which he did. Which we all did. As if he's surprised.
Which he can't be, because it was clear as day. We've been
kidding ourselves, twatting on about art and crisp bags. But we've
got to stop and face it now.

I open my mouth to tell him at least some of that, but what I
say is, 'No. Oh, no.'

Whether she happened to look out the window at the right time
or she's been phoned by someone as the news leaks, when we
step out of the van and make our way back up to Davey's gate,
there's Zelda coming striding down the hill in her painting smock
and splattered clogs, her hair streaming out behind her.

'What exactly is going on?' she says, taking in everyone with
one fierce glare. All three of the cops, both undertakers and the
two remaining musketeers shrink under the look and the voice
and the sheer presence of her. It's me her eyes settle on. 'What
have you done now?' she says, dripping with weary scorn. And
so I shrink too. She doesn't know and I won't tell her. I want to
give her these last few moments living in a world that's still got
Davey in it.

'Mrs Muir, isn't it?' says one of the new cops, a woman (pig).
'We're going to need to get in touch with Mr Muir's next of kin.'
She raises an eyebrow and pokes her tongue into her cheek. 'And,
eh, I believe you can help with that, can't you?'

'I should think so,' Zelda says. 'Why? What's wrong? What's
happened?'

'Seeing as how you're such a *close* family,' the woman says.

There's a long, empty moment as everyone waits to see what
Zelda will do. Which is turn on her heel and march back the
way she's come. Apart from the Musketeers, every single last
one of the rest of them is wearing that deadpan look that might
as well be smirking.

SIX

Barrett

'You sure you don't mind me cooking?' Gordo asks her for the third time, poking his head out the open side window of the sanny van. The awning's up and Barrett can hear the *spit spit pop* of onions on the griddle. He assumes the lass – Tabitha – can hear it too. He hopes she can tell that, never mind all the ink and metal, Gordo's still a good lad.

'"Never mind"? "Still"? Jeez, Dad!'

'Absolutely not,' she tells Gordo, with a smile he can tell has been hoisted up from the pit of her belly. 'I'll have a roll on bacon and fried egg. Brown sauce. No butter.'

'I'll have the usual, Gordo,' Barrett says. His usual is fried egg and bacon with no butter and a wee dab of brown sauce but he's not saying 'same here' and making the poor lass think he's trying it on. She's as white as a sheet right now but she's a fine-looking woman and she must get sick of it.

Gordo's set the two chairs and the wee table up where he always does when he's working Hiskith: right beside the water's edge looking over to where the track comes out of the loch on the far side. It's the best spot and, with the van as a windbreak, it's pleasant enough even on a day like this. Barrett screws his eyes up and traces the line of the horizon, dying grass as dark as the mud, dead grass as pale as the clouds. Close up under their chairs, there's still a shadow of green near the roots, but it's gone from the far hills and the sheep'll soon have it away.

'Only, I don't want to go back down the valley before I know for sure what's happened,' Gordo says. Barrett thinks that all three of them know for *damn* sure what's happened but he can't blame the lad. He's leaning right out over the counter so he can look her in the eye, squashing a basket of ketchup and a box of napkins under his chest. 'It'll go to waste if I don't cook it. Plus cops make good customers. They don't bring stuff from home 'cos of drunks and all that and they're usually starving.'

'It's fine,' she says. 'Honestly. I'm glad to have somewhere to sit out the road. Like you, I don't want to go home.' Then she makes a noise Barrett thinks at first is a smothered sneeze. When he shoots a look at her though, she's trying not to cry.

'Aye, it's a sin,' he says. 'Forty-four years old. It's a crying shame.'

The lass – what kind of name is Tabitha? – puts her head in her hands and hunches her shoulders up round her ears.

Barrett looks away again, up at the horizon, over at the black smudge of plantation in the west, the other way to the folds of hills sinking gently down the valley to the east, even straight ahead at the water, which isn't his favourite view. He's not a fanciful man but he hates the loch when it's in this mood. Flat and glassy he can appreciate, watching the clouds reflected there. He can see why people take photos, even films. He can see why people set up easels and paint it. And, when the wind whips up waves that scud across, sending up spray, he can sit and watch it like a screensaver. But on days like this when it's moving but nothing's breaking the surface, it makes him think of what's under there and, worse, what might be. It makes him think of snakes tied in a sack, rising and dropping, bulging and sinking, never bursting out but never lying still. Kittens, it used to be back in the bad old days. Was it ever puppies?

To stop these ugly thoughts, he looks away from the water. His eyes rest on the dam and he feels a jolt, suddenly remembering what's been driven from his mind.

'There was an explosion here last night,' he says to Tabitha. 'Not a big one but something went wrong in the water. Were you here? Did it wake you?'

Gordo puts a couple of paper plates down on the counter then comes out and round to join them. 'Two B & Es,' he says. 'Three teas.' When he's transferred the cups to the table, he opens the storage bit under the counter and takes out an old chip pail. He turns it upside down to make a third seat. 'That's what brought the polis up,' he tells her. 'That's what brought *us* up.'

'That cop said as much,' the lass says. 'I thought I was imagining things.'

'That's a funny conclusion to jump to,' says Barrett.

She frowns at him. She must be forty – Barrett remembers Davey saying they were all born one after the other, the four of them – and she looks her age when she frowns. 'Well, to be fair,' she says, 'I'd had a fair whack of Ouzo. But, as well as that . . . I thought you'd know about me. I thought Davey would have told you.'

'Told us . . .?' says Barrett, pushing one of the cups towards her. He's hoping she'll wrap her hands round it and breathe in the steam, even if she doesn't want to drink it.

She reaches right past the cup and takes one of the rolls. 'Why I'm back.'

Barrett wants to stop her. They should be talking about Davey, sharing memories. Then he thinks there's plenty of time for that when it's official (as if a note, two cop cars and an undertaker wasn't official enough). He leans forward to pick up his butty carefully in both hands so's not to waste a drip of yolk if it's burst.

'Divorce,' she says. 'Lost my husband, my job, my house and my son.'

'You puir wee sowel,' he says. He talks like his granny when he's trying to be consoling. He's noticed it before.

'He only told us the old stuff,' says Gordo.

'And I've got a handy history of poor mental health, so I decided it would be quite nice to go off my rocker again. When I was sitting there last night and heard a bang and a splash, I thought – I *hoped* – I'd managed it. From trauma this time. What they call "major stress".'

'But no such luck, eh?' Barrett says. He can't for the life of him think why she's saying all this. Or more like he's hoping that when the first shock of Davey's death is by her, she doesn't regret blurting such private things to a pair of strangers.

'Not so far,' she says. 'Mind you . . .' She turns and looks over her shoulder towards Davey's house. 'Bereavement's another high-scoring card.'

Gordo's face falls. He's young. He's not seen enough of life to appreciate gallows humour. Barrett gives her the laugh her brave wee joke deserves, but it comes out wobbly and turns into a sigh.

Gordo lifts his mug and says, 'Davey.'

'It should be a dram by rights,' Barrett says, lifting his own mug nevertheless.

'I'll stick to tea,' she says. 'The Ouzo, you know?' She lifts hers and clinks it against his and then against Gordo's. The memory of the three raised litter-pickers swipes at Barrett and he knows it's hit Gordo too. 'To Davey,' she says.

'Can I ask a question?' Gordo says, but Barrett gets in quick with, 'Can *I* ask a question, actually?' She didn't mind the 'old stuff' comment, true, but God knows where Gordo's going now.

She looks from one to the other and shrugs as she wipes her mouth, quite daintily, on her paper napkin. She's managed to polish off the butty and there's not so much as a drip of sauce on the paper plate.

'Have you any idea why?' he says. 'Davey.'

She takes a minute to think and then shakes her head. 'Have you? You're his friends. If it's something recent, you'd be the ones.'

Gordo shrugs. Barrett can't even bring himself to do that much.

'But I get why you're asking,' she goes on. 'It might *not* be recent. It might be the "old stuff".' She tips her head at Gordo, as if she more than didn't mind the 'old stuff' comment. As if she's grateful he summed it up so neatly. 'We didn't have the best childhood, Davey and me. Any of us really. Well, you'll know all that, if you're local.'

Not the best childhood, Barrett echoes to himself and thinks no one's going to clobber her for over-reacting.

'But then who does have a perfect childhood?' she says. 'It didn't seem weird at the time. Your life's just your life. You think every family's like your own.'

Barrett's trying to nod and look as if he agrees but he thinks he's failing. Gordo's definitely failing. He's got one eyebrow up, one down, and his mouth open. She sees it and smiles, then looks away across the water. The light's changed while they've been sitting here. The sun's higher but the clouds are thicker and so the day seems to have grown heavy. The hills have lost their silver glint and turned a flat brown. Only the loch is the same, still bulging and rolling, still not breaking. It makes Barrett feel sick just looking at it. It made him *be* sick, over the side with the rest of them jeering, that one time he went out. Ten-foot waves he could have coped with – the adrenaline would have helped – but that endless greasy slipping and rolling did for him.

'Can I ask my question now?' Gordo says.

'Sorry.' She blinks and uses the time her eyes are shut to turn his way. It makes her look robotic. 'Go ahead,' she says, when her eyes are open again.

'Why the hell were you drinking Ouzo?'

And so she's actually laughing when they hear the sound of another car. They're all smiling as they turn and watch a couple step out of a Range Rover and head for Davey's garden gate. The man opens it and steps aside to usher the woman through. The woman, already dressed in black, stalks up towards the house looking like someone headed for the gallows but carrying it off well.

Tabitha stands and wipes her hands down the fronts of her jeans as if her palms are sweaty. 'Every family's like your own,' she says again. 'Ho, ho, ho.'

SEVEN

Tabitha

I knew Johnny would come. He had to. He's the next of kin. But I never dreamed he would bring her with him. As I pull myself up the short climb to Davey's garden gate I try to prepare myself for seeing her.

My preparations are these: first the usual. I breathe in. I breathe out. I think of a meadow. When being somewhere else fails, I give the exact opposite a go. I hold my eyes wide open so the wind makes them leak tears, telling myself, 'See? You are *here*. It's *now.*' I stamp my feet down hard, telling myself, '*This* is real. It's *this* year. It's today.'

But that fails too. With one look at a strange woman, stalking on her high heels towards Davey's door, the past has rolled over the horizon like a dioxazine purp— like a purple thundercloud and engulfed me.

We're girls again.

I'm a child.

There were four of us. Wait, at the start there were eight of us. Well, right at the start there were four of *them*. Four grown-ups: Zelda and Watson in the old school at the top of the hill, Rowan and Roddie in the schoolhouse that used to be halfway down the hill but is now nearly at the bottom by the water's edge. Then the kids came along, one after the other like the teeth in a zip. Auntie Rowan had Davey, Zelda had Jo. Auntie Rowan had Johnny, Zelda had me. And there we were, one big happy family up on the hill above the waterline. Brothers, wives and cousins.

Briefly.

The brothers died. That's the first thing that put the look on the cops' faces, put the hesitation in Gordo's voice, the careful kindness in Barrett's. The Muirs of Hiskith set themselves up higher than everyone else and look what happened. I'm quoting, of course. We didn't set ourselves anywhere. I don't even know *who* I'm quoting. Them. The valley. The town.

Poor old town. And it wasn't even the first time. Away back when the mills closed, there was no point to the reservoir. Years later when the mines closed, no one needed the colliery brickworks. Same thing again. So the brick men went home to sit on the couch. Then, when the kilns were smashed and the chimneys were dropped into a cloud of red dust, when the shiny new factory rose up, they went back, meatpackers now.

Watson and Roderick Muir were the only ones who didn't climb the hill to the west of Kirkconnel where the smoke was thicker than the dust had ever been, where the meat cooked hotter than the bricks ever had. They didn't put hairnets on. Not them. Roddie and Watson took their redundancy cheques and went the other way. They bought a house and a school, long abandoned, high on the moor, miles from anywhere, and a patch of land to go with each. Crucially, a patch of freehold land. There they waited for fortune to find them.

Everyone looks for someone else to blame. It's only human. If I knew who on the council, or the electricity board, or in Westminster – someone with connections somewhere – told my dad the old reservoir was set to be the engine of a new hydro-electric scheme, I'd blame *them*. But who even knows if a real man in a blazer on a golf course ever said anything. (Why would he have said it to two brothers with their brickworks redundancy?)

Over time, my dad started blaming my uncle and my uncle started blaming my dad, like a snake eating its own tail. Or so Zelda tells me on the rare occasions that she speaks of it at all. The acrimony grew and grew like venom in sacs, she says. And when the town turned on the brothers, they blamed each other for that too.

'What do you mean?' I asked her once. 'Hadn't "the town" turned on them already?'

'Well, quite,' Zelda said. 'Pitchforks and flaming torches.' She seldom listens properly and so fairly often she doesn't answer the question you're asking.

'They turned on them when the brickworks closed, right?' I said. 'Out of envy.'

'Jealousy,' Zelda said. 'Two quite different emotions. Both

corrosive in the end. But then there was . . .' She stopped herself.
She disdains gossip.

'What?' I asked. If ever I got Zelda talking, I kept at her like
a terrier. It could be months, years, before she opened up again.
'Oh, the Seventies, Tabitha,' she said that time. 'The Eighties.
Such a dreary time in this part of the world. *Endless* strikes, you
see. *Endless* . . . muscling in.'

'Muscling in on what, Mum?' I asked.

'Exactly!' said Zelda. 'Those Kirkconnel men weren't even
redundant miners turned meatpackers. They were redundant
brickmakers. Stolen valour, in my book.'

I thought I could see a glimmer of what she was on about at
last. Solidarity in the town, an artist finding it all rather 'dreary'
up on the moor. And the upshot was that the two brothers who'd
got above themselves hadn't a friend in the whole valley.

Which makes it even sadder that they hadn't seen each other
for years the day my dad died.

I can't remember either of them very clearly. I was barely
toddling that terrible day and Uncle Roddie had started keeping
to himself long before it. Even to Jo he was nothing more than
a lighted window and a passing car when he had to go to the
doctor. (Your life's just your life. You think every family's the
same as your own.)

'But didn't he have friends?' I asked Zelda once.

'Roddie?' she said. It came out like a squawk. 'Hardly. No
one from Kirkconnel would give either of them the time of day.
Give any of us the time of day.'

'Why?' I asked.

'Small men with small minds, Tabitha,' was all she would ever
tell me.

It wasn't just the brothers doing the blaming. Auntie Rowan
blamed Zelda for having ideas above her station. Her evidence?
Our pretentious names – Jocasta and Tabitha instead of her David
and her John. Although my name's not Zelda's fault, because Jo
chose it for me. But Auntie Rowan reckoned if my dad hadn't
married 'a Zelda from an art school' – her voice curdled with
scorn as she said it – but had settled down with another Rowan,
same as Uncle Roddie did, then home ownership, cashing in,
getting rich, grand plans, fantasies, delusions and the hard crash
back to earth, none of it would have happened. I tried to talk her

out of this once. I must have been eighteen, a first-year student armed with one term's worth of psychology. I said that Zelda was quite a woman but even *she* couldn't give her husband schiz—

I didn't get to finish the word. There were so many words you couldn't say in front of Auntie Rowan by then. There were so many memories you couldn't share, as if the ending had spread backwards and stained the good times.

And there were good times. We lived out on the summer hills, going for miles standing up on the pedals of our bikes, throwing ourselves down in springy heather or nibbled grass, staring up at the endless bowl of sky above us that we owned as sure as we owned the rocks and the bracken. We owned the burns and the waterfalls with the deep ponds underneath them. We owned the good trees with branches set for climbing as if by design. We owned the dips where we could hide under awnings made from pine branches. We owned the corpse of a fox that we watched bloat and shrink until it turned into a dull mummy of itself and then into a pile of bones. We owned the nests of the grouse, the music of their flustered warnings when we got too close, the eggs, the chicks, the sudden emptiness the day they fledged and flew. We owned the sorrel that puckered our mouths and the watercress at the edge of the burns that made us sneeze. It was our world, whether we were pirates, or knights, or aliens. It was ours.

And it was even better in the snow. I'm too young to remember the winter of '78. 'Lucky you,' Zelda said dryly, one time. But I'm there in the photos along with the other three, wrapped up in duffel coats and hand-knitted scarves, mittens turning our hands into useless flippers. I swear I can remember hearing my breath loud inside the padded hood of my snowsuit, the feel of the damp cuffs making my wrists and ankles burn. But it's '84 I'm sure of. I was nine, Johnny was ten, Jo was eleven, Davey twelve. The snow came all at once, shutting the schools early for Christmas, and then the clouds disappeared and the sky was the same icy blue as Cinderella's ball gown. The sun shone down bright and magical, with no heat to melt the drifts. They stayed in peaks like surfers' waves, the caves in their hollows sparkling. We spent the whole extended holiday outside, rushing out first thing in the morning, the cold air setting fire to the toothpaste taste left in our mouths. All day we would slide about the moor on trays and binbags, making glassy runs that wouldn't melt till after Easter. One day it was cold enough for the boys to stick their nostrils shut and then blow them back open. They chased after us to make us watch, wrecking our girl game. Because of course Jo and I, posing in headbands and sunglasses, were pretending to be princesses at Klosters. Both pretending to be the same princess, I suppose. And we had the entire moor to ourselves. No one came up from the valley to join us, day after glittering day.

But let's be honest. That was summertime, plus one perfect winter and the hazy memory of one more. Usually, it was raining. Usually, the track was puddles and potholes, with bog to either side. By November, the battered bracken stalks were slippier than our glassy sledge runs had ever got and the sleet dashed us in the face, finding the seams of anything we wore, seeping through and spreading cold stains on our jumpers and cords, so, when we finally gave up and came in, we had to peel every stitch off our clammy pink bodies and run to the bathroom shivering.

So actually, although it's the moor I remember best, we must have spent whole weeks playing inside the school, the four of us, when the short days were filthy. It was always the school too. Johnny and Davey had started coming to ours when they were tiny, since they couldn't be trusted not to make noise and disturb their dad, already deep in his troubles. Even when he was dead and gone, it stuck. We never went to them; they came to us. When it rained. Which it did.

We weren't allowed in the studio, but the corridor was broad and smooth for sock-skating and we got to chalk the floor for peevers as long as we wiped it off after. We played Battleship, Cluedo and Scrabble, day after day in the old head's study with the oil heater going. We re-played that first box of Trivial Pursuit until we knew it off by heart and had to turn it into Charades to make it fun again. We drank orange squash made with hot water from the kettle, and ate the rock buns Auntie Rowan sent up in a tin. She baked and cleaned with a kind of bitterness I only recognized years later when I was still feeding Scott while our marriage ended, trying to keep things normal for Albie.

I hope Albie can say the same when he looks back, but even the worst day of our childhood was pretty good. Even days when Auntie Rowan was too angry to turn her oven on and it was toast with the hot juice, even when Zelda's music was loud enough to drown the telly and no one could agree what to watch anyway, eventually Davey would sit up straight and remind us about Yahtzee or try to teach us poker again. We had a séance once.

I don't know if Davey saw it changing. Felt it. He was fourteen when Jo declared herself too old for children's games. She took to taping the charts off the radio, hunched over the REC button on a Sunday night. Johnny was twelve, lounging on my bed, listening to her music, bouncing a tennis ball off the Pretenders poster.

I'd be outside in the hall, making jumps from clothes poles and flowerpots for the skate Olympics, with Davey on his board and me on my in-lines. We had heats and knock-out rounds. We had real medals. So maybe he missed the signs too. I think he must have. I think everyone did.

I think everyone put it down to what adolescence does to kids. *Some* kids, because Davey never changed. He stayed as dorky and sunny as ever, coming to tell me about the gooseberries ripening in the old gang-hut dip, or about black baby rabbits at the edge of the pines, a sheep with triplets down by the last cattle grid and did I want to say to the farmer that I'd bottle-feed the wee one if the ewe was struggling. Or maybe Davey changed too but, because I was still a child and he was kind, he stuck with me while the other two got to be proper teenagers. Slammed doors, loud music, strange clothes.

Then it happened.

Jo was already seventeen when Johnny had his sixteenth birthday. Not quite three weeks later, I heard Auntie Rowan's voice in our house. It was late, after midnight, and she was shouting, spewing such ugliness, bitter as lye, that I put my head under my pillow. Zelda didn't shout back but the next morning she was pale and her hand shook as she tried to cut bread for the toaster. I remember her having to shave off squint bits to make it fit.

'A family wedding,' she said, in a bright, grim voice. 'You might have overheard us discussing it, Tabitha.'

'Auntie Rowan's getting married again?' I said. 'She didn't sound very happy. Where's Jo?'

Zelda turned and looked at me as if I was messing with her,

as if I'd picked today of all days to follow Jo into the pit of sarcasm.

'Your sister is getting married,' Zelda said. 'She is marrying your cousin. *Her* cousin. Rowan wants to stop it.'

'Jo and Johnny?' I said, and even then I thought how neat it sounded, how much of a pair they made. The last few years shuffled about in my mind. It wasn't kind Davey still making time for wee Tabby, was it? It was them, Jo and Johnny, pulling away and leaving the pair of us behind them. 'Is that legal?' I asked.

'It's legal,' Zelda said. 'They told poor Rowan last night that the banns come good this weekend, since they registered it on his birthday. It's legal and it's unstoppable. Though tremendously misguided.'

'Is she pregnant?' I ask.

'She says not. Which is something.'

'So what's the rush?'

'Well, exactly. I'd rather they simply . . .'

'Gag,' I said, very glad she hadn't spelled it out. 'Mum, are you sure it's not a wind-up?'

'I suppose we'll find out on Saturday,' Zelda said. 'We're invited, apparently.'

I still didn't believe it. I got dressed and went down to the schoolhouse. Davey was earthing up a long row of potatoes in the back garden. He had mud clinging to his boots and there was that good dirt smell in the spring air, when suddenly you can tell there's living stuff in the soil, as well as the minerals that make it tangy all winter.

'Have you heard?' I asked him.

He stuck his spade in the bed as if he was trying to take off something's head with it. 'We've got four days,' he said. 'To find a priest or a doctor to talk some sense into them. Or talk to a reporter and *shame* them out of it. My mum's collapsed. How's yours?'

'A bit wobbly,' I said. 'For her. Did you know it's legal?'

'Cousins marrying cousins?' Davey lifted his shirt tail and wiped his face with it as if he was hot. Or maybe it was cold sweats from feeling sick at the thought of what Jo and Johnny were going to do. What Jo and Johnny had probably been doing for years. I looked away from his milk white belly and the thin tail of black hair that came down from the round mat of it on his concave chest. 'Yes, I know it's legal,' he said, 'but it's a terrible idea, when the link is two brothers who died in their forties of the self-same *thing*, for God's sake.' He was almost shouting. I had never seen him like this except springing a crow-trap, and even then he didn't shout until the mesh was cut and bent safely away and the poor terrified crow had battered its way up into the thermals and was gone. 'Look, Tabby, you don't need to be involved in this,' he said. 'You're too young to understand.'

'I'm fourteen months younger than Johnny,' I said. 'And he's getting married!'

Auntie Rowan came outside then, stalking over the grass in her slippers. Her face was swollen and the skin around her eyes looked sore from crying.

'Did you know, Tabitha?' I shook my head. She stared at me a long time. 'Did you hear what I told your mother last night?' Did I? I wasn't sure what I might have missed when my head was under the pillow.

'It wouldn't be legal if it was *so* terrible,' I say.

'You know nothing,' she spat at me.

'Mum,' said Davey.

I can't remember what else he said or whether Rowan said any more.

In fact, I can't remember much of anything that happened for the rest of that week leading up to the Saturday when Jo and Johnny went into the registry office as two and came out as one. When the six of us that were left became four.

I can't remember the wedding at all. I know I was there because I've seen photographs with me in them, same as the pictures of me as a toddler that snowy winter. For the wedding, I was in peach muslin, like one of the Bennet girls. Zelda called it Naples orange, just for spite I reckon, but even she had to concede that Jo wore white. It was nearly still the Eighties and wedding dresses were humongous but hers was accidentally cool because she'd made it herself and she couldn't afford enough satin to make more than a sleeveless sheath. She carried a bouquet of meadow-sweet and hawthorn blossom. That's what it looks like in the photos anyway. So she must have been out on our hills to collect it, even though, in my memory, she was already gone and I was alone in our shared room from the night Auntie Rowan shouted until the day it was over.

There's a picture of Johnny and Davey in their dad's and uncle's kilts. Davey wore a tweed jacket and a brown leather sporran, but Johnny went the full shortbread tin for his wedding day.

The worst picture of all is the one of us outside the restaurant where they had the meal. You couldn't call it a *reception*, Auntie Rowan always said afterwards, enjoying her own scorn. We're in the back garden, where a couple of wooden picnic tables with bench seats attached have been set out for the good weather that's supposed to be coming for Easter. There's an ashtray visible and a row of aluminium rubbish bins. They're almost quaint now, I suppose, when we're used to plastic wheelies, but they can't have looked quaint at the time. Jo and Johnny are in the middle, holding hands. Zelda and Davey flank them. I'm right at the edge of the shot, a peach blur, as if I'm already dropping out of focus. Auntie Rowan beat me to it. She is in bed at the schoolhouse, her throat raw from crying and her hair starting to separate into greasy strands at her parting. She hasn't bathed for days.

Jo and Johnny – they really do sound like a perfect couple; they even said their vows with their short affectionate names and Rowan moaned about that too – are headed off to Dublin for a honeymoon and then to Newcastle, where Jo is starting a course at the university and Johnny is going to a sixth-form college to do A-levels. In between, they will visit Hiskith one more time, for the infamous 'annulment tea' that ends Johnny's relationship with his mum forever, when Rowan – so Zelda tells it – started out so calm and persuasive and ended up gibbering. 'Like a monkey at the zoo,' Zelda will say with great relish. 'Just like a little brown monkey.'

I will have to rely on Zelda's report. I won't see them at this tea, because it's a school day. That's a lie. I won't see them at the tea because I'm still on the intake ward, with no passes for visits home. *That's* why, after the not-really reception that I don't remember anyway, I won't see my cousin or my sister again for twenty-five years. Not until this morning, as the clouds thicken and the wind picks up and the first huge blots of rain hit my bare head hard enough to sting, and Johnny, next of kin, comes back to identify his brother's body, bringing his wife with him.

EIGHT

Tabitha

Zelda and I are sitting in the head's room when the undertaker's van goes by. It's a high-set vehicle and so it moves along past our line of sight like a shark fin showing above the water. We say nothing. Zelda looks as serene as ever, her chin lifted to show the elegant set of her jaw and the length of her neck, her hair scraped back to show her delicate ears and accentuate the high smooth line of her brow. No. Not 'to show'. That's not fair. She raises her chin in an act of self-belief, to say she can take what comes. It just happens to make her neck look longer. And the reason she scrapes her hair back is to keep it away from the paint. I drop *my* chin when I want to drop my eyes and I pull *my* hair in front of my shoulders when I want to hide my face. It's me with the problems, not her.

'Poor old Davey,' she says. 'He didn't have much of a life, did he?'

'He had interesting work and good friends,' I say. 'He lived in a place he loved.'

'Most of that life with *Rowan*,' she says, like clockwork. I manage not to roll my eyes. Auntie Rowan has been dead for ten years but the rivalry lives on. 'You didn't know her the way I knew her, Tabitha,' Zelda adds. So something must have shown on my face after all.

Maybe she goes back into her memories then. Certainly, she says nothing when the Range Rover stops with one set of wheels hitched up on the steep verge. Maybe she thinks it's plain clothes, or a doctor. She doesn't watch as they open the doors and step down and it's not the marble glass. We've all been experts at seeing through that our whole lives. I stand up and sort of watch, through my hair. I wouldn't recognize them if I didn't know.

'Mum,' I say. She sits back and lets her head rest against the wing chair she's sitting in. Her eyes are closed. 'That's Johnny,' I tell her. 'Will I let him in?'

'Of course,' she says, frowning, still with her eyes closed. 'We must be civilized. There's no need to screech and throw plates. There never was. *I* never did.'

That's true. It was Auntie Rowan who took the vapours. Like it was Jo who said she wouldn't be back at Hiskith, casting us off because her new husband had fallen out with his mum. It's bonkers when you think of it. Maybe if I'd been well when it happened I could have helped. At least I would have fought it. As it was, back then, by the time I came up out of the depths, it felt too late. Things were set. Our new normal, horrible as it seemed, was in place. Jo was gone. Johnny was gone. Auntie Rowan was walking around like an open wound. Zelda was back in her studio. It was down to Davey and me.

'He's not alone,' I tell Zelda's closed eyes and grim mouth. 'Will I let them both in?'

'Who's with him?' she says. Then her eyes snap open and she sits up as if someone's pulled a lever.

'Will I let them in?' I say again. Why am I asking instead of just doing it? It's like I've lost my adult self and it only took a day.

'I'll put the kettle on,' Zelda says, standing. 'See what we've got in the fatted calf line, hmm?'

She's using her best drawling, above-it-all voice, her artists-are-different voice, the one she sharpened on Auntie Rowan all those years of their widowhood, praising a new 'suite', or the 'fitment' as Rowan called the unit with lights that she put in the living room in pride of place.

And then Rowan would say, 'Well, I suppose there's a lot of paint around,' when she looked at Zelda's battered leather armchairs and crocheted throwovers. And so they remained, locked in mutual judgement and umbrage, until Jo and Johnny split them like a coconut thrown at the ground, its two halves leaking rage.

Zelda stalks off towards the staffroom, past the rows of coat pegs that are still screwed in all along the walls. They've got pieces of tumbled glass bound in rope hanging from them now, the coats all hidden away in the old supply cupboard, but wellies are lined up underneath and there are still walking sticks and fishing rods, curling brushes and golf umbrellas, same as ever. I wish, as I walk towards the GIRLS entrance, that something had changed in the last twenty-five years. I dread Jo thinking Zelda has been holed up here, waiting.

This is only one of the fluttering thoughts that batter around inside me exactly like trapped crows, as I near the door. What will I say, is another. What if it's not even her? What if Johnny divorced her years ago and this is wife number two who doesn't know anything? Then I catch the birds, one by one, and hold them in my cupped hands until they gentle. I open my hands and let them fly off, each one taking a crumb of panic in its beak. Johnny's brother has just died and the only thing that needs to be said is 'sorry'. Davey is dead, darling daft Davey, and nothing else matters. Not today.

And of course it's her, not another wife chosen by a man with a type. It's my sister Jo, who I shared a room with for fifteen years, my best friend. How I've missed her.

That's what I say as I haul open the heavy GIRLS door and see them standing there. Johnny is a shock. He's turned into my memory of my dad and all the old photos of Uncle Roddie. His chestnut hair has faded to sand and he's cut the curls off and combed the strands straight back. He hasn't thickened in the middle as far as I can tell but he's bulked up across the shoulders and he seems taller. Well, of course he has! Of course he does! He was sixteen on his wedding day.

'Johnny,' I say. 'I'm so sorry.' Duty done, I turn to where she's standing beside him. I stare and stare. She looks like herself but also like a woman in her forties, with careful highlights, clever make-up, good clothes – she's actually in black already; Mars black, the coldest, deadest black. She's also got a stony look in her eye that I can't remember seeing before, even when she was locked in our room with her music and her grievance. Then she swallows hard – I see her throat dip and rise – and I realize she's frightened.

'Jo,' I say, reaching both hands out to her. 'I've missed you.'

When she hugs me I smell perfume I don't recognize, and hair products more expensive than the ones I use, but I smell lavender water too. It's on her clothes. She still irons with scented water like she used to. I squeeze her harder, briefly, before I let her go.

They walk into the house ahead of me. I even give Johnny's arm a quick squeeze as he passes and he replies with a flick of a smile for me. Then I shut the door. It feels so strange to have Jo and Johnny in the house again, and even stranger to have shut Davey out, to know that he was in that van that went by and we have to let him go wherever they're taking him and leave him alone there.

As I turn at last, I see Johnny halfway along the bottom corridor between the staffroom and the head's room, no sign of Jo.

'Where is she?' I ask him.

'I'm in here,' comes Jo's voice. She's gone into the studio and, in my confusion, I go scurrying after her. Verboten. No entry. Here be dragons. But I'm there before I know what I'm doing.

Jo is sitting in one of the armchairs. It used to be in the head's room until it got too knackered even for Zelda's low standards – her aesthetic, as she says. Now it sits by the little solid-fuel stove with the bent-tin chimney where Zelda perches to look at her work in progress and think it over. There's a tin of tobacco and a packet of rolling papers on top of the stove, filling the place with a dry scent you can feel in your teeth. It's been so many years since I was in here, I'd forgotten. I look up at the roof, half metal and half glass, and I'm sure I can see a yellow tint to the panes of the skylights, just like Jo always said would happen if she kept on smoking.

'Mum's in the staffroom,' I say, ashamed of the little tremor in my voice.

Jo rolls her eyes. 'The kitchen, Tabitha.'

'Sorry. Yes,' I say. I really have lost myself, letting my big sister scold me. 'We should go. She's waiting.'

'I'll stay here,' says Jo. 'She can come to me if she wants. It's Johnny who insisted we stop off, and it's you he wants to talk to.'

'Shouldn't you be with him, though?' I say.

'He'll be fine.'

'Are you sure? His brother's just—'

'Are you the best judge?' says Jo. I don't know what she means and so I don't answer. 'Anyway,' she goes on, 'I don't think I could stand to be in one of those tiny little rooms with her. I get claustrophobia.'

I stare at her again like I did on the doorstep, but not in welcome now, not in recognition. I'm mystified by everything about this. Jo's never been claustrophobic in her life. She looks around her with an appraising look but I'm sure that what's going on is she doesn't want to meet my eye.

'It's gone downhill a bit, hasn't it?' she says. 'Has her adoring public finally moved on to the next thing?'

'Actually,' I find myself saying, 'she's working on something new.'

'Is she indeed?' says Jo. 'I highly doubt that after all these years. And I don't see any sign of it among this lot.'

'How . . . how have you been?' I ask her, purely to change the subject.

She raises one eyebrow in that same old look of two-years-older scorn. 'What? In the last twenty-five years?' she says. 'Fine, thanks. You? Fill me in, by all means.'

'Uni, job, marriage, son, divorce,' I say. 'That's the highlights.' I wish I could say the look I give her is mildly expectant. I think it probably looks like what it is: need.

'In five words, is it?' Jo says. 'OK. Marriage, uni, house, business . . .' Then she runs out.

It's to spare her the pain of how small her life has been that I ask, 'What kind of business?'

'Why the divorce?' she snaps back, like that's the same kind of question at all.

'He met someone else,' I tell her.

'Pig,' she says.

I shrug. 'I don't know. I've never met her.'

There's a ghost of a smile on her face as she remembers the game. Then her eyes narrow. 'You skated over quite a bit there, Tabby. Starting with "uni". What about your early adventures?'

'Wh—?' I say. 'Oh. Yeah. That. Six months in a loony bin. *Then* uni, job, marriage . . .'

'Exactly,' says Jo.

'Exactly what?'

She doesn't answer. At least not quite. 'And did you ever get to the bottom of it? Mum said you didn't have a clue.'

'She did?' I ask. 'When?' Have they been in touch all this time after all?

'When we came back from honeymoon,' says Jo. 'When else

could she? Zelda said you had thrown a total flaky but no one knew why.'

'Right, right,' I say, nodding. It's peculiar the way I half have no clue what she's talking about and half understand her before she even speaks. 'So . . . "exactly" because that would make me the kind of hysterical sort who's no judge of what Johnny's going through and whether he needs you? Is that it?'

'Weddings don't usually send people off their nuts,' she says. 'Did that never occur to you?'

She says it so casually that, if I didn't know her, I'd think she was just teasing me. But I do know her.

Before I can pick my way to the point she's making, though, she has changed the subject. 'Is your ex-pig likely to come to Davey's send-off?'

'Not a chance,' I tell her.

'Shame,' she says. 'I would deck him for you.'

I smile but I keep thinking. Why is she here at Hiskith if it's not to support Johnny? Why is he here at the school when the thing he came for is over and done with down at the house? What does he want with *me*? And how can she prefer to be in here with a dozen of Zelda's paintings glowering down at us from where they're hung on the monkey bars?

She doesn't squash them in willy-nilly wherever they'll fit. She's got them in pairs, as she'll license them when the time comes, and just thinking about them makes my flesh start to crawl even though I'm facing away. I haven't deliberately looked at any of them for years. I don't have to. They're everywhere. Zelda Muir's Night and Day Paintings are, like Gordo said, jigsaws and mouse mats and tea towels and aprons. They're calendars and greetings cards and notelets and diaries. They're china mugs and melamine trays, oilcloth tote-bags and cotton cushion-covers. They're everywhere. They're like Snoopy was when we were wee.

And people love them, both ironically and unironically. People wonder about them, try to decode them, explain them, excuse them. Every so often, she'll pop up in an op-ed along with the rest of the usual suspects who could be having us on. When that happens, someone might email me to ask for my take on it all. I usually give them some variation on 'You think your family's like every other one, don't you?'

The truth is, I hate them. I blame them. I fear them. I shudder to remember back when I was tiny, when I only knew about the Day Paintings. They showed a village cradled in a dip in the hills, just like our hills at Hiskith, but it was always sunny there, unless it was snowing, always bustling with life as cheery neighbour greeted cheery neighbour over the fence, and a farmer passed through the main street, beaming down from his haycart, not minding being stopped while a child fed his horse an apple, not caring that sparrows were tweaking straws of hay off the top of his load to make their nests with. I had the cleverest, prettiest, bestest mummy of anyone, and she painted perfect pictures. And I had the kindest sister and my daddy was an angel in heaven and life was lovely.

I think I was five when I saw the Night Paintings for the first time. I thought Jo was teasing me. She told me there were secret paintings in Mummy's studio that she was allowed to see, a big girl of seven like her, but I had to be kept away from them because I was just a baby and I'd be frightened. So, one night when I woke up needing a wee-wee, I didn't go straight back to our classroom afterwards. I crept all the way down the passageway to the coat pegs. Mummy was still up. I could hear the tinkling sound of her washing up cutlery in the staffroom and there was violin music too. Bruch, I know now, but that night it sounded like fairy music, completely different from the stirring stuff she played to keep her going at her work.

I left the door open when I stole into the studio. My thinking was not to get trapped in there in case Jo was right and it was too scary. But the open door meant that I could still hear wisps of the music as I edged further and further into the forbidden room, past Zelda's armchair, stove and tobacco tin, past her easel and the table heaped with paint and rags, one lamp still lit and shining down on the crumpled tin of the squeezed-out tubes. Years later when I heard that concerto again, I felt my esophagus open as if I was going to vomit, had to cross my legs and squeeze them as I felt my bladder threaten to let go.

But that was years in the future, when I was going out with Scott. His kindness that night – checking if I was OK, summoning the waiter, asking for the music to be changed – lured me onwards to engagement, marriage, baby, complacency, rejection, heartbreak. Such a small thing to hang a life from.

The night when I was five, though. When I was only five, I saw the sunny pictures of postmen and skipping ropes, naughty robins pecking bottle tops and lucky farm children riding high on the necks of shire horses. *Had* Jo been teasing me? But then I looked further up the wall-bars at the higher pictures and felt my scalp shrink. It was the first time in my short life I had ever felt that sensation.

They were the same scenes. The streets and houses were there, garden walls and fences, even the trees and lampposts were there, in oily green and inky blue; colours I'd later learn were gentian and indigo, although at five I didn't have those words. At five, all I saw was the depthless pure black midnight of a lost village. Weeds waved in the currents, half-hiding the cottages. Fantastical fish swam in and out of the glassless windows. They were no bigger, these Night Paintings, but the emptiness once the children and milkmen were gone made them huge to my little eyes. Big enough for me to fall into and drown, they looked to me.

I stepped carefully backwards, on my tiptoes, in case someone was listening. I was sure someone was watching. And I was right. He was there in every scene, never in the middle but always somewhere at the edge: an eel, grey and coiling, with human eyes looking out at me from inside a mask.

I fled.

I ran back to our classroom and climbed the ladder to the top bunk. I sat in my muddled covers, with my knees at my ears, ankles crossed, arms wrapped tight round my shins, still shivering. Eventually, I dared to lift my head from where it had been tucked into the hollow between my belly and my thighs making my breath sound like the sea in a shell. I looked out of the window at the track leading down to the loch, the gleaming face of the water, the same track emerging on the far side again to disappear into the trees. I felt sure I would never stretch out flat again, never dare to go to sleep here on my high bed where the eel could come coiling up the posts and join me.

I was wrong about that, of course. The fear faded as fear always does. By the end of the month I was only checking three times a night that the spiky bangles of paperclips I put on all four bunkbed legs were sticking straight out to stop that eel from getting to me.

A nurse once asked me if I had spoken to Zelda about that

night, about the eel. They were forever rootling around in my childhood. I tried not to laugh at the idea. Zelda wouldn't have told me anything. She won't tell anyone. When she gives interviews she only says the paintings have already told the world everything she's got to say. Thing is, that's not true. The whole enterprise rests on a sentence she insists goes on the jigsaw box, the tea-towel label, the protective cardboard around each china mug and the paper sleeve around each calendar. 'Zelda Muir lives in a converted school above the waterline of a flooded village in rural Scotland.' That's half the secret of Zelda's success.

The other half, just as clever if much more mundane, is that she won't license one without the other so there's no such thing as a single mug; they come in pairs – one for morning coffee and one for bedtime cocoa. Tea towels for lunch dishes and supper dishes. Calendars for work appointments and after-work fun. She started the craze for double-sided jigsaw puzzles more or less single-handed.

Anyway, I don't need to ask her. I know who he is. And I was wrong about him being an eel. That long grey sinuous body was a diver in a wetsuit. His eyes looked out at me like human eyes because they were. It made much more sense than an angel in a white nightie, lounging on a cloud as if it had a built-in footstool. Because the one time Jo asked for details about what happened to Daddy, all Zelda said was, 'He drove on to the track and he didn't drive off again.' That was all she ever said with her words. The rest was in the pictures.

NINE

Tabitha

The look on Zelda's face as I open the staffroom door! She turns from the kettle with her lips parted, her expression a living leap of some emotion I couldn't name. Perhaps it hasn't got a name. Johnny is sitting at the table, with a biscuit on a plate in front of him. He's obviously accepted it to be polite, but he could no more eat it than I could.

'Jo's . . .' I begin, but I run out of words. I don't know if I'm trying to let Zelda down gently, or trying to explain to Johnny why she's not there beside him, or trying to stop Zelda wondering where she is and finding her sanctuary breached. I catch hold of my thoughts with a firm hand, picturing a leather glove, a sturdy grip. This works better than taking my thoughts to a desert or a meadow, better than giving them to birds. But only when I'm spinning off into grandiosity: sanctuary! Breach, for God's sake! It's no use at all for general freaking.

I let my firm, leather hand fall open and decide to say nothing, since Zelda might be pissed off to know there's someone in her workspace, same as I'd be.

'That policeman said you saw the envelope through the letterbox.' Johnny's voice is exactly the same. It bumps me right back to squabbling over Monopoly, all of us in the head's room with the fire lit on a miserable day. The room Jo reckons is too small to contain her.

'I'm so sorry, Johnny,' I said. 'Is it really true? I mean, I know it's true, but it's hard to believe. What happened? Poor Davey. What happened? Poor thing.' I manage to stop talking.

'It's true,' Johnny says. 'I saw him. He was peaceful, lying in his bed, but yes, it's definitely true.'

'But what happened?' I ask again.

'Suicide,' Johnny said. 'Insulin. My mum's insulin. He kept

it all these years since she died, if you can believe it. And it looks like he injected the lot.'

I feel dizzy and I can see Zelda holding hard to the rail of the stove too. It's so strange to hear Johnny talk about Auntie Rowan's medicine. About her dying. As if he was here ten years ago. For all the world as if he's been here all along, like any other son, and knows the gist of the family history. Of course, Auntie Rowan used insulin before Johnny left. And her death was public. It was in the papers, topping up the interest in 'the Muirs of Hiskith' just when it had finally begun to die down.

I know I'm fixating on that bit to keep from thinking about the other things he said. I'm a past master at running away from what I should be facing. I imagine that gloved hand again, a thick gauntlet protecting my tender flesh. I imagine it reaching out and latching on hard to the terrible cold truth. Davey has killed himself.

'Why?' I ask Johnny. 'Why would he? Was it money? Was he in some kind of financial mess he couldn't get out of? Because he never asked for help. Or was he ill and never told us? Was this his way of leaving on his own terms? Mum, did he say anything to you that would explain it? I spoke to his friends—'

'That pair!' Zelda spits the words. Maybe she's fixating on how odd his friends are instead of what *she* can't face. She's put three mugs and a fat teapot down on the table. She pushes the sugar bowl towards Johnny and then snatches her hand back, as if to deny what she's just confirmed. She knows him, remembers him, practically brought him up, used to sigh about the heaps of sugar he spooned into his tea.

Johnny smiles and says, 'Not these days, Zelda.'

'Did the letter explain anything?' I ask. She's poured a cup for me but I ignore it. The one I drank in the back of Gordo's van is sloshing around in my stomach. I think I can feel it lapping at the base of my throat. I can certainly see it in my mind's eye. But the base of my throat in this picture has got big rocks for the lapping tea to wash up against and so it might be the reservoir.

'Gremlins and Numskulls aren't real, Tabitha,' that one kind nurse used to tell me. 'Try not to think about the inside of your body so much. Look out the window at the trees and the sky.' I tried, but madness lay that way. How can you eat if you're deter-

mined to believe there's no inside of you? Why would you
endlessly hide food? And why should you deal with stinky shit
every day if it's nothing to do with you? I wasn't a toilet attend-
ant. It pissed her off royally when I said that, though. She called
me silly. She said I was being 'deliberately silly'. But I wasn't.
I was trying to do what she had told me to.

'You need to find a middle ground,' the doctor said. 'No
Numskulls. Definitely no Gremlins, but eating and drinking and
. . . the other end . . . are facts of life to deal with lightly.'

Johnny has reached into his inside pocket and pulled the letter
out. He lays it on the table. 'You tell me what it explains,' he
says and slides it over towards me, pushing it round the teapot
and milk jug as if he's playing at cars the way he used to, the
way they both used to, making *brrm-brrm* noises as they moved
pepper pots and sauce bottles around the plastic tabletop waiting
for our plates to be put down.

'Don't the police need it?' I ask him.

But I pick it up and read the front like I did through the
letterbox. 'To Whom It May Concern'. It's not sealed. It's never
been sealed. I can feel my fingers slide over the shiny band of
new glue as I lift the flap. My heart is starting to bump and I
don't understand why he wants me to read it for myself, like I
don't understand why Jo won't come into the staffroom, why
she didn't stay in the car, why she came at all, why Davey killed
himself, why Scott left me, why he wanted the house so badly,
when it was me who cared for it, did the garden, did the decor-
ating, even cleared the gutters, why he wanted Albie so badly
when it was me who washed his clothes and cooked his meals
and nagged him to finish his homework.

I don't understand anything. Certainly I don't understand what
I'm looking at, now that the unsealed envelope is lying on the
table and I'm holding its contents in my hands.

It's not a letter. It's another envelope. But this one *is* sealed
and it's not for whom it may concern. It's for me. On the front,
in Davey's messy, jagged handwriting, it says: 'Tabitha Lawson
née Muir'.

'Is this why the cops didn't take it?' I say.

Johnny nods. 'They asked me to ask you to drop it off and let
them get a copy. For the records. But it's cut and dried. The
police surgeon said it was cut and dried.'

He's staring at the envelope in my hands. I imagine opening it and finding another envelope. I hope so. I hope the next one is addressed to someone else, anyone else, so I don't have to read what Davey has written. Given my family's talent for secrets, maybe if I don't see it with my own eyes today, I'll never have to know.

But I am out of luck. Inside the envelope addressed to me is a folded sheet of paper. I glance at Zelda, back to gripping the stove rail with both hands as she leans against it. I glance at Johnny, who's turned into a waxwork of himself, nickel titanate yellow from his neck to his hairline. He's not even blinking. I unfold the paper.

It's not a letter. It's a will.

This is the last will and testament of David Roderick Muir signed and witnessed this second day of October 2015. Being of sound mind and free from influence and coercion, I hereby bequeath all my property and worldly goods, comprising Hiskith Old School, its policies and its contents, as well as my other holdings, movable estate and financial assets, to my cousin Tabitha Lawson. I appoint as sole executor Timothy Hawes Esq of Hawes, Beattie & Thom, Dumfries, who hold a copy of this will, the deeds to my property, other relevant documents and all necessary keys.

It's signed at the bottom and it's witnessed by one Barrett Langham and one Lyle Gordon.

Below the signatures, Davey has added a scrawled note: 'Tabby, you didn't deserve any of what has happened to you and I hope this helps. D.'

Helps. That word blackens and deepens until it's like a scar gouged into the landscape of the paper, until it cuts through not just the paper but the table beneath it and the floor and the ground the house is built on. *Helps?*

'What does it say?' Johnny asks and, when I move my head, the creak in my neck makes me think I've been sitting there silent and still for a long time.

'It's a will,' I tell him. 'It says nothing.'

But of course that's not true. It says plenty.

It was September the third last year that Scott told me he was leaving. He did it when we got back from our summer holiday. Even at the time, the practicality of that struck me as hilarious. I laughed out loud, right in his face. I didn't laugh again for months, maybe not until this morning when Gordo asked about the Ouzo. (Gordo. Who witnessed this will and never told me, all those hours we sat crammed together in his little van.)

For the whole of last winter and spring, once I'd faced the fact that it was true, I worked on the finances, determined to keep the house. Early summer, I was told Royal Danish were letting me go. By high summer, I knew why and was speaking to a solicitor. Later in the summer, I'd discovered there was nothing I could do. I remember reeling out of the meeting into sticky heat and the sound of an ice-cream van. When September rolled round again, I was speaking to our mediator. Mid-month, I found out the judge was going to let Albie decide. End of the month, Albie decided, plumping for his room, his stuff, his pals and his dad. So it must have been about the first week in October, right enough, that I finally accepted what was happening to me and told Davey, in one of our regular messenger chats. I told him I'd be jobless, homeless, childless – and penni-less too – if I didn't stop asking lawyers to fight it for me. I told him. I told him I couldn't cope. I asked him if he had any ideas.

But that's crazy don't say crazy mad don't say mad, nuts don't say nuts. No one could have dreamed that telling a friend – a cousin – you're in a mess would make him kill himself.

'Why?' I say again, even though they don't know what I'm asking now. 'Why would he? Why did he?'

'The cops,' Johnny says, 'think he didn't want to go to jail.'

'Jail?' Zelda's voice is sharp like a slap and it brings me back.

'They think he tried to blow up the dam,' Johnny says. 'Flood the valley and drain the loch. He must have known he'd do time for that.'

'What?' Zelda rears back as if she's been struck. Of course, unless it's hit Radio 3 she won't have heard about it yet. 'Blow up the dam?' she says, sounding dull, sounding stupid. 'Drain Hiskith? Davey?'

'There was an explosion,' I say. 'Late last night. Underwater. But it didn't work.'

'What the devil do you mean "didn't work", Tabitha?' Zelda

says. 'It might have completely undermined the dam. Anything could happen.'

I wonder why she's so upset. It's not as if the water could flow uphill.

'But anyone who bombs a dam must be hoping for something a bit more dramatic,' says Johnny. 'So then they thought *that* might be relevant. If he'd been planning it a while and then it was a failure.'

'But why would Davey . . .?' I said. I can't finish the question.

'There's really nothing in there?' Johnny says, nodding at the piece of paper I'm clutching so tight in my hand that it's buckled into origami. I hold it out to him to let him see for himself.

He smooths it and reads it. 'I'm sorry,' I say. 'And, look, it surely can't be legal.' I'm thinking if Davey did blow up the dam then he wasn't of sound mind and it won't stand. I'm at it again. Who cares about a will, a house, a reservoir? Davey is dead.

'What won't stand?' says Johnny. He's still waxen and now his voice is as bloodless as his white cheeks.

'He can't disinherit his next of kin, can he?'

'That's just children,' Zelda says. 'You can't disinherit your children. I wouldn't be so quick to look a gift horse in the mouth, Tabitha. In your current circumstances, I mean.'

'But then he definitely can't leave me the house,' I say. 'Because Rowan couldn't leave it to him. Half of it belongs to *you*, Johnny.'

He shakes this off as if he's walking through cobwebs, clawing to get the thought away from him. 'I don't think that's right,' he says. 'We asked at the time. You can leave a house and land to whoever you fancy. It's a moveable estate that the kids are entitled to get their mitts on. Cash, jewellery, priceless antiques.'

'Rowan had some lovely pieces,' Zelda chips in. 'Not my taste, but good stones.'

'Not by the time she died,' says Johnny and again I get that slight whirl of vertigo. What does he know about the end of his mother's life? He wasn't here.

'You need to believe me, Tabby,' Johnny is saying. 'I don't want the place. I didn't want a share of it then and I certainly don't want it now.'

But what he just told me is echoing in my head: we asked at the time. *We* asked at the time. In other words, *Jo* checked at the time to see if Auntie Rowan's engagement ring and garnet bracelet and pretty gold watch were coming her way. Then didn't even show her face at the funeral. Let's see, I think to myself, what *she* makes of Johnny being so generous now.

'Maybe you can come and choose a keepsake,' I say.

'Maybe,' Johnny says. He's re-reading the will for what must be the fourth time as if there's more it can tell him, like poetry or the Torah.

'Maybe these lawyers in Dumfries have got a letter that could explain a bit more,' I say. Johnny looks up sharply. It must be a jolt of hope in his face but if I didn't know him I'd have said it was fear. 'You know,' I go on, 'along with the deeds and the keys. What keys anyway?'

'It's all very sad,' Zelda says.

I can tell she's itching to get back to work. A bit of me wants to let her go and find Jo in there, see what happens next. It's like I'm hurting so bad, as this new truth settles in like toothache – Davey is dead! – that I need to spread the pain around. That's a bit of me. But a lot more of me wants to get Jo and Johnny out of the house and go down past Davey's to the water's edge to see if the van and the pick-up are still there – I haven't seen them passing – because the toothache is strong enough to be scary and I want to share it with people who'll feel it too. People who loved Davey as his aunt and his brother never seemed to.

'You look a bit peaky, Mum,' I say, in the end. 'Why don't you sit and finish your tea? I'll see Johnny out and then I might go for a walk and get some fresh air.'

I watch the Range Rover disappear over the hill before I turn back to face the water. It was easy enough to get rid of them and keep Zelda where she was. She's always open to the idea that she works too hard and should take better care of herself. Jo was champing to leave. Johnny muttered that he'd be in touch about the funeral and, with a peck on the cheek from each of them, they're gone.

I wish I hadn't just looked at those Night Paintings. I try to tell myself what I started telling myself every day once the nurse led me to the realization of it. It was the best day of one-to-ones in the whole six months, the day I felt that sweet wash of understanding surge through me. I remember laughing with the blessed relief of it. The Day Paintings, like the nurse helped me see, weren't real. Scottish mining villages don't have duckponds and blacksmiths and orchards. The Day Paintings were fantasy. So why did I ever believe that the Night Paintings were true? They were fantasy too. Light fairytales and dark fairytales, but all fairytales.

Back in the real world, there are a handful of cars parked up down by the water now, besides the sandwich van, which looks closed. The chairs are tipped up against the table, the awning is down and there's a shutter pulled over the serving hatch. A few men stand looking at the dam through binoculars. The news must be out down the valley, through the town.

Barrett's pick-up is rumbling up the track towards me. Both men are in the front seat. We meet right outside Davey's garden gate. *My* garden gate, if such a thing is actually possible.

Barrett stops and pulls on the handbrake but doesn't turn the key to kill the engine.

'He's dead,' I say to them. I should soften it for his closest friends, I suppose. 'He killed himself,' I add, hardening it instead. And then I let out an enormous braying sob. Barrett switches off the engine and they both climb down.

'Well, we knew as much,' Barrett says. 'Didn't we?'

Gordo is closer and so it's him who puts his arms round me. I weep helplessly into the grease-spattered, sauce-scented apron he's still wearing. He pats my back. Barrett pats it too and they're not in time with each other. In their awkwardness, they're not all that gentle either so I feel, after a minute, as if I'm being tenderized rather than comforted. I pull away.

'Sorry,' I say. 'I'm sorry. It's just all too much. Why didn't you tell me about the will? About the house? Never mind,' I add at their startled looks. They're nothing like each other – why should they be – a tagged and branded fox in his twenties with pitted cheeks and narrow shoulders and a pig in his fifties with hands like hams – but their expressions match now. 'Those stupid policemen think he killed himself because he tried to blow up the dam,' I tell them. The least important thing about this whole miserable day is the police making such a dumb mistake, jumping to such an outlandish conclusion, but it's easier to be angry and easier still to be angry with people who're not standing there right in front of me.

'No way,' says Gordo.

'In hell,' Barrett adds.

'It's that lot the polis should be fingering,' Gordo says, pointing down the hill at the binocular men.

'Them?' I say. 'They're just ghouls, aren't they?' Although it occurs to me that ghouls would be watching the house, not the water.

'Ramblers,' says Barrett, gesturing towards one clutch of them. 'And anglers,' with a nod at the other.

'Why would . . .?' I begin. 'I don't understand.'

'It failed the inspection, see,' Barrett says. 'The ten-year check-up. So draining it was already on the cards.'

'Drain Hiskith?' I say, just like my mum did. I feel sick. Today has had too many shocks and horrors already. I can't take any more.

'There's a public consultation document,' says Gordo. 'Online. And a hard copy in the library.'

'But they can't drain Hiskith,' I say.

'To save the cost of repairing the dam they can,' Gordo says. 'They'd use the money to replant it as woodland with a wee pond at the bottom. Amenity woodland. Walks and did someone not say camping, Barrett?'

'Glamping,' Barrett says. 'Whatever that is when it's at home.'

'And so you're saying' – my brain is moving very slowly – 'you're saying the ramblers might have tried to swing the decision by scuppering the dam?'

'Someone did,' says Gordo.

'But it can't have been Davey,' I say. Davey can't possibly have wanted Hiskith Loch to be drained. He's the last person in the world, after me and Zelda, who would want that.

'We don't think it was him either,' says Barrett.

But that's not what I mean. I'm not saying Davey didn't do it. I'm saying Davey can't have done it, couldn't have risked it, couldn't have borne it, would never do such a thing to the rest of his family. To me. I can't say any of that to these two. 'Surely Davey was on the side of the anglers,' is how I put it. I can tell that all they hear is that one word. Was. Davey was. And they're not ready for it. Davey still *is*, for this two. To stop my heart softening, to gird up my anger, because if I'm going to get through this day I'll need it, I say, 'Why didn't you tell me you witnessed his will?'

And they're back to looking like twins again, owlish in confusion.

'I've never witnessed a will,' Gordo says.

'I can't remember that I ever did,' Barrett chimes in.

'Never?' I say, and I'm shouting, suddenly. 'Can't remember? It was only a few weeks ago!' I wrestle the envelope out of my coat pocket where I've stuffed it, meaning to shake it in their faces, but the wind is sneaky up here. It rolls around the hills like a puppy scratching its back and then it'll suddenly pick up and whip litter into tiny tornadoes, make children stagger, or as now snatch a piece of paper out of your hand and juggle with it.

Gordo leaps like a basketball player and grabs it down again, grinning with the glee of all boys when they hit a target or vault a gate. He smooths it and hands it back to me.

'Look,' I say, 'let's get out of the wind, eh?'

I only mean into the lee of the gable wall but, when I come round the end of the bushes that Davey has planted to mark off the bins and toolshed from the garden proper, I see that the side door, with the smashed pane, is lying ajar. The cops haven't even secured the place.

'Should we maybe not?' Gordo says, as I push the half door all the way open. 'Or is it OK because you're related?'

'It's OK because it's my house,' I tell him, then I see what's behind the door and I stop talking, stop feeling angry, stop thinking I might cry again. I stop dead.

TEN

Gordo

She seemed like she was going to walk right into Davey's house but now she's bottled it on the doorstep. 'What?' he asks her, peering over her shoulder. 'Aw, naw!'

He's never been in this way before. Davey always used the back door and so Barrett and him did too whenever they came in for a feed after a long day on the hills, whenever they made a night of it with the cribbage board. The door to this wee pantry or scullery or whatever it is has always been closed. But now it's obvious Davey was sleeping in here. Just as obvious that he died in here. No wonder she can't make her feet step over the threshold. Gordo's legs aren't feeling too steady either.

The single bed is pushed against the far wall, but the room's so small the glass from that copper breaking in has left spangles on the grubby sheet. Jesus Christ, that sheet. It's royal blue, to match the duvet cover and the case on the single pillow, but it's black with grime in the middle where he's been lying and there's a smaller patch of greasy black in the pillow dent. There's no wee table by the bed or even a chair. Just a paperback and some screwed-up tissues on the floor, a lip salve with no lid and marks from coffee cups all over the beige vinyl like Olympic rings. That's not the worst. The worst is syringes and ampoules and ripped blister packs of something or other that the paramedics must have left behind. And it's not the weirdest. The weirdest is a Bible there by the bed. Gordo remembers everything Davey ever said about 'corporate superstition' and 'state-sanctioned magic' and yet right there on the floor is a well-thumbed leather-bound Bible with a bookmark about halfway through.

Gordo doesn't want to know any of this about his pal and wants to spare Barrett knowing. Without his glasses, the old man probably can't see all that much, so, before he can get close enough, Gordo moves to open the kitchen door, herd the pair of them through. Save Davey the riddy. Which is nuts, he knows, but he does it anyway.

Her voice is in his head most of the time so of course it's there now.

You're so nice, Lyle. You're so kind. You're so sweet.

He knew what she was going to say next back then and he wishes he could stop himself hearing the echo of it now.

You're too good for me.

It's strange coming into such a familiar room from a new direction. Even stranger to feel how empty it seems. For the first time in years, he's looking at it properly: old Mrs Muir's dishes and glasses still on the shelves of the free-standing cupboard, cloudy from disuse; the drawer below that won't shut from all the stamp albums of Davey's boyhood, the franked envelopes of his adult obsession; her sewing basket full of birdseed and plant food now; her ornaments on the high mantelpiece over the old Rayburn half-hidden by all Davey's guddle: maps and leaflets; folders and ring binders; press clippings and the albums Davey pasted them into. Gordo would wind him up, describing Google, and even Barrett joined in sometimes, telling Davey he could bookmark articles online. God knows what he was working on just before the end, Gordo thinks. There's a pile of books sitting with their spines facing out, four thick volumes covered in faded green buckram. He squints at the gold embossing on the jackets. *The Domestic Science Handbook* edited by M.C. Pepper B.Sc. Not at all Davey's usual fare. And underneath them is something even more surprising: a chunky – 'jumbo' is the word that springs to mind – pictorial history of the twentieth century, one of those bright and shiny budget books, packaged and distributed to discount shops to be stickered down to half price and bought as last-gasp stocking-fillers. Davey despised them. He taught Gordo to despise them. And yet here's a classic example of the breed sitting out on his kitchen table as if he's been using it.

The girl – woman – Tabby – sinks down into the nearest chair at the long messy table. It's Davey's chair, nearest the cooker, handy for the fridge, facing the window. 'Read,' she says, and hands the envelope to Barrett, even though it was Gordo that caught it out there, plucked it back out of the wind like an ultimate Frisbee champion.

Barrett takes out a sheet of paper and spreads it on the tabletop. He shuffles to one side as he fishes for his specs, inviting Gordo to read along with him.

It's a will. Gordo has never seen one before but it's clear enough. It's Davey's will leaving everything he owns to this woman, his cousin. It's short to the point of bald, although there's a p.s. scribbled along the bottom under the three signatures. He skips them and starts to read the note, but Barrett lets out a loud 'Heh?' and he nudges Gordo, pointing.

Gordo looks and shrugs, then looks closer. It's not his signature – it's nothing like his signature – but it's his name. Lyle M.N. Gordon, it says alongside, in printed capitals, with a date. The two men stare at each other for a moment. What does this mean? Barrett looks away first.

'Hen,' he says, 'sorry to break it but that's not my signature. Gordo?'

He shakes his head.

'What do you mean?' she says. 'You're not trying to tell me it's a different Barrett Langham and Lyle Gordon?'

Barrett sits down in one of the other chairs, the less comfortable ones left over from old Mrs Muir's day. They've got rope seats and carved rods on their backs and they're brutal without a jumper slung over them to soften the knobs. He takes a pen from the inside pocket of his fleece and pulls a sheet of newspaper closer. When he's finished, he shows her and she goes through a performance of checking one against the other, then sits back and lets out a huff that might have been laughter if there was any mirth in it. As it goes, it's a sound of utter defeat.

'That's about right then,' she says. 'That'll show me.'

She looks as if she might cry, and Barrett shifts about on his chair. Gordo knows he hates women crying. He admitted that he once took his daughters back to their mum's early on a Sunday when it was his weekend, because 'some celebrity' had died and they couldn't stop bawling. 'Not the Geldof girl, poor lass,' he'd said. 'I'd never heard of this one.' Simone Battle, Gordo reckoned, but you never know which way it'll go with Barrett – his age can be a sore point.

Gordo pats Tabitha on the back as he passes to take another chair and asks, 'Show you what?'

She sniffs and clears her throat and Barrett finally stops

squirming about, making the raffia on his chair squeak. 'Don't hate me,' she says. 'It's not that I wouldn't take Davey back in a heartbeat, but it just occurred to me, see, that if this house is mine then I've got a house for my son. I could try anyway. I could tell him we wouldn't be bunking in with his granny and it might swing it. Maybe.'

Gordo says nothing. Barrett is as straight an arrow as they come. It's hard to tell what he'll make of what just crossed Gordo's mind.

But he has misjudged his friend. It's Barrett who says, 'I won't tell if you don't. If Davey wanted you to have the house, hen, it's fine by me.'

'But,' she begins, then stops. Her eyes travel around the kitchen. From the way her head lifts and drops, the way her eyelids rise and lower, it seems like she's looking at the top line of stuff Davey keeps – kept – crammed in along the back of the worktops: folders and leaflets and reference guides to God knows all what. He's got three smoked-plastic boxes of floppy disks lined up behind the sink. And every envelope that ever came through the door. You could forgive her for quailing at the thought of living here. That's not what the 'but' was, though. She's not wondering if she really wants it. 'But,' she says again, 'it can't be that easy. What if he signed the will at this solicitor's office? The one with the deeds and the keys. What keys, by the way? Do you know? Won't he . . . Mr . . .'

'Hawes,' says Barrett, looking at the will again.

'Hawes, right. Won't he have *seen* the witnesses? And need to see them again?'

'I don't think so,' Gordo tells her, but the truth is all he knows about wills comes from films and the telly.

'Why don't I go with you?' says Barrett. 'We walk in, I introduce myself, see what he makes of me, play it by ear.' Gordo would have said that if he'd thought of it. He should have said something anyway. The next chance he gets, he'll definitely say something. Because, with Barrett's words, her face has cleared. It's more than cleared. It's lit up. As if Barrett's just handed her a present.

'You're less keen?' she says, turning. She must think Gordo's silence means he's scared to stick his neck out for her. Barrett's looking at him as if he's spat in her cider.

'I'm like you,' Gordo says. 'I'm asking myself "what keys"?'
She stands and goes back towards the wee pantry Davey's
been sleeping in.

'The key for this door's in the lock,' she says. Then: 'Oh God,
I can't bear it.'

'Look,' Gordo says, leaping up, 'at least let me chuck out the
needles and swabs. At least let's get rid of that, eh?' *You're so
kind.* He goes to the kitchen bin to lift the lid but for some reason
it won't open. He fumbles and scratches at it, getting hot at his
neck to be fluffing so simple a task. He's relieved when she
waves him away.

'Not yet,' she says. 'Not right now, eh?'

'You were saying?' says Barrett gently. 'About the keys?'

Tabitha shakes her head. It's as if she's literally shaking Gordo's
nonsense about tidying up out of her head and getting back to
what matters. She heads across the kitchen towards the hall. After
a minute she shouts back, 'The back door key's in the lock too.'
Her footsteps go up the passageway to the front of the house.
She doesn't shout this time but when she comes back she says,
'Front door key's hanging on a hook right inside. Has Davey got
locked cupboards somewhere? A strongbox? A safe?' She says
the last word sheepishly, as if she feels daft for asking.

'Why not have a quick check round and see?' Barrett's done
it again. He's thought of the right thing to say and said it, making
her smile. Gordo stands up. It's never bothered him before that
Barrett decided where they would pick and Davey took care of
the pickings, leaving Gordo to tag along, foot soldier, redshirt.
But he doesn't want to start off that way from the get-go.

'I'll have a shufti round the upstairs if you check down here,'
he says and heads for the hall before they can stop him. Apart
from anything else, he wants to be the one who opens the doors
of the bedrooms Davey seems to have abandoned in case there's
anything even worse behind them than the state of that pantry.

From the ground floor you can't see beyond the bend at the
bottom of the staircase and so he's not ready for the sight of
main flight. Both sides are stacked with junk: loose papers,
envelopes, leaflets, pamphlets, same as the kitchen worktops, and
also fat Jiffies and those stiffer ones, stuffed with shredded paper
that go like a Hoover bag bursting if you rip them. Whatever this
is, there's plenty of it, because besides the Jiffies there are

old-fashioned parcels made up of brown paper and wrapped with string. Gordo threads his way up the middle of the stairs between the two walls of packages. It's just as bad on the landing except it's boxes up here: crisp boxes and biscuit boxes, stacked up like the walls of a fort, leaving only a chicken's foot of three thin pathways to each of the bedroom doors. He goes to open the nearest one and feels the prang in his palm as the old iron handle stops dead. It's locked. So are the other two.

When he gets back downstairs, Tabitha is standing by the living-room door and Barrett's bent over checking the keyhole. 'Well, that's the mystery of the keys solved then,' he says. 'Same upstairs, is it?'

Gordo nods. He doesn't tell Tabitha what he's seen on the stairs. No point pissing on her chips. She's had a bad enough day. *You're thoughtful. You'd make a great daddy.* 'Same in there?' he asks, pointing at the door on the other side of the passageway. It was the heidie's study when this was the schoolhouse, Davey once told them, then his mum's sewing room, where Davey said he 'stored stuff'.

'So much of this is just weird,' she says, trailing back to the kitchen. 'Did he seem OK to you recently?'

'People hide it though,' says Barrett.

She shakes her head. 'Not just the suicide,' she says. 'Why would he lock up rooms when he lived alone?' It doesn't seem like it's rhetorical, because she looks back at both of them, hoping for an answer. Then she gives up, and says, 'And why would he forge your signatures on his will instead of just asking you for real? And why the hell would he blow up the dam?'

'Aye, but at least that would help explain the will,' Barrett says, dropping into a chair. He looks exhausted.

She's frowning and blinking like she doesn't follow, but Gordo does. He's kicking himself for it not occurring, and so he starts speaking before Barrett can pile in and look like the oracle. Again.

'*If* Davey set the explosive device,' he begins, 'to wreck the dam and tip the balance towards draining the loch and making it woodland, he'd not want Barrett and me to know he was up to something. He knew we'd fight to the— Well, fight hard to keep it water, keep it' – he almost lets the word 'sacred' out but manages to say – 'intact. Wouldn't we, mate? Eh?'

'But so would Davey,' Tabitha says. 'He would never interfere with the loch. It must have been someone else. An activist.'

'An idiot,' Barrett says. 'Look around!' He swings an arm as if they're not in Davey's kitchen with old Mrs Muir's net curtains hiding the view. 'If this is a good place for trees, where are they? Miles of moor and barely a blade of grass can stand up in the wind. There's never going to be a forest glade up here. Wind farm, maybe. And the ramblers must know that.'

'You'd think,' Gordo says. 'Anyway, it's not as if they're short of space to roam even with the water.'

'That's a good point,' Tabitha says. Gordo tries to keep his face neutral. 'And it's not as if their country walks would be improved by a permanent low tide and a ruined village. Plus whatever's fallen in over the years coming back up again.'

Barrett starts back as if she's scalded him and Gordo thinks *he's* made a noise in his throat, helpless not to.

She hasn't noticed. She goes on talking. 'So I don't see the ramblers risking it. And it's obviously not the anglers. But Davey? No way.' She considers it for a moment, then nods as if she's convinced herself. 'So whyever it was he forged your signatures, it wasn't to stay off your radar while he bombed the dam. No. Way.'

'OK,' Gordo says. She can believe she's convinced him if she likes, so long as she stops talking about it. 'What I don't understand is why he would forge our signatures when he must have known his brother would contest the will. Because wouldn't that mean the witnesses would definitely have to come forward, swear under oath, all that?'

'He won't,' she says. 'He's already told me he wants nothing to do with it. Davey must have known that. Somehow.'

'He won't?' says Barrett. 'Are you sure?'

'He only came because the cops asked him to and he's gone again now. He's gone.' She's talking quietly now. Gordo thinks she'd be talking even if she was alone. She'd talk to herself, just to get the words out of her. 'I don't know why he came back, even once. He could have met them at the morgue or the undertakers. I don't know why *she* came back.'

'Your sister,' says Barrett gently.

She looks up. 'You know I haven't seen her since their wedding, right? 1990. I never even saw a photo until Facebook. But they're

savvy with the settings and even that was the odd blurry shot at
a hen night. Twenty-five years. And they've only been in Annan.
They've been forty miles from me, fifty miles from her, all this
time. I don't even know what either of them does for a living.
She came to the house she grew up in today and didn't even . . .'

'She sounds as hard as nails,' Barrett says. 'I mean, I know
there was bad feeling when they got married.' She laughs at the
understatement. 'But Davey always said it was his mum kicking
off. Not your mum and definitely not *you*.'

'I was creeped out,' she says. 'We were more like brothers
and sisters than cousins, all a year apart and living up here with
no one but ourselves. It was gross to think of Jo and Johnny . . .
like that. And it was weird too, you know? My sister waiting
until his sixteenth birthday and then picking him off like a sniper?
What I remember most at the time was thinking "what's the
rush?" and being embarrassed. Not angry. Yeah, you're right,
none of it came from me.'

Barrett says nothing and Gordo doesn't speak for a while
either, letting her stay in her memories. But someone's going to
have to say something.

*You shouldn't hang back so much. You've as much right as
anyone else to be talking.*

'Was she pregnant?' he asks at last. Barrett puts his thumb in
one eye socket and all his fingers in the other and kneads at
himself.

'I don't know,' she says. 'The months after the wedding are
kind of lost for me. But I remember Davey saying, when I had
Albie, that he was the future of the family. The only one. So I'm
guessing not. Thank God, probably, eh?'

'Or maybe she lost it,' Barrett says. 'Seventeen and sixteen is
gey early to get married, unless there's a reason.'

'If I'm ever in the position to ask her, I'll ask her,' she says.
'There was talk of a funeral so it won't be another twenty-five
years before I see her again.'

Gordo can see Barrett gearing up to say more. He *shouldn't*
hang back. He *is* as good as anyone else. And he *would* have
made a great dad. Plus Tabitha's nearer Gordo's age, probably,
which is another reason it should be him who speaks. 'There's
worse things to do than get married when you're young and
pregnant,' he tells her. 'Since you were talking about Davey and

the loch, here's why I can't believe he did it. Why neither of us can.'

She frowns and right enough that doesn't make sense unless you know. So he tells her.

'When I was sixteen, and my girlfriend got pregnant, I asked her to marry me.'

She's still frowning.

'She wasn't as strong-willed as your sister,' he goes on. 'Or I wasn't as reassuring as your cousin, maybe. Either way, her mum got round her and made her break it off. She sent my ring back.' Gordo touches his chest and then freezes. He's just given it away that he still carries it with him after all these years, but with any luck she'll think it's on a chain or in a pocket, not through a piercing. Most engagement rings wouldn't work for that. But the best Gordo could do was a thin hoop of gold with a speck of a diamond.

It was perfect for me!

She was right. Her hands were fine-boned and tiny and that delicate ring looked just right.

'But what's that got to do with Davey?' Tabitha says.

'She killed herself,' says Gordo, the only way he can, hard and loud. 'She drowned herself and the baby. The peanut, it would have been, as early as all that. She left her bag and her shoes on the dam and jumped in with stones in her coat pockets. That's a guess. She must have though, eh? Weighted herself down with stones? Because she was a good swimmer and the instincts take over.'

Tabitha turns her head as if she's in a dream and looks towards the front of the house where the loch lies. 'Davey knew?' she says. Then she turns to Barrett. 'What about you?'

'Not so bad,' Barrett says, like he always does.

'It's not a competition,' Gordo says, like he always does.

'I'm divorced,' Barrett goes on. 'I was divorced, all done and dusted, kids settled into the routine. But then I met someone else and my wife, my ex-wife, took against it. Search me why, because it was her that left, not me.'

Tabitha waits while he gets himself together to say the rest.

'We shared custody of the dog as well as the kids, don't laugh. Bess went to my wife, my ex-wife, when the girls came to me and I kept her the rest of the time. It wasn't ideal, since it meant the girls never got to see her but my wife, my ex-wife, got a puppy too, a rough wee mutt, but they love him. Bess was a flat-coated retriever. Lovely dog.'

He stops again and she waits again.

'My wife was a farmer's lass,' he goes on. 'She'd have been happier with a farmer from the get-go. It was bad enough when I was in the forces but when I took up with my wee gardening business she was mortified. Anyway, farming background.'

Gordo is trying his best to stay calm but the way Barrett's spinning this out is making him dig his nails into his palms to keep from screaming. He managed to say the love of his life and their unborn child were in that loch quicker than Barrett can tell the tale of a dog who'd surely be dead by now anyway.

'She brought Bess up here one weekend when the girls and me were away at my sister's,' he's saying now. 'And Bess loved a swim, you see? Couldn't keep her out of the sea, lochs, rivers, bloody open-air pool on the front at Portobello one time that nearly got me fined. So she let Bess in for a splash about and then . . . she shot her. Farmer's lass. Crack shot that she was. Still is probably.'

Tabitha's quiet and still, her mouth dropped open. 'But,' she says at last, 'why?' Barrett doesn't answer. 'And how do you know? Did she confess? Was there a witness? Because she'd get more than a fine for that.'

'Not her!' Barrett says. 'Confess? No, she sent me a photo of Bess in the water,' he says. 'And the shell. Swears blind she didn't, mind you. Phoned me up all flustered and blubbing saying Bess had run away.'

'And there's no way she could be telling the truth?'

'None,' Barrett says. 'That dog wouldn't run away if you set off a bomb und—'

He stops as they all remember together, what it is that Davey did, *if* he did it, before he lay down in that filthy wee bed and started opening ampoules of ancient insulin. He certainly did *that*.

'I am so sorry about your girlfriend,' she says to Gordo. She turns. 'And your dog.' At least she's put them in that order. 'And, look, if it turns out Davey did try to blow up the dam, I want to apologize. Speaking for him, because I'm his cousin. I'm so sorry if he did something so rotten to hurt you both so much.

When you thought he was a friend. We're not the most normal or sorted out people in the world. The Muirs.' She pauses. 'I thought Davey was different.'

'Let the police track down all the leads, eh?' Gordo says. 'Maybe it was some rewilding lot that did it; not the ramblers at all. Maybe it was hearing the blast that tipped Davey over. They need to pay for his life if they did that to him.'

She's shaking her head. 'It wasn't spur of the moment,' she says. 'He wrote the will. He forged signatures. He put that note on it.'

'Still no need to apologize,' Barrett says.

'On behalf of the family though,' she says.

'He was our friend,' says Barrett. 'Best friend I ever had.' He looks over to check and Gordo nods slightly. 'So, if he tried to drain the loch, he didn't do it to hurt us.' He holds up a hand. 'Hear me out. I knew him, see? We both knew the bones of him, Tabitha. *If* he did it, he did it from . . .' He gives an awkward laugh. 'From love.'

'I don't understand,' she says.

'Maybe he knew better than we do that recovering remains is better than letting them lie there forever.'

'Pretty tough love,' she says.

'But love all the same,' says Barrett. 'Maybe it's a case of . . . How would you even put it, Gordo?'

'He knew we needed it to come up more than we wanted it to stay down there,' Gordo offers, surprised at how it comes out like a practised line when he's never said anything like it before in his life.

'The thing I *don't* understand,' Barrett says, 'is why now. Gordo's girl died fifteen years back and it's ten years coming up for Bess. I don't know what changed suddenly.'

Tabitha gasps, as if she's sewing and she's pricked her finger, as if she's chopping food and she's sliced into her skin. 'I came back,' she says. 'That's what changed. He thought he knew what I needed too. I've done it again. It was me.'

ELEVEN

Barrett

Since when were country solicitors open on a Saturday morning? Barrett does not know but the text comes through from Tabitha at ten past nine to say Timothy Hawes is expecting her at eleven o'clock and did he mean it about chumming along.

Do you need a lift? he texts back, laboriously. *Or were you thinking of meeting in town?*

Cheshire Cat at 10.30, she texts back. *Thank you!*

Which gives him a problem. He selects speed dial three – his ex is in there after both his girls but still before anyone else – and texts: *Are either of them up yet? I could pick them up in Dumfries mid-morning and save you.* Then he deletes *and save you* and hits send.

She doesn't answer. She might even decline the offer and insist on bringing them right to his door, like it says in the custody agreement. She would drive a lot further than that to avoid helping him out. Or maybe she's making him wait for the sake of it. He suspects they're both still in their beds, forty-five minutes before she's supposed to be dropping them off. They can sleep as if they've trained for it. Both of them can lie in a wreckage of homework, iPads, make-up bottles and dirty clothes, tangled in charger flexes, curtains wide open, sun beating in, updates pinging beside their heads, and them sleeping like the angels they still are, like longer, thinner versions of the same chubby wee angels that used to sleep tangled in teddy bears and hair ribbons.

In the end, it seems the call of a Saturday morning outweighs the cost of making Barrett happy.

Not ideal, she texts back at almost ten o'clock. *Because I need a word with you about something. But if you think we could have a* short *discussion for once instead of an inquisition, meeting in town could work. When/where?*

11 at the Cheshire Cat on Queensberry St, he answers. None of
the rest of it is worth dignifying. He knows that. But still, he can
feel his pulse beating in his throat as he deletes the chain of
messages. He should probably stop off at one of those caravans,
get his blood pressure checked. And his cholesterol too. Which he
also blames her for. If she'd back off, or drop dead, he could maybe
live on salmon and broccoli, but it's only a dram and a curry that
stops him from smashing his fists through the door some days.

Eleven o'clock should be OK, he tells himself. He only needs
to let this Hawes bloke see his face and hear his name and it'll
be clear if they're going to get away with it or if Davey's ruse
is a bust. When his phone buzzes again, he predicts to himself
that she'll be making some crack about eleven o'clock being late
– not mid – morning, but it's Gordo.

Where's on the docket today? It's Davey's phrase and it hits
him hard.

Was Barrett going to tell him about the surprise Saturday
solicitor? He likes to think he was. He surely wasn't going to
keep quiet and spend the morning with Tabitha, just the pair of
them? His girls were going to scupper that anyway.

Hawes the lawyer's squeezed T in today, he texts. *So I'm doing
that*. There's a long silence, phone comatose, then he adds, *She
only told me ten minutes ago. I've been sorting out the handover
with ex*.

He's forgiven. Gordo texts, *When and where are we meeting
her? Will I pick her up from Davey's?*

Barrett shakes his head as he thumbs in the rendezvous. Gordo's
willing to clank up the track all the way to Hiskith in the sanny
van and then trundle the lass all the way down to Dumfries in
it? That's pretty clear then.

So's the fact that Gordo's first to the Cheshire Cat. When
Barrett lets himself in, after a bit of business to get through the
door beside two women struggling with their brollies, Gordo's
sitting at the best table, the round one in the bay window, tense
with the effort of repelling all other customers.

'Just the two of you, is it?' one of the brolly women asks, as
Barrett sits down.

'No,' Gordo says. 'We're just the first two.' Barrett hides a
smile behind one of the laminated menus. The lad's showing off
for her before she's even got here.

'Of how many?' says the other woman. Barrett thought it died out with his mother's generation, this sharp-elbowed fierceness. It used to get his mum and granny into jumble sales right at the bell, like it got them money off clothes with miniscule marks on them. It's not going to get this pair a seat in the window today, though. Gordo's like a wall.

Tabitha arriving sends them on their way by sheer force of numbers. She takes her kagoul off neatly, folding the wet in on itself and ending up with a square she can tuck into the outside pocket of her bag.

'Thank you both for doing this,' she says before Gordo cuts her off.

'It's nothing. Signing was nothing and this is nothing either.' His voice is too loud and he stares too hard. Then he leans forward and whispers, 'You never know who's listening.'

'My sister,' Tabitha says, 'can't lie for toffee either. Never could. That's what made it such a surprise when she announced the wedding.'

'Either?' Gordo says.

'Let me do the talking, I think she means,' Barrett says and earns a grin.

Gordo flushes but it takes the wee waitress a while to write the order and by the time she's gone Barrett reckons he's over it.

'Do you think he'll hand over keys and deeds today?' Tabitha says. 'And a letter. If there is one.'

'Keys maybe,' Gordo says. 'Deeds no way. It'll have to go through probate. Just a formality,' he adds, 'given what Johnny said. There's no one else, is there?'

She shakes her head. 'Roddie and Watson were the only two brothers, and Auntie Rowan's sister never married. She's a nun, but like a Buddhist nun, you know? Shaves her head and all that.'

'So a pretty straightforward probate process,' says Gordo.

'I hope,' she says. 'I told my son about it last night.'

Barrett searches for something to contribute but comes up short. He hasn't been googling wills, like he now knows Gordo has. He could always ask how long probate takes. It looks good for a man to ask questions. Women love that. Although he's quoting dating tips now, he realizes.

Da-ad. Predatory much? You're here to support her!

As the thought rings in his head, someone knocks on the steamed-up window right beside him, a loud boing that quiets the entire café. Peering through the rivulets, he sees them. The pair of them are huddled under one buckled umbrella, heads close together, mouths moving although he can't hear a word of it. His heart detaches from his ribcage and rises up into his throat, just like it always does, bringing tears to his eyes. Then they head for the door and he sees *her* standing staring in at him, taking in Gordo, with a curl of her lip, then physically starting to see that the third one at the table isn't Davey. She hurries after the girls.

'I know we're early,' says Sorrel. 'We were going to Markies for treats.'

'Nice try, Dad!' says Willow. 'Sneaking a quiet coffee without us.'

'What's the hot chocolate like here?' Willow asks the waitress who's just brought the coffees.

'And a panini,' says Sorrel. 'Just plain cheese and chili sauce on the side.'

They've got their roller-bags with them, like they used to when there were toys they couldn't leave behind. He can't imagine what's in them today. They've more clothes at the police house than he had in his entire childhood.

'What pretty names your daughters have,' Tabitha says and smiles at his ex-wife.

'Can I have that quick word?' she says to him, with a smile for Tabby that could knock her teeth back in her head it's so tight.

They go over to stand in front of the cake cabinet where the noise of the espresso machine will cover whatever it is she's got to say. This also means they have to stand quite close and it's troubling. Inches away, he can see the green flecks in her brown eyes and smell the coffee and toothpaste on her breath. He gets a twinge of the vertigo he used to think would fade one day, after the divorce, but now believes is his for life.

'Who's that then?' she asks. No attempt at subtlety.

'Friend of Gordo's,' he lies, and it works. She turns until Tabitha is out of sight.

'Look,' she says next, 'I wouldn't do this, but I need you to take the girls.'

He frowns at her. 'I'm taking the girls.'

'I mean for a few weeks. Maybe a month.'

He wants to ask why – he's only human – but he doesn't want to ask anything that might make this miracle dry up and blow away. 'Of course. Happy to. Do they know?'

'I need to go to Portugal,' she says. 'There's been a death in the family and there's a lot to sort out. We're hoping we can keep the villa but it's not straightforward.'

'I'm sorry for your loss,' Barrett says. He's trying to think which one of her relatives lived in Portugal or was thinking of retiring there. It can't be her parents, they're not the type. They'll move to a bungalow on the farm when her brother takes over, but no further.

She shifts from one foot to the other and says no more. 'We'll be out of the house by Monday,' she says. 'Sorrel's got a key for them to pick up whatever they want. I didn't make them pack before I asked you.'

As if he would say no, Barrett thinks, before that 'we' hits him. She's seeing someone. She's seeing someone with a claim on a Portuguese villa and so she's steaming right in to make sure he gets it.

'What about the dog?' he says, watching closely for a flash of guilt in her face.

'I've kennelled it,' she says, which is more evidence than a guilty look could ever have been. There's no good reason for her to keep her dog out of Barrett's hands, as they both know. And who calls their own pup an 'it'?

'You've no need to go to that expense,' he says. 'Tell the kennel I'll pick him up. The girls'll miss him. Missing you's going to be bad enough.'

They're coping with the prospect so far, he sees. They've got their arms up and out in that strange scarecrow pose that means they're taking selfies. With Tabitha, he notices. On her phone. He wonders if she's more Gordo's type after all. Gordo's watching the show, saying nothing.

Barrett flinches and checks his watch. 'Eh, mind your time,' he says, going back over. 'Gordo? It's nearly eleven.'

'Are *you* not going then?' Gordo says. 'To do the talking?'

'I'll wait here with the girls,' he says.

Tabitha glances at his ex and he thinks she understands. She's

another one like him, picking her way through the ruins, scared
to piss off the one with all the power.

'I just need to text this photo to Albie,' she says, thumbing
buttons. Aye, she's just like him right enough. Sending photos
of his girls to her teenage boy to tip the scales in her favour.

'So you're mine for a month?' he says to the pair of them,
mostly so Tabitha hears it. He's sure she types a wee extra few
words beyond what she was going to.

'We tried for Porto but she's not having any,' Willow says.
'You'll need to make it up to us for getting a trip to the sun
snatched away, Dad.'

'I can be bought with Pandora charms,' says Sorrel.

'You can be bought with Buenos,' Willow says, shoving her
sister hard with her shoulder. They're sharing a chair. He hasn't
seen them sit on a chair each with both legs straight down since
the last time they were strapped into boosters.

'That's me away then,' their mum says and they leap up to
fling their arms round her, getting in the way of the waitress
bringing their chocolate and paninis. They swerve to help with
the tray and thank her over and over again, tell her it looks lovely.
They're lovely. Barrett thinks. Even though they're 'a lot'. A lot
of what, he asked once and got nothing but a 'Jeez, Dad' in
reply.

Then all at once Tabitha's gone, Gordo's gone, *she's* gone and
it's the three of them, like it's going to be for weeks on end.
Barrett feels his chest burn with a depth of feeling he could never
admit to anyone. A phone on the table buzzes and rattles and he
picks it up.

'Dad! That's Tabby's. You can't answer her phone!'

'Rent a grip, Dad! See if you like it!'

'She's probably phoning it to check where she left it,' Barrett
says and swipes it open.

It's a text from an Albion Lawson. *Davey's house sounds cool*,
it says. *Is there still fishing?*

He smiles at his daughters. 'You've just made someone's day.'

'Would that someone be you?' says Sorrel.

He shakes his head, still smiling. 'That too. But no.'

They tease him and pretend to pout. He zips his lips and
refuses to tell them any more. Maybe he would get sick of it
eventually but he's still enjoying it when the café door opens

and Gordo ushers Tabitha back in. Her face is pale grey like wet
Polyfilla and Gordo's eyes are wide with panic. Neither of them
has put a hood up or used an umbrella coming back from the
lawyers either. Their hair is plastered down and dark.

Tabitha stares around the interior of the cafe, even busier now
as the last of the coffees meet the first of the early lunches. At
last, her eyes light on Barrett and she stumbles towards him.

'Right,' he says, plucking twenties out of his wallet and shoving
them at the girls. 'Marks. Treats. Something for movie night
tonight. And get some dog food. We're picking up Uggy.' They're
mesmerized by the money, and the dog news, so they're gone
before Tabitha sinks into her seat and begins weeping.

'Did he twig?' Barrett asks Gordo. 'Did he know?'

But Gordo gives back a cloudy look as if from far away. It
takes three blinks – and all the while Tabby's still crying – before
realization dawns. 'Oh!' Gordo says. 'Right. You mean did Hawes
know I'm not a witness? No, no, nothing like that. Davey went
in on his own to drop off the will and other stuff for a deed box.
Keys and papers and all that. It's fine.'

Barrett is aware of a loosening under his ribcage. Not until
this moment has he admitted to himself he was scared of the
trouble they could all get into, covering up an inheritance fraud.

'So what's wrong?' he asks.

'There was a letter,' Gordo says, then ducks his head to try
and catch Tabby's eye. She's looking down into her lap as if she
can hide the fact that she's crying from all the other women in
here. 'Tab?' Gordo asks softly. 'Can I tell him?'

She sniffs, a deep, wet, choking sniff, and nods. But then she
plucks a paper napkin from the fan of them held up between the
sauce bottles and blows her nose. 'I'll tell him,' she says. She
looks up and Barrett sees that the make-up he didn't know she
was wearing has run down her face.

'You're needing a wee dicht, hen,' he says. She scrubs at her
cheeks with the crumpled napkin until the black streaks are gone
and her skin is as rosy as an apple.

'The letter,' she says, then sniffs one last time and clears her
throat. 'It's a confession.'

'He tells you why he did it?' Barrett says, thinking 'confession' is a funny word to choose.

'He doesn't tell me why he did it,' she says. 'And I can't

believe he did it. But I read it plain as day, typed out in black and white. Signed.'

The knowledge creeps over Barrett that they're not talking about suicide any more.

'Maybe not here, eh?' he says. But, as he looks around, he sees that the lunchers are deep in their own conversations. 'Or quietly, at least,' he adds.

'He killed Auntie Rowan,' Tabitha says, as soft as breathing. 'It's all in the letter. He tranqued her, and took all her insulin away so she went hyper while she was passed out. He killed his mother and kept it quiet for ten years.' She nods slowly and then a smile spreads over her face, as if she caught sight of an old friend. 'Nothing's what it seemed to be,' she says. 'He's not who he pretended to be. It's all a trick. It's a trap. There's no Jesus. Not now. Not ever. Not just "no Jesus at the moment". Never! Do you see?'

PART TWO

November 2015

TWELVE

Tabitha

It feels like last year and it feels like yesterday I was in that lawyer's office, then in the café ranting about Jesus. Poor Gordo. Barrett took it in his stride, funnily enough. You wouldn't think a gardener would have the 'relevant resources' as I used to call it in my job, but maybe it's from wrangling those girls of his.

In the 'careful what you wish for' department, after all the trying to lose my marbles, thinking it would be better than facing the truth about my life, it was bloody awful when it happened. The sick feeling as everything slid out of my grasp. I had forgotten what it was like. They say that about childbirth, don't they?

Today, two weeks later, as I prepare to return to Hawes, Beattie and Thom, I'm girding my loins to stay calm, no matter what fresh surprises might lie in store. All I want is to walk out with the keys to the locked rooms in Davey's house. My house. Nearly. Probate will take a lot longer than we thought but Tim Hawes said on the phone yesterday there's no real reason to wait. He had to check that Johnny truly wasn't going to challenge the will, and he had to wait for the official verdict of suicide – in case it was murder and it was me, I suppose. When they said they couldn't find his laptop, I thought they were hinting at an intruder, but apparently that's normal for a suicide these days. He probably chucked it in the loch, they told me.

With the cause of death and next of kin squared away, there's nothing stopping me. I'll pick up the keys, the deeds, and that letter. I'll use the keys in the locks, I'll lodge the deed with a different solicitor, because one more trip to Hawes etc., is enough for a lifetime. And the letter? Oh, I think I'll burn the letter. Now I've definitely decided I'm not going to do the right thing, I don't want documents lying around waiting to jump up and bite me.

I never thought major fraud would be such an easy step, but

turns out I barely hesitated. All it took was one text from Albie hinting that he might come back and live with me.

I turn over in bed on the last morning I'll wake up in my old room. I know I've been dreaming about Jo again. I can feel the past suck at me like quicksand, so I get firm with myself. I breathe in. I breathe out. I think of a garden. I tell myself I am remembering, that's all. I can't *feel* the pictures on the wall bars along at the other end of the house. Of course I can't. Even though I could swear the floor tilts in that direction and, unless I'm careful, unless I brace myself, I'll roll all the way there and tumble into one of those Night Paintings for good this time.

If I stand up on my bed, I can see the corner of Davey's garden wall and my heart . . . sweetens. You'd think it would sink, seeing what a titchy distance I'm going. But for some reason it doesn't take me like that at all. I float on the wonder of how near it is, how easy to get to. My heart feels as fresh and light as a line of washing billowing about inside me. I feel . . . cleansed.

I feel – if I let myself, and I think I will – as if flakes and plaques of some nameless murky substance have lifted from where they coated my insides, shrinking as they dried, pulling me out of shape, stifling me. Looking at the corner of Davey's garden wall is like swishing myself out with clean water, like you would rinse out a red wine carafe with grains of rice to dislodge old stains. The clear, bubbly water swirls around inside me until I can breathe all that dried-on gunk out of my pursed lips and let it drift off and dissolve in the air.

'There are no *plaques* inside you, Tabitha,' the nurse said one day when we were sitting in the hospital garden. 'There are no flakes of anything. And you can't breathe water. In or out.'

As if I didn't know that. I tried to make her see what a big step it was for me to fill with clean water and not panic. I tried to explain that it was mud from the loch that had dried in my mouth and nose. Strands of weed and little clumps of algae shrinking and crackling in my ears, but she didn't want to hear that either.

'You can't fill yourself with water,' she insisted. 'And you don't need to. You are perfectly clean inside, just as you are.'

I breathed out to show her, but she didn't even notice. Of course, I knew, deep down, that it was only the vapour of my breath I could see, pluming out in front of me like those old pictures of God jump-starting Adam. I did know. I'm not *nuts*.

Gordo took some convincing, mind you, two weeks ago, in the café that rainy day. Eventually I managed to explain it was just a figure of speech. 'When I was transferred off the intake ward,' I told him, 'after my assessment, and was put on the ward where I stayed until I came home, my key nurse was introducing the other patients and she told me there was "no Jesus at the mo". We had the seventh wife of Henry the Eighth – another Catherine, as if he hadn't had enough! – but no Christ. Not right then. I thought it was the funniest thing I'd ever heard. Elspeth and me both did. Whenever things got lively on the ward, or if someone was sad, I used to think what a shame it was that we had . . .'

'No Jesus at the mo,' Gordo said. 'Uh-huh, I see.'

'It sounds,' Barrett said, 'like something out of Dickens. How come you were locked up? Instead of getting a therapist and a wee prescription.'

I was still struggling for an answer when his girls came back, drenched and giggling, carrier bag handles looped round their wrists, making their hands turn purple. He forgot all about me.

He's not the first one to make that mistake. People are kind; they assume I'm talking about 'depression' and 'anxiety', even when I've said 'hallucinations' and 'psychosis'. Even when I've tried to tell them what a spree it was, they still imagine me sitting with a tissue balled in my fist while I tell a doctor how I'm feeling. I let them. I don't want to tell strangers I've just met, or not quite strangers who might turn into friends, that I thought I was a mermaid, Miss Mirror's gal pal, happily coupled up and living in the loch, spied on by Mr Moon and his hostage family I never got to see. No one needs to hear that my throat was full of mud and weeds and that inside my head my voice sounded like someone blowing down a straw into the bottom of a glass of water. 'A fart in a bath,' Elspeth said once, and we laughed until red dots broke out all over our eyelids, same as from screaming.

It wasn't until a nurse taped me on her little Walkman and played it back, that I started to doubt myself. I couldn't hear the bubbles on the tape. Same as when I picked the wax out of my ear and showed her tiny crumbs, swearing they were long, sodden tongues of pond weed. It took that same nurse snapping a photo of me holding a pile of mud and weed in my outstretched hand and showing it back to me. I peered at it and couldn't see anything, not even the crumb of wax hardened to that cadmium orange. It was too small to show up in the photo. All I could see was my fingertip and behind it my face, eyes wide and mouth grinning, so delighted about showing her.

'When I started to get better,' I told Gordo and Barrett in the café that day, 'it was like a mantra. An affirmation, except we didn't talk about affirmations back then.'

'*That* was a better world,' Barrett broke in to say, then put his hand up to cover his mouth.

'I told myself I had to do it on my own, there was no one coming to save me. No grown-ups were going to lift me up and take me away from the bad stuff this time. There was no point waiting for a miracle.'

'Ahhhh,' Gordo said. 'No Jesus.'

I nodded. 'Not at the mo.'

I'm looking forward to seeing them again today. They've been busy the last two weeks. It was half-term and the weather picked up, so Gordo's been trundling Peace and Bacon to car parks beside all the popular walks, starting with coffees and rolls at dawn and not pulling the awning down until the last slice of cake's sold and the tea urn's empty. Barrett's been hard at it too, raking, chipping, burning, clearing, stacking logs, pressure-washing patios, giving lawns their last cut for the winter.

Me? I've been down an online rabbit hole: the websites and message boards of ramblers, anglers, birders, rewilders and something called forest bathers, who you'd think would be pro-water but aren't actually. And, unless all these clubs have got hidden political wings, I can't see anyone going as far as getting explosives on the dark web. Oh, they sling some muck below the line and they sometimes get off carbon and habitats and on to football and independence, but no worse than that.

Which brings me back to suspecting Davey.

The police are no help. Whatever it was that went off, it sank afterwards and there's nothing in the budget to get it up again, not when they've got a suspect and he's dead. I'm glad of that. It would be hard work to keep believing the divers were only divers. On these dark days when we lose the sun at three, they could be anything.

Zelda always grumbled about the winter light. She might still be grumbling but – and maybe this is why Davey's house doesn't feel too close – I hardly see her. And if I hardly see her when we're under the same roof she's not going to be in my pocket with two hundred yards of steep track separating us.

For the last two weeks, she's been a warm kettle, a rumbling dishwasher, a steamy bathroom. So the chance hasn't arisen to talk about Davey's funeral yet. I suppose I'll have to make it happen this morning before I go. I suppose, too, that I should check she's actually OK, that it really is her 'work' and maybe the fact that she's processing Jo and Johnny's visit, Davey's death, my return . . . I need to check she's not in a world of quiet pain, falling down a silent chasm.

When Uncle Roddie was struggling, see, when he turned into a cleared throat through the wall and the smell of shaving soap left behind in the bathroom, Auntie Rowan covered for him. Johnny and Davey told me all about it. Rowan told *them*: about him coming into their room and kissing them goodnight, singing lullabies as they slept. She said he was getting help, getting better, getting to miss his brother. Maybe it was true, but his brother drove on to the track and didn't drive off it and, when he heard the news, Uncle Roddie threw a rope over the upstairs banister and stepped into thin air.

It's not my memory, this memory, because I was a baby. It's made of other people's rememberings and retellings, my over-hearings and half-listenings. But it's strong enough to spring me from my bed and along the corridor, hoping Zelda's still at her breakfast in the staffroom.

I'm out of luck. Yesterday's paper is folded back at the cross-word and the teapot is still vaguely warm inside its cosy, but she's gone. So I head for the studio, knock and wait. She can't be deep into it for the day, I think, so she won't get too annoyed at the disturbance. The way she sweeps the door open and breathes out hard through her nose at the sight of me, you'd never know.

'S-sorry,' I say. 'I wanted to catch you before you get stuck in. I'm off this morning, remember?'

Zelda glances behind herself the way I would look at a pot on the cooker, as if something in her studio's going to spoil if

she steps away from it, then she draws the door to and points
me into the belly of the hallway, where the old coat pegs and
cubbyholes are still there above the low benches.

'So I was just thinking,' I go on, 'about his funeral.'

Zelda strikes a pose. I think. Or maybe that's not fair. Maybe
she's just trying to keep a hold of herself. In any case, she lifts
her chin and shows me her profile against the light. It's impres-
sive, although less so for me of all people because it's my profile
too.

'I haven't been able to stop thinking about it,' she says. 'So
many clues and I missed them all, in my grief and pain.'

I say nothing and try to keep my face blank in case she turns
to look at me. What clues is she talking about?

'When Rowan told me Roddie had no intention of coming, I
didn't even ask to see him, try to talk him round.'

Oh. That funeral. Clues about that. She's lost in the past,
talking about the terrible day when my dad died. The terrible
days, plural, I suppose. Terrible weeks. Such awfulness that I
suppose I should be glad I can't actually remember it. And maybe
she'd forget too if she didn't keep painting him, there at the edge
of every dark picture.

'But the thing is, Tabitha,' she goes on, 'it had been that way
for years by then. Roderick's reclusiveness, I mean. It barely
registered how strange it was. There's such a thick cloud sometimes, in new grief.'

She says this to me as if I'm not feeling my way through a
cloud of my own right now. Then she takes a deep breath and
shakes her head as if to clear it. 'If I had known Rowan was
about to die, ten years back, I would have sat her down and tried
one last time to clear the air about all that.'

All that. What mild way to refer to the most twisted little knot
in the whole delicious-horrific scandal that put the Muirs of
Hiskith on the map: the fact that Auntie Rowan, God alone knows
why, didn't tell us Uncle Roddie killed himself the same day
Dad did. All the time Zelda was waiting for the Fiscal to give
the verdict on *Dad's* enquiry – suicide, of course, in the end,
because the rest of the plan didn't work – Rowan quietly dealt
with the much more straightforward suicide in her own house,
called a doctor, had the body taken away, waited for a death
certificate. Which came, because hanging yourself all alone in

your own stairway, apparently, makes for a lot less fuss than driving yourself into a loch, at least the way my dad did it. Uncle Roddie was cremated a full five days before my dad was put in the ground. And everyone accepted that our uncle wasn't there for the same reason he hadn't been anywhere for years and years.

'So you never pressed her about it?' I ask Zelda now. 'You never actually found out why Auntie Rowan did it?'

'Oh I know why she *did* it,' Zelda says, tossing her hair. We might have the same hair but I've never learned how to take it from over one shoulder to over the other just by moving my neck in the right way. I have to flip it with my hand and look like a teenage cliché. So I don't. 'She did it to make me look histrionic, and herself stoic. She did it so that all the prurience – the reporters and gawpers – were round me like flies, and she escaped. Rowan wasn't as meek as that simpering look on her face would have you believe.'

'That's pretty harsh, Mum.'

'She was one of the most scheming, conniving women I've ever . . . Well, I'm glad to say I haven't spent my life in any kind of henhouse at all, so in fact she was one of the *few* I've ever met. But it's true. Manipulative to the nth degree and quite vicious when thwarted.'

'Or,' I said, 'maybe she did it so that all the sympathy wouldn't leach away from Dad and go to Uncle Roddie instead.' I don't know why I'm arguing exactly; if I could believe Rowan was some kind of wicked witch that ruined Davey's life, it would help me understand what he did to her.

'What sympathy?' Zelda barks. 'He got none! His name – *my* name – was dragged through the mud. Thank God it was then and not now. That's something. Articles in the paper and letters to the editor. It would be hideous these days, with things the way they are.'

I nod, but Davey's suicide, which you'd expect to kick up plenty of 'prurience' – a great word for it – has gone pretty much unmarked. Maybe the death of a single man, a loner, and a bit of an oddball, doesn't get the public's blood pumping the same way as my dad's dramatic exit from life.

'So,' I say, 'when we hear about the funeral arrangements, will we go together? Or would you rather drive separately in case we want to leave at different times?'

'How do we drive separately in one car?' Zelda says in quite
a different voice. No more musing, no more regretting. This is
a voice that puts me back in childhood just as thoroughly as
when I think about Uncle Roddie, and my dad, and that awful
time I can barely remember. It's the same cold, bored tone that
used to ask me if I'd paid more for the holes in my jeans, if I
knew that vegetarian cheese might as well use the rennet of the
dead calves along with their stolen milk, if I wanted an honest
assessment or cod praise of the finger painting I'd brought home,
the poem I'd copied out in my best writing, the ornament I'd
moulded out of salt dough for her birthday.

'Davey left me his car,' I remind her.

'Of course,' she says. 'And his rather pretty cottage. With its
very pretty garden.'

I wait to see if she's going to say more. It's not like Zelda to
chat for nothing. 'I do hope you're not going to dismantle it,'
she goes on at last.

'The house?' I say. 'Why on earth would I do that?'

'The garden, Tabitha,' she says. 'To make it easier to look
after, or to follow some fad for "decking" or "features".' She's
got some nerve. The playground outside her own house is still
the same zero-maintenance asphalt it ever was. 'Or to make
provision for a "kick-about",' she finishes.

I can't decode the tone. It's not quite sarcasm. But she definitely doesn't want to be seen as someone who can say such words
without the quotation marks. I smile anyway. Even Zelda being
so much herself, distilled and spotlit, can't take away the fact
that I might indeed need to make space for a kickabout. I'm
getting my son back today.

There's just this second and final visit to Mr Hawes' claustrophobic office to get through first. This time, Gordo's waiting
in the café and Barrett's coming with me. He insisted. I think
he wants to double-check that Hawes didn't meet the other will
witness. It's like how you have to touch a plate after a waiter
tells you it's red-hot. Barrett checks the handbrake when someone
else is driving too – subtly, when you're turned towards your
seatbelt or you're unlocking the door.

But he's a reassuring presence, in spite of that or because of it,
and the office isn't the shock I'm braced for when a receptionist
ushers us in. The bookshelves full of legal volumes are the same,

the heavy curtains, the dark furniture, the smell of leather polish, and a plug-in air freshener that doesn't quite cover the faint sourness of an old bag-style Hoover. But I'm fine. My palms stay dry and my neck stays all one colour instead of going what Albie once called 'pink giraffe' when he was at that filter-free age. I smile again at the thought of him. Barrett, in my sight line, smiles back.

'I think it was the letter that made me freak out last time,' I say.

'Well, duh!' says Barrett. 'Or maybe I mean "derp",' he adds. Thirteen nights he's had his daughters in the house. They're flanking Gordo in the café right now, loath to miss the chance of a hot drink with sprinkles.

'So, can you take the papers, when Hawes hands them over? I'm going to destroy the letter. But I don't want to touch it till I'm ready. I'll take the keys.'

When Mr Hawes arrives, though, neck and neck with that same receptionist who's got a coffee tray now, he is carrying much more than a letter and a keyring.

'What's all that?' I ask. The flat, Portland-grey boxes, three of them in a stack, are making the arms of his suit jacket dusty with that brownish, bookish dust I thought you only got in libraries.

'Deeds,' says Mr Hawes. 'As requested, although I have to advise you that even if you want to store them with your own solicitor, it's a better idea to have me transfer them direct. There are insurance implications if they go missing or are destroyed while in the possession of a private individual.'

He's really pissed off with me. I was so floored by the letter last time I didn't register how pissed off he was. But it's loud and clear now. He even glares at the coffee tray as if he wouldn't have wasted hot water on someone not sticking with his firm, even though it's only instant, with smeared granules up the sides of the cup where it's slopped a bit in transit.

He's unlocking the top box and lifting out old, yellowed papers, long envelopes tied up with faded pink tape and bundles of something or other tied with brown string like a granny parcel.

'You could just leave it all in the boxes,' I tell him.

He's delighted I did so. He was hoping I would. He smiles thinly and says, 'These deed boxes belong to Hawes, Beattie and Thom. Have you brought a bag of any kind with you?'

Of course we haven't. In the process of making two manage-
able bundles out of it all, one for Barrett and one for me, I glance
at a new-looking document that's come out of the third box and
see 'wayleaves, third-party, boundaries, sporting and minerals'.

'What's this?' I ask Hawes.

He gives it only the most cursory look and says, 'Title of the
northern parcel. It's approaching production, so wherever you go
you should look for a specialist. The adjacent lot is ripe for
afforestation too. In fact, I was in the process of securing permis-
sions for Mr Muir, alongside the main project.'

'What?' I say, just as Barrett says, 'What the hangment?' about
the paperwork *he's* holding.

'It really is not the ideal time for a change in representation,
Ms Lawson,' says Mr Hawes. 'No one is better placed than me
to complete the purchase programme Mr Muir and I have been
working on all these years. And if I can let my professional mask
slip for a moment, it would bring me considerable personal
satisfaction to do so too, in Mr Muir's memory. In Davey's
honour.'

'What?' I say again.

'Blow me!' says Barrett. His daughters haven't made very
deep inroads into his vocabulary after all.

It takes twenty minutes, all the nasty instant coffee, and a bit
of googling before I've got it through my head: Davey didn't
just own the old schoolhouse and its patch of garden. He owned
the moor. For years on end, from before Mr Hawes even worked
here, Davey had been buying up hill farms, bits of commercial
planting, grouse acreage, old native woodland, and even the
allotments with the pony sheds and chicken houses down by the
bridge. All the farmers, from the Kirkconnel road right up over
the top to Muirkirk and as far west as Cumnock, were either his
tenants outright, or at least they were renting grazing from him.

And the main project? The thing I can't even begin to get my
head round? He was trying to buy the reservoir. Mr Hawes was
helping.

'But . . .' I say, and then can't think of anything to add to it.

'But that's not . . .' Barrett manages before he runs dry too.

'It's Scottish Water's right now,' Mr Hawes agrees. 'Although
there are a number of stakeholders, as ever with an asset such
as this. However, it wouldn't be the first time a disused reservoir

has passed into private hands. Community ownership is more usual, and there's a ticklish negotiation about future use and stewardship. But, in a nutshell, if they can sell it to someone who'll spend his own – her own now, of course – money on either upkeep or conversion, or at least take over the job getting grants . . . then all the better.'

'Stewardship,' I say. That one word has snagged on my brain like a hooked trout. I catch Barrett's eye. Because no matter how badly Scottish Water or the council or Holyrood or the other stakeholders want to offload Hiskith, they'd never sell it to someone whose stewardship included trying to blow up the dam.

'This is a lot to take in,' Barrett says. 'Can I ask a question?' Hawes inclines his head, gracious now that he's rattled us so thoroughly. 'Would any of the sellers or other interested parties be likely to have got in touch with Davey direct? Or would it all definitely have come through you?'

I nod in silent agreement. If Davey heard that his plan was a bust, that might make him angry enough to set an explosive. Or gutted enough to want to die.

'You're wondering if he heard that the sale fell through,' says Mr Hawes. 'It's not *Location, Location, Location* up there, Mr . . .'

'Langham,' Barrett says and there's a flash of recognition in Hawes's eyes.

'It's not a "hot market",' he goes on. 'It would be most unusual for anyone to "back-channel" bad news to Mr Muir. But, as you know for yourself, he liked to be as independent as he could. Viz: drawing up his own will and having it witnessed without the benefit of my expertise.'

Barrett stares back at the man. I know he's thinking, 'Here it comes, if it's coming.'

'Can *I* ask something?' I say. Watching Hawes subject Barrett to scrutiny is making my pulse pick up. Hawes turns to me and once again inclines his head. 'Is the will definitely legal, if it's so home-made?'

'Oh yes. Davey was never independent to the point of foolishness. He knew that a will must be watertight, since there's no possibility of further discussion. He brought it to me when it was done. I went over it then.'

'Was-was the note already on it?' I ask him. 'The note to me at the bottom of the page.'

'I was sitting in this chair and he in that one when he wrote it,' says Hawes. He looks misty, which surprises me.

'Can I ask another question?'

His head dips.

'How could he afford it?' Davey got into freelance coding early, as soon as he'd finished at the tech, and built up a business. He never worried about money, but he didn't earn enough to go buying up acres of Hiskith Moor, surely.

Hawes gestures at the piles of paper. 'What do you think the rest of *that* is? Davey was good at games. He lived online, like a youngster, as you know. Indeed it took a will – that most solemn of contracts – to make him stop emailing me and actually drop in for the dram he deserved, after all the business he put our way. Would *you* care for a wee something, Ms Lawson?'

I shake my head, but I think I understand Hawes a bit better now. He's got the mawkishness of a serious boozer. Why else would a lawyer want his clients cluttering up his office instead of emailing everything, unless to give him an excuse to start drinking.

'So . . .?' I say. 'Games?'

'Stock,' says Hawes.

'Stock?' says Barrett. I know he's thinking of cattle and sheep. I hope he doesn't say it and embarrass himself.

'Some dull fare. Boeing, Visa, Amazon. But he likes – he liked – a punt too.'

'Are . . . are you telling me Davey was rich?' I say. I hope it sounds like what it is: bewilderment at how he lived, at the dirty sheets on the single bed, at the twelve-year-old hatchback, no matter that I'm grateful to have it. I hope Hawes doesn't mishear me and think I'm finding out fabulous news about my amazing life. Because I'd rather have Davey back. Once again, I remember that I've got Albie back and I feel the smile that's attached to the thought of him like he was once attached to me, by a thick life-giving cord.

'Sorry to have to disabuse you, Ms Lawson,' Hawes says, mistaking my smile right enough. 'Davey wasn't rich. *You're* not rich. He might have been if he'd kept his shares or reinvested wisely. As it stands, he owned a great deal of very low utility land and not much else.'

'But if he was going to buy Hiskith Watter?' says Barrett.

'By mortgaging every last inch of the rest,' Hawes says.

'And Johnny knows this?' I say, feeling the need to make sure, even though the only reason I've waited two weeks is so Hawes could make sure for me. 'When you met Johnny, you did make it clear it wasn't just the cottage he was giving up?'

'*Phoned* Johnny,' Hawes says. Maybe it still smarts that he missed the chance to pour a whisky for the bereaved brother of such a valued client. 'But yes, I told Mr Muir that his brother had been buying up bits of land.'

I feel my eyes widen. *Bits of land?* I think of endless miles of road and the moor stretching away all around it. Mr Hawes is looking at me with the first twinkle I've seen in his beady eyes. He's smiling again too, if a bit wolfishly, and suddenly I need to get out of here. If this lawyer knew that Davey killed his mother and had no right to the little house he sat in, trading his stocks and converting his profits to acres, he wouldn't be grinning.

So maybe it's to salve my conscience that I do a 180-degree turn, tell him he's my solicitor, and ask him could he please keep all the deeds and the rest of it in his nice grey boxes for me and do I need to pay rent for them, which makes him laugh and tell me they're not safety deposit boxes and document storage is free.

'I'm not buying the reservoir, though,' I say. 'Sorry if that was going to be fun to work on.'

'Very wise,' says Hawes. 'Not that your holdings as they stand are trouble-free, but rights-of-way, fences and farmers' rent are nothing compared with a decision to drain or not drain. Whenever you can avoid pitting hobbyists against activists, you've done a good day's work, Ms Lawson.'

'Tabitha,' I say.

He smiles for the third time. 'It's not a name you hear.'

'My sister chose it,' I tell him. 'I was named after her favourite baby on the telly.'

Unbelievably, Mr Hawes puts one of his index fingers on the tip of his nose and wiggles it. He's defrosted completely since

I've given him back my business. I try to smile, as if my heart hasn't just shattered like sugar-glass at the memory of Jo leaning into my playpen and doing exactly that to me, to my nose, before I was old enough to understand why.

THIRTEEN

Tabitha

I couldn't have arranged it any better if I'd tried. Albie's in the café by the time we get back. He's sitting opposite Gordo and the girls, who're ranged around the bench seat against the wall. He's mesmerized by them, like a charmed snake, like a cat on a windowsill looking out at a bird table, like a beaver hearing running water, a mosquito smelling fresh sweat. Like the creature he is – hormones and instincts and millennia of evolution a whip across his back. He's helpless in the face of them. I feel one tiny twinge of unease and then shake it off as Gordo winks at me. If he thinks it's funny, it's OK. He was a fifteen-year-old boy not so long ago. Still, I check Barrett quickly. He's noticed but he's smiling too. Over his shoulder, I see Scott waiting by the counter to pay for his coffee. So it's not quite perfect. But the cup is a takeaway.

I've been dreading this moment, seeing him again. Maybe it's the after-effects of too many shocks already, but it turns out the sight of him barely touches me. His face, his voice, the way he's bouncing slightly on the balls of his feet dying to be done with me; he's close enough in the crowded café for me to smell his moisturizer, the stuff he calls aftershave, but I'm untroubled by it.

And smell's always been my worst thing. I used to sneak into the bathroom and take the top off my dad's Blue Stratos for years, uncapping it and drinking in that rank hit of musk and alcohol. It faded eventually, sitting on the windowsill with the sun beating in, but Zelda didn't get rid of it until Jo and Johnny ran away, until after the night of Auntie Rowan's frantic visit and all the shouting. It was one of the many things that was different when I got better and came home.

There won't be too much to talk over with Scott this morning, I think, heading his way. We've already decided Albie would pack his stuff into Scott's big car, our family car as was, and we'd swap keys here on neutral territory. Scott's going to take my car home. Then, after Albie's unpacked at the schoolhouse, I'll drive to our old house and swap back again. The last bit took some wrangling. Scott wanted to bring mine back and pick up his. I didn't want him at my new house. He didn't want me at his place in case, I think, his girlfriend saw me. But I reckoned that was the price of wrecking a marriage – the ex-wife existing and all that.

'I'll leave your keys in the glovebox,' he said, coming over. 'You've got two sets, right? And you put mine through the letterbox, eh? We'll be out.'

We. I know a lot of people banish the word 'I' from their vocabulary as soon as they're in a couple, but it wouldn't kill him right now. I'm so irritated by this it takes me a minute to decode the rest.

'When?' I said. 'How do you know you'll be out? I've got no idea when Albie's going to get round to unpacking. You know what he's like.'

'We don't need to wait on Albie. You can unpack the car and store the boxes. Best way to get him moving, if you dump it all in the middle of his floor. So. Later today?'

'Weather permitting,' I say, to be mean. One reason Scott caved so easily about following me is he hates driving our road when it's rough, and today's shaping up to be a humdinger. Hail the size of peas was falling when I drove down, the wind scudding it up into heaps at the base of the walls. And the forecast is for the temperature to rise all day then plummet tonight, so the hail will turn to rain and then freeze.

'Weather permitting,' Scott agrees. 'Don't drive back down if it's really bad. And not in the dark.' He pauses. 'I'd hate anything to happen to the Sorento.'

Barrett's at my elbow, and I hear him breathe in deep as if he's going to say something. I get my goodbyes started, all but driving Scott out the door with them.

'So that's the pillock that let you go,' Barrett says, when we're alone again.

'The Sorento!' I say.

'I know what *I'd* like to shove through his letterbox!'

'It's so lovely not to be embarrassed anymore,' I say. 'I've

dreaded him mentioning anything to do with driving ever since
we sold our Skoda for scrap and upgraded. The word "car" hasn't
left his lips since. "Park the Volvo", "Time to service the Mazda".
Ssh!' Willow and Sorrel have gone off to the toilet together,
breaking the force field, and Albie's making his way over. I'm
not going to turn into one of those badmouth mums, no matter
what kind of ex-wife I am.

'Mr Langham,' he says, 'can I get you a latte?'

'Barrett,' says Barrett. He's not laughing or even smiling, but
his eyes look like he's got fairy lights in them. 'I'll take a latte
if you're dead-set on treating me.'

'You're going to have to have a talk, you two,' Gordo says,
as we join him. The table's wrecked. Balled-up teacake wrappers,
napkins torn and formed into flowers, crusts strewn, half-empty
cups of hot chocolate growing skins.

'What about?' I say, with a glance Barrett's way.

'Not to each other. To them. To him. Safe sex, enthusiastic
consent, the morning after pill. I'm not kidding. You weren't here
to see it.'

'I had the talk with Albie when he was seven,' I said. 'It started
with a gay teacher and snowballed.'

'They could teach me,' said Barrett. 'They *did* teach me what
HPV was. Don't fret, Gordo.'

He draws a breath to remind us what can happen and what
can go wrong when it does, then he lets it go and uses the next
one, a smaller one, to say, 'Aye, it's changed days even since
me, I suppose.'

I've been meaning to ask him, or maybe it's just nice to have
something else to think about for a minute, so I say, 'Even when
it *was* you, was she religious or something? Her family?'

He shakes his head. 'Christmas and Easter,' he says. 'I didn't
understand what she did. It broke her mammy. They moved away.'

And so I end up feeling selfish and I'm glad I've got so much
to tell him, to take his mind off things. 'Can you drive up with
me – just us two?' I say. 'To let me bring you up to speed. And,
Barrett, you take the kids?' I hesitate. 'You were coming, right?
I mean, did I actually invite you? I meant to.'

'Aye, we're coming,' Barrett says. 'We wouldn't let you be on
your own, with the lad.'

That takes some working out. If I was absolutely on my own,

it would be kind to come with me. But me and my son getting into our new home is the sort of thing even old friends wouldn't want to crash. Do they think I'm too fragile to cope with going back into the place Davey died? Do they think Albie will hate the place and want to leave and I'll have a meltdown when he tells me?

'Alb?' I say, when he gets back with Barrett's coffee, 'have you ever actually been inside Uncle Davey's house?' I remember afternoons in the garden, a hammock swinging between the crab-apple tree and a cleat on the gable end, a jumble of old deckchairs, their canvas faded and their wood dried pale over summers of sun and rain. Scott wasn't often there. (He and Davey circled each other like strange dogs in the street. I was never sure why.) When it was too cold for Davey's garden, likes of Christmas and New Year or Zelda's birthday in February, we'd always sit in the heidie's office at the school and Davey would come to us.

'Why?' Albie says. 'What's wrong with it? I'll have my own room. That's all I care about. And decent Wi-Fi.'

'Brilliant Wi-Fi,' Gordo says. 'Well, it's a dish, like. He had it for his work, but you could stream the World Cup and Netflix at the same time and not even slow down his IDE.'

I smile to think of Barrett watching his football and Gordo watching his superheroes while Davey worked. 'What's an IDE?' I said.

'Integrated Development Environment,' Gordo and Albie say in chorus.

'That clears that up,' says Barrett to me, and then the girls are back.

While we're getting out of town, I concentrate on the road. The rain is hammering down and spraying back up again, so the grit they've only just spread is pinging the shiny paintwork of Scott's *Sorento*. The other drivers are a flustered collection of full-beams, fog-lamps and nothing at all, including some silver cars invisible in the wing mirrors against the shining road.

'Bampot,' Gordo says as one of them passes and nips back in three feet ahead. 'The sanny van isn't cool wheels but at least I know everyone can see me.' He gropes under the seat and lets it back so he can stretch out his legs. 'Right then. What is it?'

As we cross the bypass, I start filling him in.

'Davey's been buying land,' I begin. 'All round Hiskith. Been going on for years. And recently he was trying to – or at least thinking of – buying Hiskith itself. Hawes just told me.'

'Buying the reservoir?'

'Even if it meant selling everything else. Selling wood that's nearly ready to chop down for a profit, Hawes reckons. Plus this other bit of land good to plant up. Farms that are paying rent. He was trying to convert it all into ownership of the loch.'

Gordo takes his time thinking this over. 'To . . . be the one who gets to say "drain it"?' he goes on at last.

'Or to be the one who gets to say "never drain it",' I add.

'And so . . . the explosion . . . Did he find out that they wouldn't sell to him?'

'That's exactly what I thought!' I chance a quick look over. He looks delighted for some reason, then alarmed, and I look back at the road just in time to see us drift towards the white line. I'm out of practice with this car. Thank God I'm not going to have to reverse-park it. 'Except Hawes said that was unlikely, because it's all very official and nine-to-five Monday to Friday. But then he also said Davey liked to do things his own way. And I quote, "like his will".'

'Christ!'

'Exactly. We didn't pursue that avenue.'

Gordo laughs then spends a while thinking. 'Maybe Davey just lost heart,' he says eventually. I like the rhythm of his conversation. He takes his time, not afraid of a silence.

'Could be,' I agree. 'Maybe he got news about a community bid, or gossip from someone about a grant, or heard that Scottish Water were definitely keeping it for the anglers, or some alliance was definitely draining it for the wildlife. Maybe he'd just had enough.'

'Guilt weighing on him,' Gordo says. 'About his mum.' It's my turn for silence. 'And . . .' He won't fill in the rest, so I have to.

'And he knew I was desperate, so he reckoned he could balance his books a wee bit: leave me a house and do me some good? It doesn't outweigh what he did . . . to Auntie Rowan . . . and telling me about it was a rotten move. Poisoning the gift, daring me to do the right thing. Man, if I believed in spirits and I had a Ouija board, Gordo!'

'I never thought the man I knew could do something like that,' Gordo says. 'Leave you a house and make sure you felt bad for taking it.'

'Oh, *that*?' I said. '*That's* what you can't believe?'

'And because I can't believe he did that, you bet your bum I can't believe he did the rest.'

'Blew up the dam?' I say.

'Or killed his mum.'

'The police think he did the dam. They're happy to close the case.'

'I know,' Gordo says. 'And he confessed to the killing. But . . .'

'But,' I agree.

'Apart from anything else, *why*?'

'She was . . .' I begin. 'She was a very unhappy woman. And she didn't make life easy for the people around her. So my mum says anyway. I just remember her as "one of the adults", you know, like you do.'

'She had a lot to be unhappy about, to be fair,' says Gordo.

'But I think my mum meant before. Before Jo and Johnny. Before Roddie even.'

We sink into another comfortable silence, listening to the slosh of grit and puddles under the wheels, the rain battering on the roof, until we're through Sanquhar and over the bridge. We're away from traffic now, it's true, but we're away from lights as well, from lines on the road, from shops and houses and signs of life. We're climbing up into impenetrable, colourless wet as far as we can see, into a settling chill that makes Gordo shudder just once in his still-damp clothes. I flick the heater on to high, steaming the windows and making the grey draw even closer and even thicker, as if we're sinking instead of climbing, as if we're dropping through water. Like we're tied to a rock.

I strike up a new conversation to quench that thought. 'You'll have noticed we didn't bring anything back from Hawes with us.' Gordo nods, whether he noticed or not. 'He was chuffed at the idea of carrying on being my lawyer, like he was Davey's, and it seemed like a good plan to keep on his sweet side.'

'No need to muck up your new place with a load of crumbling old documents anyway,' Gordo agrees. 'Are you planning to change it much?'

I haven't thought about it yet, is the truth. I suppose if Albie wants to decorate his room, whichever room he chooses, I'll try to afford it. And I won't be happy until I've made Davey's pitiful little downstairs bedroom into a pantry again. But it's only now that I really start to wonder what I'm going to find behind the locked doors. Vintage charm? Retro funk? I can't remember in detail what it looked like. Boring, I think. What Zelda calls bourgeois. That unit with lights under the shelves. A three-piece suite.

'I can help,' Gordo says, when I haven't answered. 'Barrett can help. It's the quiet time of year for both of us now. As long as I get to the school gates most days, Monday to Friday, I can suit myself at the weekends till Christmas.'

'Christmas?' I echo, thinking Christmas and sanny vans don't go together.

'Oh yeah. Park at the edge of the German markets and pick off the locals that want the candles and toys but can't face the bratwurst. It's a good time for me. And then folk go on a lot of walks after Boxing Day. I make rich cakes and serve hot apple juice with cinnamon sticks in.'

I think anyone this enterprising could be making money every day, rather than helping me scrape wallpaper off Albie's bedroom, and maybe he knows I'm hesitating because he goes on, 'We owe Davey a lot, Barrett and me.' Then he stops and makes an odd little creaking sound as if he's trying to hold his breath but some of it is getting out.

'I know,' I say. 'I'm exactly the same. You think about Davey, the Davey you knew, the one who . . .'

'Sorted all the litter himself and took care of getting rid of it, never made Barrett and me take a turn.'

'Right.'

'And knew how we felt about Bess and Allison. Never asked questions. Pretended he didn't notice the odd tear.' I know Bess was the dog so I make a leap and assume Allison was the fiancée. 'And then we're supposed to believe he went and tried to blow up the dam. That's the thing I can't get past. Allison's grave. That's how I think about it. He desecrated Allison's grave.'

'So she's still in there? They never . . .?'

Gordo shakes his head.

We're past the allotments and paddocks now and, as if the

ghost we've summoned is real, the temperature drops again. The wind thins. I've done this journey thousands of times: in the back of Zelda's car, in the school taxi – four of us kids costing the council a bomb, in Scott's first wee banger, then driving myself, driving Albie in his baby seat. It catches me out every time the way the altitude and the loneliness twine together. We're ten minutes from the town and we might be driving over the moon.

'I need space,' I used to tell the nurses. 'I need out. You don't understand.'

'You need sanctuary,' one of the more creative ones once told me. 'You need cradling, holding safe. You need the hospital, Tabitha. "Asylum" wasn't always a dirty word.'

'I need the moor and the sky,' I said. 'The wind on the water. The hill behind the hill behind the last hill I can see.'

She called the doctor to check my dosage. She thought I was babbling and for once I wasn't. I was trying to tell someone who'd never seen Hiskith what it's like here.

After we've been quiet a while, I break in on Gordo's memories and ask, so tentatively it's like I'm coaxing a fox cub out of hiding, 'Can you still see the beauty of it, up top, even though it's Allison's grave, like you said? Is there comfort? Or do you come up here just to be near her?' Because, as much as I need friends, it's not healthy for him to keep returning to where she died. To base his business there, any chance he can, spend his leisure time there too.

'It's complicated,' he tells me. 'Isn't it?'

I smile at that. I like the way he folds me into what he's living. What Barrett lives too, to a lesser extent. It *is* complicated and who knows better than us? My dad died in that dark water. My Uncle Roddie killed himself in the house I've inherited. Auntie Rowan died there, breathing her last pear-drop breath as her body shut down. And now Davey has died there too, in that heart-breaking bed, full of the very insulin that could have saved his mother's life.

I used to think the most understandable thing Jo and Johnny did was leave Hiskith as soon as they could, even if the rest of their choices mystified me. I used to think Zelda had a chip of ice where her heart should be, to stay on and paint the place over and over again: the sweet lies in the Day Paintings and the dark lies in the Night ones. I used to marvel at Davey, so benign, so composed, with his gentle smile and the way he whistled through his teeth as he pottered about. I used to wonder why Hiskith hadn't touched him when it had nearly destroyed me.

And yet here I am, headed home to make my life there. 'It's complicated,' I agree.

'It's beautiful,' says Gordo, like my acknowledgment has given him permission. 'Just because it's not a chocolate box.' He stops speaking so abruptly I turn to see what's wrong. 'Sorry,' he says, seeing me looking. 'I know she's your mum. It just bugs me.'

'What does?' I say, taking my eyes back to the road.

'That village she paints. It's fake. It's like something from the Cotswolds; nothing Scottish about it anywhere. Why couldn't she paint the real thing?'

I think of the Night pictures and bite my lip on the answer.

'There's a proud history in this valley,' he said. 'In these hills. She could paint that.'

'She'd never sell a painting of today,' I say. The high-set seats in Scott's car let us see over the walls into the fields. Drenched, muddy sheep are standing about miserably with their feet sunk in puddles made oily with droppings. 'I'd rather be a cow than a ewe,' I say. 'They're in the byre till spring. Standing on straw. Eating muesli. Basically.'

'You don't get cow people and sheep people,' Gordo says. 'Pigs and foxes, Davey always said.'

I had forgotten it wasn't my private classification system. Of course it wasn't. The youngest of four, I made up nothing for myself. Every bit of my childhood was joining what had started without me: wearing hand-me-downs; pretending to remember the fun they'd had when I was too wee to have had it with them; cajoling them to keep doing the things they'd grown out of.

As we rattle over the first cattle grid, I try to remember who first called them 'bum-rufflers' but of course that was long before I could speak. I've got as much chance of deciding who first made up the name for the pee-in-a-stool, for the place at the hairpin bend where three fields meet. 'Giza' we called it because the walls are thick at the bottom and sharp at the top, quite like pyramids when you're small and looking up at them. Maybe I could ask Jo, at Davey's funeral. Or maybe I could ask Jo to meet me for lunch every once in a while. Maybe this loss would finally bring us . . . not close, but near enough to help with remembering.

Except I'll be living in the house that should be half hers, owning land I've no right to.

Beside me, Gordo sits up straighter in his seat and cranes his neck, just like we always used to do whenever we came back after a trip, to catch that first glimpse of the water as you crest the hill.

'We used to say "I think I can, I think I can,"' I tell him. 'When we were kids.'

'Davey never stopped saying it.' And so we both chant 'I thought I could, I thought I could' as I freewheel down past the school towards home.

'Will we wait for the rest of them?' Gordo says, once we've parked but before we've girded ourselves to step out into the cold. That thin wind is ruffling the water into ridges without breaking it up. I've never liked the look of the loch when it does that. It's hard not to imagine that the water is fighting back, resisting the air. That the water has consciousness, that it's got a plan, got a stance, got a view of what it'll take and what it won't, no matter how hard the weather tries to prevail. Of course, I know that's insane. Water has no mind of its own. It's the one who's underneath the surface – beyond Miss Mirror – that you need to watch out for.

'Let's go!' I say, a bit too loud and a bit too fierce, grabbing the handle and wrenching the door open.

'Physical activity, Tabitha,' one of the nurses used to say. 'A walk, a cuppa, even a pee. If you can just distract yourself before it takes a hold.'

As I scurry, I pick over the big bunch of new keys. 'Let's open one locked door. I'd rather know why Davey locked them without Albie watching. He's a big lad but he's only fifteen when you get right down to it.'

And so we go straight to the living room, where I try four keys before I find the right one. When the lock gives, I send a look of mock fear to Gordo, except it's not really mock at all.

'What do you think?' I say.

'I have no idea,' says Gordo. 'You?'

I try to imagine, but when I let my mind float over the possibilities, all I can picture is dark corners, wet skin, hair like weeds, and burbling rushes of speech in a thrash of water. Which is silly, even for me. The diver eel in the Night Paintings, Miss Mirror lit by Mr Moon, are nothing to do with Davey and nothing to do with this new house of mine.

To prove it to myself, I throw the door wide.

FOURTEEN

Gordo

He's facing the wrong way when the door opens; he's looking at Tabitha. It's her rearing backwards, hands flying up to clap over her mouth, that makes him snap round to see what she's seeing.

The sound of Barrett arriving barely registers. Car doors slam and the kids' voices lift in the endless chirp and tussle of them shaking down into knowing each other, but Gordo takes one faltering step forward and then another into the darkened room, the noise as meaningless as birdsong, no louder than the rushing blood he can't ignore.

I'm here, I'm with you, she says, although she's not.

You're not alone, she says. But he is.

Tabby clicks the light on. She can just about manage that much, threading her flattened hand in along the wall beside the door jamb.

'What is it?' she says. 'I don't understand.'

Gordo takes another step. It's the last of him thinking he knows who Davey was. It's the end of him thinking the three of them were all the same.

'I don't either,' he says, as his eyes travel over it. Of course, in one sense there's no mystery. It's litter. It's neatly packed Tesco, Asda, Safeway, Sainsbury, Lidl, Aldi and Iceland carriers, stacked like breezeblocks with the open ends facing them. Inside – he moves closer – it's crisp bags, sweetie wrappers, juice pods, yoghurt tubes, cellophane packs from sixers of buns and scallop-edged fans from bouquets of flowers. It's every kind of plastic crap. He can see the pack-rings tidily nested, fours and sixes, held tight with bread bag ties. He sees the bread bags and bagel bags, moulded trays for cakes and biscuits, breadsticks and choco-lates. He sees a tower of tiny white tables, fairy-sized. They're pizza-box lid supports and there must be twenty of them. There must be as many of them as the Three Musketeers ever found in the car park, or by the path, or on the moor where some bunch of lads had been camping.

'What the f–laming hell's this?' Barrett is standing beside Tabby in the doorway. The kids are in the kitchen, laughing and kidding; Gordo hears them at the usual volume again as if he's come back from a trance.

'He kept it,' he says. 'I think he kept all of it. He didn't sort the recycling and take care of discarding it. He kept it.'

Barrett's face screws up as if he's embarrassed to hear Gordo talk so daft. He starts shaking his head. But Gordo points to the stack of tiny, white, plastic spacers.

'Fairy tables,' Barrett says.

'It's mostly crisp bags and sweetie papers,' says Gordo. 'Like we always knew it was. Some juice bags. Some bread bags.'

'The occasional tray from a big box of Christmas biscuits,' Barrett says looking at the nearest pile of brittle, coloured plastic. 'Oh Davey boy.' He turns to Gordo. 'He kept everything? *Why?*'

'The list of whys is growing and growing,' Tabby says. She sounds as if there's no power in her voice, as if the words are drifting out on her breath. When the kitchen door opens, she flinches.

'Mum? Have you got the keys to the bedrooms? Can I pick one? Have you got dib—?'

Tabby clicks back into gear as if she's had a slap in the face or a bucket of cold water. It must be a mum thing. 'Albie,' she says, 'this is the living room. It seems Uncle Davey was hiding a bit of a hoarding habit, so the chances are you're not going to be able to sleep in any of the other locked rooms tonight. We can go to Granny or we can go to a hotel. Or, we can camp in the kitchen. And tomorrow we'll start clearing. OK?'

There's a struggle going on inside the boy and it shows on his face. Disappointment, disgust, anger and embarrassment are wrestling for control of him. Gordo thinks if it was just his mum and him, he'd be throwing a strop and asking to go back to his dad's. But things being what they are, all he cares about is what those two girls are going to think of him *now*. Gordo can remember feeling like that, would spare the boy if he could.

'Oh. My. God,' Willow says. They've come from the kitchen and they're right behind their dad to either side. Like they've always been, it seems to Gordo, since they were short enough for him to cup their heads in his hands. Now Willow can hook her chin on his shoulder.

'Open another one!' Sorrel says. 'Mrs Muir, do you want to give us the keys and we'll check over the rest of the house?'

The boy's catching up quickly, blinking but nodding. 'We'll check it out, Mum! You sit down and have a cuppa and we'll see what else . . .'

'We should film it,' says Sorrel. 'People love hoardage.'

Tabby's staring at Barrett. It's a parent thing, Gordo thinks. Tabby can't tell Sorrel to shut it, because she's not her mum. But Barrett can't tell her either because the last thing he needs is the girls flouncing off to phone his ex and call him a bully.

'You make the tea and *we'll* check the rooms,' Barrett says. 'Albie, lad? You could always stay with us tonight till you start getting straight.' He drops a wink at Tabitha as the three of them trail back to the kitchen.

'Maybe it's just one room,' Gordo offers, as Tabby fits a key to the door opposite. It's the place Davey used to use as a work-room until he moved to the kitchen instead. He said it was because his laptop did everything and he didn't need a desk-top monitor and stack anymore. Didn't need a printer when you could send everything digitally. Gordo hopes he was telling the truth.

He wasn't. As Tabitha pushes the door open, a pall of strange stink rolls out over them. It's familiar but Gordo can't identify it until Tabitha clicks the light again and he sees more bags, mostly clear and all stuffed with fag ends. The smell of the old tar and nicotine stuck in the filters is making a guff strong enough for his gorge to rise.

'Douts!' Barrett says. 'What the hell was going on in his head? Tab, I swear we had no idea about any of this.'

'It's not all fag ends,' Tabby says. 'Look! This bag's cigars.' She sounds as if there's hysteria bubbling under the surface, and not too far under either.

'Are you OK?' Gordo says. 'You could wait through with the kids and we could check out the rest of the . . .'

She smiles at him. 'I'm fine,' she says. 'I mean, for me. I don't blame you for wondering.'

Gordo feels a flush creep over his face. Of course she blames him for wondering, for checking. It must be shit to have everyone look at you like a bomb that might go off any second, just because you had a wee rant a month ago. 'Sorry,' he says. 'What's in that?' he asks Barrett, who's undoing the flaps of a cardboard box.

'Batteries,' Barrett says.

There are camping gas bottles too and a few tyres. A stash of air-gun pellets Gordo remembers finding, the three of them, one cold Sunday morning. There are enormous plastic sacks, like lumpy beanbags made for giants, full – when Gordo checks – of aerosols.

Barrett looks back across the hall to the living room and nods. 'Plastic,' he says, pointing. 'And this is hazardous, I reckon. Carcinogen-laden filters, dead batteries, pressurized containers. The lead pellets aren't hazardous, but Davey hated guns. Even air guns. It was like him to put them with the rest of the mucky stuff.'

'What's left for upstairs?' Tabby asks, with a look to the ceiling. 'Or maybe it's not too bad. If the bedrooms were stuffed, wouldn't the plaster have given way?'

It turns out the ceilings are sturdy in this old house. All three bedrooms are at least half full. The big back room over the kitchen is given over to metal and glass. It's mostly foil and coke tins for the metal but Barrett says he remembers a roll of flashing they found one time dumped by the roadside as if it fell off a workie's pick-up bed. The shards of glass are safely stored – Gordo recognizes these big bins from the council dump and wonders how Davey got them. Whole bottles – vodka and whisky, some Bucky, endless ranks of Hendry's and Barr's as well as Coke and the rest of them – lie on their sides like a wine cellar, a whole wall three deep and nearly as high as the ceiling. Gordo doesn't care for spiders and he feels his flesh creep at the thought of disturbing them after all these years. They must be ancient, some of them. Nobody drinks cream soda these days.

The first front bedroom isn't so bad. It's a pretty wee place that reminds Gordo of his granny and grandad's house with the steep coombs and frilly tops to the curtains in the dormer window. And it's full of clothes and shoes; so not actually full at all, because days and weeks would go by without a single garment being left behind on the moor. Stood to reason.

Most of it was always single mittens from toddlers, lost and not missed until the family was on its way back home. Wee hats and scarves were just about as common. The shoes were a mystery. Babies' shoes he could understand. Pairs of shoes he could nearly understand, if someone changed into new walking boots and couldn't be bothered carrying the old ones. But single adult shoes had always puzzled him. How could anyone tramping up Hiskith not notice they'd lost a shoe? Was it pranks maybe?

'Christ!' says Barrett. 'Gordo! There's that wellie full of sick.'

Gordo feels his face screw up but, when he turns, he sees that the single black Argyle pluch, a farmer's wellie, is fully sealed inside one of the big see-through bags.

Barrett stretches the plastic over the top until it's smooth and peers in. 'Christ,' he says again, and looks up at Tabby, with a twinkle in his eye. 'We couldn't agree on this at the time. It was in the passing place just near the brow there. I thought it was a practical solution to a wee bit of car sickness. Gordo reckoned they could just have pulled over and got out.'

'It's a bit of a waste of a wellie,' Tabby says. Like Barrett, she sounds as if she's starting to find this funny.

'Not if they buy them from a charity shop for exactly this,' Barrett says, like he did the day they found it. They didn't pick it up. Davey said it wasn't safe to assume car sickness and if it was norovirus it could clout the lot of them. He said he'd get it later, not let it ruin their walk. It was gone the next time Gordo came up and he thought no more about it. Now here it is, must be four years later, happed up in plastic and sitting in Davey's old bedroom.

'Wrappers, glass, metal, hazardous and clothes,' Tabby says, looking over her shoulder at the last of the locked doors. 'What else *is* there? I can't think what's going to be in there, can you?'

Gordo doesn't even know what he's looking at when the door is open and the room is in full view. Home-brew is his first thought. There are huge tables, covered in cloths as if they're altars, and on top of a couple of them are big black bins, four in all, taps screwed into them at the bottom, tubing leading to demijohns. But it's not beer in the demijohns. It looks like tea. It looks like tea in all the full and stoppered demijohns that are laid out around the walls, three bottles high with planks in between like boards holding up tiered cakes at a wedding. There are altars in the middle of the floor too, a row of them as if Davey was starting to build a wall across the room. And it's warm in here. Warmer than the rest of the house apart from the kitchen, with a low buzzing sound he can't quite place although he knows it's familiar.

'What . . .?' Tabby says. 'What the hell is *this* now?'

'We didn't know,' Gordo finds himself saying. 'I mean, he was an odd duck, was old Davey. No point denying it, eccentric for deffo, but no more than Barrett and me. No more than any other bloke with a hobby. No more than nine out of ten other coders and gamers. Tabby, we didn't know he was—'

'Carrying on the family tradition,' she says, with a wild note in her voice. 'Mad as a hatter. Nutty as a fruitcake. Off his rocker. Out of—'

'Maybe,' Barrett says, stopping her. Gordo wonders how long she could have gone on, how many ways of saying it she might have collected over the years. Not now, but sometime, he'd like to know. 'And maybe not. Those are worm bins. That's worm tea he's been collecting in those bottles.'

'*What?*' Tabby says, and she turns a hunted look on Barrett as if she suspects him of messing with her.

'Worm composters,' he tells her. 'Waste in at the top, fertilizer out at the bottom.'

'Food!' Gordo says. 'It's food, Barrett. That's what else there is that we haven't found already. Sandwich crusts. Apple cores, orange peel. He *said* he composted it all, right enough.'

'Oh well then,' Tabitha says. 'That straightens it right out, doesn't it?' Her voice is rising. 'He's brewing worm compost in the master bedroom. In that case, I take it back about him being clinically fucking insane!'

It's the first time Gordo's heard her swear and he reckons it's out of character because a call comes up the stairwell. 'Mum? Are you OK? The tea's ready.'

'He was making sure the floor didn't go,' Barrett says. 'The way he's got these bottles and the . . . whatever that is under the cloths . . . laid out around the edge and across the middle? He was following the joists.'

'What does that change?' Tabby says, but she's not as belligerent now, not as sarcastic. It's like she actually wants an answer.

'Let's assume for now he had a reason,' Barrett says. 'Let's assume he had a reason for all of it. Just for now.' He's prising the lid off the nearest bin and Gordo steps forward to look inside too. He's braced for the sight of a seething mass of worms and he reckons that's what Tabby thinks is in there too because she turns away. But Gordo looks into the black plastic maw and it's nothing so dreadful. It's not dreadful at all. It's neat apple cores, completely cylindrical as if they've been done with a machine. And it's neat squares of sandwich and disks of orange peel that look as if they've been stamped out with a biscuit cutter. There are even squared-off bits of chocolate bars, no gnawed ends, no teeth marks. If Gordo had to guess, he'd say Davey bought the food and prepared it for these bins like a chef.

'Where are the worms?' he says. 'Did he forget the worms? I know you were sticking up for him but if he forgot the worms . . .'

'Down a bit,' Barrett says. 'As they should be. He's making proper compost and tea. It's an odd place to do it, I'll give you that—'

'Oh God, no!' Tabby cries out and they both wheel round, the bin lid falling back down with a soft whomp. She's holding the edge of the cloth covering one of the big oblong tables. 'Look,' she says and lifts it. It's not a table underneath at all. Probably none of them are tables. Gordo counts seven around the walls and there's two in the middle of the floor, on the joists like Barrett said. And *this* is why it's warm and why there's humming.

'A freezer,' he says. It's a chest freezer with a lift-up lid, as big as a sarcophagus. As soon as he has the thought, Gordo can feel the hair on the back of his neck start to bristle as his scalp shrinks.

'Is it locked?' Barrett asks, as if he's hoping they all are – with stout padlocks so there's nothing for it but to call the police.

Tabitha shakes her head and shoves the cloth off to fall in a heap down the back. She grips the handle and tugs the lid up, releasing a billow of cold air into the warm room. 'Oh!' she says, softly.

Gordo stands as if his shoes are locked to the floor like ski boots in bindings. All he can think of is the number of people lost in the lake over the years. Tabby's father, and did he ever hear how exactly the uncle died? And poor Bess. Even Rowan – who he knows died in her bed – is going through his head. Round his head more like, as if the image is a pinball. More insane yet is the thought of Davey himself somehow not in the

Co-op undertakers in Dumfries where they know he is, they *know* he is, waiting for Tuesday.

And of course, Allison. Allison. The real reason his mind is whirling on full speed and sending his reason flying out of him. Allison was never found. What if *Davey* found her? What if Davey found her, and Tabitha's dad, and Bess. He feels his vision start to blur.

Shush, shush now, she says. *Don't be upset. Forget me and live. Do that for me. That's all I want.*

'Huh.' Tabitha is looking into the freezer, frowning slightly but surely not facing what Gordo's been imagining. 'Why would he do that then?'

Barrett's standing beside her, looking down into the clouds of cold that are still drifting out, although more gently now. 'It explains how neat the worm portions are.'

Which is such a nutso thing to say it gets Gordo over there, peering in too. At a top layer of Ziploc bags with the same chewed crusts and orange peel and apple cores and bits of chocolate in them as the worm bins. Except not quite, actually.

'Why didn't he just freeze everything?' he says.

'Probably did to start with, till he ran out of room,' says Barrett. 'How long do you think he's been at it? I mean, you've been litter-picking nigh on fifteen years, Lyle. How long do you think Davey did it on his own before you rocked up?' Gordo shrugs. 'He needed the worms because there's no room for any more freezers, I reckon. There's no room for any more anything.'

'So why didn't he *compost* everything?' Tabitha asks.

'Cleanliness?' says Gordo. 'Maybe he didn't fancy folks' saliva all over his veg plot.'

'But that's insan—' Barrett begins to say, then rubs his hand over his mouth.

'Oh, Davey,' Tabby says. 'Is *this* why he died? Not the loch? Not a fit of conscience for Auntie Rowan? Maybe it was just . . . cumulative. Maybe he just tipped over, like you would, if this was your life and your house was full and you didn't know what to do next.'

Gordo finds himself nodding. Briefly. He stops because what she's saying makes no sense when you think about it for a minute. Why would any man who'd got his house in this mess and didn't know how to stop, blow up a dam on his last evening alive?

'We should get downstairs to those kids,' Barrett says, as a gale of laughter, three voices in chorus, rises up from below.

'Right,' says Tabitha. 'To celebrate Albie's arrival in our lovely new home.' Her voice is far from steady. 'Our fresh start. My new beginning. Champagne all round, I say.'

FIFTEEN

Tabitha

But, even after all that, I'm still happy when I go back into the kitchen and see Albie standing at the sink with a tea towel in his hand. If he was here alone he'd be on his phone. These two girls, Barrett's girls, are good for him. *They're* tidying up and so he's tidying up too.

'We've been very careful,' Sorrel says. She has put on an apron, one I recognize from Auntie Rowan's day, and she's twisted that long hank of honey-coloured hair into a rope and tucked it into the bib bit, out of the way.

'We're cleaning up the stuff that definitely isn't important and leaving everything else,' Willow adds.

'Important how?' says Barrett. 'Please,' he adds, as Willow holds up the big brown teapot.

'There was only Carnation milk,' Albie says, 'so I diluted it down like it says.'

I try not to react, but if my son knows what to do with tinned milk apart from pour it on ice cream neat so it makes a shell, then he's only known for twenty minutes and only because he hopes it's the sort of thing that's going to impress whichever one of these two it is he's going for. I hope it's one. I hope it's not either. Or both. Only, maybe that's me being old. If I ask him, maybe he'll say 'Jeez, Mum!'.

'Important,' Sorrel says, 'like clues.'

'To *what*?' Gordo's voice squeaks on the word.

'It's *Sherlock*'s fault,' says Barrett. 'They've never seen a minute of *CSI*, whine at me for putting it on, but that daft tosh had them glued.'

'Yeah, but everybody's saying Mr Muir tried to blow something up,' says Sorrel. 'Dale McCardle's dad's a cop, and he said Mr Muir blew up a bridge? There's biscuits.'

I'm not sure I'll be able to swallow the tea, never mind solids.

If there really are any clues here, they might be clues to a matricide, not just a half-arsed home-made bomb that didn't even work. 'So what did you leave?' I ask. 'What did you think was a clue?'

'Well,' says Willow. Then she looks at her sister. They're such a matched pair, so similar to look at and the same sunny nature, for all I can see. Barrett moans about them but I can't remember Jo and me ever pitching in to clean up a grubby kitchen.

'That pile of books for a start,' says Sorrel. She gestures to the sideways heap of almanack and domestic science training manuals that's sitting so inconveniently far back towards the middle of the kitchen table as if to leave room for something else right in front of Davey's chair.

'I've got to agree with you there,' says Gordo. 'I noticed them too.'

'So at first we thought it was to angle a laptop for a video chat, right?' Willow says. 'No up-nostril shots, no extra chins, right?' From the way Albie is nodding I can tell he's only just learned about these considerations and he's distracted, thinking about how he's been looking on video chats before now.

'So we looked for his laptop,' Sorrel takes up. 'To check.'

'But he's got an external camera on an extender,' says Willow.

'What?' Barrett says. 'How do you know? His laptop's gone.'

'His laptop's hanging on the back of his bedroom door,' says Albie. 'That room, I mean.' He points to the corner of the kitchen where the pantry door is flat back against the wall like it's been since we first burst in here the morning after he died.

'We checked it out in case he didn't have a password,' says Willow.

'But duh,' says Sorrel.

'So we put it back,' Albie adds.

I am so relieved to hear that they haven't been on Davey's laptop, I think I might have turned pale.

'Sit down, Mrs Muir,' says Willow.

'Lawson,' I say. 'Ms. Or Ms Muir. Or Tabitha. Tabitha would be best.' Lawson feels pointless now that it's over with Scott and I'm living here again, one of the Muirs of Hiskith again. It seems silly to deny it. But I can't be *Mrs* Muir. That was Auntie Rowan and it's still my mum.

'Sit down, Tabitha,' Willow says.

I obey and smile at her. 'So why was Davey looking at a twentieth-century almanack and . . . whatever those are?' Sorrel takes a big breath and uses it to say, 'We don't know. Which is a major clue, right? Exhibit A.'

'No,' Barrett says. 'This isn't a telly programme, So. It's Tabitha's cousin that she loved. A pile of books isn't a clue.'

'But Dad—' Sorrel begins.

'What else did you leave?' I ask them. The bounce will get kicked out these shining girls soon enough. I don't want them taken down a peg on my account.

'Exhibit B,' Willow says, marching over to the worktop near the sink. 'The bin!'

'Oh yeah,' Gordo says. 'I noticed that the other week too, when we were first in here.'

'What's the problem?' I say, feeling my throat soften at the thought of what they might have found but, even as the idea rises, I'm wondering why there's no smell to go with it.

'It's back to front,' says Sorrel. 'Look.' She slides the bin out from under the worktop and shows us the hinge. 'It's the wrong way round. That's weird.'

I've just said I don't want to flatten them so I try to agree, but the truth is I can think of ten reasons Davey might have it that way: to stop an animal from opening it; to make him think twice about chucking stuff out that he could recycle; a simple mistake after he changed the liner.

Except he didn't have any pets and he obviously thought a lot more than twice about everything to do with waste management – my heart flares and then drops at the thought of dealing with the rest of the house – and we know he hadn't just changed the liner when he died, because as Sorrel toes open the lid with the pedal, we can all see the polystyrene disc from a shrink-wrapped pizza and the balled-up cellophane too.

'OK,' I say. 'I'll bite. What's the explanation?'

Willow shrugs, an extravagant Gallic gesture complete with pushed-out lips and a tiny raspberry sound. 'Dunno,' she says. 'Again. Which *is* a big clue, Dad, whether you like it or not.'

'And now Exhibit C,' Albie says. His voice is sombre and the girls watch him without a spark or a smirk between them. He leans over and reaches under the table. When he emerges again, he's holding a tall cardboard tube in his hands. It looks like the kind of box good whisky comes in except that it's got no branding on it – just a marble pattern in shades of Portland and Oxide. Blue and grey, I probably should say. I know what it is. I've seen them before. I helped Scott choose one for his mum, although we went with a print of hydrangeas and irises that time.

'Only we don't know who's inside,' Sorrel says. 'The initials are R.W.M. So it might not be a clue. It might just be weird and icky.'

'It's neither,' says Barrett. 'It's adult life and if it bothers you, that should tell you something.'

'Don't be like that,' I say. 'They're fine. They're grand. But it isn't a clue,' I tell the girls. 'It's nearly forty years old. It's my Uncle Roddie, Davey's dad.'

'Or his mum maybe,' Sorrel says. 'Rowan, right?'

But I remember Auntie Rowan's funeral all too well and I shake my head. 'Definitely his dad. There was a lot going on when he died and he must have got forgotten about.'

'I wonder why he didn't put the ashes in with Auntie Rowan though,' Albie says.

I know. Because he killed her. Because there are limits, even for a murderer. And Davey couldn't put his beloved father in with a woman he hated. And he must have hated her, mustn't he?

'Mum?' Albie says. I've been quiet for far too long.

'Maybe he didn't want buried,' I say, plucking the theory out of nowhere. 'Maybe he wanted scattered.'

Albie nods. 'So we should scatter him. Poor old thing.'

'We will,' I say. 'Let's ask Granny, make sure she doesn't know different, and then we'll scatter him on the moor.'

'Or in the loch,' says Willow.

I say no, louder than I meant to, and I think Gordo and Barrett have chimed in too.

How the hell are we going to explain *that* to the kids, I'm wondering, when Sorrel says, 'Was he scared of water? That's weird, living here.' And the moment is past.

'But the bin and the books, right?' says Albie. 'We're on to something there. And . . .' He pauses. 'We saved the best till last.'

'We did,' says Sorrel. 'Exhibit D.'

'A secret code,' says Willow, slipping a notebook on to the table from where she's been holding it in her lap.

'We found it in with all his philately stuff,' Albie says, nodding towards the shallow dresser drawer where Davey kept his collection. 'Mum, did you know he hoarded whatjamacallthems as well as real stamps?'

'Franks,' says Gordo. 'He said it was shortsighted to ignore them, because . . .'

'. . . they're today's Penny Blacks,' says Barrett. 'Only ephemera to . . .'

'. . . the ephemeral,' says Gordo.

'Anyway,' Albie says. I think most of that went over his head. 'This book was in there, with stuff that mattered to him. So we checked it out. In case it was passwords. It's not.'

Willow opens it, turns it and shows us the first page. 1268773. 1318385. 1238079. 'It goes on and on and on,' she says.

'Any idea?' I say to Barrett and Gordo, who're reading over my shoulder.

'Not a scoob,' Gordo says.

'PINs?' says Barrett. 'We should let Timothy Hawes see it. He might know.'

'It could be phone numbers,' I say. 'Without the first bit.'

'It's not,' says Willow. 'We checked.'

'OK,' I say. 'Exhibit D.'

But all of a sudden I feel as if I can't take much more of this. I open my mouth to break up the party, but Barrett beats me to it. 'Right, Tab,' he says. 'Why don't you go for a walk? Go and ask your mum about the scattering right enough. Leave this to us. Girls, you help Albie get unpacked. Gordo, if you'll drive down with me, I'll pick up my truck and trailer and see what we can get hauled off.'

'Hauled off where?' I say. It comes out as a yelp.

'I've got connections at the dump,' Barrett says. 'I'll get one lot good and gone and see about having a skip delivered.'

'Da-ad!' says Sorrel. 'Connections at the dump? It's nothing to brag about.'

'But should we maybe not?' I ask him. The girls and their 'clues' have got to me. 'Should we maybe tell the police?' I say. 'Leave it undisturbed until someone's seen it?'

No one answers me. Maybe the kids don't really believe that this is any more than a game. Barrett and Gordo know otherwise, but maybe they can't face more trouble. Or maybe the kids can't see the connection to the mystery they know about. Who bombed the dam? Davey's hoarding doesn't relate to that in any way I could see. But then how could a bin and a pile of books either? A crematory tube and a book of numbers? When I think about it, how could any of these so-called clues relate to anything?

'I am going to go for that walk though,' I say. 'Albie, do you want to come to Granny's?'

The look on his face is comical and I take pity on him, pretending he has to be around to supervise unloading his belongings. Besides, I need the time to think. I let myself back out the side door, telling Barrett, who's come to see me off, that I'd love him to get rid of that single bed first out of everything, even the worm bins.

'I'll bring an airbed up for the lad,' Barrett says. 'And I've an old Z-bed you could use meantime, if you don't mind the thought that it came from my mother's house in the year dot.'

I don't mind the thought of a Z-bed at all. I hope it's one of the really ancient ones with a tabletop that turns into the headboard and a chintz skirt that hides the folded mattress when it's not in use. Maybe I could get one of my own online for when Barrett takes his back again.

So, although I thought I needed solitude to howl, as I turn out of the gate I find myself smiling. And instead of heading straight up the hill to the school, to ask Zelda about ashes, and numbers, and books and a back-to-front bin, I make my way towards the water, feeling strong enough to let the thoughts come if they want to. I'm feeling unbelievably strong, actually. I feel as if my feet are planted in the ground instead of just resting on top of it, like what happens if you stand in wet sand and let the tide slosh in and out around you. The same thing happens in the soft mud of the loch too, but no one who knows what's under there would do that for fun, like they do at the seaside.

The first thought to pop into my head as I stand there feeling my eyes and nose start to run in the cold, watching the rain dimple the surface of the water, is why didn't Auntie Rowan's death trigger a post-mortem? If there was any chance that her death wasn't natural causes, wouldn't there have been an investigation? Because there definitely wasn't. And times have changed since my dad and Uncle Roddie died. Back then it might all have been a bit on the nod – small-town coppers wanting to not upset the family, even that small town, even this family – but ten years ago there's no way Rowan would have been tidied away as quick and neat as the two Muir brothers had been.

So, maybe just maybe, just possibly, Davey didn't mean it literally. Maybe – going downhill, overwhelmed with life and still hurting from all the things that still hurt me, he had started blaming himself for her dying. Can I let myself think that, like I let myself look at this water and see only the pockmarks of raindrops on the surface, as if it's a puddle, as if there's nothing under there?

I know better than anyone how guilt works on you. And Davey was grown-up when Rowan died. I was a child, barely walking and talking when it was me. I got that dinned into me. 'You were a baby, Tabitha. You were a tiny little girl. You couldn't have changed anything or stopped anything. It wasn't up to you. Eat your crusts and say your prayers, Tabitha.' Elspeth and I used to joke that life on the ward wasn't that different. Eat your crusts and say your prayers. Eat your pills and talk honestly to your key nurse. And if you decided to eat your own hair, like Elspeth did once, and you say to the doctor that one of the orderlies served it you, there was no harm done. 'They know we're all insane,' Elspeth said after the mild scolding. 'What do they expect?'

When I stop thinking about Elspeth, I start thinking about Barrett. I decide the only reason he's chasing about the country-side – fetching a trailer, calling in favours at the tip – is that he knew more than he's letting on about how peculiar Davey was getting. He knew, but he's not so normal himself, mooching about a loch where his dog drowned.

And if *he's* odd, we need another word entirely for Gordo, mooching right alongside him, at the spot where his fiancée drowned herself and took his unborn baby with her. That's why they're helping: guilt and remorse because they let it get this far. And they no more killed Davey than he killed Rowan, than Tabitha killed her daddy, underneath Miss Mirror, all those years ago.

I catch that thought in my leather gloves and squeeze the life out of it. I take it to the middle of the desert and drive away. I tie it to a tree in the deepest bit of the forest. And I don't breathe at all – in or out – until I'm done.

SIXTEEN

Tabitha

The rain stops, suddenly, like it sometimes does, leaving silence, and leaving me staring at the flat reflection of the cloudy sky, exactly the same colours as that tube of ashes. I turn away, rattled to be feeling so much dread in the daylight. It's normally not till the sun goes down and even then it's like the memory of a fairytale someone once told me: Mr Moon and his captured family; Miss Mirror's shining face; and *him*, somewhere at the edge, always watching.

I trudge up towards the school, promising myself I'll download a talking book for bedtime, or something soothing off Radio 4, something to stop Bess and the fiancée from taking shape and joining the rest of them. I'm glad I can't remember the fiancée's name. That'll help me.

But then I think 'Allison' as I push open the gates of the playground and make my way to GIRLS. I can hear the music before I open the outer door into the vestibule. Violins are soaring from the old paint-splattered beatbox Zelda still uses in her studio, so loud that the discs – perhaps they're tapes, even – crack and break on the crescendos.

'Mum!' I shout from the coat pegs. 'Mu-um?'

There's no answer and, maybe it's because I want a new start where I'm an adult and all the memories of childhood are puny against my resources and my understanding, but I open the studio door and walk in. Or maybe, I realize too late, it's only because I want to be more like Jo, who strolled in here and sat in the armchair, free from all the rules that hung over us when we were wee and still hang over me. Wanting to be more like your sister isn't exactly mature, I think to myself, but it's too late to back out now.

I breathe in paint, linseed oil and turpentine, then glance at the little stove wondering why the dry baccy isn't overwhelming everything. The tin is there and the papers too, but the stove isn't lit. I can see my breath.

Maybe Zelda can't feel the chill because she's working on something so big that she's bending and stretching instead of just standing. It must be five foot tall and much wider; I can only see her legs and her feet. There's no clue from the back of the canvas or the stretcher but I can tell from the paint on the palette she's holding out to the side like she always does that it's a Night Painting. The worms and splats of colour are Mars, Van Dyke, Asphaltum, Prussian, as I long ago learned to call black and blue, bottle green and chocolate brown.

I was so scared of those strange names when I was tiny. I thought they were people hiding in the studio, people I never saw. The same doctor who named all the cats made me admit they were colours, powerless to harm me, made me use their names all day every day until it became a habit. But the names weren't the only problem. I hated the look of the palette when she introduced it to me, not understanding how the mixed gobs of paint had got there, only knowing that they looked like spat-out gum stuck to the ground, the hawked-up phlegm that I fled past when I saw it on the street in the winter. The first time I saw an oyster my heart hammered, remembering the colours of Zelda painting clouds. I could no more have swallowed it than I could float.

'Why are you *in* here?' Zelda's squawk brings me back to reality, like a slap. She's standing between me and the canvas now, still holding the palette hooked over her left thumb and pointing the brush at me like a wand. If it *was* a wand, if she could curse me for interrupting her work, she wouldn't hesitate.

'Sorry,' I say, as I so often do when I'm starting a conversation with her. 'I called out but you didn't hear me over the music. Mum, aren't you cold?' Her hands look dark and papery and once again the thought occurs to me that she's trying to save money.

'I'm working!' she says, casting one panicked glance back at her picture, 'and you can't look!' As she snaps her head to the side and then to the front again, her hair swings out. The tips trail through the paint and flick thick drops of it on to the back of the canvas. She doesn't notice.

'I don't want to look,' I assure her. 'I know you won't let me. I'll stay over here.'

She's making visible efforts to calm herself, which is strange because she usually plays the artistic temperament card when-ever she can. Maybe she really is trying something new and she's beginning to doubt whether it's working. The more I consider this the surer I get, because this canvas is truly enor-mous and she's been painting smaller and smaller in recent years. I know why: the jigsaws and tea towels are where she makes her money and the one time she was told her painting wouldn't 'reduce well' she got angrier than I've often seen her. Since then she's been painting them the right size to start with. Not today, though.

'What *do* you want?' she demands crossly. 'If it's more than a nosey.'

'It's about Davey,' I say. I cross to the armchair by the kettle and settle into it.

Zelda watches me and then goes back behind her canvas again. 'What about him?'

'Lots of little things.' They seem *so* little now that I don't want to mention them. I make myself. 'Why would he have bought domestic science training manuals from the 1930s?'

'Those are Rowan's. They were her mother's before that. She was convinced they'd be of interest to an antiquarian bookseller one day. So deluded.'

Any more deluded than an artist who makes a modest living from jigsaws but still nominates herself for the Turner Prize every year? 'But why would Davey be reading them?' I say instead of that.

'Perhaps he was going to let a dealer see them.'

I shake my head even though she can't see me. 'No, it's not that. Because the other book in the pile is the cheapest discount-outlet almanack.'

'Wobbly table?' says Zelda and laughs a smoky laugh at her own wit. She goes on. 'Tabitha, I wouldn't try to make sense of Davey's possessions, if I were you. The last time I saw his kitchen I thought hoarding wasn't far away.'

I laugh now and the hollow sound of it makes her pop her head back round to look at me.

There's no point beating about the bush. 'He's got carrier

bags full of litter he picked up on the moor,' I tell her. 'Freezers full of leftover food. Hoarding is in the rear-view mirror.'

'I haven't been further than the kitchen since Rowan died, you see,' Zelda says. 'He always came here when we wanted to see one another. Or if he needed anything.' She pauses. 'Or if I did. I'm not denying he was good to me. Tree pruning and logs and what have you.'

'But you never got the sense that he was struggling with anything?' I don't know from one minute to the next whether I'm trying to convince myself Davey was basically fine and no one could have foreseen what happened, or if I'm gathering evidence of him sinking for years, a miracle he lasted as long as he did, and no one could have helped no matter what.

'Struggle and Davey are not two words I'd put in the same sentence,' Zelda says. 'He worked when he felt like it, he pottered in his garden, he roamed about with those peculiar friends of his. His life was without care, as far as I could ever see.' She twists up her mouth into something like a smile. 'Don't wear yourself out looking for explanations, Tabitha. His genes were not his friends and whether you think it's *all* nature or part nurture too, he was dealt a poor hand.'

I'm glad when she pulls her head back behind the picture again, because I can feel myself gaping. Davey was dealt the same hand I was dealt, so it's hardly reassuring to hear Zelda say no wonder he took his own life. Maybe she'll play this conversation over to herself later and freeze in horror. More likely it'll never cross her mind again.

'I better get back,' I say, when I've recovered myself. 'I've left Albie unpacking.' I leave a pause for her to fill with grandmotherly clucking about how much she wants to see him, her only grandchild, with demands to know when I'll bring him up for tea.

'I shall see you at the funeral,' she says. 'I'm glad we're expected to wear black and not "celebrate his life" by dressing like children's entertainers.'

'Where did you hear that?' I ask. Surely Jo and Johnny haven't been ringing her up for chats.

'I heard nothing and so I inferred the standard procedure,' she says, quite sourly. She hates to be caught out in little fibs. She has a disdain for the kind of self-serving stories others employ to save face. It's one of many things she finds bourgeois.

So, while I've got her on the ropes for once, I ask her, 'Why were Uncle Roddie's ashes not buried with Auntie Rowan?'

'*What?*' She shrieks it.

'Or scattered years before?'

'Why on earth are you asking about Roddie?'

'Do you know what he wanted?' I say. 'Because we've found him, still in the house. It seems sad.'

'He could be scattered with Davey,' Zelda says, calm again. 'I hardly think Johnny will want one of them at each end of the chimneypiece.'

'One last thing,' I say, standing. 'Whenever you *were* in Davey's kitchen, over the years, like you said, did you ever throw anything in the bucket? A teabag or a biscuit wrapper or whatever?'

Zelda's head re-appears around the side of the canvas. She stares at me. Well, of course she does. I can't believe I've swallowed the notion of clues, like another teenager instead of the adult who shouldn't be indulging them. 'What?' she says again.

'No?'

'Tabitha, I know you've been through a difficult time what with one thing and another.' She hesitates. 'Are you in regular contact with your doctor?' That's as near as she'll ever come to saying what she means.

'No, it is, then,' I answer. I leave, with her coming to stand by the canvas as I pass near it, like a bear protecting a cub from a predator. Not at all like a mother trusting her daughter not to glance at a painting.

So maybe it's sheer cussedness that tempts me round to the outside of the studio to where there's a potting bench against the wall under the high windows. If I climb up on a plastic chair and then the tabletop, I can just about see in. I stand on the balls of my feet and steady myself with elbows on the stone sill.

She's back at work, dabbing little dots of paint on to the canvas then considering the effect with her head on one side like a bird planning to pull on a worm. I peer at the picture to see what it is that she was guarding so fiercely, but it's just another of her Night Paintings after all, the same as dozens more that she's painted, then sold, over the years. I suppose it's mildly interesting to see one half-finished. Apparently she paints a realistic ruined village scene and adds the nightmare later. And perhaps she washes over the paint after it's on, to make that dreamlike wateriness that's become her trademark. At the moment, this one is a fairly plain looking landscape with stars and moon above, mud and shadow below, skeletal trees joining the top and the bottom of the scene like Frankenstein stitches.

As I turn round on the bench to clamber down again, I can see the tops of the same real hills as the ones she's sketching into that murky scene and suddenly, in comparison to this place, Davey's house feels sure, safe and . . . wholesome, is the word that pops unbidden into my head. Even with nowhere to put a bed except the kitchen and God knows how much work ahead of me to make it a proper home.

Looking in through the kitchen window when I get back, I could convince myself it was a family: two dads and three kids busy playing a parlour game, the table covered in ripped and crumpled scraps of paper, all five of them scribbling.

'What's going on?' I ask as I join them.

'We decided to have a crack at Davey's password,' says Albie, looking up. He leans over and hands his phone across the table to Gordo who's sitting at the laptop. 'Three more to try.'

Barrett and the girls look up from their jottings. Willow crosses her fingers and her legs and arms, until she's wound like a rag being squeezed dry.

'How can you crack a password?' I ask.

'We started out just trying everything we could think of,' says Gordo. 'Dates, names, favourite books, films, games . . .'

Of course. They must have talked about it all out on those hills over the years. 'But maybe he made passwords like you're supposed to,' I say.

'He didn't,' Gordo says. 'We used to argue about it. I make up different passwords for everything. Barrett and Davey use the same password for everything. Except that Davey changed his a lot, and Barrett . . . well.'

'*Will&So*! So safe, Dad!' Sorrel says.

'Ah but the O is a zero, So,' says Willow. 'MI6 couldn't get past that!'

My password is BabyBoyAlbie. With a zero too.

'But then,' says Albie, 'we found another clue. Gordo says

it's a clue anyway. Pile of books, back-to-front bin, book of number codes. And now . . .' He waggles his eyebrows and brandishes a small, black, leather-covered volume. It looks vaguely familiar.

'Another notebook?' I say.

'It's a Bible,' says Albie.

'It was on the floor in the pantry when we first came in,' I say, remembering. 'But Davey—'

'Exactly,' says Albie. He holds his hand up as I start to interrupt. 'That's what *he* said.'

Gordo takes up the tale. 'Couldn't wrap my head round why he had a Bible handy. You'll know this, Tab. He had no time for it. Not even the stories as stories. And yet there's a Bible with a page-marker in it and a highlighted line.'

'Hey!' I say. 'That's not what the numbers are, is it?' I point to the little code book lying open, face-down, on the table. 'Book, chapter and verse?'

'*That's* it, Mum!' Albie says.

'What?' I say. 'I cracked it?'

'No,' says Sorrel. 'The numbers are too long. One three three eight two seven five doesn't fit the longest book with the most chapters and the most verses no matter how you slice it.'

'But you're thinking like a detective, Mum,' says Albie. 'Way to go!'

I share a look with Barrett. No one patronizes you quite like your own teenage kid.

'As I was saying,' Gordo cuts in, 'a Bible with a bookmark and a highlighted line. Proverbs, Chapter twenty-six, verse eleven.' He waits to see if that means anything to me. I shrug.

'The grossest bit in the whole thing,' says Sorrel, from behind the twisted rope of her crossed arms. She's holding them up in front of her face while she watches Gordo type.

'"As a dog returneth to his vomit, so a fool returneth to his folly".'

'Ewwww,' says Sorrel. 'Do dogs even do that? Uggy doesn't do that.'

'Pigeons do it for them,' says Barrett.

'Dad! Ewwwwwwww!'

'And so we're trying to turn *that* into a password,' says Albie.

'Because why else would an atheist have a Bible verse high-lighted?' says Gordo.

'And how's it going?' I ask.

Albie lets out a long raspberry, but he does it with his cheek, not his tongue, for the first time ever.

'Maybe that's for the best,' I say. 'Uncle Davey wasn't well. His laptop might be upsetting.'

But, even as I speak, there's a ping, and a gasp from Gordo. The kids all cheer.

'I'm in,' Gordo says. 'Dogsvomit, with zeros for the Os and a 3 for the S. Sorry,' he adds, with a glance at Sorrel.

'Don't open anything,' I say. 'Not while the kids are here.'

'Mum!' Albie says, 'This is really significant. Keeping however many years' worth of crap until your house is bursting at the seams is full-strength for most people, but it's not as meaningful, for Uncle Davey, as choosing a boot-time password for your whole account. He left the Bible to make *sure* we got in. There's definitely something worth seeing on there.'

'I agree,' Willow says. 'I think there's method in all of it. Dad told us about the freezers.'

I frown at her. The freezers and worm bins seem to me to be the craziest thing of all. The split between clean food in neat shapes and dirty food with teeth marks? If I'd been on the ward with someone who did that, I wouldn't have blinked. 'You're very kind to say so,' I tell her.

'But there really *is* method,' says Sorrel. She has unwound herself and is shaking the pins and needles out of her arms.

'There must be,' says Albie. 'If the Bible's a clue to his password, and the book of numbers are clues to something and the stack of books and the bin are as well, even if we haven't worked them out yet, then the however many years' worth of crap have got to be clues too.'

I know there's a flaw in this argument but I could no more explain it than I could float.

I catch myself. That's the second time I've thought that today.

'Fly, Tabitha,' the nurse said. 'No more than you could fly. People *can* float. People *do* float as long as they don't thrash about too much from panicking.'

'So why do I say "float"?' I asked her.

'Why do you think?' She had never spoken so kindly to me.

'I don't know,' I said. 'Why don't I know?'

'You do know,' she told me, still kind. 'Give yourself permission, Tabitha. You really do.'

'I wish,' I say to all of them sitting in the kitchen waiting for me to speak, 'I wish I believed in séances. I would summon him. There's so much I want to ask.'

The knock at the door makes all of us jump and then makes the three kids giggle and flap their hands as they recover from the fright. I try to laugh with them, because it seems so much like something that would happen in a play. I don't quite manage it.

It takes another half minute for me to remember that it's my house and realize that no one else is going to get up to answer the door. I can feel my blood in my legs as I go out of the kitchen and along the passageway. But when I open up, it's a farmer standing on the doorstep, a woman I vaguely recognize from times I've been behind her on the track and times I've stopped at a field gate to help block off her sheep as she moves them.

'Tabby, aye?' she says. 'Lorna. I was sorry to hear about the lad. Terrible thing. I wrote to his brother as soon as I heard. Your . . . cousin, I suppose you'd say.' There it is, same as ever. That pause that reminds me my cousin is my brother-in-law. At least she doesn't smirk. 'And he wrote back saying it's come to you. So I was wondering if you knew yet what the plans are. Davey was a fair man, and he said we'd always have first refusal, but it's your shout now.'

SEVENTEEN

Tabitha

Because of course, I'm not just an owner of property. The tenant farms and commercial plantings mean that I'm a landlord. I must have been mad to think I could off-load Hawes, bring my deeds back to the house and deal with it all on my own. I'm on the phone to him ten times that first week as the letters start arriving: from Scottish Water, from SEPA, from DEFRA, from some other bunch I've never heard of and can't find by googling. I take photos of everything and text it down to Hawes, Beattie and Thom. Then Tim Hawes, so he tells me, sends out letters saying Mr Muir's estate is in probate and nothing's going to happen till it clears. I told the farmer, Lorna, as much, over tea in the kitchen that day, as she looked around the rest of them and tried to sort us all into a shape that made sense to her. 'Crack on as usual,' I said. 'Let's wait for probate to go through and then we'll see where we are. I'm not for making waves.'

Emptying the house is a nice human-scale distraction from all of that and Barrett's been as good as his word, hauling off trailer-load after trailer-load to the tip for me, while Gordo takes care of catering. Or, if he can't justify parking the van at Hiskith for the day, he sends up supplies with Barrett in the morning: thick soup, trays of brownies so rich I cut them as if they're fudge, coffee in insulated cups with woolly jackets on top, so I still have to blow on the foam when Barrett hands one over the garden wall to me. *I have* got *a kettle* I text to Gordo one Thursday, embarrassed at so much giving, despairing about ever paying it back.

A mouse died in that kettle once, he texts back. I never know whether he's joking, but I soak it with bicarbonate of soda before I make Barrett's tea. It would be easier to brush it off as a wind-up if it wasn't for the stuff we *do* find, day by day, as we chisel down into Davey's hoard. Of course mice have nested in it, shredding paper and cardboard into cities of linked nests. Moths have been in the clothes, long gone now but leaving coloured dust behind them as well as the casings of their grub babies, dried out like the husks of a crop. I take to wearing a mask and gloves as I ferry it all out to the trailer. Willow and Sorrel have walked away from the cleaning completely, preferring to keep on at the 'clues', although today they're out on the hill with Uggy and I've let Albie join them, mostly because he didn't ask; just pleaded silently with his eyes the same way he used to plead for sweeties from his seat in the supermarket trolley.

I've completely given up thinking about clues for myself, trying to get the place cleared before the funeral. If we'd found anything on the laptop, it might have been different. But after the euphoria of cracking the password, we hit the ground with a thump. There was nothing. Gordo and Albie both checked for hidden files – down the back of the couch, Gordo called it – and pronounced the laptop clean of anything useful. They were so sure that, after I'd copied what I needed on to mine, I took it down to Tim Hawes and handed it over to help him get a better idea of what Davey was up to with what Hawes calls his 'holdings'.

'It's not really a surprise,' Gordo said. 'His laptop being clean. I mean, he left a literal letter, on paper, folded in an envelope, in a file, at his lawyers. And he left the clue to his password in a paper Bible with a cardboard marker.'

'But when we use the oh so significant Bible to crack the password . . . it all fizzles out,' I say. 'Doesn't that trouble anyone else? It troubles me.'

'What letter?' said Albie.

So I changed the subject. It's not hard to distract Albie these days. Mention Willow, or Sorrel, and he's gone.

And I can't blame him for being smitten. They're lovely girls. And Albie's not the only smitten one, if I'm honest. I've never made friends this easily before. My family and my past always combined to make me wary of new people. I could never decide whether it would be better to live where people remembered everything about me as soon as they heard my name or live where I was a total stranger, but I always knew Castle Douglas was the worst of both worlds. Just too far for everyone to know but not far enough for no one to know. So I got in the habit of hanging back. I wonder if Annan, fifty miles south, where Jo and Johnny have been all these years, was too far and too near as well. I'll ask them. When they come back. Like a dog to vomit. For the funeral.

When I get there, on a crisp day that's more like winter than the usual November murk, Jo's alone, sitting in the front row in a velvet hat and a Quinacridone violet coat with a velvet collar. Zelda ushers Albie and me into the pew ahead of her and comes in behind us, obviously needing a buffer. But, for all that, she's staring so hard at Jo that her eyes are starting to water. You hear people say 'drinking in' about a really avid stare but this is even more than that. She's devouring her daughter, gobbling her up. Maybe she pushed us in first knowing she'd need bodies between them to stop her from eating Jo alive, crushing her bones in the hug her arms have ached for, twenty-five years now.

'Where's Johnny?' I ask Jo.

'He's sick,' Jo says. 'Going at both ends. Nothing to be done about it.' I feel myself draw back in case she's got it too and she's breathing it all over me, but she shakes her head. 'Don't worry. It's his IBS. Nothing catching. Anxiety makes it worse so it was odds on he'd be down today.'

I try to believe her. In fact, I go further. I try to tell myself that if anxiety and grief are killing his insides today, maybe that was why he didn't turn up for Auntie Rowan. But Jo never showed her face then either.

That day was bleak beyond belief, with lashing rain and bitter cold, and Rowan was set on a burial. 'Her last chance to bend us all to her will,' Zelda said. I'll never forget the look of everyone huddled round the grave, shoulders hunched like roosting vultures. The grave dirt was covered with Astroturf but it was so wet that mud leaked out along the seams and turned the bright obnoxious plastic to a colour worse than honest earth could ever be. The rain hammered on the coffin lid and Davey hung his head and wrung his hands. He had wanted to pay for a gazebo but knew from speaking to Rowan over the years she thought they were an insult to what she called 'the departed'. It offended her to think that no one would be cold and miserable for her.

I'm so glad we're not at the cemetery today. This place is

beautiful, strange as that sounds to say about a crem. It's like an upended Viking ship, stripped down to the bones, with a lot of glass and a view of gardens. The wood inside is pale and there's no fake velvet or flock anywhere. Albie's been dreading it, his first funeral, but he visibly relaxes as he looks around. I give him a grin and he nods back at me and mimes a phew. I'm as relieved as he is. I hate that moment when the curtains close over the coffin. Here, when it's time, the coffin moves as smooth as a skater on new ice and gently disappears from our view behind another bit of arty wood that's almost a sculpture.

Once it's gone, I sit back and feel my spine start to unknot, although I wasn't aware that I'd been holding myself tightly. In fact, I haven't really been paying attention to anything. The order of service tells me there have been two hymns and a poetry reading since we sat down. I turn to the back of the sheet to see if more's coming and the photograph there makes me catch my breath. It's the four of us, leggy kids in drainpipe jeans and aertex, sitting in a row on the drystane dyke outside Davey's side door. He looks fifteen or so, the same as Albie now, so I must be ten or eleven, not quite grown into my big teeth yet and with arms so skinny that my elbows are their widest point. We're holding ice lollies, the home-made ones from Rowan's freezer. No vans ever came up our track back then, long before the car park and the walks. Long before the jigsaws and tea towels, I suppose I mean. Jo's got her lolly in her mouth, sucking it hard, and Johnny's laughing at her. I can't help seeing the crudity in it now, and the way Davey's staring at the camera with his jaw set and his knuckles white tells me he knew at the time they were playing games with whoever took the photo. I'm oblivious as I was so much of the time, smiling a wide, wet grin with my lolly held off to the side and a few strands of my hair sticking to it.

'What made you choose these photos?' I ask Jo in a murmur. 'Weren't there any good shots of just Davey?' The picture on the front is a recent selfie of him in his garden. He's wearing sunglasses and looking out from under a baseball cap with his head tilted back. He's holding up a haulm of newly dug potatoes. They're in sharper focus than he is.

'What better portrait of Davey?' Zelda says. 'The garden was his pride and joy.'

'Compared with the house anyway,' says Albie, released back into snark now that the coffin has disappeared from view.

'So I do hope you're not going to traduce his memory by changing it,' Zelda adds. 'You'd do better to honour him and his generosity by acting as custodian of his vision.'

It's really not like Zelda to labour a point this doggedly. That's always been the best thing about her: she's so caught up in herself she doesn't nag anyone else much. But that's the second time she's warned me not to wreck Davey's precious garden. She can't even see it from the school.

'His vision?' says Jo. 'He's hardly Capability Brown.'

'So why put that potato pic on his order of service?' I say. 'That's exactly what I'm asking.'

'Have *you* got pictures of Davey?' she asks me. It's a good question. It's been a long time since we were that kind of family. 'I reckon he'd have wanted the spuds to be seen,' she goes on. 'And the other one? Might as well give folk something to cluck about since they're going to cluck anyway.'

I don't know what 'folk' she means. Behind us, standing as we stand and watching us as we walk out, are about twenty-five mostly strangers. Tim Hawes is there and an old man I think I recognize as one of the doctors when we were all wee, probably long-retired now. Lorna is there with her family, out of her farmer's waterproofs and looking uncomfortable and unlike herself in a print dress and black jacket. A few of the others might be more tenants. None of them have been up to see me yet, if they are. Maybe Lorna took it on herself to pass on my message around the rest of them.

My eyes find Gordo and I smile. He's sitting with two women I don't recognize. From the fact that they haven't dressed up I'd say they were health workers, maybe care workers, people who go to a lot of funerals semi-officially. But I don't know why they would be here. Davey wasn't getting regular care for anything, as far as I know. He was in good shape; the autopsy confirmed it. I make a plan to talk to them if I get the chance, in case Gordo hasn't quizzed them already.

Barrett's there with the girls, of course. I feel Albie wanting to stop and sit down with them as we go past, but I put my hand under his elbow to keep him walking all the way to the foyer, where we stand in a row – Jo, Mum and me. I let Albie wait outside in the gardens for us. No fifteen-year-old kid needs to be on a receiving line. Not for an uncle.

'I'm so sorry for your loss, so sorry for your loss, so sorry for your loss.' It's different voices but they all sound the same as the same words are repeated to the three of us, before each of the twenty-five guests moves on to the collection box and starts rootling in wallets and purses for money.

'How did Johnny decide which charity?' I ask Jo, in a lull.

'Scottish Wildlife Trust?' she says. 'I reckoned it wouldn't offend anyone and it wouldn't make anyone feel bad about not putting fifties in. Children's cancer and all that is a lot of pressure. And "Hot Dates For Scruffy Weirdos" don't go in for publicity.' I can't help it; I feel myself start to crack and dip my head to hide it. I've missed her without knowing it, all these years. Missed the way she could surprise me: older, cleverer, funnier.

'Oh now, Tabby my love,' says the nearest woman in the line, taking a hold of me under my chin and lifting my head. 'Don't take on. He's in a better place. And God never gives us more than we can bear.' I have no idea who this is.

'Good of you to come, Alva,' says Jo and then I *do* recognize her. She was at school with us and, judging by the records I've copied from Davey's laptop, she rents one of the paddocks down by the bridge and keeps a few animals there.

'Jocasta,' Alva says, making the point that it's only me who gets an endearment. She gives Jo a long look as if she's considering what advice would fit best *there*, but she thinks the better of it and moves on to Zelda.

The next woman along grabs both of Jo's hands in hers. 'Welcome back, Jo,' she says. 'You've only been down Annan way, I heard. But welcome home.'

'Thank you for coming,' Jo murmurs. She tugs but her hand is held fast.

'What have you been doing with yourself all this time?' the woman says.

Marriage, house, business, travel, I think. I put my own hand out to move this nightmare person on.

The nurses are next but when I read the logo on their polo shirts it says 'Nithsdale Veterinary Clinic'.

'We've missed seeing him since Ed died,' one of them tells me.

'Sorry?' I say. 'Who died?'

'The fox cub. Ed Sheeran. Davey nursed him all winter, borrowed an old crate and feeder left over from before we upgraded. But it was no use in the end.'

And now I'm close to tears for real. He must have been so lonely, nursing a fox, sorting his litter, putting automatic stamping patterns into spreadsheets. Why were men such hopeless friends that neither of this two coming towards me now knew what a state he was in? I glare at Barrett and Gordo as they approach and, to cover the fact that I don't want their hands in mine or worse their kisses on my cheeks, I introduce them both to Jo.

'We've met,' says Barrett.

Jo looks at him coldly. 'I don't think so.'

'I never forget a face,' says Barrett. Jo's look gets even colder but she adds nothing to her denial. 'Ach it's a small world and Nithsdale doesn't pump it up any,' says Barrett, relenting.

'I don't live in Nithsdale,' says Jo, quick as a dart. 'I'm at Annan.' I've no idea why it matters to her. They're just making conversation. No one's exactly been scintillating as they've shuffled past us.

'Must be the family resemblance,' says Gordo and Jo's cheeks flame bright red. She looks beyond them to where Tim Hawes is waiting to pay his respects.

'I am so sorry for your loss,' he says. 'Davey was a remarkable man. I'm glad I finally got to give him that dram I'd been owing him.' The man's got a one-track mind.

Hawes doesn't come to the purvey; maybe he knows the whisky's a blend. Neither do the two vets I thought were care workers. But there's no stopping the rest of them. The tenants and the locals who've come for a gawp all pitch out of their cars and into the Manor Hotel, where a slick funeral tea is waiting for them. The staff, as you'd expect in the nearest pub to a crematorium, have got it down to a fine art: the head waitress clocks them as they pass and guesses how many cuppas, how many wines and how many orange juices, with barely a glassful going to waste. The trays of still-hot sausage rolls and still-damp egg and cress sandwiches are out on the tables before the coats are off. Zelda and Jo sit stony-faced and shoulder-to-shoulder in a booth facing the room. They're not talking to each other, but they're allies in their determination not to talk to anyone else.

It looks like it's up to me to circulate, although why I have to bother at all when we've just done the reception line I've got no idea. But I remember Zelda going round the tables at Auntie Rowan's do, and I think I remember Auntie Rowan and Zelda together going round when it was my dad, Rowan in lambswool and serge, Zelda in something she told me was bombazine, both of them despising the other. But there's that same thing again – I don't remember it. I can't remember it. I just remember being told some of the highlights. Such as one of the Kirkconnel old timers starting a long anecdote about a suicide just after the war and no one being able to stop him. The Ancient Mariner, Zelda called him. When he died, years later, and it was in the local paper, she threatened to go and latch on to his wife 'at *her* darkest hour'.

'Have you everything you need?' I ask the first tableful. The milk jugs are those titchy ones with no proper handle and the tea looks stewed; I couldn't drink it without a good glug of milk to calm it down.

'Don't you fret, Tabitha love,' says a stout woman I don't recognize. So I move on.

'Will I ask for another plate?' I say at my next stop. This lot, four tenants I reckon, have stripped the sandwich and pie platters already.

'Naw,' says one of the men, definitely a farmer from the look of him. His face is a map of broken veins and his lips are so dry they look salt-crusted. He's wearing a suit and tie he's no doubt been wheeling out for funerals since he wore it to his wedding.

'Don't worry about us,' his wife says. 'You must be up to ninety.'

It's an odd thing to say at a moment like this. I'm sad and I'm tired, but I've no idea where she thinks anxiety might be coming from, unless she knows more than I do about getting Davey's estate settled. The confusion must show on my face, because she continues, 'Where is he? Tell me there's someone stopped back with him. Tell me he's not been left on his own?'

She puts a final mouthful of sandwich in after this and chews methodically, watching for my reaction. Her husband is dabbing up crumbs of sausage-roll pastry with a wetted finger. The other couple at the table for four are munching too. I feel myself start to sway backwards. It's as if they're watching a show and enjoying snacks while they're at it. But why they're baiting me, I've no idea. Of course we've left him alone. That's how it works. No one stays while they do what they're doing with Davey's body. Even if he was buried, the gravediggers wait until the family have gone before they fill in the hole. What are these four asking me?

Gordo has come up beside me and put his hand under my elbow. 'OK?'

'Your mother can hold the fort if you need to go,' says the old man. He's finally finished his sausage roll and he's cleaning out around his gums with the blade of his tongue. 'Or your sister could go.'

'What's up?' Gordo says.

'Of course, you weren't here back then,' says his wife. 'Lyle, isn't it? With the van? You're too young to remember last time.'

'What are you talking about?' I ask her.

'When it was your father,' says the fourth member of this little coven, piping up for the first time. 'And his brother couldn't cope with the news and now here's Davey away and no sign of Johnny. *Is* someone with him? To make sure?'

'For fuck sake,' says Gordo and I kind of love him for the look the word puts on their four faces. 'Johnny's not feeling well and had to stay at home. Don't be so . . . Christ, I don't even know what to call it.'

But I'm not managing to shrug it off quite as easily as he is. I cast a look around the packed tables and realize that fully half of them are watching me, none of them with pity, as if they're agog for me to break down in public. I wonder how long it would be before the phones came out, if I did. As Gordo draws me away, I mutter to him, 'Yeah, but they're right, aren't they? My dad killed himself and then his brother killed himself and Davey killed himself and Johnny's alone and—'

'Shush-shush,' Gordo says, as if I'm a baby who's woken up grizzling. 'Your dad and his brother were neighbours and they'd both been ill for years. Davey and Johnny haven't even seen each other for yonks and Davey had some kind of brainstorm to make him do what he did. They're nothing like.'

As his words wash over me, I breathe in, I breathe out, I repeat my latest mantra. Book, bin, Bible, I say. Books in a stack, stats in a book. Paper. Plastic, compost, frozen. Metal, clothing,

wellie-full-of-sick. It's like a jingle. A nurse told me once that
it doesn't matter what words you use. Mind you, she was lying.
Elspeth managed to choose words that got banned, pretty much
every day. Funny while they lasted, though.

Gordo's still talking when I tune back in. '—because I'm
sitting with them. They were just making chit-chat, you know?'

'What?'

'Here.' He steers me over to where Lorna is sitting with two
kids about Albie's age who've got the look of being dragged to
something they couldn't care less about. Both of them have
phones in their hands under the table. Gordo must have been in
the fourth seat, in place of a missing husband.

'Tell Tabby what you just told me,' he said. 'She's been getting
herself upset about how long Davey was planning it.'

'Less than a day,' Lorna says. 'He had a repairman out the
self-same day he died. And not for a regular service either. To
fix his broken washer.'

I blink. 'How do you know?' I don't trust any of them
now after those four ghouls had Johnny dead in a copy-cat
suicide. If Lorna merely saw a van pass on the road, I'm not
convinced.

'He had to stop for my ewes,' she tells me. 'Then didn't the
cheeky bugger try to sell me a service deal while I was up to
my oxters, telling me the call-out was going to set Mr Muir back
a packet, seeing as how he didn't have a plan.'

'See?' Gordo says. 'Who calls in a washing-machine
repairman . . .?'

'. . . if they've decided to top themselves?' Lorna finishes.

'Mum!' says one of the kids. 'We're at his funeral!'

But all I feel is a slump inside. Because this explains the
back-to-front bin in the kitchen that the kids thought was a clue
to crack the case wide open. A repair guy took it out to get at
the pipes and then put it back the wrong way. Nothing more than
that. Like the laptop is as clean as a whistle behind its password,
and the Bible verse meant nothing.

'It shouldn't bother me,' I say, walking away from Lorna's
table. Gordo is still at my heels, like a little dog, or rather he's
bumping against me like a little buffalo in a watering hole, gentle
but insistent. I don't know why I think 'little'. He's not little.
He's not even all that young. But I find myself looking for Barrett.

He catches my eye and slides out of his seat to come and meet us, Willow and Sorrel right behind him.

'There's plain-talking and there's plain-talking,' he says, when he gets to where we're standing. 'And I know this lot are mostly farmers and countryfolk, but God Almighty.'

'What?' I say.

'That bit that's shovelling pies into her gob was on and on about hoarding prescriptions,' Barrett says. 'She's part-time in the Sanquhar chemist's for pin money and she thinks she's Big Pharma.'

'Pin money? Jeez, Dad!' Willow says.

'Christ, where's she going now?' says Barrett.

I look over to where a woman in a camel coat is leaning in, talking at Jo and Zelda, who are wriggling out of the other end of the booth. I don't usually see a resemblance between them, if it makes any sense to use the word 'usually' after all these years, but right now they're bearing down on me with identical expressions on their so-different faces.

'She has got a point though,' Sorrel says. 'If Mr Muir had handed old Mrs Muir's medicine back in after she died like you're supposed to, it wouldn't have been there for him to use.'

'Opportunity drives the stats,' says Willow. 'That's why it's so bad in America. Like that's why farmers kill themselves over here more than other people do. Because they've got shotguns. If you take away the means, the numbers plummet.'

'Opportunity,' I say, nodding. 'Exactly. Davey wasn't planning this, no matter what notes he wrote to me. He got his washer fixed the day he died.'

'Christ!' says Barrett. 'Of course he did. I saw the bloody van. I pulled over for it.' He shakes his head, disgusted with himself.

Jo has reached us. 'Have you heard the topic of conversation raging round this room while they suck down the free booze and gorge themselves on the free pies?' she says. 'They're enjoying the idea that my husband's jumping off a cliff and I'm here letting it happen.'

'Worrying,' I say. 'Not enjoying.'

'They've no respect,' says Zelda. Then she catches her lip and translates into something less bourgeois. 'No elan.'

'Maybe you should both go,' I tell them. 'I can bring a piece of cake back wrapped in a napkin.'

'Cake?' says Zelda.

'Aren't we having a cake?' I ask her. Then I wonder if there's ever cake at funerals or if I'm maybe thinking of weddings. The truth is I'm thinking of neither. I'm thinking of ripped open syringe packets and needles. I'm thinking of little vials of insulin littering the pantry that Davey was using as a bedroom. I can't think of anything else. But I don't know why. Except that Davey *didn't* hoard medicine. He didn't hoard anything willy-nilly. He kept some things and discarded everything else same as anyone. He kept far too many documents about the history of Hiskith, in all those boxes up the sides of the stairs, but the local studies library have taken every last one. It wasn't junk. He kept seven years' worth of his financial papers. Like they tell you to, and no more. He had no out-of-date tins in his cupboards and no old shoes under his bed. He hadn't even kept any other medicines from Auntie Rowan's day. The bathroom cabinet had disposable razors, an opened six-pack of soap and a tube of toothpaste. There was a bottle of Head-n-Shoulders by the bath and a flannel screwed tight into a rope and stuffed behind the taps. If he'd kept insulin and needles for the ten years since his mother died, then this plan was in the back of his mind all along. That must be what's bothering me, mustn't it? I nod. Must be.

Only, it isn't. The thing that's actually troubling me is right on the tip of my brain. I'm reaching for it, when Barrett says, 'Ah, shite!'

'Dad!'

'The washing machine,' Barrett goes on, ignoring her. 'That's another clue gone.'

'What clue?' says Sorrel.

'The bin,' he tells her, with a forgivable note of triumph in his voice. 'The washing machine repairman put it back the wrong way round.'

'Huh,' says Willow. 'Good deduction.' She sounds as flattened as I feel, but she rallies. 'Still two left though. Books in a stack and stats in a book.'

I must have said my jingle out loud at least once then. It seems to have caught on. But they think they're solving a suicide. Vandalism, at worst. What if they do it and find out they've solved a murder? I remind myself of what I decided: Davey meant it metaphorically. He didn't kill his mother by withholding her insulin. With that thought comes a flash so real I blink to protect my eyes. Once it's past, I reach again for what's eluding me. Those vet nurses, and the syringes . . . but it's gone. Whatever I almost dragged up to the light is tucked back down in the murky sludge again, hiding.

EIGHTEEN

Barrett

Usually, this time of year, he pesters customers for work clearing gutters, raking leaves, gritting paths when the bad weather starts. Otherwise, once he's oiled his tools and locked his mowers up in the garage till spring, he's at loose ends. He's known for a while he should join something, take something up. He went as far once as to put on his tracksuit, faded and shabby, and show his face at the school gym for a badminton ladder. The shock of how breathless and sweaty he got before the first game was over! There he'd been thinking gardening all season kept him fit, but as he towelled off his dripping head in the boys' changing room, all he could think of was tea-breaks, the sit-on with its grass box, the leaf blower, the garden vac. He'd not touched a rake for years and nobody went in for double-digging anymore. Other than that one foray, he mostly sat in and waited for his days with the girls to come round, waited for the weekends with the other Musketeers, refused to feel lonely.

He'd take loneliness now. Willow and Sorrel wake up as if someone's fired a starter pistol, yakking and laughing from the get-go, rousing the dog. They're the only kids in the world, Barrett reckons, who've got no truck with headphones; their music and fitness coaching, their endless true-crime podcasts, fill his house morning till night. And they can't possibly be catching any of it. They never shut up and listen.

He used to think their voices filled his thoughts when he was apart from them. 'Jeez, Dad! Eww!' He knows better now.

'Dad?' Sorrel says one day. 'If I got pregnant, would you make me leave school?'

'Dad?' Willow pipes up another time. 'If one of us passes our driving test first will she get insured for your car? And if that costs a bomb cos it will cos kids like us are forever totalling cars, will the other one just never get a shot?'

Once, they both come in from the school bus saying, 'Erin in our class got a tattoo and she told her mum it was an "ephemeral" and it's not. It's a real one and now her mum says she's spending Erin's money that her grandma left her on a removal. She can't do that, can she?'

And he's lost his escape, his retreat, his sanctuary. No more days of Gordo, Davey and him out on the hill, standing braced against a scudding wind that brings tears to his eyes and dries them on his cheeks. No more huddling in the sanny van watching sheets of pale rain sweep over the landscape until there's nothing to see except that endless grey curtain of water and nothing to hear except the drumming on the roof and the chuckle of instant streams down the sides of the track, streams that swell to torrents and churn with soil, streams that leave a flotsam of litter over land they thought they'd cleared, streams that freeze overnight into glittering silver snakes, creaking when you step on them, half-thawing and re-freezing every cold night until they're thick and glassy, hiding in pockets of shadow for months, sending the sheep skittering.

Now, going up the hill with the girls quacking away in the back seat, he's headed for Tab's latest worries and Gordo's latest theories. He's headed for the mounds of litter his friend saved and sorted and the endless task of piling it all into the trailer without his heart breaking.

They've cleared the room that used to be Davey's office, the one that was full of fag ends and batteries. They were the first to go, neck and neck with the freezers and worm bins. Barrett knocked up a row of compost stores outside and come summer there's going to be plenty to spread under Davey's crab apple trees and gooseberry bushes. They got the tins and bottles out of the big back bedroom next, since the lad fancied that one, well away from his mum. That's the room in the house that's most sorted out, so the three of them and Uggy head straight to it when it's raining, like it has been every day since the funeral, like it could for weeks yet, as Barrett knows from winters by.

The living room's nearly done too but it's taken all his clout at the tip to get his pals to accept so much landfill, no deposits to get back, no recycling value like the other stuff. He'll take along enough bottles of whisky to go round, when he drops off the last load, whenever that is, whenever they finally mine all the way to the floor of the final room. Although surely the clothes and shoes will be easier than the stacked packets and the walls of bottles. Maybe they'll finish it today.

'It's good of you to come with me again,' he says, glancing at the girls in the rear-view mirror. 'Not getting bored?'

Four innocent eyes gaze back at him. Six if you count Uggy, but the girls are doing such a good job of butter wouldn't melt they manage to make the pup look shifty in comparison. 'We don't mind,' Willow says. 'We like it up there. It's like . . .'

'*Wuthering Heights*,' says Sorrel. 'Plus we're trying to get Albie to take us up to meet the witch.'

'We'll soon be finished, mind you,' says Barrett. 'And then Tab might want some privacy.'

'But even when the house is clear, Dad,' Willow says, 'that won't solve the mystery.'

Barrett says nothing, as if that's going to stop them.

'And we didn't know when to come right out and tell you this but it's not going to go away so maybe we should just say it.'

Barrett considers this a good while before he speaks. It's hard to believe there's anything this pair don't let fall out of their mouths as soon as it enters their heads. He reckons he better brace himself.

'Well, you've got to tell me now!' he says, acting more light-hearted than he feels.

'Albie doesn't think his uncle killed himself,' Willow says.

Barrett feels his breath leave him in a rush. Right, he thinks; they're still on telly-style drama. They're just having fun.

'And when we solved the back-to-front bin that backed us up,' says Sorrel.

I solved, Barrett thinks, but doesn't say.

'So I bet if we crack the number code in that notebook and work out about the manuals and almanack, they'll confirm it,' says Willow.

How, Barrett thinks, but doesn't say either.

'And we think Tabitha is right about the Bible too.' Sorrel again. They might not have decided when to say this but they certainly worked it up into a double act.

'That it's too significant to only be a clue to the password,' says Willow, 'when the password doesn't tell us anything.'

'Some people turn to the Bible when they're in despair,' Barrett says.

'Yeah, but not to that bit,' says Willow. 'Ewww.'

'And what have we just said?' says Sorrel. 'We don't think he *was* in despair. We don't think he blew up the dam either. He was trying to buy the reservoir and that would have scuppered him.'

'So we don't think it's fair to let everyone believe he did the bomb,' Willow adds. 'Plus it means the real bomber getting away with it.'

'And a murderer too.'

Barrett wishes he was on a motorway doing eighty, or seventy since the girls are in the car. There's nothing like driving in bad weather and heavy traffic for demanding all your attention no matter who's rabbiting on at you. But they're trundling over the cattle grid at a steady twenty-five and there's not another car or so much as a sheep in sight for him to concentrate on, so he's got no excuse to leave this, like he was going to.

'Hang on now,' he says. 'This isn't a telly programme. Davey was a real person with a tough life and a sorry end.' He gives their reflections a stern look. It only works on Uggy who hangs his head and then curls up facing the other way. 'And Tabitha hasn't had her troubles to seek either. You've not to go upsetting folk. OK?'

'What about Albie?' says Sorrel. 'He gets a say, doesn't he?'

'Oh, is that right?' Barrett gives them another hard stare in the mirror. 'You're sitting back to see what Albie wants, eh? You're not leading him one way or the other.'

'He wants it all to come out and get sorted once and for all,' says Sorrel. She might be misunderstanding him accidentally on purpose, Barrett reckons. Her eyes are wide enough. Butter wouldn't melt.

'It all?' says Barrett. 'Once and for all? What have you kicked up, the three of you?'

'Don't you know about his family, Dad? His grandad and his great-uncle? And the creepy incest cousins? It's got to stop with Davey, Albie says. And we agree, don't we? So?'

Sorrel nods solemnly and, before Barrett can decide where to make the next dent in this drama they're whipping up, they each get a text and drop their eyes to read it. 'Aw no!' Willow says. 'Dad, can you hurry up?'

'What is it?' says Barrett. 'Is Tabith— Is everything OK up there?' He couldn't hurry no matter what they say though. The rain isn't coming down in those grey veils now, it's pounding the roof of the car and turning the windscreen opaque with thick splotches like a colourless animal print even as the wipers whine away at it. He can feel the extra weight as the open trailer fills with rain faster than it can seep out at the tailgate hinge.

'Albie's dad's been,' Willow says. 'What's his name? Scott.'

'So what?' Barrett says. He's never heard anything about the man that would make him worry. A tool, right enough, kicking his wife out and losing her job for her but that sleekit kind doesn't usually turn physical when the divorce is cold ash and it's all settled. Unless Tabitha's been holding back the worst of it, like women do, ashamed of who she chose, ashamed of staying until *he* decided it was time to go. Or maybe losing his boy has sent him over the edge.

'*Dad!*' Sorrel grips the back of his seat and her daft nails scratch his neck. Barrett swings to the right just in time, as a dark car emerges out of the grey and barely misses the trailer. Both cars lurch to a skidding halt. Uggy starts whining. It's the Sorento Tab borrowed to bring Albie's stuff home.

Barrett jabs the passenger-side window open and leans over. The driver of the other car is moving again, edging past them. 'Put your fucking lights on, you moron!' Barrett shouts at him. 'It's shitting wi' rain!' He finishes off with a blare of his horn and then grinds his gears getting off the soaked grass and back on to the gravel. The girls are creasing themselves in the backseat.

'You should be a weatherman!'

'You go, Dad! That's him told!'

Barrett's so flustered he only realizes the window's still open when he clocks Uggy with his head out, snapping at the drops of rain.

Inside the schoolhouse the girls kick their boots off and shrug out of their jackets then disappear straight off upstairs. For once Barrett's glad because Tabitha is white and strained-looking, holding on to the edge of the porcelain sink.

'I ran into Scott,' he says. 'Nearly! Missed him by inches.'

'You got the good deal,' says Gordo, appearing in the doorway. 'He's torn a strip off me and he's left Albie in bits.'

They all hear the twittering and rumbling start, up in the big bedroom, as the girls set to soothing their friend. All three of the adults find themselves smiling. It's easier when you're young, Barrett reckons, but he has a go anyway. 'I wouldn't have tried to miss him at all if I'd known he deserved a knock. We should text more, like that lot.' He jerks his chin upwards. 'What's happened?'

'Cassie's dumped him,' Tabitha says.

Barrett sends a silent prayer of thanks up through the floorboards to his daughters. He's listened to the other side of this conversation enough times. He knows what to say.

'What's that got to do with you? Or Albie? Why's that made him drive up here on a day like this?'

'I didn't answer his texts.'

'How come?' Barrett says. 'Doesn't take long to type "tell someone who cares".'

Tabitha rewards him with a smile. 'He wants me back,' she says. 'Both of us. Back home.'

'I want a Lamborghini and Angelina Jolie,' Barrett says.

'Too high maintenance,' says Gordo and pauses. 'They'd never have parts in stock. They'd have to send to Glasgow.'

It's an old joke from Musketeer days, but it makes Tab laugh.

'The thing is,' she says, 'last time he wanted something – me homeless so I'd lose Albie – he got it. He made sure and got it. And I'm on thin ice. I'm only keeping this inheritance by hiding what I know.'

'You're on firm ground,' Barrett says. 'Not thin ice.'

'Yeah,' says Gordo. 'Scott couldn't have found a letter Davey left at a lawyers' for you. Never mind now that you've burnt it. Let him spin.' He's starting to sound a bit better and Barrett decides not to ask about the 'strip' Scott tore off him.

But Gordo offers it up anyway. 'You can't seriously be thinking about going back to him. Has he always spoken to you the way he spoke to you today?' He turns to Barrett. 'He didn't know anyone else was here, because I parked the sanny van down the bottom. So when I came in he thought I was staying. You know. Slept here.' He turns away sharply before they can see his face change colour, but his neck changes too and so they watch that.

'And what?' Barrett says. 'The same bloke that took up with

a side-piece when you were still married blew his stack about you maybe having a boyfriend after the divorce? What did he say?'

'Ocht, guff about telling the court I hadn't squared away a new partner before exposing Albie to him.'

'As if . . . I don't know what!' Gordo says. 'And Albie's nearly sixteen anyway.'

But Barrett can remember some of the wording in the custody and access agreements from his own divorce, and he can't be as breezy. Of course it's meant to stop sleazers getting in with mums of wee girls, but they can't say that, can they? So if this Scott decided to kick off, Tab could be looking at trouble. 'Did you tell him different?' he asks her.

'*I* told him,' Gordo says. 'Just a pal, helping get the house straight. Wanker.'

'Good,' Barrett says. 'And is the lad OK?'

'Solid,' says Tabitha. 'Stronger than me. Doesn't want to go back in the slightest. I thought he'd be bored rigid up here in the winter. I was wondering how to get him through till it was summertime. You know? Those light nights and the peace and the gorse and the birds?'

'We know,' Barrett says.

'But he's fine,' she says. 'Best Wi-Fi of his life and I don't care what they're up to. As long as it's three of them we don't need to worry, eh?'

Barrett thinks about telling her that the three kids are spinning wild tales, hunting out secrets, digging around in old graves, God knows what they're going to unearth. But he catches himself. The worst the kids could find would be details of a sorry tale Tab knows all too well. You could even argue it's time for the lad to know it too.

'Right then,' Gordo says. 'If you're not packing and going back to Mr Resistible, can you come and help me? I don't know whether to chuck it all or sort it into donations, cotton you could compost, and landfill for the pick-up's last load.'

When Tabitha bursts out laughing, Barrett can't follow the track of what's tickled her. 'You're turning into Davey!' she says, when she catches her breath. 'Sorting clothes! Composting cotton!'

'But only the clean stuff!' Gordo says.

She inhales hard and lets it go as a sigh. 'I don't know. Let's see. Is any of it worth trying to save?'

The kettle is singing. Tabitha makes six mugs of tea and they troop upstairs, dropping off three and a packet of Jaffa cakes with the kids.

'OK?' she asks Albie.

He nods, although Barrett can see he's been crying. Crying like a boy cries, scrubbing at his face until his skin looks sore. 'He's a tosser, Mum. I love him because he's my dad but that doesn't make me blind or stupid.' Barrett recognizes the line, more or less, from Willow and Sorrel talking about one of their reality shows. For sure, Tab doesn't recognize it coming out of her son's mouth. She can't get her lips to form an answer; she just nods and backs out of the room again with the tray.

'They've been good for him,' she says as soon as the door's closed. 'He's showering every morning too.'

'They're good kids,' Gordo says. 'They always were. When they were tiny, they used to pick up caterpillars on the path and put them safe in the verge. Remember that, pal?'

Barrett nods but the truth is he doesn't remember those days very clearly. Like he doesn't remember their babyhood at all. He was reckless with the gift of them back then, back when he thought he'd sleep under the same roof every night until they were married. He didn't think on college or gap years, although he's braced for them now. It wasn't until he was clinging to every other weekend and Tuesday nights, starting to bargain for Christmas before the summer was over, that he started drinking them in. When they were fat toddlers saving hairy caterpillars from ramblers' feet, it was Gordo who never missed a word or a look from either. It was Gordo who knew what it meant to lose what you loved. Gordo, who had lost it almost before he'd taken in the news that it was on its way.

'Right,' he's saying now, taking a pull from his tea mug as if it was a pint of cider, the china clinking against his lip ring, 'if it wasn't raining, you could pull round the side, Barrett, and we could drop it all out that wee window, right into the back. Clothes wouldn't lift the whitewash off your gable wall, Tabby.'

But the rain, that Barrett thought couldn't get any heavier, has found some extra welly and the sound of it hitting the slate roof above their heads is even louder than it was on the car. The wind is raging and whirling, sending lashes against the windows on both sides of the room and then sucking the other way so the panes rattle. He goes to the bigger one in the dormer and checks the catch. If it blew open in this the glass would shatter. Down on the reservoir apron, Gordo's van is rocking as the gale buffets it. Unbelievably, someone has got out of a parked car to look and see if Peace and Bacon is open. As if Gordo might be in there, brewing coffee and grilling burgers. They give up soon enough and scuttle back to the steamed-up little hatchback they came in. Barrett watches them do a three-point turn that takes them within feet of the rocky edge, and then drive up the start of the track, wiping a porthole in the condensation on their windscreen.

'At least you can be sure your flashing and sarking's all good,' he says. 'Rain like this would find a mousehole.'

'Don't talk about mice!' Tabitha says. 'I'm still getting over the nests in the paper. And don't let on to the caterpillar fans back there but I'm fine with snap traps if it means I never hear another one skittering about the bare boards at night.' She shudders and turns to see what Gordo's doing.

'So *are* we just clearing the lot then?' he asks. 'I mean, single mittens and that's not worth saving, but what about this sort of thing?' He's holding up a Fair Isle jumper, the old-fashioned kind that's the colour of porridge. It must have untied itself from round someone's waist when they were walking on a warm day. No one would chuck it away deliberately.

Tab leans over and rubs a piece of it between her fingers. 'Real wool,' she says. 'Hand-knitted. I see what you mean.'

So it ends up taking them most of the morning. Barrett does bring the pick-up round but parks it on the gravel hard against the living-room wall. Each time he's stuffed a black sack full of ragged T-shirts and balled socks, those single mittens, dozens of them, and the baseball caps that have come sailing off of countless heads on windy days over the years, he opens the sash and lets the sack drop straight down. None of them split and none of them miss. He doesn't admit it, but he's enjoying it. It's like plunking rocks off a bridge, which he always preferred to skimming flatties. He likes the gulping noise the water makes when a big rock hits it and he likes watching the tube of water rise up and scatter after the impact.

There's knickers, of course. Gordo and him knew there'd be knickers because they were usually there to find them. Tab colours when she finds the first ones. 'Bit out of the way for hammered lassies squatting, isn't it?'

'They come off the heather,' says Gordo. 'Ken up where the heather's so thick, up by the old forester's track to Muirkirk? We always reckoned it was courting couples lying down on it and then not finding their keks again after.'

'I should have brought tongs up from the kitchen,' is all Tab says. 'Or gloves.' She shudders as she picks them up and stuffs them into the bag Barrett's holding open.

'Your hands'll be like those bowls of peanuts on the bar in pubs,' Gordo says.

She stares at him, then lifts her hands and stares at them.

'Tab?' says Barrett, before he's distracted by a noise at the doorway.

It's Willow, poking her head in with a worried look on her face. Uggy's with her and he looks worried too. He keeps pushing his nose into her hand to let her know he's there. 'Dad,' she says. 'Can you answer a question?'

'Shoot,' Barrett says.

'What can you get DNA from?'

Before Barrett can answer, Tabitha makes a sound like the air whooshing out of a punctured tyre. It sounds painful, hissing over her clenched teeth.

'Tab?' he says.

'DNA,' she says, still staring at her hands. 'Oh my God! DNA!'

She shoots to her feet from where she's been kneeling by the shrinking mound of clothes and belts and shoes and bags.

'What is it?' says Gordo.

'We need our heads looked at,' Tabitha says. 'The fag ends! These knickers! The food! The worms and freezers! It wasn't about cleanliness and it wasn't insane. The chewing gum and everything.' Sorrel and Albie have overheard and they crowd into the room. Uggy is picking up on the excitement, his tail going round like a propeller as he wheels about snuffling at each one of them in turn. Gordo is nodding as if he's trying to rock his head right off his neck. And finally Barrett understands. Davey cored out the middle bits of the apples, gave the clean cylinders to the worms and kept the bitten edges, full of teeth marks, covered in saliva. He kept the chewed bits of crust and the chewed bits of chocolate. He kept the messy little dabs of gum, covered in saliva all over. For the DNA.

'Wow!' says Willow. 'He saved anything that might have DNA on it?'

'Which should be rank but it's cool in a way,' says Sorrel. 'I wish I'd met him. He sounds really interesting.'

'Why did he do that, Mum?' says Albie.

'Because . . .' Tabitha says. Then she smacks herself in the head. 'Oh my God! Two in one. *This* explains the Bible. He saved DNA because he thought someone who had been here before was bound to come back.'

'And revisit his own folly!' says Gordo.

'Like a dog returning to its own vomit!' Barrett finishes off.

'I knew it,' Albie says. 'His boot-time password! Didn't I tell you it had to mean something.'

'But who?' says Tabitha. 'Who was it he expected? What was he saving God knows how many years of junk in case of?'

'Oh,' says Willow. She shoots a look at the other two kids. 'We might know, actually. We might know who he was waiting for.'

'*Ten* years of junk, Tabitha,' says Barrett. He's sure which crime Davey believed he could solve. It's Bess. It has to be.

'Why, what happened ten years ago?' says Sorrel, her eyes so wide Barrett can see the separate flicks of liner above and below her lashes. He hates that but he's got to admit it's skilfully done. He folds his lips in and says no more. He's never so much as hinted to the girls what happened to Bess.

'Auntie Rowan died ten years ago,' Tabitha says.

'But that was natural causes, wasn't it?' says Albie.

There's a hell of a silence then. Barrett reckons if she could stuff those words back in her mouth she would do it. Gordo saves the day.

'It's not ten years,' he says. 'It's fifteen years. I bet you. If we'd looked at the oldest sell-by dates on the wrappers, or if there's newspapers or anything, it'll be fifteen years.'

'Well, what happened *then*?' says Sorrel.

'I was born!' Albie says, in mock bombast. Then he catches himself. 'It's not, is it, Mum? It's not to do with us? With me?'

'No,' says Gordo. 'Nothing to do with you being born, Albie. It was something else altogether.'

Then Willow says, 'But we think it's much longer than that actually, don't we? We think there's a secret from long, long ago. That's what we came to tell you. That's why we need to know if you can get DNA from . . . well, from ashes.'

'Ashes?' says Tabitha.

'We should explain,' Sorrel says. 'We should have explained before but Albie's been kind of bottling it.'

'What?' Tabitha says.

'He thought you would notice the charge on your credit card bill and work it out without him having to tell you,' Willow says. 'But you haven't, have you?'

'Oh!' says Tabitha. She's relaxed like Barrett unbuckling his belt after dinner. 'Albie? What have you been buying?'

'Records,' says Willow. Barrett will never admit to them that, in the moment, he thinks they mean LPs. 'From MyGov.'

'Who?' says Gordo.

'Scotland's People?' Sorrel tells him. 'It's like the sexy-pathetic new name for Register House. Online anyway.'

'You've been buying records?' Tabitha says. 'Of what?'

'Well,' says Willow. 'They only do birth, marriage and death. And the thing is . . . the thing is Albie tried to get a copy of a death certificate – didn't you? – and it's too weird but you can check for yourself, it looks like his uncle didn't actually die.'

NINETEEN

Tabitha

I don't lose it. That's the first thing. But, for a minute or two, I feel madness nip at the edges of me, too heavy to cart off to a meadow, too big to hold in gloved hands, too solid to breathe away. I feel the floor tilt as if it's going to upend and tip me into chaos, but somehow I manage to keep my feet braced on the flat of the carpet and keep the air of the room quiet beyond my ears. Inside my head's another story. There are alarms and clackers and hooters going off, a party in Funtown. But it's OK. For one thing, a dry lump of madness too heavy to lift isn't the thing that scares me. And for another, I manage to hide it all. Barrett and Gordo are watching me but they don't look worried.

Garfield, I tell myself. Garfield and the other one whose name I don't know. It's not Mungojerrie and it's not Rumpleteazer. It's not Macavity and it's not Rum Tum Tugger. Trying to think of that second cat's name has got me through worse than this. Even if 'this' is finding out that Davey's still alive and I've lost my new house, and he'll never forgive me for throwing away all his stuff, and now I'll have to tell the police that he murdered his mum, and—

'Bullshit,' says Gordo. 'Sorry, but seriously. I saw him.'

'No, you didn't,' I say. 'Even *I* didn't see him. I saw the envelope and then that copper went in on his own.'

'Tabith—' says Willow.

'The cop had no reason to lie though,' I say. 'And the undertaker wouldn't go along with it. We had a funeral, for God's sake!'

'Tab—' says Sorrel.

'Why are you claiming to have seen him?' I ask Gordo. 'Did you go in with Johnny to do the ID? Wait! That's right – Johnny ID'd him.'

'I didn't see him here,' says Gordo. 'I didn't see him at the morgue either. I saw him at the undertakers, the day before the funeral.'

'Johnny let you do that?'

'I didn't ask,' Gordo says. 'I went on spec.'

'Why?' says Barrett.

'I wanted to. I couldn't face losing . . .' He looks at Willow and stops talking. I carry on and I think Barrett does too. Couldn't face losing someone else without viewing the body.

'How did you get in?' I ask.

'Told the wifie on the desk I was his partner and the family were being rotten about letting me say goodbye.'

'Genius,' says Willow. 'Sneaky genius. But that's not—'

'She took pity on me, swore me to secrecy and gave me ten minutes,' Gordo says.

'But if you'd let—' says Sorrel.

'So I know for a fact that Davey Muir is dead,' Gordo says, cutting her off. 'You've mucked up asking for the right certificate, probably.'

'No, we haven't,' says Willow, bristling. 'If you'd listen! I know *Davey*'s dead. I didn't mean that uncle. Sorry. I mean Albie's Uncle Roddie. Great-uncle if you're nitpicking. I don't think *he's* dead. Roderick Muir? There's nothing in the records for him.'

'Alb—' I start to say, then I notice that he's gone.

He's sitting on his bed, with Uggy beside him. His laptop is discarded on the beanbag he uses as a cup-holder, tray, coffee table, footstool and sometimes pillow when he's slumped on the floor for hours streaming or gaming. I've found him, in the morning, still with his headphones on and still with his console in his hands. Maybe once he's settled I'll try to put some ground rules in place. It can't be good for him.

'Son?' I say. 'I'm not angry. You should just have asked. I'd have handed over my card to let you order duplicate records. It's about time this family had everything stored in a file fair and square. But you shouldn't let yourself get talked into things, you know.'

I'm treading lightly, so lightly I think I might have to explain what I mean, but he's nodding. 'I'm not,' he says. Then he screws his nose up. 'OK, I was. They were all for it and I went along.

But I had to, Mum. I wanted to understand what happened to
Uncle Davey. And it's my family at the end of the day. Even if
it's people I never met.'

'Like Uncle Roddie? And Grandad?'

'Exactly,' Albie says. 'Except it might not be too late to meet
Uncle Roddie. He might decide to turn up one day. He might
returneth.'

'Alb—'

'Because he definitely didn't die the same day as Grandad. Or
the day after. Or the day after that. Or before. I've checked six
months either way, in case they got it wrong. He didn't die,
Mum.'

'Of course he died,' I said. 'It must be a mistake in the records.
A glitch. We'll phone them up on Monday. Albie, we found his
ashes.'

But Albie is shaking his head. 'He didn't. That story – heart-
broken at his brother's suicide, hanged himself, Auntie Rowan
keeping it quiet – it's not true. And it *was* a bit bonkers.'

'Son,' I say, 'of course it's true. You weren't here. I was. I
was only wee but Roddie and Grandad were here and then they
were gone.' Even as I say it though, I'm wondering. Roddie was
gone already – a shadow in the passenger seat, a lighted window,
clothes on the line – so I suppose . . . then I catch hold of
myself. 'Davey and Johnny were here in the house, Alb. Their
dad died.'

'And no one knew?' Albie said. 'No one saw the undertaker
or the doctor or the police?'

He's got a point. Why did none of us ever see the same kerfuffle
down at the house as we were suffering up at the school? Cop
cars and black vans. 'Albie, you don't understand,' I say, trying
again. 'You don't know what it was like. The chaos of your
grandad dying like that. Our house was like . . . as if it had been
picked up by a giant and shaken. We were living on bread and
jam. Nothing was real. We forgot to feed the goldfish or top up
their water until they were gasping in two green inches over the
gravel.' Why the hell am I letting myself think of a goldfish tank?
'You don't know what it's like when something so awful happens
that nothing makes any sense anymore.'

Albie stares at me and waits. 'Neither do you,' he says finally.
'How many times have you said it? You don't remember anything

except what you were told. And whatever you were told you swallowed it whole. Your dad, your uncle, everything.'

'Everything?' I say. 'Like what?'

'Like Davey killed himself for no reason whatsoever,' he says. 'He was waiting for someone to come back, saving DNA in case they did, and then he just kills himself? That's insane.'

'Albie, Albie, Albie,' I say, as if I'm trying to stop him talking, even though he's sitting silently now. I just wish he hadn't said 'swallow'. 'One thing at a time,' I say. 'It wasn't for no reason whatsoever. I maybe should have told you before now, but Uncle Davey believed he was responsible for Rowan's death. He believed he killed her. He died from the guilt of that belief.'

Albie is shaking his head. 'Your family stories are all nuts, Mum,' he says. 'I trust the records office. Auntie Rowan's cause of death was established, same as everyone else's. And Uncle Roddie didn't kill himself the day your dad died.'

The day my dad died. I feel pressure in my ears. The weight. The cold. I struggle to take the next breath and don't quite make it.

'Which leaves the question,' Albie says, nodding towards his open wardrobe door, 'who's that in there?'

My heart is about to burst out of my chest from the need to breathe as I turn, slow as the tide, to where he's pointing. Then I see the cardboard tube of ashes, sitting on the hat shelf, and I do let some air go and watch as it bubbles up in front of my face.

'We brought it up here to take a bit of it and bag it up without you knowing,' he says. 'But then we didn't know if you could get DNA from ash and the internet's off, because of the weather, so Will came to ask you.'

I take my chance at a gulp of dry air. What's drier than ash, after all?

'Can you?' Albie says. 'If that's not Roddie in there, could we find out who it is? Because whoever he is . . . Or she is . . . Or they are . . .'

That's Willow and Sorrel speaking. I smile at him, still wobbly but not sinking now.

'You *can't* get DNA from ash,' I tell him. 'But the thing is, cremated remains are not ash like from a bonfire. They're more like grit. There will be wee tiny bits of bone or even teeth, and there should be DNA in those. We can confirm that it *is* Roddie and that the records office made a boo-boo.'

'Boo-boo?' says Albie. 'You're talking to me as if I'm five.'

'Fine,' I say. 'You're fifteen. Is fifteen old enough to look for yourself. Or will I?'

He rubs his nose. 'OK,' he says. 'I'm five. I didn't know there'd be teeth.'

I cross to the cupboard, my legs as heavy as if I'm wading, and I reach the cardboard tube down. I twist off the lid, which makes a tight squeak and sets my teeth on edge. Inside is a plastic bag sealed with a black bread-tie. I ease it out and hold it up to the light.

Inside is about half a kilo, I reckon, of the softest palest powderiest ash. It looks like something I've seen many times before. I start to untwist the tie, ignoring Albie's soft moan from behind me. The smell is unmistakable. 'Alb,' I say. 'This is Fuller's Earth.'

'What?'

'Women used to use it for face packs in the old days. Auntie Rowan used to use it. Jo and me used to use it. It makes you look like Groot.'

'So it's not Roddie then,' Albie says but, before he can gloat, I hear a shout from the other room. Uggy sets off along across the landing in full protective panic. Then comes the scurrying sound of one of the girls moving at a trot in her sliders. It's Willow.

'Come quick,' she says. 'Dad's found something terrible.'

They've been busy. The mound is down to a few little piles hardly bigger than sorted laundry ready for the machine. Gordo's standing at the window as if he's just dropped another bagful down into the bed of the pick-up. The sash is open and he doesn't seem to realize that he's getting wet as the rain blows in. Barrett is in the middle of the floor on his knees, hunched over something I can't see, cradling it. Uggy stands by, staunch but troubled.

'Albie, take the girls downstairs,' I say. 'Feed the dog.' I hold up a hand as they start to protest. 'OK! Girls, will you take Albie downstairs for me and give Uggy some biscuits? Thank you.'

When they're gone, I drop down beside Barrett and put my hands on his, trying to open them, but he's clutching so hard at whatever he's holding that I can't make any headway. A tear falls, hot and shocking, on to my knuckle and I take my hands away.

'What is it?' I ask him. 'Gordo?' But Gordo's still staring out of the window into the rain. When I look back at Barrett, finally he has opened his fists and spread his palms. Lying over them is a plain length of worn brown leather; a belt, I think, until I see first how short it is, next that it's got a silver medallion attached to the buckle end. I don't need to read it to know, but I read it anyway. BESS. And a phone number.

'Why would he keep this from me?' Barrett whispers. 'How could he be so cruel?'

'It's what he did,' says Gordo. As if talking has made him realize he's getting drenched, he slams the window down and turns towards us. 'He found things and he kept them.' He's got something in his hands too, a bulky sodden bundle. 'Look,' he says, holding it out. It's a coat. That cold pink colour that had such a moment a few years back, quite a few years back, now I think about it. It's got a black velvet collar and black-velvet-covered buttons. That's right. Black and pink like an old-fashioned hatbox was the hottest look for a while. I try to think exactly when that while was and, remembering my swollen pregnant feet jammed into pink ballet flats with black piping, I'm suddenly convinced that this coat is fifteen years old and that I know who it belonged to.

'Allison?' I say, searching Gordo's face for a sign that this isn't real. That none of this nightmare is actually happening. I'm sinking again.

Gordo nods. 'He watched her leave her stuff at the water's edge to throw me off the scent and then he watched her drive away. Hey, maybe that's who he thought would come back.'

'I don't understand,' I say. 'Why does finding her coat mean she drove away?'

Gordo, moving the pink bundle to one hand holds out the other one to me to help me up. His fingers are wet but he grips hard and I don't slip.

'Look,' he says, pointing out of the window. I have no idea what he's trying to show me. How could the water, a decade and a half later, prove that someone did or didn't jump in? That someone was or wasn't pushed? That someone did or didn't drown?

'I can't,' I burble at him. 'I'm sorry. I can't look at the loch. Any more than I could float.'

'Fly, Tabitha,' the nurse said.

'Why did I say float?' I ask her.

'You know why. Let it out now.'

'Don't look at the water,' Gordo says. 'Look at the car park.'

That I can do. I wade over to him and peer through the rain. A little hatchback has stopped by Peace and Bacon and someone is out in the wet struggling with the padlock that holds the serving-hatch shutter down. It's a woman, middle-aged from the look of her, wearing a good mackintosh and long shiny boots with stacked heels. Why would someone like that want to knock over a van for the float?

'Here she comes,' Gordo says, as the passenger door of the hatchback opens and a second woman gets out, head tucked down tight against the rain. She's got a plastic bag in her hands and she holds it open for the first woman, who drops something in. Then together they manage to lift one of the wiper blades on the van's windscreen and tuck the bag safely under it.

'Oh,' I say. 'She was trying to feed a note in through the gap in the shutter? That makes more sense. Slightly. But what's it got to do with the coat or the collar?'

'Christ!' says Gordo. He throws the sash up again and leans out so far I'm scared he's going to topple.

'What's wrong?' says Barrett, looking up at last.

'I don't know,' I say. And I *don't* know. How could I? But I *do* know, because what else could make him sound like that?

My vision is blurring and the last of my breath is leaving me in big, fat, burping bubbles. I jam my fingers through the back belt loop of Gordo's trousers and tug at him.

'Oh Christ,' he says again.

I wiggle myself down beside him and lean out, instantly soaked, my hair plastered to my head and rivers of cold rain coursing down the neck of my sweatshirt. The outside of me is drenched. My inside is so deep I'll never get back to the surface again. 'What is it?' I say, because I really shouldn't know.

'That,' he says, pointing at the hatchback where the two women are standing in deep conversation, oblivious to the rain, 'is Chrissy McCabe. Allison's mum. And that, beside her, is a woman about my age, I reckon, the same height as Chrissy McCabe with a run that I recognize. That way she ran from the car to the van? With her feet kicking out to the side. I used to call it a "shilly-shally". She ran like that even on sports day.'

'Oh my God,' I gurgle, with the last air I'll ever have in my lungs. 'Are you sure?'

'Look in the back seat of the car,' says Gordo.

'Nooooooooooo!' I scream into the black water. 'I can't do this!'

'You can,' the nurse said. 'You can face this. No one can fly, Tabitha. But you can float. People can float.'

'People can't float if they're wearing a snowsuit,' I hissed at her. 'And if they're buckled into a booster seat in the back of a locked car. Sometimes people need their mummy to jump in and grab a rock from the loch bed then spring back up and smash the window and release the seat catch and haul them, waterlogged snowsuit and all, up to the surface again.'

'You can't actually remember any of that,' the nurse said. 'You were too small. Toddlers don't lay down long-term memories of the type you're reporting.'

'It was traumat—' I used to say.

'You might well hold trauma. I'm sure you do. But you can't remember your mother picking up a rock and pushing off the bottom, can you?'

I remember frowning at the nurse, feeling it start to crumble even though I didn't know why. 'Even if you weren't too young, you were in your baby seat in the back of the car. You couldn't have seen that happen. Someone told you and you imagined it. Do you see?'

'But no one would tell that to a little child.'

'Someone must have.'

'Who would do that? Who would do that to me?'

'Let yourself remember,' the nurse said. 'You're safe and you're strong and I'll help you.'

'I'm not,' I wailed. 'Help me.'

'Oh God,' says Gordo. 'God help me.'

'You're safe,' I tell him. My voice has lost all its bubbles and snapped as dry as a twig. 'I'm strong,' I tell him. 'I'll help you.'

'Look in the backseat,' he says again. 'See that? See that light?'

I squint hard. It's still shitting with rain, like Barrett said, but

I *do* see it, glowing just below the level of the window and shining up on the white shape bent low over it. There's no mistaking the size of that light, the angle of it, the distance from light source to surface reflecting. That's a teenager, deeply engrossed in a phone.

PART THREE

December 2015

TWENTY

Tabitha

E very year for my whole life, every single Halloween when
I lived here, I would come in drookit to the bones after
guising down at Auntie Rowan's and think the weather
couldn't get any worse.

Then, on my birthday, in November, I'd scrap plans for a party
when folk's mums and dads started saying it was a hell of a drive
up Hiskith 'in all this' and instead I'd end up at the ice rink, just
the four of us again. Chippy tea after and ice cream from the
Italian.

And still I'd say to myself December couldn't have anything
left to throw at me. I'd say this Christmas would be blue sky
and white frost, air so still you could hear the grass squeak as
it froze ahead of the sunset. I'd look forward to skating on the
pristine ice of the loch, (in skates Zelda would produce from a
secret cupboard, the perfect size for me). I imagined every detail.
Opening my advent calendar in the morning with my breath
blooming in the cold air of our classroom; rushing outside with
a red scarf and matching gloves on to make a snowman in the
playground. Hot chocolate, toasting forks, soft, thick socks and
a duvet on the couch in the evening.

It never happened. The doors on my advent calendar curled
open on their own in the damp and the morning air smelled of
the Calor gas we kept on all night to stop the pipes freezing.
Outside, the water rose and rose and the rain haemorrhaged down
until every burn in the bowl of hills gushed as if the gods had
lanced them, washing mud and sticks and rabbit corpses into the
loch to churn there. And even that one time it *did* snow and the
twenty-fourth of December was like a glittering Christmas card,
our power went off, and everyone had the flu. The turkey sat in
the fridge till nearly Hogmanay before Zelda had the strength
and the stomach to cook it. That's the truth behind the magical

memory of sledging and sunshine that I hang on to. We were sitting in the dark because the long valley memories made the ironmonger save his lamps and stoves to help the striking miners. We were swallowing ground glass because no one from the Kirkconnel chemist would trail up to Hiskith with a prescription for our sore throats. 'Reap what you sow,' the chemist's snippy wife told Zelda when she phoned down. As if moving out of the town meant we could all die up here and her conscience wouldn't trouble her.

So it's ludicrous that this December is surprising me. Maybe it's because I've been away for nearly twenty years.

Or maybe it's the kid.

That first day, after we saw him hunched over his phone, Gordo went storming out to bang on the windows of the little hatchback, to lie down under its wheels if that's what it would take to stop Mrs McCabe driving off. I sank back on to my heels and tried to squeeze the worst of the water off me. It was all on the surface. None of it was inside me now.

'Barrett,' I said. But he was looking down at the dog's collar lying in his hands. 'Allison's back,' I whispered. 'Allison McCabe.'

'Who's Allison McCabe?' said Sorrel, appearing in the doorway. 'Did Gordo just go out?'

'Who *is* Allison McCabe?' said Albie. 'Mum, you're drenched.' He looked from me to Barrett. 'Oh, hey, is that Bess's?'

Barrett lifted his head at last.

'They told me she was buried up here after she died. Did you know Uncle Davey kept her collar? Looks like you didn't.'

'Uncle Davey . . .' I started to say. But I was saved from having to think up the end of the sentence by the sound of the back door opening and the unmistakable bustle of multiple people getting themselves in out of the rain.

'Ta-ab?' Gordo's voice came faintly upstairs, wavering like a thread of smoke. I left Barrett to his musing – it was a bloody *dog*, I wanted to tell him – and trotted down to the kitchen.

Gordo was waiting in the hall. He hadn't put his coat on when he went out and his army surplus jumper was soaked dark and hung down, dripping on the lino. His face was blank, spotted all over with rain that he didn't seem to have noticed. As I watched him, a drip rolled down his nose and trembled on the end. He didn't seem to notice that either. When he tried to talk, his mouth gobbled on empty air. Instead he flung an arm out to show me the way into my own kitchen.

There was a woman (pig) I would have put at my sort of age who had already found the tea-towel drawer and was dishing them out to dry hair. She threw one at Gordo and I was relieved to see that his reflexes worked. He put up a hand to catch it.

The other woman (also pig), looked younger than him, from good genes maybe. She seemed terrified. Her eyes were strained, her shoulders hunched, and she watched Gordo closely. But I didn't think it was him she was scared of. The only other time I could remember seeing a woman with that same strung-tight yet exhausted look on her face was in the relatives' room on the children's ward. I was waiting for Albie to come round after a routine appendicectomy. No one asked the scared mum what her kid was in for. We brought her tea and turned the telly off when the music got too jaunty.

Remembering that and recognizing Allison in the memory, I turned to the third stranger who had arrived in my house. And suddenly all was clear.

He was rubbing his face and hair dry on one of Davey's threadbare tea towels and when he finished he left it draped over his head as if he'd been cast in a nativity play. He hadn't rubbed any roses into his cheeks but I didn't think he was naturally sallow. I didn't think he was white from the cold day or the shock of seeing Gordo either. His colour was the solid grey-yellow of mutton fat and his face was puffy, so distorted it was impossible to say if there was a pig or a fox or even a horse underneath. His fingers, not holding a phone now, rested slack on his wet jeans.

'I'll put the kettle on,' I said. 'Cup-A-Soup? Hot chocolate?'

'Are you Lyle's—?' said Allison.

'Friend!' I said, too emphatically.

'I thought his friend was a man,' she said, turning to her mother.

'It makes no difference!' Gordo had found his voice. 'None of that matters. Just tell me what he needs. Tell me where to go. Where to sign.'

The girls were back. They came tumbling into the room like

a pair of puppies and finally the kid looked up. He snatched the tea towel off his head.

'We heard you say chocolate!' Sorrel batted her eyes.

'But not Cup-A-Soup because blerk.' Willow made a retching sound and I found my eyes flitting to the kid again.

'Go back up,' I told the girls. 'I'll shout when it's ready.'

'Do you want to come?' Willow said to the new arrival. They're such nice kids. I can't believe what Barrett says about his ex-wife, when I look at the girls she brought up.

'How many stairs?' Allison said.

Willow frowned as if she didn't understand, and maybe she hadn't given him a close enough look yet.

'Fifteen,' I say.

'Take it easy,' she told her son. 'Take it slow.'

When they'd gone, Gordo went off like a wind-up toy. 'Seriously, never mind filling in the gaps. Plenty time for that. What is it that's wrong? Because that's why you're back, right? What is it he needs? Because tell me where to sign. Tell me where to go. I'll open my veins with a spoon. I'll drill out marrow with a corkscrew.'

'Shush, shush,' Allison said. 'Calm down and let me tell you.'

'It's not as if you're scared of needles,' Mrs McCabe said. I couldn't think what she meant, until I saw the way she was looking at the ink on Gordo's arms, where he'd pushed up his wet sleeves. I took an instant dislike to her, standing here in my house insulting my friends.

'Mum, for God's sake,' Allison said, saving me the trouble.

'Whatever he needs,' said Gordo. 'As soon as I can do it.'

What he needed, Allison told us, in such a dry, formal voice that she could have been talking about planning a trip or changing the route she takes to work, was a liver.

'Partial liver transplant,' she said. 'I checked myself out first, of course, but we're not a match.' I could tell from Gordo's face that he was thinking of motorbike crashes and donor cards, a family weeping and a grateful stranger.

'You can donate a bit of your liver when you're alive,' I told him. 'It grows back. And the bit you've donated grows to be a full one. That's right, isn't it?' Allison and her mum were both nodding.

'Sign me up,' Gordo said. 'Book me in.'

'Well,' said Mrs McCabe, 'first we need to check, don't we?'

Gordo went still, like a hare, except not even his nostrils were twitching. Then slowly he swivelled his gaze until he was looking at Allison. 'Do we?' he said and, although the words could make a question, they hit like an anvil.

Allison – I saw this because I was watching her so closely – flushed up in a tide from the round collar of her jumper to the roots of her hair where it was pulled back off her face in a scrunchie. 'In case your blood type doesn't match,' she said. 'Because it's not a sure thing. I'm AB positive. What are you?'

Gordo shrugged and both Allison and her mother frowned briefly, the same quick tug on both sets of brows.

'I don't know either,' I said. I reckoned they were so steeped in the intricacies of illness now, that they'd forgotten what it was like never to think about the blood in your veins. 'But I'll get checked if Gordo isn't a match. It *is* just blood type, isn't it?'

Why did I say that? Allison was looking hard at me, doubting my claim to be only a friend all over again. But it was nothing to do with Gordo. It was this woman, so scared of losing her son, and the memory inside me of the way I felt when I thought I'd lost mine even to alternate weekends and shared-out holidays. 'What's his name?' I asked.

'Oliver,' said Allison and Mrs McCabe in chorus.

Gordo winced. He'd never have called a boy Oliver, clearly. 'And what is it that he's got?' he asked. 'Do they need to check that it's not genetic? If my liver's shot with it too, that would be worse than useless.'

'It's not genetic,' Allison said. 'It was viral. If *you're* not a match and *you're* not a match' – she turns to me – 'we could move on to the girls.'

'Mum, for fuck sake.' Oliver was back at the kitchen door. 'They're not my half-sisters. They don't even live here.' He crossed the room and sat in a chair with a good view of Gordo. 'Steep stairs,' he said.

'Sorry,' said Allison. 'I thought they were yours, Gordo.'

'It is a bit hard to work out who's who,' said Oliver. 'To be fair.'

'It's my house,' I said. I tried not to speak to him as if he was a toddler but he looked exhausted and he sounded confused. 'Your – Gordo, Lyle, your dad – is a friend. And

so is Barrett, upstairs, and the girls are his. Can you have a
hot chocolate?'

I didn't even know what I was asking. It was just a vague
sense of fat and sugar and caffeine and I might have been thinking
of spleens anyway.

'So it's me or nothing,' says Gordo. 'Unless, like I was asking,
it's genetic.'

'And like I was answering,' Allison said, 'it was viral.'

'Hepatitis,' said Oliver. He hauled in a deep breath and sighed
it back out as he said the next bit. 'And then glue-sniffing, to be
fair.'

'How the fuck do you catch hepati—?' Gordo tried to ask.

'Please, no need for that,' said Mrs McCabe, although she'd
said nothing to Oliver's outburst. How ill must a kid be for his
granny not to scold him for swearing at his mum? As ill as this
one, leaning back in the chair, his chest hitching from the pain
inside him. 'I caught it off a lass,' he managed. 'The fun way.'

'—in this day and age, I was trying to ask,' said Gordo. 'Aren't
you jabbed for it?'

Oliver said nothing but cast a look at his mum from under his
lashes.

'Is there somewhere private I can talk to you?' Allison said
to Gordo. She meant away from me. Her mother was drilling me
with hard eyes, daring me to speak.

'There's been enough secrecy,' said Gordo. 'It's time for some
openness.'

'I agree,' I said. So brave when it wasn't my family, our secrets.
'How much does Oliver know about Hiskith?' I asked them and
both the women drew in a breath so sharp over their teeth that
it hissed.

'Nothing,' Allison said. Then belatedly: 'What do you mean?'

'So what did he think had happened to *me*?' said Gordo.

'Sitting right here.' I smiled to hear the first bit of teenage out
of the boy.

'The usual, was it?' Gordo said 'Deadbeat dad, slunk off into
the undergrowth. Plucky young mum doing her best on her own,
was it?' His voice was rising and the sounds from upstairs
dropped. The rest of them were listening. 'Did you tell him that
to keep him away from me? So you could not vaccinate him and
let him catch Christ knows what all and then let him out sniffing

glue, without me saying, "Hang on, Allison. Maybe don't kill our kid, eh?".'

'Right,' said Mrs McCabe, getting to her feet. She brushed the front of her fleece top as if to get rid of crumbs although she hadn't eaten anything. It must be a habit. Maybe she was troubled with dandruff. But she was brushing so strenuously she was almost hitting herself. It made me think of banging the chalk dust out of a blackboard cleaner. 'You've made your position very clear,' she said. 'Your lifestyle is clear too.' She turned on Allison. 'I warned you.'

'What the fuck?' said Gordo. 'Aye, I know I've made my position clear. Where do I sign, when can we start, I said. And I'm not even asking why or where she's been. But honest to God, am I supposed to clap her on the back and say "Well done, Alli. Top job." As for my lifestyle, what the fuck are you even—?'

'Can you all just stop?' Oliver said, and he said it so weakly that it cut them off like a switch. I put the cocoa down at his side and he flicked up one side of his mouth in the closest thing to a smile I think he could muster.

I didn't think I'd see him again after that first day. But once he'd had a good night's sleep and calmed down he looked a bit brighter and Allison's let him back half a dozen times now. She's sending him here to be with the girls, doing exactly the same as me so I can hardly fault her for it. I don't know what Barrett told *them* but I sat Albie down and filled him in good-style.

I wish I could say I did it with a heart full of sorrow but the truth is that telling my boy Oliver's grey face and careful breathing came from unprotected sex and mucking about with aerosols felt the same as buckling him in to his car seat or fastening his bike helmet.

'Plus the mad anti-vaxxer angle,' he said. Because of course they'd all been listening. Even Barrett, apparently, hung over the banisters.

I considered defending her. I remember sitting in the surgery with Albie on my knee and my eyes squeezed tight shut as the nurse snapped her gloves on and swabbed his chubby little arm with the alcohol wipe, a wipe so cold he was crying before the needle got anywhere near him. I remember lying in the dark staring straight up, listening to him snorting and snuffling in his

cot beside me, willing myself not to sleep. Willing myself even
harder not to look anything up online, knowing I'd be racing
through the night to A & E if I so much as let myself glance at
it.

But I *didn't* defend her. I was thinking of Gordo, and the last
fifteen years, all of Albie's life – all of Oliver's life – grieving
over that dark water. My heart hardened. Not to the girl who ran
away but to the woman who stayed away, lied to her son, then
came pelting back again when she needed something.

She's going to get it. Gordo's a match and the surgery is set
for the first week of the new year. He's doing the same as I did
after the infant vaccinations: googling nothing. He's read the
leaflet until it's nearly ripped along its folds, but not one more
word. Still, anytime he's not busy, you can tell his mind is dicing
and shredding and mincing and grating it all into smaller and
smaller pieces and still not managing to shrink the fears down
enough to sluice them away.

So it's partly for that reason we returned to the mystery. To
take Gordo's mind off it, here in the dead time of the year before
Christmas brings folk up walking in the hills to be sold soup and
mince pies. But partly too, it's for me. I can't get over that day
when Oliver came. I was drowning as deep as I'd ever drowned,
gasping for breath and swallowing water, then in an instant, my
voice was clear and I was helping Gordo. Hard as I tried to deny
it, it's true.

And I did try. The angriest I ever got on the ward was when
one of the nurses told me I should maybe 'focus on something
outside myself'.

'She's basically calling me a spoiled brat,' I said to Elspeth.

'Bitch,' Elspeth agreed.

'She's basically telling me to pull my socks up and get on
with it.'

'Cow. You should report her.'

'I should. I could focus on *that*. See how she likes it.'

So, even though I've decided freely and independently to take
on solving a mystery, still sometimes I remember her face
simpering at me, and get myself well pissed off again. Just
because I had given up hope of someone saving me, that didn't
make it OK that no one tried. I hide all of this turmoil from
Gordo too.

Mysteries, plural, I should say. There's the mystery of Uncle Roddie's missing death certificate for one thing. And the two remaining clues: the stack of books and the book of stats as the kids have taken to calling them. They're just as convinced as ever that there will be answers to both. And somewhere along the way, so subtly I can't say where it began, so gradually I'm boiling like a frog before I've even admitted I'm in the pot, they've all decided Davey didn't kill himself.

'Because didn't the back-to-front bin confirm that he wasn't suicidal?' Albie says. 'And didn't the Bible and the hoardage confirm that he suspected someone else was coming back to do dread deeds?'

'He left a note,' I say, ten times a day. 'And we know why: even if he was wrong, he believed he killed his mother.'

Albie shrugs this off and goes back to persuading. He's completely convinced there will be an answer that explains everything. He's been treating me gently while he wears down my defences, but he's determined all the same. He speaks about what he calls the matrix mystery – Gordo nodded approvingly at this term – of Davey. It's hard to disagree. Davey's whole life is one unanswered and – as far as I'm concerned – unanswerable question. If I wasn't scared of losing the house, I'd be tempted to tell everything I know to that copper from the station in Kirkconnel. It would blow my whole family up, probably, but it would shake the truth loose too. Of course, then I'd have to go and see Scott and offer to chalk Cassie up to a midlife crisis, say I was willing to try again if he promised to try too.

I'm thinking about this one early morning standing at the kitchen sink running the water hot to steep last night's dishes. I imagine the view from our house in town, the row of terracotta pots with herbs in, the neat garden and the lap fence, the single maple tree in one corner, chosen for maximum impact. Then I let my gaze sweep up over the rise of the hill to the ridge, the soft black of the shadowed ground against the hard black of the sky, hours before dawn. Satin and velvet. Leaning over the taps, I can just see the third black of the water too, oiled silk. I turn my head as a square of yellow leaps into the dark. Up at the school, Zelda has switched her bedside light on. I wonder if she's looking this way, seeing my yellow square – Hanza yellow, maybe Cadmium Light – knowing I'm up too. I realize that it takes

Zelda in my mind to make me think paint names instead of colours now. For that reason – for lots of reasons – I find myself smiling.

Still, I check with the other party involved. 'Albie,' I say later, when he's stooped over his cereal bowl, his elbows wide and his head low, making the journey from bowl to mouth a short one.

'Sorr-ee!' he says, straightening. 'Jeez, Mum!' That makes me smile too.

'You do like it up here, don't you?'

'Everyone likes it up here,' he says. 'Even the nutters who want to drain it love it. And even the other nutters who want to kill fish would rather kill them with a scenic backdrop.'

It's getting easier to believe Davey's innocent of *that*, at least. I've met some of the ramblers and anglers now. I thought they were harmless when I looked at the websites, but now I've had some of their more exuberant pamphlets pressed on me. I can see that a few of them have gone too far into their own worlds.

'They throw most of them back,' I tell Albie. *Kill fish!* I knew he'd be knocking on vegan's door sooner or later, with Willow and Sorrel leading the way. 'Anyway,' I go on, 'what would you say, now you've had a chance to mull it over, if Dad and me got back together?'

He drops his spoon and wipes his mouth with his cuff. 'Seriously?'

'That's what he came to ask me, that day he came.'

'Yeah, because she dumped his arse and he panicked. But why would you go "Oh, OK then. Give me a minute to pack"?'

'For the sake of the children,' I tell him, in a comedy voice with a throb in it. 'Hence why I'm checking in with you.'

Albie shakes his head. 'I keep telling you, Mum,' he says, and he gives me a kind look that makes it hard not to laugh at him, 'I get on fine with Dad, guy to guy. Golfing or watching football. In a couple of years, I'll buy him a pint. But it's one thing to be a laugh and handy on a five-a-side team. It's another thing to be partner material.' I'm trying hard to believe this is my fifteen-year-old son talking to me. 'So how about if I keep him in the dad zone and you keep him in the friend zone. You could do better, you know.'

That's *definitely* Sorrel and Willow. And there's far too much in it for me to deal with. Settling for Scott all those years means of course I don't deserve better. And if the woman he left me for left *him* then doesn't that mean his value's dropped even further from where it was before?

'What was she like? Cassie?' I find myself asking. I was scrupulous about not doing this when she might be his new stepmother but it doesn't matter now.

'Dunno,' he says. 'I never met her.'

I look over with a smile starting, thinking he's being kind and funny, thinking she must be gorgeous and successful and he doesn't want to tell me, but he's not wearing his joke face.

'Seriously?' I say. 'She didn't move in?'

'How can you not know?' He's still young enough not to feel responsibility, not to see that *he* is where my life and Scott's life touch now, the only conduit for information.

'Or stay for a weekend?' I suggest. 'You didn't ever go out for lunch with her?'

'Her and me?' says Albie. 'And then get our nails done?'

I've had it completely wrong. All this time I've been telling myself Scott had fallen deeply in love with his soon-to-be second wife. She as deeply with him. But really he discarded me like one of the drinks cans or crisp bags Davey found out on the moor. The humiliation engulfs me.

'So you're OK up here?' I say to Albie, when it's started to subside. 'In the cold and dark and Granny and everything?'

'And Olly and Will and So,' he says. 'And Gordo and Barrett for you. And anyway, it's cool. It's different.' He casts about for a way to explain it to me. I think he's forgotten that I grew up here and I understand. 'Do you think I should go and *see* Granny a bit more? I always feel like I'm interrupting.'

'I'll invite her down for tea one night,' I say. 'One night when it's just the two of us.' But, even I say it, we both hear the sound of the sanny van and the pick-up breasting the top and Albie jumps up to brush his teeth before the girls spill out and come to greet him. They're huggers. They've turned him into one. He even gives me a quick squeeze right now as he's passing.

It feels right to have the four of them here – Albie and Olly, those two girls. It's just like the old days with the four of *us*, lying around in the warmest room waiting for the rain to stop, playing cards for buttons, laying elaborate schemes that never get past the planning stage.

'You know,' I say, as he goes past again after what must be the most cursory teeth-clean ever, 'by the time the spring comes, Olly might be able to go out on the hill with you on good days.'

'Looking for clues?' he says. 'I think all the good clues are in the house. Or online, actually.'

Which puts me back in the rat-run of mysteries again, in the maze of questions none of us can answer. About Roddie, about Rowan, about Davey. Even if I stay away from any thoughts about my dad and me, I'm still back in the fear that all of this is built on lies and when they crack, I'll lose everything.

'Face your fears,' the nurses used to say – the nicer ones, not that smug cow. 'One at a time,' they told me. 'You'll see.'

But that was when my fears weren't real. Or weren't in the future anyway. Although, I realize, nothing that's come to light so far – the hoarded junk, the Bible verse, the fixed washer, Allison and Oliver – has put my new life in jeopardy yet.

Start small, I tell myself. The dog. Start there, for practice, and see where we get to.

TWENTY-ONE

Gordo

He knows being watched could get pretty annoying pretty quickly. Oliver – bloody awful name; what was she thinking? – isn't as feisty as the girls or as sarky as Albie – another heinous name in his opinion – but he doesn't want to heap up extra woes on those bony shoulders. They've got enough pressing down on them. It nearly broke Gordo the first morning after the three of them turned up, when Olly – he was trying out 'Olly' to see if it was better – came into the kitchen in his striped pyjama bottoms and his ribbed white vest, his shoulder blades like folded wings and his collar bones like a pair of drumsticks lying on his chest. Whatever it is making his cheeks so puffy it's having no effect below the neck. Or maybe he's just got chubby cheeks and it's the colour that makes it look wrong.

As he thinks 'chubby cheeks' he feels another wave of rage surge up and wash over him. It's an exhausting thing to experience when you can't shout or throw your arms about or even swear really. What he *wants* to do is take Allison up the hill on the other side of the loch and scream at her for twenty minutes about the baby needing to be burped, and the toddler scraping his fat knees when he fell over, and the kid who learned to play football and Fortnite, and the boy full of questions about shaving and girls. He wants to jab his finger at the water's edge where she left her stuff and bellow at her so loud that she's knocked to the cold ground.

The first time he thinks this he hears her voice soothing him. *Of course you're angry*, she says, *it's normal to be angry.* And that makes him even angrier. She's come back in the flesh and taken away his comfort. He can't ever listen to that voice again now.

That makes him want to take her by the arms and shake her

until she rattles. He wants to pull her hair. It's like being seven again.

But of course, for the boy, he does none of it. He does nothing. He lets them stay in his house, mother and daughter in his double bed, Olls – another failed effort – on the spare room single and himself on the couch, huffing over from one shoulder to another all night long, seething. In the daytime he takes the boy up Hiskith, small talk in the van, driving over the cattle grids as if he's got a load of eggs on board, delivering him to the girls and Albie like a temple offering. And always so careful not to watch.

The only time the small talk grew big was when Oliver said, 'I can't believe she's letting me go with you every day. But it's best all round, ken?' Wisps of Glasgow in his speech, surprising Gordo every time. 'It's as tiring for them – the both of them – as it is for me.'

'What's tiring?'

'Watching and asking and offering and checking all the time. I'm not going to keel over with no warning. It's daft for them to keep nipping at me.'

So Gordo is twice as careful to be breezy; careful not to notice what he's eating; careful not to count off the pills he swallows every four hours, the size of tiddlywinks some of them; careful not to ask where he's going when he leaves the room. But he checks the weather forecast and he's never been gladder to see day after day of that black cartoon cloud on the ten-day page, thick drops coming out of it sideways.

Anyway, he doesn't need to watch the boy to know how he is. He can feel him through the hairs on his arms as if fatherhood has turned him into an octopus or a carnivorous plant. He can tell from the sound of his breath if he's comfortable, if he's drowsy. He heard him fall asleep one night driving down, glanced away from the road just in time to see those long lashes drop to his cheeks.

'Did she ever tell you why I wasn't there?' he asks today, as they crest the hill and Oliver sits up at the sight of the water before them. It's Gordo's favourite too, this winter Hiskith Water after days of rain. The oval, like a mermaid's mirror, is gone and in its place is an angry crab, the year-round burns swollen to pincers and eight new legs made of seasonal streams. Somehow, when it's extra wide and extra deep, it's easier not to think about what's under there. And of course now he knows what's not under there after all too.

'I didn't *know* you weren't there,' Oliver says. 'When my mum and—' He stopped and swallowed hard. 'Did you know she got married? I was four. I can't even remember a time before him. So, when my mum and—'

'You can say "dad",' Gordo tells him, hoping he won't.

'When my mum got divorced,' he settled for, 'I knew *he* wasn't there anymore.'

'And when all this started up, first stop was my . . . I don't think I *can* say it, you know. Not to you, anyway. But, like I'm telling you, the first stop was his new place to see what his blood type was. Because it is just blood type. It only ends up being relations because who else would do it, to be fair. And it's not even blood type totally because O people can donate to anyone. Kidneys too.'

'O people like me,' Gordo says. Never been prouder to be so ordinary, he thinks to himself. Still, it takes him a minute to get over being second choice. When he's in charge of himself again, he says, 'Did you not wonder why they never came back to Kirkconnel? Your grandad was born here. The graveyard's full of McCabes.'

'I didn't know. Granda McCabe's buried in Wishaw.'

That pulls Gordo up short. He never thought to wonder where Allison's dad was the last few days. Now that he thinks about it, he assumed big Ally McCabe was at his work in some Post Office sorting facility, keeping out of Gordo's way. It's sixteen years, but Gordo will never forget the night they told him about the pregnancy. 'You walk in here, bold as brass, smirking at me and telling me you've forced yourself on my wee girl?' Gordo said nothing, just simmered with a milder version of the same rage boiling in him now. If he'd left it to Allison alone to tell them, he'd have been accused of cowardice. And he only started smirking when Big Ally assumed it was all Gordo's doing.

'Nobody forced anybody, Dad,' Allison had said. Gordo watched the man make an effort not to take his flat hand off her, watched him realize Gordo could see the struggle. Maybe that was the moment their fate was sealed. If Gordo had hung his head and said sorry, maybe they'd have been shoved down the aisle and set up in a bedsit. Maybe life would have taken a different tack entirely.

'Same back anyway,' Oliver says. 'Didn't you wonder where *I* was? Where *she* was?'

He's pulled up on the verge outside Davey's gate, but instead of switching the engine off, he slips the handbrake and lets the van coast to the water's edge in neutral, then stops again.

'I didn't know about you,' he says.

'She didn't tell you she was pregnant?'

'See over there?' Gordo says. 'See where the path dips down so it's right near the edge? Where those big square rocks are?'

Oliver turns in his seat, wondering what the path round the loch's got to do with anything. And so Gordo tells him.

'Jesus fuck,' Oliver says, with a scornful laugh in his voice that Gordo thinks he should say something about. He doesn't. 'Wow.'

'I probably shouldn't have said.'

'Away and get,' Oliver says. '*You* don't need to worry what *you* say or do for a good bit. You never sent us packing when we turned up. You're sleeping on the couch in your own house. You're getting sliced open and stapled shut. She's the one – and my gran too – who need to be watching what they say, keeping on *your* right side. Running away like that and then waltzing back in! Why would she do it? You were up for it, weren't you?'

'I was so up for it,' Gordo says. 'I spent my Saturday money on an engagement ring.'

'So why would she run away? What was she running from?'

Gordo muses later that the thought occurs to both of them in the same instant: if Allison could do that, what else might she have done? He turns right round in his seat to give Oliver a close look. He even undoes his seatbelt to face the boy. What meets his eyes is Oliver doing the same back, looking at Gordo's hairline and eyes and teeth and chin, taking an inventory.

'Blood type O,' he says.

'And you're B,' says Gordo. He doesn't need to tell the lad to google it; the phone's out already.

'Possible,' Oliver says. 'An O father can have a B son. Thank fuck for that, eh?'

'It wouldn't make a difference,' says Gordo. He knows this is true, knows it to his guts. To his liver.

'Still, though,' Oliver says, with his head bent and his thumbs flying.

'What are you doing?'

Oliver holds out his phone and Gordo reads the text super-imposed over a photo of a blue-eyed baby in a knitted hat. *Private DNA paternity testing. Free kit. £99 three-day service.*

'Can you read out your credit card number?' Oliver says. 'Christmas post and all that, we better get going.'

Gordo wonders at all this calm and manages to get himself het up close to tears, assuming it's illness stopping any sulks or strops. When the order's through, they back away from the water's edge and head to the schoolhouse. Once inside, he overhears Oliver, halfway up the stairs, say 'You will not *believe* what I just found out!' and he feels his shoulders drop, understanding. Any discovery at all – even his mum's teenage games – is welcome if it gives him a titbit to offer the girls.

'You look happy,' Tabitha says. She and Barrett are in the kitchen, the last of the box files of Davey's old paperwork spread on the table.

'Getting things straight with the boy,' says Gordo. 'Listen, something's going to be delivered here in a few days' time, addressed to me. A wee parcel. I hope that's OK. It's just with houseguests, you know.'

Tabitha shrugs. She's different from Allison's mum and Allison herself, both in his memory and now they're back. Tab doesn't pry. He thinks maybe it's because she's got secrets of her own but then he thinks that would make Allison the least nosey person in the world.

Anyway, he doesn't want to think about Allison at the start of a day with his friends, the sound of the four kids upstairs. He looks around the kitchen and can't put his finger on what's changed since Tabitha took over from Davey. She hasn't decorated or added ornaments or anything but this is a cosier, more welcoming room than before. Maybe it's the dog, lying on a folded blanket in front of the Rayburn. But it's happening down at his house too; the two women are doing something that's changing his house from a bachelor pad back into a cottage again. It bothers him that he can't point to what it is.

'I told him,' he says, as if to remind himself that there are more important things in life. 'About the bag and shoes by the loch. About me thinking she was dead. I didn't want him wondering why I never tried to find them.'

'How did he take it?' says Tabitha.

'He took it upstairs to tell the rest.'

Tab smiles, laughing silently.

'It's bombshells all round today then,' Barrett says. 'Tell him, Tabby. See if *he* can make sense of it all.'

'Tell me what?' says Gordo.

Tabitha folds the tea towel she's been using, folds both sides into the middle so the pattern's at the front, then hangs it over the oven-door handle. It's probably no more than things like that that have changed. 'It's all too much,' she says. 'Roddie, Rowan, Davey – all of them dying with a great big question mark over them.' She never includes her dad, Gordo thinks, and that's surely the worst one of all. 'So,' she goes on, 'I decided to start with Bess. Solve that and go from there.'

'And where have you got to?' Gordo says.

'Brace yourself,' says Barrett.

'The weekend Bess died was the same weekend Auntie Rowan died,' Tabitha says. 'Ten years ago. The second Saturday in May.'

'Whoa!' says Gordo. He doesn't know what it means but it must mean something.

Barrett nods, approving of this reaction. 'I knew it was roundabout the same sort of time,' he says. 'But May's my busy month and I couldn't have sworn to it.'

I could swear to my date, Gordo thinks, and her voice says *because you're caring* before he can stop it.

'When I got the chance to come up here again,' Barrett is saying, 'and Davey told me his mum had passed on, I was still thinking Bess would come back. Still thought she'd run away. Remember? We made posters.'

Gordo remembers perfectly. He printed them out on the library photocopier and put them in plastic sleeves from a file folder. He went out with Davey's staple gun and stuck them on lampposts and bus shelters. He remembers folding over the tops and taping them shut, then changing tactic when he saw how the rain still found a way to get in. It made more sense to turn the plastic folders upside down and leave the bottom open so they didn't fill with condensation.

'It was weeks later I got the photo and the cartridge casing through the post,' Barrett says. 'I'd forgotten the timing to be honest. But you see what this means?'

Gordo doesn't see anything, so he waits to hear more. At last, Barrett carries on. 'Witnesses,' he says. 'There must have been a doctor and an undertaker at least, coming and going. They could have seen her, seen the dog, heard the shot.'

'Best-case scenario,' says Tabitha. 'And we can ask my mum too. She phoned me the night Rowan died. She might remember a car, a dog. Have you got a picture of your ex-wife?'

'What does that mean?' says Gordo. 'Best-case scenario?' Tabitha is wiping down the worktops now, carefully gathering breakfast crumbs into her cupped hand. She opens the window and shakes the cloth outside.

'For the birds,' she says, noticing him noticing her. 'And then you say it'll attract rats. And I'll say let's get a feeder then. And you say the birds will mess up the washing.'

'Who's this? Your mum?' Gordo asks.

'Scott,' Tabby says. 'I never realized what a sweetie-wife he was until I got away from him. You know the next one's slung her hook already?'

'Worst-case scenario,' Barrett says, very deliberately, 'doesn't bear thinking about, but we've got to face it. A dog disappears. Same day, someone kills his mother.'

'If he did,' says Gordo.

'He confessed,' says Barrett.

'To something,' Tabitha adds.

'Worst-case scenario,' says Barrett again. 'Person who kills his mother has got the dog's collar.'

'That's not a scenario,' Gordo says. 'That's a summary.'

Tabitha has poured a bit of bleach into the basin and laid the dishcloth in to steep. Now she's refilling the kettle. 'We need to ask ourselves seriously if Davey shot the dog,' she says. Gordo glances over to see if Barrett's offended by this string of bald words, but if anything he looks relieved *he* didn't have to say it.

'It doesn't make sense,' Gordo says. 'If Davey decided that day was the day to kill his mother, why would he do something public, outside the house, noisy, guaranteed to draw attention if someone saw him?'

'Bess knew this house, right?' Tabitha says. She's standing swishing hot tap water round the teapot, waiting for the kettle.

Gordo can see a tea cosy ready to be used too. And the teabags are in a paisley-patterned tin, instead of a ripped open box. He's changing his mind about trying to live like this. It looks like a lot of trouble. All he would need to do for Oliver is have the latest games and let the lad take a lager every now and then. Unless he'll never be able to drink any booze at all for the rest of his life, once he's got two thirds of Gordo's liver growing inside him. 'What are you thinking?' he says.

'Just that if Bess was scratching at the door trying to get in and Auntie Rowan was dying or already dead, maybe Davey panicked.'

'Panicked and sent her off into the middle of the loch after a stick to make the shot a challenge?' Barrett says. 'It's not like it was me with her. *I'd* wonder why his door was locked and he wasn't answering. But all he had to do was ignore Bess and ignore the ex if she came up the path. A dog walker whose dog has disappeared is going to hang around a lot longer than otherwise. This scenario *doesn't* make sense. It was my ex like I always knew.'

'And Davey found the collar like he found Allison's coat?' Gordo says. 'Either when Bess washed up—'

'Or,' says Tabitha, 'actually like he found the coat. If the collar was removed first.'

Gordo is trying to think it through. 'Can I see it?' he says. He knows Barrett. He knows it'll be in his pocket. And he's right. Barrett hands the collar over and Gordo turns it in his hands.

'I don't think this has been submerged,' he says. 'Do you? We've found enough old boots at the edge over the years to know what waterlogged leather looks like.' He hands it back to Barrett who rubs his thumbs over the soft, chamois-feeling surface where the top layer has worn away. 'So whoever killed Bess took it off beforehand.'

'Why would she do that—' Barrett begins.

'To make ID harder,' says Tabitha.

'—if she was going to send me a picture?' Barrett finished.

But there's an idea growing in Gordo. 'Have you got the photo on you?' he says. And of course he does. 'And have you got round as far as Davey's stamp collection, Tab? Or is it still in the drawer there?'

Tabitha shrugs and so Gordo goes over to the free-standing cupboard where there should be a magnifying glass in the stamps and franks drawer. He brings it back over to the table and bends over the snap Barrett has laid there. He tries the main lens, then the lens-in-lens, and is just about to give up when Tabitha offers a suggestion. 'Couldn't you take another photo, zoom in and then up the clarity?'

It works. It works so well that even Barrett gathers courage to look head-on at the photo he's been carrying around all these years without ever so much as glancing it.

'She's wearing it!' says Gordo.

'So, if you're sure about the state of the leather,' says Tabitha, 'this is a photo of Bess enjoying a swim! It's a happy picture. Look. She's in the loch, splashing about, wearing her collar. This is nothing to do with the day she disappeared.'

Barrett takes the magnifier and applies it to Gordo's phone screen, to the blown-up and clarified and lit and brightened rectangle, where they can all clearly see the lighter band of Bess' worn brown collar against the wet black of her fur.

'I'll go even further,' he says. 'That's not Bess.' He's blinking fast and he glances to the window in a way that makes Gordo's chest hurt. It's as if he thinks maybe Bess is going to turn up again like Oliver did, after ten years missing.

'So whoever killed Bess, they didn't do it in such a public way after all,' says Barrett. 'I took a photo I was too scared to look at properly and a cartridge that could have come from anywhere. I made a misery out of them and carried it on my back for ten years.'

'Whoever?' says Tabitha. 'Barrett, it *must* have been Davey.'

'He hated guns,' Barrett says.

'But he might not even have shot her,' Gordo says. 'He might have . . . Well, look, we don't need to think about that. But the only thing that makes sense is that he killed her somehow. Like you said, because she was being a pest and he didn't want anyone at his door that day of all days.'

'But landing yourself with a dog to get rid of exactly when

you don't want to be arousing suspicion . . . that makes no sense either,' says Tabitha.

'No more does getting your washing machine fixed when you're going to kill yourself,' Barrett reminds them.

'Or keeping years' worth of DNA, when you're the killer,' says Gordo, 'or keeping fake ash or drawers full of bloody franking marks, but he did that. Face it, Barrett. We thought we knew him and we didn't know him at all. He was a complete fucking nutter. No offence, Tabby.'

'None taken,' Tabitha says. 'If any of us was normal, they'd be a black sheep in the Muir family. Complete fucking nutters are ten-a-penny.'

Gordo opens his mouth to argue back, ashamed to have started her down that path, but he can't think of anything to say. The old witch with her creepy pictures, the married cousins who ran away, the man who strapped his baby into the car and tried to drown them both, the man who hid for years and then killed himself over the death of a brother he never saw, the friend with a house full of worm bins, keeping trophies from others' grief. Tabitha, with her months on the mental ward, was the plain vanilla Muir.

He'd forgotten about Albie. But now the kitchen door is opening and there he is standing with the girls behind him and the sound of Oliver's slow tread catching up too.

'Mum?' he says. 'Can we talk about something? Two things actually.'

'Olly's solved the stat book,' says Sorrel. Gordo feels his chest swell with pride.

'And is that the book stack?' Oliver says, pointing at the manuals and almanack still sitting there on the table where they've left them. 'Because if it is I've solved that too.'

'Three things!' Willow says, her voice lively enough to make Uggy stir in his sleep.

'No,' says Oliver. 'The stack and the stats are the same thing. So it's only two.' He sits down in what was Davey's seat and pulls the chair in close. 'I can't reach,' he says.

'Short arse,' says Albie. Gordo opens his mouth to flay the wee shite for that, till he sees how much Oliver loved it. It must be great to get some normal piss-taking instead of all the care and caution.

'You try, Tabitha,' Oliver says.

'Ohhhhhhhh!' says Willow. 'I get it.'

'Sit like I was,' Oliver says, 'and rest your arm on the books.' Tabitha strains forward to lay her forearm along the top of the pile.

'No, not like that,' Sorrel says. 'Elbow on the tabletop and back of your hand on the top book. See?'

Gordo doesn't see anything at first but then something about the awkward balance of Tabitha's wrist and the sight of her inner forearm, her veins blue against her white skin, triggers a memory.

'I see it,' he says.

'Read a number out the stats book,' says Oliver.

With a flourish, Willow cracks open the little notebook full of codes and says, 'One, three, two, eight, six, seven, two.'

'Or,' says Oliver, 'a hundred and thirty-two over eighty-six.'

'Blood pressure!' Barrett says.

'Blood pressure. Well done, Dad. You got there,' says Sorrel.

'And the seventy-two?' says Tabitha. 'Oh! Pulse.' This last is with a half-turn to beam at the others.

'Well done, Ol,' Gordo says.

'And you see what this means, don't you, Mum?' says Albie.

'You're saying why would someone who's going to kill himself care about his blood pressure?' says Gordo. He's been so caught up in the kids' little drama, the slump of disappointment settles on him very heavy.

'That too,' Willow says.

'Lots of reasons,' Tabitha says. 'Habit. Or maybe he knew he was ill and he always meant to leave on his own terms before he had to go to hospital.'

'Yeah but, Mum,' says Albie, 'he wasn't ill. Because the post-mortem said everything that he had going on, didn't it? The lung stuff from the chest infection. The benign lump in the back of his knee. What was it called?'

'Baker's cyst,' Gordo says. 'He showed us when he was worried it was something worse.'

'If he had heart problems they'd have put it in the post-mortem report,' Albie says. 'So he was taking his blood pressure regularly enough to keep the books stacked up, even though he didn't have high blood pressure. Which means he was trying to stay healthy. And who tries to keep healthy if they're going to kill themselves?'

'I don't want to burst your bubble,' says Tabitha, 'but you can spend twenty minutes finding just the right anniversary card for a man you already know has stopped loving you. So you could definitely check your blood pressure every day, planning a couch to five K and a suicide at the same time.'

'That's pretty bleak for the weans to hear,' says Barrett.

'And FTMI, Mum,' says Albie.

'Anyway,' says Oliver, 'that's not really the point. We found the stack of books for Davey to rest his hand on. And we found the notes of his daily readings. Ask yourselves the question.'

Gordo whistles between his teeth and watches the light dawn in Barrett's eyes, even though Tabitha is still frowning.

'What's missing?' Oliver says, after he's given her a fair chance to get there on her own.

'Ohhhh!' says Tabitha. 'The blood pressure machine.'

'The blood pressure machine,' says Albie. 'It's gone.'

'Maybe the cops took it,' Tabitha says. 'Maybe it was on loan from the hospital and the cops took it to give back to them.'

'Tab,' says Barrett, 'have you ever tried to return a commode or a pair of crutches to the NHS? I have. It takes months.'

'Or maybe,' Tabitha says next, 'when he decided to kill himself, he threw it away.'

'Threw it away,' says Willow. 'Are you serious? He didn't throw anything away. He killed himself with insulin from the steam age.'

Tabitha stares at her, frowning.

'Except we think this proves he *didn't* kill himself,' Sorrel says. 'We think whoever murdered him didn't want it known that he was concerned about his health. So *they* took it away.'

Gordo is still watching Tabitha, to see how she copes with this. She's in analytical mode. 'What is it?' he asks her.

'Something keeps bothering me,' she says. 'And I can't quite . . .' She shakes her head. 'Anyway, tough as it is to believe Davey killed himself, it's even harder to accept that someone else killed him. Davey? Sweet daft Davey? Why would someone want him away?'

'Old secrets,' says Albie. 'Old scandals. Old lies.'

His mum is watching him very closely, wondering. Gordo

reckons, what corner of Muir family history he's uncovered now.

'It's just we kept searching the records,' he says. 'Especially after the Fuller's Earth thing. And we've found Uncle Roddie's death notice. Finally. But now we don't know what to do.'

TWENTY-TWO

Tabitha

'You look like you need a cuppa,' Gordo says. The understatement alone makes me laugh hard enough to worry everyone. And then because the girls don't drink tea – although, as Barrett says, they'll suck down green matcha if it costs enough – Albie starts pouring orange juice and because Sorrel tells him how much sugar is in orange juice, which according to her is more than you'd find in cola, I end up out at Davey's herb bed picking mint leaves to infuse for them, and trying hard not to think about where a dead dog might have ended up if she didn't drown.

Davey's herb bed hits me in the gut. I remember him putting wee tiny satellite strawberry plants to root in pots whenever the big plant sent them out. He's been doing it with the mint too. And he's put straw over the crown of something tender – I won't know what it is till spring – and set sheets of glass over the creeping thyme to keep the worst of the rain off. 'It's not the cold, Tab,' he used to say. 'It's the wet.' How can he have done all this work to see a five-foot-square patch of herbs through till spring if he wasn't going to be here to see it? Why *would* he care about his blood pressure? And where's the monitor gone? And what *about* the washing machine?

Back inside, once everyone's got their drink of choice, I nod to Albie. 'Right. Death certificate.'

'Right here,' Albie says. 'We printed it out.'

I feel as if a death certificate should be more special-looking, and maybe the originals are but this is just a piece of A4 paper with black writing in boxes and print at the bottom far too small to read, plus the angry-looking signature of someone whose job it is to put his name to these things all day every day.

'Suicide by asphyxiation,' I read. 'That's what we always believed. He hanged himself from—' I stop, because the truth is he hanged himself from the banister rail Oliver was just holding on to as he made his way downstairs.

'It's the date, Mum,' Albie says.

I check it and it says 4 February, which is what everyone in the family, everyone in the valley, everyone who ever read a newspaper and thrilled at our misfortune, has always known. The same day as my dad killed himself and tried to kill me. The same day that Zelda dived down into the cold water as the car sank and got one of the back doors open and unbuckled my booster and brought me up to the surface.

'The year,' says Albie. For once the girls are quiet, leaving it up to him to present this, whatever it is. They look solemn and Willow nods at the paper I'm holding.

'1972,' I read, off the third box in the date line. 'That's wrong.' I look up at them. 'OK, so that's wrong. That's a typo. That's why you couldn't find it when you went searching. They've put the wrong date on. He died in 1977.'

Albie is shaking his head. 'It's just not the wrong date, Mum. It's in the wrong place too. In the wrong order in the registry.'

'So . . .?' I say.

'So Uncle Roddie died in 1972.'

'But he can't have,' I say. 'He can't have. I was born in '75 and I *remember* him.' I'm breathing so hard I can feel the force of the air coming down my nostrils and I can see the rise and fall of my chest. Any minute one of the kids is going to giggle. But I've got no choice. For all my big talk about the mysteries helping me stay on an even keel, right now I'm scared if I don't concentrate on my breathing, counting it in and counting it out, I'm going to detach and go spinning off like a sycamore seed. I don't want the kids to see that. Not any of them and definitely not Oliver, who's staring at me out of his pale, round, puffy face making me think of Mr Moon and his hidden family. I breathe in. I breathe out. I think of my forest, my meadow, my desert.

'Desert, Tabitha?' the nurse said. 'Why not a beach?'

'Because the tide comes in,' I told her. 'Because I'll drown.'

They never learned. They never even tried. Over and over again in the group relaxation classes, they'd say 'Think of a lake, a lazy river, a babbling brook.' I stuck with my desert. My cats. (Cats hate water.) My stationery cupboard full of dry paper.

Garfield and . . . I think to myself. Did I once know the name of the other one and I'm trying to remember? Or have I never known and I'm trying to find out for the first time? Because that doesn't make any sense. You can't forget what you never knew. And you can't find things out by concentrating. But that thought is far too close to home. That kind of mind trick is what made me slip my moorings and drift downstream in the first place.

Time for some cold, hard facts.

I don't remember Uncle Roddie *at all*. At. All. I've seen photographs of him, and I've been told about him. My whole life I've been told about him. I've been invited to take part in stories about when we were all together. And even that's hazy, like everything is when you're tiny. Did I remember when Auntie Rowan and Uncle Roddie went to London? No, I only remember a car going past and Zelda saying they were in it. I remember Johnny and Davey at our dinner table, getting their baths with us, in their jammies drinking warm milk with us, whenever Uncle Roddie was having a bad day.

But even those memories can't be real, because they're buttoned on to memories of the school taxi spitting us all out at the same spot and the boys coming into our house instead of going down the hill to their own house. On school days. Which I started when I was five, in 1981, four years later than the day in February of 1977 when my dad died and I didn't.

That's all it takes for me to finally realize that this perfect bauble of memory I've been swimming around in is no more than a dandelion head, scattered and gone at a single breath. I don't remember Uncle Roddie's bad days like I remember the school minibus and the warm milk. I remember Uncle Roddie's bad days *and* his good days like I remember being in the car with my dad as it went down and down, the tug of the door and the screeching as Zelda wrestled me out. I wonder if Davey . . .

That's the thing about death. The grieving, the funeral, the lawyers, the clearing of the house . . . they are all such wonderful distractions. You do all that busy work and inside yourself you believe that, when it's finished, things will go back to normal again. Right there, what I wondered was if Davey, who was four, remembers him. What I wanted was to find Davey and ask. Because I've accepted that Davey is dead. But not until this moment have I accepted that Davey is gone.

'So,' I say at last, 'if Roddie died in 1972, even Davey wouldn't be old enough to remember him.'

'February 1972, Mum,' says Albie. 'And you know when Uncle Davey was born. Think about it.'

I've never been any good at this. I always need to work it out on my fingers. I'm forty and I was born on 9 November 1975. Johnny is a year older than me, Jo a year older than him, and Davey is just ahead of Jo, four years older than me, born in December.

'We should mark his birthday,' I say. 'We always used to make sure and keep it separate. The fifteenth was Davey Day and Christmas started the next morning.' Then my brain catches up. The others got there before me and are waiting.

'Hang on,' I say. 'If Uncle Roddie died on the fourth of February in 1972, and Davey wasn't born until the fifteenth of December, that's . . .'

'Forty-four weeks,' says Willow. 'We counted.'

'That's . . .' I say and then I run out of steam. It's possible. If Auntie Rowan was newly pregnant when Uncle Roddie died and then the baby was late, later than they'd let a first pregnancy go nowadays . . . 'But why would Rowan pretend her husband was still alive?' I say. 'For four years. That's not denial. That's not grief . . . That's insane.'

'Is it?' says Albie. Barrett nods as if he understands the question. Maybe he does. Maybe they all do. Certainly, they're all staring at me as if I alone have missed something. I was used to that, being the youngest one, but it shouldn't happen here today with four kids and Gordo. I shouldn't be the baby, the straggler, missing the jokes and falling behind, even though I'm less than a year younger than . . .

'Ohhhhhhh!' I say. 'I see. I get it. Johnny. If Uncle Roddie died while Rowan was pregnant with her first son. He can't be the father of her second one. Is that it?'

'Oh, come on, Tabitha!' says Sorrel. 'Engage brain!'

'Yat!' says Barrett as if she's a sheepdog moving before the whistle. Uggy looks up, wondering if the scolding is for him. I didn't mind what Sorrel said.

'Think about it,' says Willow. 'Her husband dies. She doesn't tell anyone. She has a baby. She still doesn't tell anyone. She has another baby. Then she finally tells the world that her husband has died a couple of months back. And here are his ashes in a canister, except they're not.'

'You're saying Davey definitely isn't his either?' I can see how much more plausible that is and I can also feel something else too, something off to the side, that I've missed. 'Do you think Davey knew all along? Or do you think he found out ten years ago and that's what made him so angry with his mum?' It's the first hint of a motive. 'Because he was still calling me his cousin in his will and if all this is true we weren't cousins at all. We weren't anything.'

That vague feeling off to the side is getting closer now and sharper, as if I'm twisting the focus adjuster on a pair of binoculars, just about to feel the same leap of panic I used to get lying on the rough grass up the hill, twiddling the lenses after Davey handed them over to me. Every time I saw a deer or a grouse or a stranger suddenly right there in front of me, clear and close, I would feel the hitch in my chest. 'Atavism,' Davey called it, explaining that we evolved to avoid predators and we haven't had time to de-evolve just because of magnification. I shake the Davey memory out of my head. It's too confusing to let sweet moments like that drift in. I feel a flash of anger. No wonder I obsess on the unseen Moon family faces and the name of that damn cat, seeing as how I don't think anyone in my life ever told me straight who they were or what was going on.

'All the memories,' I say. 'I *remember* Uncle Roddie. And my dad. Only, I can't. I never questioned why Rowan worked so hard to make the four of us believe we remembered. But it's because planting memories is all there was, isn't it? He wasn't *there*.'

'He wasn't there,' Barrett says.

'It makes sense of a lot of things,' I say. 'Why she was so . . . rigid. So bloody clenched. Why she was so bothered about what people thought when there was no one there to think it.'

Except there was someone, wasn't there? Someone who thought plenty and usually said it too.

I stand up and slip out to the back hall, waving them all back from me as they threaten to follow. I take Davey's old sheepskin coat off the peg where it's been hanging for all the years I can remember, and I shove my feet into a pair of his wellies, short blue and yellow

ones, made for sailing; God knows why he had them because he
never so much as put out on the loch in a dinghy. None of us did,
too scared of what we'd see if we looked over the side. I wind his
scarf round my neck and over my head to keep the worst of the
weather off and let myself out the back door. Uggy has noticed
me moving. With a dog's instinct for the prospect of a walk, he
noses out in front of me and sits with his breath clouding the air,
waiting for me to decide which way to go.

The half-hearted day has given up completely. The sun is
already behind the hill and the temperature's going to keep dropping until it's full dark at five o'clock. I turn away from the water
and face into the teeth of a wind that's clattering down from the
top, bending the bare hawthorns into boomerangs, making my
eyes water and my nose stream. I pull Davey's scarf up over my
face and set myself into the hill at a sharper angle, wishing I
had a lead on Uggy so he could pull me. I'm tired out by the
howling and buffeting by the time I get into the playground and
I rest with my head against the stone for a minute.

Inside GIRLS, as I lift my awkward sheepskin arms to start
unwinding my scarf, I hear a cry. Beyond the inner doors, probably on her way back to the studio from a loo break or headed
for an early lunch, Zelda is standing frozen and wide-eyed, staring
at me with one hand clamped over her mouth. I shrug off the
coat as quick as I can, finish peeling the scarf away, then I go
to her.

'Mum? Did I give you a fright?'

She has lowered her hand and put it against the wall to steady
herself. 'What are you doing?' she says. 'In his coat, in his scarf,
wearing his boots. What were you thinking?'

It takes me five solid minutes to persuade her I meant no harm.
To turn her from this shaken, scolding thing back into my drawling
mother.

'I didn't know you believed in ghosts,' I say. 'How can you
live here if you believe in ghosts?'

'How could I not believe in ghosts, living here?' she snaps
back. I think about it for a moment: my dad, my uncle, Rowan,
and now Davey. She doesn't even know that Allison McCabe is
alive.

'I need to talk to you about Uncle Roddie,' I say to her, when
it looks as if she's going to go back into the studio and leave

me standing here. I expect her to take me into the staffroom, or even into the head's room, if the fire's already lit perhaps. But she sinks down on to one of the benches under the row of cubbyholes and looks up at me, more weary than I've ever seen her. 'About when he died.'

It seems to me that a shadow passes over her, or maybe it's just that her eyelids drop a little and it takes the light out of her eyes. I know how easily my eyes can lose their sparkle in photographs if I'm caught at the wrong angle. Those deep sockets she's got and passed on to me. Hooded eyes, Jo called them when she was being mean. They can be glamorous if you're lucky, cadaverous if you're not. 'She's got Bette Da-avis eyes,' Jo would sing at me. I took it all at face value. When she was ten, then twelve, her milkmaid looks were what the pretty girls in picture books and Disney films looked like and I agreed that she had won the prize. I hated looking like the wicked stepmother and Cruella de Vil. Now, when I think of her carefully made-up face at the funeral, I can see that she was always trying to get her eyes to look more like mine.

'Are you listening?' Zelda says.

'Yes,' I blurt. 'No, sorry. I was thinking about taking after you. And Jo taking after Dad. And Davey taking after Auntie Rowan. And that leaves Johnny.'

'Leaves him?' says Zelda. 'What do you mean "leaves" him?'

But I don't know what I mean so I say sorry again and tell her I'll listen if she starts over.

'When Roddie died,' she tells me, 'I had rather a lot on my mind, if you remember. Rather more, in fact, than I've ever told you.'

'No,' I say. 'Sorry. I know I said I would listen, but that's not what I mean. I don't mean I want to talk about that time we've been saying is when Roddie died.' Her eyes widen enough to let the overhead light catch them again, so they flash at me. 'I mean I want to talk about when it was that Uncle Roddie actually died. Because it wasn't then. It was much earlier than that. Mum, did you really not know?'

'Did I really not know what?' she says. She's trying for her usual self but she's failing badly.

I want to shake her and so, to stop myself, I walk backwards and let myself sink down on to the pee-in-a stool.

'Did you really never wonder why you hadn't seen Uncle Roddie for all those years?' I say. 'You can't have seen him at the hospital when Davey was born, or when Johnny was born. You never gave him a lift down to the town or caught sight of him when you went to borrow a cup of sugar.'

'What are you talking about?' Zelda says. She's looking me straight in the face and she sounds sincere, but she can't be. Can she?

'Mum,' I say. 'Uncle Roddie died before Dad. Years before Dad.'

She casts about for her next move. I see her do it, glancing from side to side, her mind going like a hamster in new bedding.

'I asked weeks ago if you were in touch with your doctor, Tabitha,' she settles for at last. 'And you didn't answer me. Or do you have a *key worker*?' Her mouth twists as she says it. 'Someone you can call as-and-when?'

'Don't dismiss me!' I say. 'Mum, we've downloaded a copy of his death certificate. He was dead for years before Auntie Rowan finally told us. *Years.*'

'That doesn't seem at all likely.'

'You know what doesn't seem likely?' I say. 'That you could have been watching out the window for cops and doctors arriving to deal with Dad, and never catch sight of them coming to deal with Uncle Roddie too. How would we have missed the coming and going down at the house? Up here at the school it felt like a hundred people a day trooping in and out. And that was when he didn't even die here. If Roddie had died in the house, how could we miss all the investigation and the clearing up? Look at the amount of people who came when Davey died!'

'Oh, everything's more fussed over these days,' she says. 'Endless boxes to be ticked and forms to be filled.'

'It was the Seventies,' I insist. 'Not the dark ages.'

'Well, then it was the Seventies *whichever* year he died,' she says. 'Why didn't we know, no matter when it was?'

That's a good question and it stumps me. 'February, 1972,' I say. 'What was going on then? Is there any reason you were distracted? Away from Hiskith? Could you have missed officials rolling up to deal with Roddie dying?'

There's no mistaking the flash in her eyes this time.

'What?' I say.

'It was an Olympics year,' she says.

But she's not fooling me that easy. 'Come off it,' I say.

'But it's as you say, Tabitha. We were up here, the four of us, no children yet. We had only just moved in and we saw one another most days. I don't see how any such thing could have happened without us noticing, except for when it did. When your father's death was consuming us all and we missed the other tragedy.'

She has half-convinced me. 'I did wonder if maybe it was dealt with quietly because he was a local lad and no one wanted to upset the family. Only they went a bit too far the other way.'

'No one such as who?' says Zelda. 'The village police? The locals? Kirkconnel? Hardly. They'd have had a field day just to spite us.'

That sounds unlikely to me. I always reckoned this famous animosity Kirkconnel is supposed to harbour for the Muirs of Hiskith was half Zelda's delusion and half Rowan's paranoia. So the two brothers moved out and didn't go to work in the factory? So what?

'But then *that's* true no matter when, isn't it?' I say. 'The police wouldn't have spared you upset when Dad died either. So there's no reason not to accept that Roddie died when his death certificate says he did.'

'And why exactly would Rowan tell such a monstrous lie?'

'Seriously?' I say. It's hypocritical after how long it took the penny to drop into me, but it's different: I was a baby. I can't believe she doesn't know already, or at least suspect. She's staring at me. 'Because she had two children to explain away.'

She frowns.

'Do you see what this means? Uncle Roddie wasn't Davey's father. He couldn't be. Or Johnny's, obviously.'

Suddenly it seems to have got colder and darker. I've been so obsessed with Davey: what Davey knew; what Davey learned; whether Davey had a motive for the thing he said he did. I haven't spared a thought for . . .

'Johnny,' I say. 'Oh my God, Mum. Johnny! If Uncle Roddie isn't Johnny's dad then Jo and Johnny aren't cousins.'

She stares at me in silence for a long time. 'Then one has to ask oneself,' she says at last, 'what the hell Rowan was doing up here before the wedding, screeching like a fishwife, demanding

that I stop it, offering to pay Jo off. Threatening. Bellowing.'
She pats her smock pocket looking for her baccy tin and papers.

'I don't know,' I say. 'It doesn't make any sense.' I feel like
I've been saying that all day.

Zelda lifts her chin and stares down her nose at me.

'Well, then there must be a mistake in the paperwork. Of
course, Roddie died when we all know he died. Of course there's
not some ridiculous ancient secret that you've cracked by down-
loading some silly digital nonsense. It's all keyed in by exhausted
contract workers in Mumbai being paid per entry and cutting
corners.'

'No secrets?' I say. 'No *secrets*? Mum, I think Davey
killed . . .' But I can't say it. 'A dog. And buried it, and pretended
it drowned.'

'Buried it in his garden?' Zelda's voice is like a wisp of smoke
trembling in a breeze. 'Have you dug it up? Are you searching
for it?'

'No,' I say.

'Well, don't,' she says. 'Don't go digging in Davey's garden.
Promise me.'

'I'm only guessing that's where she's buried,' I say. 'But how
else would he get rid of it? Maybe it's out on the hill. On the
moor. But the ground's so hard there and the soil's so thin.'

Zelda has put her hands on her elbows as if she's trying to
hug herself or as if – I see this when she starts rocking – as if
she's soothing a baby. 'Oh God,' she says. 'God help me. When
will it ever end?'

'What's wrong?' I say. And then I'm sure I know. 'Mum, when
Auntie Rowan died, that weekend when she died, you don't
remember a dog barking, do you?'

But she's looking at me with eyes so blank it's as if there's a
film over them. I don't think she heard me. 'There's nothing but
tarmac here, you see,' she says in that same small voice. I have
no idea why she's telling me that, as if I didn't know. 'So I grow
my herbs in pots and I grow my tomatoes in barrels.' I know all
this. I have no clue why she's saying it. Or what it's got to do
with Bess.

'I've never told you,' she says. 'I've never told anyone. Promise
me you'll keep it secret if I tell you now'.

If I wasn't already on the pee-in-a stool I'd have to sit down now. Zelda doesn't share confidences. Or insecurities. She doesn't ask for promises.

'I had a miscarriage,' she says. 'Late. I laboured. And afterwards I buried . . .' She stops talking and works her mouth for a while as if she's got something stuck in a tooth and needs to dislodge it discreetly. 'I buried . . . him' – she takes a gasping breath – 'in the garden of the schoolhouse. Under a rose. That beautiful yellow rose by the bottom gate.'

'Oh Mum,' I say, standing and going over to her. When she puts her hand out I assume she's going to push me away but she grasps mine and pulls me close to her. 'I'm so sorry,' I say softly into her hair, as I kiss her parting. Her scalp smells of smoke and paint and the same faintly sulphureous tang my own oily hair gets if I leave it too long between washings. '*Why* didn't you tell anyone though? Do you *mean* "anyone"? Didn't you even tell Dad?'

She jerks her head up so hard that I catch the tip of my tongue between my teeth and feel blood in my mouth. 'What are you talking about?' she says. 'How could I tell your father? Your father was dead. Your father was gone.'

'So . . . whose baby was it?' I say.

'What do you mean?' she says again. 'Why would you ask me that?'

I stare back at her, feeling my reason start to fray. Dead men can't be fathers. What is she trying to tell me. 'When, Mum?' I ask her. 'When were you pregnant?'

'Then,' she says. 'It was then.'

'And what made you miscarry?'

'That,' she says. 'It was that. I lost my son and my husband that day but I saved y—' She stops herself but it's too late. I back away, stumbling over my own feet, and sink down, missing the stool and keeping going until I'm crouched on the floor with my back against the wall and my knees at my ears.

'You were pregnant *then*? When he died? When you dived down and got me out? And you—?'

'I didn't *dive*,' she says. 'Good God, I'm not reckless enough to go head-first, Tabitha. I scrambled my way down there and scrambled my way back. And it wasn't saving *you* that did it. It wasn't physical. It was the horror of *him*. You have to believe me. You can't be silly about it after all these years.'

'But then why didn't you tell me?' I say, my voice rising in a wail as pain and guilt sweep through me.

'You were a baby, darling,' she says. 'And your daddy took you with him to die. What kind of mother would have told you about a brother?'

'But why did you tell me *that*?' I said. 'Why did you tell me *anything*?'

'Not this again!' she exclaims. 'I didn't tell you, Tabitha. I told you a thousand times that I didn't tell you.'

'But then how do I know?'

'Rowan told you. Out of sheer viciousness, because why should she be upset alone if she could hurt someone else. I was so furious with her. But it was too late by then. Little jugs with big ears.'

'I don't remember Auntie Rowan telling me that,' I say. 'I don't remember finding out. I don't remember not knowing. I can't make any sense of what I knew and didn't, what I remember and can't, what happened when or why or . . . or anything.'

'Lucky you,' Zelda says. 'I wouldn't mind some hazy memories. I wouldn't complain if some of this clarity departed.'

I've never felt sorry for Zelda before today, strange as that sounds. She was married to a man who was off his head, widowed young, had one child elope and another lose her marbles, lived up here with only Auntie Rowan for company, when they hated each other, was judged and smirked about every time she showed her face anywhere else, but still I didn't pity her. She was too bull-headed about her art, too canny about her licences, too scathing about everyone else's shortcomings.

I feel awash with pity now. I forgive her the self-absorption that let her believe Uncle Roddie was reclusive, when in fact he was long gone. I forgive her for not paying attention to Jo and Johnny's plan to marry, paying even less to Auntie's Rowan's 'screeching' which we now know was bogus, designed only to make the lovebirds act like the cousins she pretended they were. I forgive her letting me sink into illness until I was on that ward.

She'd lost a baby, late enough to know it was a son. Late enough to labour. I've never had worse than a missed period when we were trying and even that grief held me like a vice.

'Are you going to be OK?' I say after the silence has stretched so thin it's frozen.

'I?' she says. She sounds like herself again. Ninety-nine people out of a hundred would have said 'me'. 'I'll be fine as soon as I get back to work. I'm doing something quite new. It's artistically challenging and I expect it to be financially rewarding too. Not that I let those concerns sway me, as you know.'

As I hear, I think. As you insist repeatedly. 'Yes,' I say. 'You told me.'

I leave her to it, picking up Uggy from the playground on my way and heading down the hill to my packed houseful. I need to work out how I can ask for a day off them visiting me. When I invite Jo and Johnny to tell them the news, it needs to be just us three.

TWENTY-THREE

Tabitha

It works out perfectly, mostly because Albie won't hear of Davey Day. He reckons someone who killed his own mother shouldn't be celebrated and it's hard to argue. Except that it's still hard to believe Davey did it. It's hard to believe any of this happened, from Auntie Rowan and her secret fancy man in the Seventies to the bomb at the dam a couple of months back. From my dad taking me with him as he drowned, to my mum grieving her husband and her son and doing both alone. But I can't think about that for too long because when I do it claws at me like a nameless cartoon cat.

So. Albie decides he wants a real Christmas tree and the McCabes are planning to decorate Gordo's wee house to within an inch of its life too. Barrett says he can get a trade discount at a tree farm down by New Abbey where he swears the spruces are so fresh there won't be a single needle on the carpet by Twelfth Night. And off they go. Quietly, Barrett tells me that he's going to let the girls decorate his house because he can read the signals coming from Portugal and he reckons his ex and her newbie are planning to stay there until the new year.

'She texted me and told me about some midnight ritual with baked fish,' he says. 'Like I care. First time it's not been pure admin since the split. You wait, Tabby. The next text'll be they've been given a pair of tickets for it. Then it'll go down well with the mayor if they show their faces.'

'That's France though, isn't it?' I say. 'Where the mayor rubber stamps deeds and planning?'

'Aye well,' says Barrett. 'Star-gazey pie's flipping Cornwall. She never did bother to get her stories ready before she served them.' He glances behind himself to make sure the girls can't hear any of this. They're in the old scullery just inside the back door, where they've decreed Davey would store his 'Xmas Dex' if he had them, alongside the ladders and half-used paint tins, the toolbox he kept so neat and orderly, the windbreaks and deckchairs I remember from trips to the Solway when we were all still together. There was so much stuff to get four kids and two adults through from mid-morning till the sun went down and the chippy started calling. We were happy, it seems to me as I remember it now. Two widows, two kids who barely knew their father, and two kids – it turns out – who didn't know their father at all. But still we were happy. I decide I'll remind Jo and Johnny of the good times before I drop the bomb.

I'm watching out the big back bedroom window for the Range Rover half an hour before they said they'd be arriving. Or maybe it's nearer the truth to say I watch Barrett's car leaving with Albie on board and then I stay put looking out at the rain. It's another filthy day. There are crows trying to fly in it, struggling against chaotic gusts, looking like broken umbrellas. I don't know why they can't take shelter and wait it out. Maybe they're migrating and the call of the murder is too strong to resist, the thought of flying all the way down to Africa alone too unthinkable. Or wherever it is they're going. Davey would know.

When I see a tiny little lime-green car, the size of a fridge magnet crest the top and start its descent, I think we're just as bad as the stubborn crows. Someone decided last night they were coming up Hiskith today and this torrential rain hasn't stopped them. I hope they get back down. I don't like the look of the track, starting to run all the way across instead of just down the sides like it does from October to April. It's more like a stream with a pebble bed now, than a wet road, and I can tell from the swathes of shadow that the grit and rocks are moving where the water's nudging them. Soon there'll be a beach at the steep turn, gravel as deep as the snow gets when the wind drifts it, and the track itself will be pure mud. Fine for us who know to keep two wheels on the verge, where the grass roots anchor the grit, but no way the driver of that fridge magnet will think of it.

And actually, I don't like the look of the verges either. They're getting a sheen on them, as they saturate. I should go through to the front and check the car park. The last thing I need when I'm trying to talk to Jo and Johnny is some clueless dog walker chapping my door because her car's floating away. It could be even worse: she could be an angler. Or a rambler. Someone glad of any excuse to bend my ear about draining or restocking. Someone eager to gossip about the explosion, share the theories that are still swirling on the message boards.

As I turn to go though, I see the little car slowing, long before the bottom of the track. It's stopping right here at Davey's gate, two wheels on the verge, two wheels on the track as if the driver knows exactly what to do up here in the winter. Then the door opens and it's Johnny. And the other door opens and it's Jo.

'Where's the Range Rover?' I shout as I caw them in from the back door. 'Did that wee thing get up the brae OK?'

'That wee thing's got four-wheel drive and a lower centre of gravity,' Johnny says. He's probably trying to get out of the weather but he brushes past me as if he's making a point – that this was his house once and it's only mine now because he said so. I'm forced to step back and press myself into the wall out of his way. Jo makes an apologetic grimace as she scoots past in his wake.

'The kitchen will probably be most . . .' I start to say, but Johnny has already made his decision and he's headed for the living room. It's clear now but still far from comfortable and the fire's not lit so the air's damp. He looks around with an unreadable expression on his face. Is *he* remembering happier times? My plan to bring up seaside trips has withered inside me.

'Can I put the kettle on?' I say.

'Thanks. That—' Jo begins but he cuts her off.

'Can you just give us whatever it is you want to give us and let us get going?'

'Give you?' I say, stupidly. I run over what I'd texted and I can't think why he'd assume I'm giving them anything.

'Or else why couldn't this be a phone call?' says Johnny. 'What have you found? In your archeological dig.'

It's news to me that he's been told about the hoarding. Maybe Zelda mentioned it to Jo at the funeral. 'Noth—' I say. 'Well, plenty but nothing for you to worry about.' I glance at Jo. 'I wish you'd let me make you some tea. Or . . . what's the earliest you've ever started drinking, barring Christmas Day? Because I need to tell you something and it's going to be quite a shock. So prepare yourselves.'

That's got them. Johnny stops looking annoyed and goes still, watching me as if I'm a snake charmer. I find myself choosing the furthest away chair. Charmed snakes still strike sometimes, don't they? I smile at Jo, but she's watching me pretty avidly too so I decide to fix my gaze on the wall in between them before I start talking.

But where *do* I start? I wish I knew if Jo would never have wanted kids no matter what or if she decided not to chance it because of the cousin problem. Only, why wouldn't they have adopted, or used a donor, if that was all that was stopping them? Marrying your cousin is legal after all and so surely the agencies couldn't have penalized them for it. 'Creepy' isn't a good reason to deny a child a happy home. Even if the family resemblance makes this case extra-weird.

I catch my thoughts as they start to spin this same old nonsense. Because of course Jo and Johnny don't actually – *can't* actually – have a family resemblance, can they? They're not related. It's just that they're both pigs. Or maybe Auntie Rowan only chanced it because her fancy man looked a bit like her husband. Her late husband. I've got to gird myself and tell them.

'Albie,' I begin, 'has been looking into our family tree.' It seems a mild enough start but, unless I'm mistaken, both of them lose a bit of colour, Jo from behind her blusher and Johnny from his whole bare face. 'And here's the thing. Uncle Roddie . . . Your dad, Johnny . . . wasn't . . .'

'Wasn't . . .?' Johnny says. 'Wasn't what?'

I take a huge breath and say the rest of it in one long, smooth coil of words as if I've swallowed an eel but now it's coming back out again. 'I think when you said you were going to get married Auntie Rowan went ballistic not because you were cousins, but because you're not, genetically speaking. I think she went ballistic because she was scared the truth was going to come out and everyone would know and she'd be shamed, which sounds old fashioned but there's no other way to account for it, because she knew the truth, didn't she?'

For a moment neither of them says anything.

'Uncle Roddie died before we thought he did. Sorry, Johnny, I mean your dad. I don't think he was Davey's father either. I know this must seem completely mad, because you think you remember him. But *I* think I remember him too and I definitely don't. I can't. We all just remember what we've been told about when we were tiny. And I'm sorry but Roddie was dead and you can't be his son. So I know it's a shock, but it's good news in a way, isn't it? Because you're not cousins. And, Jo, maybe it's not too late. You're only forty-three and that's nothing these days.'

I wonder if I've gone too far, even for a sister. But she doesn't look angry or upset. She looks like I remember her looking, amused, torn between affection and scorn. She's looking at me the way she looked at me when I couldn't tie bows in my shoe-laces so I tried to glue them together. When I didn't understand a dirty joke so I laughed in the wrong place, way before the punchline.

'Too late?' she says. 'Too late for an adorable little baby all of my own? So I can be just like you?'

I don't know what to say to her. I can't understand what she thinks is funny.

'We know we're not cousins,' she goes. 'We thought we were until Rowan came up the brae like a fiend from the depths of hell to stop us getting married.'

'She told you?' I say. 'But so what was the problem then? I remember her screaming her head off. I'd never heard her in a state like it. Not even when we felt-tipped the wallpaper.'

'Oh come on, Tabitha,' Johnny says. 'Get a clue.'

'Go and make that tea,' Jo says. 'Give yourself a bit of thinking time.'

'I don't understand,' I said.

'Are you still on the happy pills?' says Johnny. 'Because you might want to take a look at the dosage.'

'Don't be a prick,' says Jo. 'Tabby, if Uncle Roddie wasn't the boys' father, cast your mind back. Rowan's living up here, middle of nowhere, doesn't work, not much of a one for clubs and societies. And anyone that drives up and parks at her gate is going to be seen by her darling sister-in-law. So how does she manage to have two babies?'

I shrug. That's the thing about a taboo. When it's working properly it makes itself unthinkable.

'OK, try this,' Jo says. 'We were all too young to remember that Uncle Roddie wasn't there. Davey wasn't four and you were a baby. And Mum is . . . Mum, right? Away with the paintbrush fairies. But how do you think Auntie Rowan could have hidden a missing brother from Dad?'

'But she must have,' I said. 'Otherwise Dad would have known.

And he didn't. Wait! Are you saying that that's why Dad killed himself? Because he found out? Oh my God, Jo! Is that what happened? It was the other way round? Roddie didn't kill himself because his brother died? Dad killed *him*self because *Roddie* died? Because Roddie had been dead for years and Dad hadn't questioned it? Was it guilt? Grief? Like a brainstorm? Oh, Jesus. Our poor dad. He should have phoned the doctor and got himself some help. He could have weathered it. He could have gone for a break somewhere and had some therapy and got over it. Couldn't he?'

Jo's face is all scorn now, no affection left anywhere. Johnny looks as if he's only just managing not to laugh at me.

'What?' I say.

'Our poor dad,' he says, mimicking me for some reason, mocking me for some reason. 'Our. Poor. Dad.' It slides into focus for the briefest moment and then slides back out again, like I'm back to Davey's binoculars again. And also there's a memory of the daily morning group on the intake ward, me asking everyone about their families and the nurse telling me to stop it because I wasn't the only one with 'issues around close relationships' and I had to be a good member of the group and learn to be gentle with the rest of them, walk carefully around their tender spots. I remember feeling this very same sickness and telling the nurse I had inherited a genetic propensity to mental ill health. It was my brain chemistry. It was nothing to do with relationships and everything to do biology. I told her that. And she nodded and smiled, walking carefully around the tender spots I was busy telling her were non-existent.

'I'm going to put her out of her misery,' Jo says, and I turn to check that she doesn't mean it literally. This day has become such a hall of mirrors – another day in Funtown, I hear Elspeth whisper to me – if Jo had picked up the poker or found a cricket bat somewhere I wouldn't even have gasped. 'What Auntie Rowan told Mum,' she goes on, 'at the top of her voice, in quite a small house, where you were wide awake, Tabitha, was that Johnny isn't my cousin, like Davey wasn't your cousin. What she told us is that they're our brothers.'

It slides back into focus and this time it clicks.

There goes the story of my life. As it leaves it chuckles like a shingle beach when the tide goes out. Garfield and . . .?

'Yes,' I said. 'I know. You're right. She did. I heard her. I knew.' I pause. 'And then I didn't. And now I do again.' I need a longer pause. 'Oh shit, I knew! That's what I was running away from, isn't it? That's why I lost my marbles? That's why I can't remember the wedding and I wasn't there when you came back for that tea.'

'Tea?' says Johnny. 'What the fuck are you dredging that up for?'

Why is he so angry?

'And why the fuck would you go off your trolley when it was Jo and me who wanted to get married?'

I stare at him. Why would I? Why did I?

'Are you going to be all right?' Jo says.

But how can I answer her? After the creak of the focus adjuster and the click of the truth, all the stories draining away, now there's a cloud of bluebottles in my head, or maybe it's a flock of ravens. Whatever they are, they whirl as if I'm a tornado . . . I am holding on to the edge of the chair so I'm not swept up into the air and turned to confetti. How come? I ask myself. Why am I not drowning?

'Did Davey know?' I say, finally, after I've been breathing a while and all the crows and bluebottles have flown off again. I'm still on dry land, I note.

'Why?' says Johnny. 'Do you think that's what he meant by "any of this"?' I must frown because he goes on. 'In the note, on the will, like you told me. Well, you showed me. "Tabby, you didn't deserve any of this". You think that's what he meant?'

Jo is glaring at him but he's so intent on me he doesn't notice.

'I don't think so,' I say, casting my mind back to when I read those words. That's not exactly what it said. Close enough though. 'I assumed he meant was I didn't deserve what Scott did to me. Losing my job and my house. Losing my son, like I was going to until I moved in here.'

'Right,' says Johnny. 'Shit. Of course. That makes much more sense.' And now he does glance at Jo, and he shrinks under the look she's still firing at him. 'What?' he says, managing to get a bit of umbrage going anyway.

'Way to bring it all back up again,' Jo says.

'Bring what?' I say. 'It had to be the Scott stuff. The rest of it happened to everyone, not just me.'

And then, finally and yet suddenly, I see. I see what Johnny blundered into. I see why Jo is glaring at him. I see it all as if I'm a bird, or a drone anyway, looking down at a whole landscape laid out beneath me. I see everything that's there: the pale ribbon of road; the dark smudge of trees; the white dots of sheep. And I see what's always been hidden too. The water's nothing when you're up above it looking down. I can see clean through it to the rooftops and garden walls below its surface. I can see the missing bit of the track. It doesn't disappear and reappear at all. It's there to be followed.

'Tabitha?' Jo's voice comes from a long way away.

'One of the nurses,' I say. I take a deep breath as if I've used up a whole lungful even to say that much. 'One of the nurses once asked me why my cousins getting married was such a bombshell. And I knew she had it wrong.'

'Because you thought we were sibs,' says Jo. 'Because Rowan screeched it at us.'

'But Johnny's right,' I say. 'Why would that be bad enough to put me on a locked ward? It's shocking and creepy and I still can't get my head round it but it's not a nightmare. Not like the other things Rowan told me that night. Screeched, like you said. Not like the fact, that whether my dad had two kids, as I thought up till then, or four, like I was hearing for the first time, he only took one with him when he decided to die.'

'Oh, Tabby,' says Jo, and it's a voice I haven't heard her use since she came back. It's my sister speaking.

'But at least I only hurt myself,' I say. '*Did* Davey know all along? That we're brothers and sisters. Because if he didn't, and then he found out, that might make sense of why he did what *he* did.'

'Why he killed himself?' says Johnny.

I swear on the life of everyone I love, I'm not thinking when I say what I say next. I don't mean to be cruel. If I wasn't reeling I'd never have let it slip out of me. 'Why he killed Rowan,' I say.

Strangely enough, it's Jo who stands up and runs out of the room, straight out of the house and away. I can hear her feet smacking on the wet path and scattering the gravel. Johnny stays where he is, slowly changing into an effigy of himself as the words sink in.

'I'm so sorry,' I say. 'I am so, so sorry. He told me in a letter that he left at the lawyer's office along with the keys and the deeds and all that.'

'He confessed to killing our mum?'

I nod.

'Did you believe him?'

I open my mouth but he deserves a better answer than *I can't but I must but I can't*. It's exhausting even to be thinking it. 'I do,' I say. 'He had a motive, if he found out Rowan's secret. He had the opportunity. He had the means. He confessed. He killed himself. There's no reason to doubt it's true.'

Johnny says nothing.

'I didn't know, the day he died,' I go on. I hate the sound of my voice, justifying myself, pleading with him to absolve me. 'When you said you didn't mind about the house and you didn't want a share of the estate, I didn't know then. And afterwards, when I found out, all I thought about was that Albie could live here. I didn't think of you.'

Finally, Johnny comes to life again. He looks up at me, frowning and says, 'What?'

'Because it wasn't legal for him to inherit the house in the first place,' I say. 'Benefitting from his crime. So he couldn't leave it to me. I can't own it. It's yours.' And so I'll go back to Scott and take Albie with me. And we'll both forget what we've said and carry on.

'Are you sure about that?' Johnny says. 'The legal bit.'

'Barrett and Gordo agree with me.'

'Who?' he says. And then: 'The witnesses to the will. Right?'

His recall of that will is astonishing. But maybe it's burned into his brain because of the day. He had just identified his brother's body. Not everyone is like me, dumping months' worth of memories when they get a shock. Not everyone's life story is full of holes from where they've ripped bits out.

'Right,' I say. 'The friends whose names are on the will.'

Johnny puts his head on one side. 'That's a weird way to put it.'

I consider coming clean. I consider telling him that the witness signatures are forged and so the will is a fake and that's yet another reason I never had a claim on this house or the chance of a new life. Then I remember what I've just discovered. If

Davey was my brother, same as he was Johnny's brother, why shouldn't I keep this place that no one else needs? This place where I've somehow bedded myself into so deep that I can hardly remember the years in my neat villa with Scott and the double garage and the acres of beige carpet to live my beige life on.

'Are you happy, Johnny?' I find myself asking, needing the reassurance. 'Knowing what you know. Knowing you shouldn't make a family together.'

'We're happy our two selves,' Johnny says. 'So that's not an issue, thank God. Tabby, I've loved her my whole life, as long as I can remember, and she's loved me. It's only here that it feels weird for us. It's only at Hiskith it feels wrong. That's why we never came back.'

I didn't know it was their decision, after that tea. I always thought Rowan banished them.

'That's why,' Johnny goes on, 'we won't be back again after today.'

I nod. I get it. Hiskith is different. Zelda has always said it's the only place she could thrive. And look at how Gordo and Barrett keep coming back and bringing their children. No matter what horrors resurface, they can't stay away.

'You could come and see *us* sometimes,' Johnny's saying. 'Or meet Jo in town, for lunch. Pictures. Nails.' He knows he's bumbling, trying to imagine what two sisters would do together for fun. He doesn't seem to mind that I'm smiling at him.

'I'll phone her,' I say, knowing this will never happen.

'Speaking of,' says Johnny, getting to his feet. 'I better go and check on her.'

We say our goodbyes and I watch him make his way over to the gate, to where the little lime-green car is steaming up from Jo's breath. Despite everything, there's a bounce in his step and a sort of brio in the way he swings the gate open. He looks as relieved as I am.

TWENTY-FOUR

Barrett

He had offered exterior installation for a couple of years, stringing LED icicles over gable ends and making sure wire reindeer were securely anchored on front lawns, but it was awkward work, usually in filthy weather, and going round taking it all down again in the pits of January was even worse. So it's been a while and he expected to find choosing three trees in the rain tiresome. Maybe it's the kids' enthusiasm infecting him, but he's enjoying it even now three's turned into seven and Willow and Sorrel won't commit until they've seen every specimen from every angle. His fingers are stuck together with pine sap and there's rain and needles up both sleeves from him lifting his arm to twirl the trees round and round.

When Tabitha phones him, he hands over the task to Gordo and goes to shelter under the corrugated awning where the netter's waiting.

'What's up?' he says and then doesn't speak again for a full minute as Tabby pours the news, raw and ragged, into his ear.

'My mum knew,' she says, at last. 'She's known for twenty-five years that a brother and sister are married to each other. I want to go up there and shake her till she rattles. Or else change my phone number and change the locks on all these doors and brick up the back windows and buy a four-wheel drive and come and go on the forestry track to Muirkirk so I never see her again.'

'Shoosh, shoosh now,' Barrett says, as if he's soothing one of the girls after a nightmare. 'Calm down, Tabby. You're OK. They're harming no one. Put it out of your mind.'

'Of course I'm OK,' she says. '*I'm* fine! I'm better than ever, because I've just finally worked out what happened to me when I was fifteen. *You* know this, Barrett. You know how much it means to have things make sense at last. Even if it's shit, a good sniff works like smelling salts. I'm finally OK!'

'Great,' he says. 'Good point, well made.'

'Only, I've just told Johnny I think his brother killed his mum. I just blurted it out. And I don't think he even took it in. He said it didn't change anything. About me keeping the house. But maybe when he calms down again, and tells Jo – she rushed out; she wasn't here – maybe he'll think twice and I'll be homeless. And then I'll—'

'Hush now,' he says again. 'Try to stay calm. We'll be back soon and we can talk it all through.'

'You're definitely coming up?' she says. 'The track's bad.'

'If I can get this pair to make a decision about these bloody trees!' Barrett says, trying to cheer her up. 'They all look the same when they're covered in tinsel.'

And, because she manages a tiny chuckle, he's feeling pretty good when he hangs up and goes to re-join the party.

He's feeling even better by the time they're headed home with seven trees and enough wreaths and swags and bunches of mistletoe to open a grotto. She phoned *him*. Not Albie and not . . . anyone else. He doesn't let the name 'Gordo' take shape in his thoughts, but he finds himself, if not singing along to the carols on their app, then at least tapping his thumbs on the steering wheel and nodding. They've a way with them, these girls of his. Willow has called Albie, set the call to video, then propped her phone on the dashboard, so the two carloads of kids chat and laugh all the way.

They drop off one tree at Gordo's. Barrett doesn't think Allison and her mother are there; the house has got that cold, unlit look about it. Still, when Gordo comes back out and climbs into the driver's seat of Tabby's car, he looks as if something happened in the two minutes he was inside. Barrett watches him in the rear-view mirror for a moment and wonders whether he could take the phone off speaker and ask what's wrong, but then 'Santa Baby' comes on iTunes and he hasn't the heart to interrupt them.

They're three trees lighter again after he leaves the big one and one for each of the girls' bedrooms propped at his own back door. The rain is torrential now and they'll be a bugger to dry off before he can take them in but at least they'll be clean and it'll help them stay fresh. Barrett doesn't understand the point of a real tree indoors but then he's not much for house plants at any time of year. He's had to train himself to appreciate a load of pots messing up a patio, same as a load of bushes draping over the edge of the lawn. If it was up to him, he'd have green stripes and rows of veg at one end. He keeps all of these preferences hidden from his customers, his daughters (Jeez, Dad!) and now from Tabitha too as she starts to take over Davey's garden. Davey knew. He'd watch to see what Barrett made of him mowing round vetch in his grass until it had finished flowering. He never said anything, but the quiet smile told Barrett everything. The quiet nod Barrett gave the smile told Davey everything back. This is how men are friends, closer and warmer with every unspoken thought.

Barrett is struggling with memories like that one now. They keep surfacing and they've got teeth. There were so many secrets, such an iceberg mass under Davey's smiles and the few eccentricities he allowed to show. Murder? Suicide? Bombing? Barrett's been so busy making sure Tabitha is coping, and watching to check that Gordo doesn't go under with the new weight on *his* shoulders, he hasn't admitted the state he's in himself. Of course, if he let a peep about it out to the girls they'd be all over it like a rash. They'd have him reading books and filling in quizzes, they'd have the house full of scented candles and life coaches yammering in his ear when he was trying to sleep. It's not going to happen.

But he can admit to being glad it's nearly Christmas. Load of nonsense he'd have said any other year – *has* said, *every* other year – but it's what he needs right now. The lights and ribbons, the terrible music and the sachets of mulled-wine flavour to put in your coffee, the hairbands with antlers and the glittery jumpers – he'll take all of it. He half wishes it would snow like it does on the films the girls are watching every afternoon. Or maybe it's the same film over and over again. He couldn't swear to it either way. He's even been stockpiling the kind of presents he thinks will go with this orgy of fake, American cheer, particularly proud of the flannel pyjamas he's got hidden away: red ones with Santas for Willow and blue ones with polar bears for Sorrel. Secretly he's got a third pair, pale grey with pine trees, and if they don't laugh he's going to wear them.

What he wants to organize next is the day itself. He can just see Tabitha and the mad old bat sitting together with a capon, Gordo at the mercy of Mrs McCabe – she looks the sort to buy it all in trays for the microwave. Barrett is glossing over his own 'pierce film and stir' years. He's going to cook a stuffed turkey this year if he has to stay up all night to do it. And he's thinking if he buys one outlandishly big he can use that as a lever to make sure they all get together. After the year it's been, anything else would be wrong.

'Dad?'

He knows it's not the first time she's spoken. She's got that look of suppressed hilarity on her face. He supposes he's glad they find him entertaining. Sorrel's smirking too.

'Will?' he says.

'Have you heard a word we've been saying? Are you zoned out? Are you safe to drive?'

They're a year off their provisional licences (thank God!) so they don't know about muscle memory and using your brain for other things while you drive safely. The truth is he's been miles away in his own head all the way up from the town, past the allotments, past the farm, on to the smaller road, over the grid on to the track. He doesn't bother trying to tell them.

'What is it?' he settles for instead.

'Ollybobs is texting from the other car.'

'Does he know you call him that?'

'His dad picked up the post when he dropped off the tree and gave it to him to hold.' Willow steams on as if Barrett hasn't spoken.

'He's opened it.' Sorrel is reading off her phone. Barrett assumes it's 'text one text all' and briefly he wishes he knew how to set that up for Gordo and Tabitha. He'll brave the scorn and get the girls to show him.

'It's from the DNA place,' Willow says.

'Tell him not to speak to Gordo about this while he's driving,' Barrett says. 'If it's bad news.' He's looking in the rear-view mirror again. The car behind is trundling along at a steady speed, no weaving.

'It's good news,' Willow says. 'Ninety-nine point nine-nine. Father and son. So that's nice, eh?'

Barrett feels the relief wash through him like an aspirin shudder.

'And plus,' Willow says, 'Bobsie hit the wrong button, *he claims*. So, as well as the cheek swabs for him and Gordo, he got these acid-free envelopes for hair and nails too. Eww, right? Right.'

'And so,' Sorrel says, 'he put hair and nails in them and sent the whole lot off. Cost double but Gordo didn't know he'd saved the card details because, you know: boomer.'

'Gordo is twenty-nine,' Barrett says. He's a bit proud that he knows what a boomer is, which he supposes proves he is one. 'I don't know what you're saying. Did they check for drugs or something?' It's the only way he can think of that hair and nails could cause an upset.

'Da-ad! Not *his* hair and *Gordo*'s nails!'

'Not *Gordo*'s hair and *his* nails! What would be the point of that?'

Barrett thinks now that he can see the opening to the path this is leading down. 'What then?' he says anyway.

'One of Dead Davey's hairs from his gross comb that's still in the bathroom. Ewww.'

'And Albie's nail that he clipped off and dropped in the glassine baggie. Still ewwww, by the way. But a great way to triple check that Roddie wasn't Davey's dad. Because if he was, Albie and Davey would be related. And if he wasn't, they wouldn't be.'

Barrett, after the phone call from Tabitha, knows exactly what's coming. Davey and Albie are closer relations than they should be. Uncle and nephew. 'None of this stuff is one hundred per cent, you know.' They're almost at the house now, over the second cattle grid and just about to crest the top. He's hoping the ridge will shelter them from the worst of the wind. It's tiring to drive with the rain lashing this hard, and it feels like it's coming at him from all sides.

'Right. Well that all checks out,' Willow says. 'The register was right. Roddie died too soon. Davey is no relation to Albie. Happy days.'

'What?' Barrett takes his eye off the road to search out Willow's face in the mirror.

But she's looking at her sister. 'What did they call it, So?'

'Ambient correlations,' Sorrel reads off her phone. 'Statistically insignificant ambient match as expected in a settled population. Eww. Small-town inbreds in other words. But not related.'

'I don't understand,' Barrett says. 'Albie, Tabitha's son, is no relation to Davey, Tabitha's . . .?' Brother. He manages not to say it.

'Understand what?' Willow says. 'That's exactly what we

worked out. The auntie popped up, by the way. Tabitha's sister. But that's it.'

'Yeah, it's like we've known since we found the death certificate,' says Sorrel. 'But it's definite now. No "digital error" like everyone was saying. *We* knew that, didn't we, Will?'

'And it's like Tabitha said,' Willow adds. 'A motive. Dead Davey found out his mum's secret and *crrrrk!*' She makes a slashing gesture to go with the sound.

'Those poor kids!' Sorrel says. 'Jo and Johnny. They thought they were cousins all these years and so they didn't have any babies. And now it turns out they weren't and they could have.'

'They should have had DNA tests at the start,' says Willow. 'Everyone should, like in America.'

'It would blow the lid off every family in the world,' says Barrett. He can't understand it. Tabby found out from Jo that the four Muir kids were siblings. But Olly just found out from a DNA test that they're not? It makes no sense. 'Hey,' he says, as the thought hits him, 'is Albie in this round robin?' He's passing the old school now and the other side of the hill has made no difference. There's still water drilling on the roof and streaming down the windscreen.

'Round robin!' Willow says. 'Yes, we're texting Albie too. Why wouldn't we?'

'Tell him not to text his mum,' Barrett says.

'Too late,' says Sorrell. But, even if she hadn't, Barrett would know, because as he slows at Davey's gate he sees Tabitha out in the garden, coatless and hatless, standing there in her slippers on the squelching grass, with her hair plastered flat and her phone in her hand, her white face a mask of bewilderment.

Gordo reaches her first, leaving Oliver to get himself out of the car and out of the rain however he can. Barrett tells himself he's not making a point by going over to the lad with a golf brolly up, taking care of him like his father should. Oliver is still clutching the envelope the news came in, hastily rucked open with a thumb, the precious piece of paper inexpertly stuffed back in, looking like those posies of tissue paper women put in the tops of gift bags for some reason Barrett's never been able to fathom.

'That's a relief then,' he says, nodding at it. 'But you do know he meant what he said, lad? It would have made no difference.'

Oliver smiles. 'Not like this lot, eh? What's the hell's going on with them all up here?'

'Nothing you need to worry about,' Barrett says. 'The ones that made the mess are dead. All that's left is walking wounded.' But, as he speaks, the wind lets up for one of those strange quiet moments, so that the rain comes down in a sheet instead of lashing and spattering. He looks through the veil of it, up the hill to the old school, thinking about the woman who lives there, with her paint and canvas, and with the endless ripples of all her decisions. How could she have let siblings marry, Tabitha asked him. But how could she have let strangers think they were siblings? Barrett can't pick his way through this.

Inside the kitchen, Tabby is pale and shaking. She jumps at the sound of the wind banging in the chimney, the sudden stink of oil as the draught makes the pilot light gutter before it steadies again.

'I take it back,' she says. 'About a good sniff of true shit always helping. This is the truth at last, see. And it hurts like hell.'

'What do you mean?' Barrett says.

'He wouldn't kill one of his own kids,' Tabitha says. 'His sons or his daughter. He didn't "try to kill me because I was special and he was nuts". He tried to kill me because he was evil and I was nothing.'

Barrett is swiped by a wave of relief that he didn't say anything to the girls. He'd have made a fool of himself. Because of *course* Jo can be Johnny's sister without Tabitha being another one. Of course there's no contradiction between the sibling marriage and the DNA of Albie and Davey. People don't know who their fathers are – that's the whole problem of everything, isn't it? And Tabby looks like her mum. Two fine-looking women even if they're miles from each other in every other way, every way that counts.

'Maybe it was because my mum was pregnant again,' Tabitha says. 'Maybe he wanted rid of the cuckoo. Because maybe he didn't mean to die. Maybe he meant to leave me there and get out of the car. Maybe.'

'So why didn't he?' Oliver says. 'If he meant to get out of the car, what would stop him? And why would he do such a dangerous thing in the first place? Instead of just chuck— Sorry.

But hypothetically, you know? You live near a loch and you want to . . . harm . . . a child? Why wouldn't you just . . . I don't want to say it.'

'Well then, you're a good kid,' says Tabitha. Oliver tries to shrug it off. It's probably something he's not heard very often since he wrecked his liver with glue. 'You're kind,' she goes on, and he drops his head, studying the envelope he's still holding bunched in his fist, tidying it up a bit. Tabitha watches him.

'Do you want to see them?' he asks. 'Albie's results.'

Tabitha frowns at the envelope and shakes her head. 'It's good news when you think about it,' she says. 'If I'm not related to either of those men who killed themselves, then I can't have passed on the bad genes to you, Albie.' She laughs. 'On the other hand, I can't blame the bad genes for going off my trolley about a bit of bad news and never quite getting back on again.'

No one manages to think up an answer to that one. So Barrett changes the subject. 'Did Davey know?' he says. 'Any of it?'

'He must have,' Tabby says. Barrett hides his smile. Subject successfully changed! '*That's* the motive for killing his mother. *And* the motive for leaving everything he possessed to me. You know something? Johnny guessed. He guessed it was nothing to do with Scott and the divorce. He guessed that didn't "deserve any of this" meant *this*. Nearly drowning. Going nuts. Not knowing who I am.'

'But how *could* Davey know?' says Gordo. 'He was the oldest one but he was still wee when your dad . . . died.'

'I'm sorry I said that about you drowning,' says Oliver.

Tabby waves it off, then glances again at the envelope bunched in his hand. He holds it out but she doesn't take it. She just stares and stares.

'He could have . . .' Willow begins, then dips her head. 'I mean, couldn't Davey have done what we just did? DNA testing?'

Tabitha's head snaps round and her eyes flash. 'Yes!' she says, leaping up. 'Oh my God, yes! I *knew* that envelope was bothering me!' She's over at the dresser rootling around in the stamp drawer. When she whirls back round she's holding a pale blue, almost grey, envelope with a faint shadow of a tree design over half of it. She takes it to where Oliver's sitting and holds it out. He opens his fist and holds out its twin.

'He knew.' She sounds triumphant. Even though the envelope is empty it's enough to convince her.

'But knew what?' says Sorrel. 'Knew he wasn't related to you? Knew the "cousins" were actually siblings?'

'He couldn't have known that,' Albie says. 'How could he have got samples from Jo and Johnny when he hadn't seen them for yonks? But yeah, he must have taken a hair or something from you, Mum. Compared you with him. And that's why he decided to make you his heir. Because you "didn't deserve what happened". Like you said.'

'No baby deserves drowning,' says Tabitha. 'No matter who her dad is or isn't. Davey didn't need to check anything to know that. Otherwise, yeah. I suppose it must have been me and him he tested.'

'I don't know though,' says Willow. 'I mean, this house wasn't exactly hygienic, was it? There *could* have been hairs. Old combs from Johnny. A toothbrush. Davey wasn't known for throwing things away. He could have had the tests done on everyone. Well, maybe not Jo.'

'Oh, he could have found a scrunchie or something of Jo's if he'd ever got half an hour in the school on his own,' Tabitha says.

'Tabitha,' says Oliver. 'I really am sorry I said that about drowning.'

Barrett glances at Gordo, asking silently if he knows what's wrong with the boy. Gordo shrugs.

'Yeah, Mum,' Albie says. 'You know you've said "drown" twice now after Olly said it. You're making him feel bad.'

Tabitha chews her lip and waits a good while before she answers. 'Don't feel bad, Oliver,' she says. 'I'm fine. It's healthier to talk about what happened plain and square. My God, that's one thing I thought you young ones knew.'

'So why do you keep saying "drowning"?' Albie asks her.

'OK, nearly drowning,' says Tabitha.

'I'm *sorry*,' Oliver says again, and the pain in his voice is so clear even Barrett feels a tug in his chest.

'I don't understand,' says Albie.

'I don't understand what you don't understand,' says Tabitha and the jaunty tune of it clashes badly with the words. 'The man we've been calling my dad strapped me into my baby seat and drove his car into the loch. Zelda jumped in and got me out. He drowned. She had a miscarriage. We always thought his brother hanged himself that day when he heard the news. We know now he'd hanged himself years before and my dad took up with his widow. When he decided to drown himself, he took me with him because I was the . . . fruit of his wife's affair. What a hypocrite, eh?'

'But he didn't,' says Albie. 'Mum, how can you not know this? I get why you never talk about it, but you're really telling me you don't know?'

Barrett looks round the ring of faces. He's not the only one that's lost. Gordo and Tabitha are squinting in confusion too. It's only the four kids who're as alert as ever.

'Know what?' says Tabby.

'He drove his car down a siding on to a railway track and stopped it,' Albie says. 'Granny clambered down and got you out.'

'Clambered?' says Tabitha.

'Right,' Albie says. 'He got . . . a train came.'

'No,' Tabitha says. 'He drove on to the track and never drove off. That track out there that disappears. My mum scrambled down. That's what she told me. *Scrambled* down. She paints it. In the Night Paintings. She paints him. A terre verte eel. He's in every single one. But I'm not, because she got me out.'

No one speaks. Barrett scrapes his brain for a way to break this sickening silence but there's nothing.

'No, Mum,' Albie says at last. 'There was a report. We found it online. And . . . you don't scramble through water.'

'Granny did,' Tabitha says. 'She went into Miss Mirror. Mr Moon saw her. She got me away from the diver eel and brought me back to air and cats and Jesus when there is one.'

'What?' says Albie.

'I can't,' Tabitha replies, except it's not a reply really. Not in any way that makes sense to Barrett. 'I can take cousin to brother to no one. I took what Rowan said. I coped in my own way. For years. And I forgot. And then even when I remembered I coped again.' Her voice is rising. 'But I didn't imagine those pictures. They're all over the walls. They were there every day of my childhood and now they're everywhere! Mouse mats and tea towels and novelty condoms!'

She's shouting now.

'And I'm not taking this! I'm going home to Elspeth where I don't need to take any of this. I can't do this.'

'What?' says Albie. 'Mum, you sound—'

But Barrett manages to get him up out of his seat and hustle him out of the room, shoves the girls after him, tells them to look after Oliver and stay away. He'll bring them snacks but they've got to stay upstairs.

'Come on, Tab,' he says when they've gone. 'You've come too far to give up now. Come on, eh?'

'No,' she says. 'I won't. I can't. And you can't make me. I'm going back where I belong. I won't live here where nothing makes sense. I'm going back to the cats and the cupboard and I'm staying this time.'

He phones the old school on the landline to get that mad old bat down here with some answers. Gordo's on Tabitha's phone to Scott to ask about her doctor. To find out if there's something she could take to help her. Tabitha huddles in the corner in Davey's battered armchair, visibly shrinking or so it seems to him, as if she's trying to turn into the hardest, smallest version of herself, make sure nothing can touch a soft part of her ever again.

TWENTY-FIVE

Tabitha

'Are you yourself again?' Elspeth is here, cackling. I smile too. She always said that, mimicking the prissiest of the nurses. Then she'd say, 'Who the hell would want to be me again if they'd managed to stop? Or you, Tabby. No offence.'

And I'd say, 'None taken.' And it would be true because she was right. (When I was having Albie and someone mentioned getting my figure back and I said, 'Christ, I hope not!' I found out that mums haven't got the gallows humour nutters do.)

'None taken,' I say, out loud in the dark. But Elspeth is gone.

So it's quiet when Zelda comes into my bedroom and draws up a little chair beside me. There's an empty glass from the port and brandy Barrett gave me. And there's a bowl of water plus a flannel to dip in it and wipe my face, sore and sweaty from crying. Zelda does exactly this but she wrings it out too hard with those strong, artist's hands, so the loops of the terry-towelling scrape the raw skin under my eyes.

'I thought I remembered Uncle Roddie,' I tell her.

'How could you? You weren't born.'

Weren't born. She's admitted it. Just like that, the old story is swept away.

'I thought I remembered sinking into the cold water,' I tell her. 'Watching it seep in around the windows and start to fill the car. I remember you lugging me out and kicking like a frog. All the bubbles from your breath were fizzing in my face and then our heads were up in the air again.'

'How could you remember anything? You were a baby.'

'I know that now. It was one word. Track. One single, ambiguous, sneaky word and I made a whole life's memory out of it. Why didn't we speak about it? Ever? Even once? How is it possible?'

'Art is a demanding mistress,' she says.

'And that's another thing. You painted it. You paint it. You paint the diver eel in every painting.'

'What do you mean?' she says. 'What's a "diver eel"?'

'But you paint him!'

'I've never explained my art, Tabitha. It speaks for itself.'

'You paint Dad.'

'I don't explain my art,' she says again. 'But if you insist and I suppose I owe you this much. I paint my son, Tabitha. Grown up big and strong.'

I keep my breathing steady, check in on my breaths and my blinking. When I'm sure my voice is calm, I go on. 'Mum, why did you let Jo and Johnny get married?'

'Why not?'

I can't see her face. She's in silhouette against the window and there's enough sunshine getting through the bruised-looking clouds to give her a shimmer as the light picks up the wiry hairs escaping the main hank. Her shoulders are shining too. She must be wearing satin.

'Because they're brother and sister,' I say. 'Auntie Rowan told them. Told you. Told me. That's what she screeched that night before the wedding. Part of it.'

'Part of it,' she agrees. 'Of course, she also told you your father tried to kill you.'

'Yeah,' I say. 'I realize that now. I didn't know. And then I did. And then I didn't. Because it broke me. And somewhere along the way I forgot who told me too.'

'So I suppose I backed the marriage to destroy Rowan's peace of mind,' she says. 'For vengeance. To pay her back for what she had just done to you.'

She sounds fierce and I wallow in it. That fierceness is all for me.

'Weren't you scared of them having children? Or did you know they didn't plan to?'

'Assume I knew,' she says. 'If thinking so helps you.'

We sit in silence awhile. 'Davey knew and it broke him,' I say at last.

'Davey knew what?'

'That him and me—'

'He and I.'

'—weren't related.'

'What?' It's a harsh sound. Like a crow's squawk.

'If only I had wanted to marry Davey, or if only *Jo* wasn't Dad's daughter, it would all have been OK. Except then Dad would have tried to drown Jo.'

'Drown?'

'That's right, no. Kill. Under a train. Instead of me. But the rest of it is true. I'm not Dad's. I know I'm not because Albie and Davey aren't related. Davey sent samples off, and Albie has too now. They are not related. Which means I'm not related to Davey.'

'That means we don't know who *Davey's* father was,' says Zelda. 'It doesn't mean there's a question mark over who *your* father was, Tabitha. Good God! Is that what nonsense you've been imagining?'

'But then why did he want to kill me?' I say, but I'm not really thinking about that. I'm thinking about Davey and Rowan, a fox and a fox. Jo and Johnny and Roddie and Dad. Pig, pig, pig, pig. Her and me, two horses. 'There's no point in children looking like their mothers, is there?' I say. I'm watching her, bright and brittle in the backlight. 'It doesn't get you anything. No matter what Albie looked like, I'd know he's my son.'

'And you are my daughter,' she says. 'Of my body. Made of me. Nothing else in the world is as sure as that and nothing will ever take it away. It's the fundamental truth, Tabitha. Remember that. Know how much I wanted you. Know how hard I worked to have you. Know how hard I worked to keep you. *Nothing* can take it away.'

It sounds like a lullaby, so soft I could believe it's inside my head. I let it soothe me.

When I open my eyes again it's dark outside, properly dark – not just the gloom of a bad winter's day. She's gone but in her place is someone just as familiar. His silhouette, the sound of his breathing, the smell of his soap and the oil he uses on that leather jacket he's wearing.

'Scott?'

'I've been waiting to talk to you,' he tells me. The bowl of water is still sitting there, the flannel still floating in it, but he doesn't bathe my forehead for me. 'You had visitors.'

I'm not surprised he couldn't sit in the same room as Zelda. Even when we were married she terrified him.

'What was she doing here?' he says.

'My mum?' I'm thinking she's got a hell of a lot more reason to be here than my ex-husband.

'Of course not your mum!'

'Willow?'

He flicks his head as though there's a fly at him.

'Sorrel?'

He lets his breath out in a sigh.

'Elspeth?'

'Don't try to be cute, Tabitha,' he says. 'Elspeth is dead.' I know that. There's no need to fling it at me. 'But no one else has been here,' I say, although since I was out for hours I can't be sure. 'At least, I don't think so.' He's got me questioning myself and I try to rally, because my days of letting Scott scold me should really be over. 'Mrs McCabe?' I say. 'Allison? How do you know them? They haven't been near the place for fifteen years.'

'Don't mess me about,' he says with infinite weariness. 'What was she doing here?' This is the first moment I think maybe I'm asleep and dreaming. Not hallucinating. There's no mistaking that: the lavish surround-sound of a voice I've conjured; the bright, hard edges of things that aren't there, like my brain's using a budget green screen.

'Her son's father is a friend of mine,' I say, thinking of Allison still. 'He's not well. Or her grandson's father, if it's Allison's mum you mean. Or her father's my friend, if it's one of the girls. His name is Barrett. You've met him.'

'You're spinning,' Scott says. 'You're talking drivel. She doesn't have a son. What girls?'

'Who doesn't?' I ask him.

He makes that irritated noise – a kind of snarl – that he started making about five years ago, whenever I overreacted about something. He was the judge of what counted as overreacting, naturally. 'Cassie,' he says at last, 'I don't understand how you even know each other.'

'I don't know anyone called Cassie,' I say. This whole conversation is beginning to unsettle me.

'Did she just happen to drive up this road and knock on this door? A coincidence? Is that what you're trying to see if I'll swallow.'

'Maybe she lost her dog,' I say. 'Or maybe she found a dog and she thought it was mine.'

'What?' He spits the word just like Zelda did. Or maybe like she's going to, if she hasn't been here yet. I don't seem to know what order things are happening in. 'She hasn't got a dog,' Scott says.

'Or a son,' I say. 'Poor thing.' Then I think for a minute. 'Who?'

'*Cassie*,' says Scott.

'I don't know anyone called Cassie,' I say again. 'Who is she?'

'No one now,' Scott says. 'I told you. She dumped me.'

I think I sleep again for a while after that. In fact, I know I do, because the final visitor is definitely me dreaming. Davey is here. He's sitting in the same seat where Elspeth, Zelda and Scott were but I can see every detail of his face, although there's no light on and he should be in shadow. He's done the usual half-hearted job of shaving, leaving spikes at the corners of his mouth to be stained with soup and coffee, and picking a random point on his neck to give up and call what's left chest hair. It makes me smile even as I want to smack him. Or wax him. Plug both nostrils and ears with twists of paper and get rid of those horrible little ferns he's growing.

Instead of me grooming him, he starts tending me. He dips the cloth in the bowl, but it's muslin now, not towelling, and it's ass's milk he smooths on to my head. I've never seen ass's milk, but I know that's what I'm feeling.

'What's it going to change?' he says. 'If you pull it all to pieces? The dead stay dead.'

'Oh they do, do they?' I ask him as I open my eyes. Just like that, he's gone.

'What did you give me?' I say to Barrett as I wobble my way downstairs, once I've got my dressing gown on and my feet in my slippers. He must have come from the kitchen when he heard me moving. Surely he hasn't been standing waiting there at the foot of the stairs all the time I've been gone.

The house is cold. I need to face the cost of heating the whole place through just once to get going. A fire in the kitchen and a radiator plugged in in the bathroom leach all their warmth into the passageways and barely take the chill off. Already the few

Christmas cards I've tried to prop open on windowsills are curling in the damp and falling over. This poor old house needs to be warmed to its bones.

'Where's Albie?' I say.

'Gordo needed to take Oliver home for a rest so they all went.' Like Olly's going to get much rest with Albie sitting on his bed, hogging the console, or with those girls painting his nails and trying out scalp massages, but they don't seem to get tired from fifty apps open and everyone with different music on. None of them.

'You slept then?' Barrett says next. He sounds uneasy.

'I slept,' I said. 'But my dreams were escalating bonkers. My mum visited. Fair enough. And I dream about Elspeth all the time. But then Scott rocked up! And Davey!'

I'm only one step up from Barrett now and weirdly he's not moving aside for me.

'Did I do right letting him in?'

'Did . . .?' I say. 'Davey?' Suddenly all I can think of is that I've never been alone with Barrett before. And I haven't known him all that long. And all I *do* know about him now is that his wife left him and he's been a good friend to someone far from normal. Before he can answer or I can say more, there's a noise from the kitchen.

Barrett shuffles closer to me and says in a whisper, 'He's still here.'

I follow him along to the kitchen door walking as if I'm still asleep, that dream walk through soup, through treacle. If Davey is in the kitchen, I will know that I'm ill again and I need to call someone. Albie can stay with his dad. Barrett and Gordo will take care of the house. Zelda might visit and bathe my face with milk.

My eyes are squeezed shut but I can tell when I pass through the doorway, because the bright kitchen light has turned my eyelids orange inside. I relax my face and let my eyes open.

'Scott!' I say. 'I thought I dreamt you!'

'You sounded off your tits right enough,' he says and behind me, Barrett – sweet, kind, normal, lovely Barrett that I can't believe I suspected of . . . whatever that was – rumbles in his throat, annoyed at the crudeness. It annoys me too, if I'm honest. Offends me. Scott divorced me and we're nothing to each other, so he doesn't get to suspend politeness when he speaks to me now.

'What do you want?' I say. My memory of our conversation is hazy to say the least.

'I want to know what Cassie was doing here,' Scott says. 'What are you up to?'

'Barrett, is that Allison's mum's first name?' I say, turning to him.

'I've already told you she hasn't got kids,' says Scott. 'Who the hell's Allison?'

'No need for that,' Barrett says.

For a minute the pair of them look each other over, considering the next move if it's not to be backing down. Barrett is older, but fifty is still when older means seasoned, long before it starts to mean weakened. He's no taller but he's broader and his hands, roughened with work, look capable.

Scott's fingers look made for typing, but he's got the arrogance that comes from a posh car, a good shirt, a set of karate lessons for his last birthday.

I let my head rest against the back of the chair and leave them to it. Cassie, I think to myself. Scott's ex, who dumped him like he dumped me. But I meant what I said. She's never been here and I don't know any other Cassies. I don't know any Cassandras and the only Catherine in my life is shortened to Kate.

When I straighten up again, the moment seems to have passed. Barrett's sitting down and Scott has crossed his legs.

'Look, can you just go, please?' I say to him. 'I'll be in touch about Albie's Christmas presents and then we'll need to get into a good routine for his weekends with you and maybe a weeknight. Tuesdays would be good when he's got practice anyway—'

'Why should my weeknight be the one when he's out?' Scott says.

I really and truly can't deal with him now. 'Whatever. We'll fix it. Could you go?'

He folds his arms and crosses his legs as if that's going to anchor him more securely in his seat.

'Come on, pal,' Barrett says. 'Lady's made herself clear. On yer bike, eh?'

It occurs to me to ask him if he's ever worked as a bouncer, because this is straight off the script of every chunky bloke in black whoever stood at a club door. It works on Scott. At least, he stands up and zips his leather jacket closed.

'I'm leaving because you look done in,' he says, 'but not until you tell me why Cassie was here.'

'She *wasn't*. Today, my mum was here and Barrett's daughters were here.' I am not lying. This day has been so long and strange, I believe what I'm saying completely. 'And if it's not today then Mrs McCabe was here and Allison McCabe. And a farmer called Lorna was here once—'

'I saw her,' Scott says, cutting through me. 'And if *you're* not messing with *me*,' he says, gripping the back of the chair and drilling me with a hard stare, 'you need to watch out. She might be messing with you. She's always been obsessed with you, Tabby.'

'Obsessed how?' I ask. 'I didn't think she was interested in anyone but you. She definitely wasn't fussed about Albie one way or the other.'

'All about when you were away before. And your dad and your uncle. It was her talked me into what happened, you know. Guilted me into it, telling me it wasn't safe for you to do what you did for a job. I'm sorry.'

'She talked you into it?' says Barrett. 'What? She hypnotized you? Be a man and take responsibility, for God's sake.'

It makes no sense to me. And Scott's babbling doesn't explain it. I nod at him the way I used to nod at Albie prattling from his car seat when I drove him home from nursery. Not even that, actually, because that was plump with affection and these are thin little nods, like swatting a fly. But similar in a way, because I'm using most of my brain for other things now as I did then. 'Why,' I say, in a lull, 'would a woman who didn't even move in, didn't want more than you had, wouldn't even agree to meet Albie—?'

'Albie's never met the woman you left your wife for?' Barrett says. The look he gives Scott is like salt on a slug.

'What's it got to do with you?' Scott says.

'I'm divorced and I'm a father,' says Barrett. 'There's ways and ways, son. Especially for an only child like your Albie. My girls have got each other.'

I love him for that 'son'. I love him for how much Scott hates it. He's glaring at Barrett. Then, as I watch, his expression changes. I look over to see why. Barrett's eyes are wide and his mouth is hanging open.

'You forgot someone,' he says. 'It was me mentioning my two girls. You forgot a visitor.'

'Who?' I ask.

'Oh, Tab,' he says gently. 'What's "Jo" short for? It's not Joanne, is it?'

'Jocasta,' I say, and then I sit up straight so fast that I feel a muscle rip in the base of my back. 'Scott, have you got a photo of Cassie?'

He considers lying. I can see it flit through his brain clear as day. In the end, he decides he'd rather get to the bottom of this than pretend he's cool enough to delete pictures of past loves so quick. He fumbles through his phone and passes it to me.

'That,' I say, looking down at the photo of her smiling in a baseball cap and a vest top, an ice-cream cone in her hands, a harbour sparkling behind her, 'is my sister.'

TWENTY-SIX

Tabitha

'Will you be OK on your own for a bit?' Barrett says, once we've listened to Scott's car whining its way up the track, in what sounds like second gear. He always did overreact to this road.

'Where are you going?' I say. 'I mean, yes of course. Sorry. You don't owe— But the way you said it sounded specific.'

'Very,' Barrett says. 'But I don't want to tell you till I've checked. So . . .?'

'I'll be fine,' I assure him. And the unbelievable fact is, I think it's true. I'm going to cook. Make a big fridge curry out of everything in there and get it cleared for the Christmas shop. 'I'll put the radio on,' I say. 'I might even bake something. I'll be grand, really.'

'Because did I ever tell you I actually saw the washing machine repair van, the day Davey died?' he asks me.

I shrug. I can't remember.

'Of course, it didn't go in at the time because it wasn't significant, if you see what I mean. So I never looked to see what the company was called, from the sign on the side of the van. But now I'm thinking two things: first, that was the last person who talked to Davey and I want to hear what he's got to say. And second, didn't he ask for directions at one of the farms or holdings? I can go door to door and get the company name. Track him down.'

'He didn't ask for directions,' I say. 'He got held up when Lorna was moving her ewes. But she might remember.' It seems like a bit of a shunt up a siding, but I don't tell Barrett that. Then I put both things he's said together and notice they don't add up.

'So if that's what you're doing,' I ask him, 'what is it you don't want to tell me?'

'Trust me,' he says.

And I can't help smiling, because I do. I trust him and I trust Gordo. I trust Albie too except for how he's digging into what seems to him like a puzzle, a lark, a story, but is actually my life, still raw and still with the strength to hurt me. Who else do I trust? That might be it, actually. I think about Zelda – was she there? Did I dream her? – and her towering claim about how much she loves – except she never said 'love', did she? That's the one thing that makes me sure it really was her, sitting there beside me, writing her own lines. I'd have given her 'love' to say, if it was me. It doesn't hurt that I can't trust Jo. It's been a long time since I could.

Still mystifying though. If she hated me enough to take my job, and my home and my son with this elaborate game, then why didn't she make Johnny contest Davey's will? I got a nicer house and my son back again and she just sat and watched me.

And she didn't seem to have any hatred in her when she arrived the day Davey died, nor at his funeral, nor when she came here after I asked her. She was odd – if it even makes sense to think of what's odd and what's normal when you waltz back in with your brother-husband after twenty-five years of ostracizing your family. I put it out of my mind and turn to my ingredients instead.

I'm deep into measuring when Gordo, Albie and the girls come creeping back in, as if they're trying not to wake a bear. The relief on their faces when they see me standing over a bowl of flour and butter puts a smile back on my face.

'Don't worry,' I say. 'I'm fine. I'm baking it out of my system.'

'*Can* you bake, Mum?' says Albie.

'We'll see,' I say. 'Is Oliver still resting?'

A cloud passes over Gordo. So it's to take his mind off it, as much as anything, that I fill him in, once the girls have borne Albie away.

'Jo was your husband's girlfriend?' Gordo says, wide-eyed. 'Your sister was Scott's affair?' It's worked. No bit of his brain is on Oliver now. 'Why?'

'Why did she hook him?' I ask. 'Or why did she dump him?'

Gordo takes a moment to think this over and then says, 'Both, really.'

'Well, she hooked him to get influence, to ruin me. And then, once I was ruined, she had no need to keep him.' I've deliberately set it up to see if he notices the same problem I did.

'But that makes no sense,' he says, like clockwork. 'You're not ruined. You got Davey's house, and so you got your son back. And OK you've still lost your job, but you got Davey's mad collection of land and stocks and stuff. Tim Hawes might call it "low-value" but I bet if you sold it, you'd be laughing.'

'So ruining me wasn't the point.'

'And actually, why would it be?' says Gordo. 'To be fair.' He's started saying that because Olly does.

'I don't know,' I tell him. Then I try to explain the way I'm feeling. 'There's so many different angles. So many secrets and lies. All the way back to before I was even born. I can't believe that this latest doesn't have to do with the old stuff in some way.'

Gordo nods. Then he stands and goes to the stamps and franks drawer, comes back with a pen and a pile of junk mail, blank on the backs. 'Right,' he says. 'What do we know? In order.'

'Uncle Roddie died before his boys were born,' I say. 'Per the DNA test. They're *my* dad's. Except God knows who "my dad" actually is, because Watson Muir wasn't related to me, which we know because Albie wasn't related to Davey, also per the DNA test. Except my mum said I *was* my dad's, and it was *Davey* who wasn't. Except that doesn't explain why he – Dad – wanted to kill me but not Jo. This was a good idea, Gordo. Your turn.'

'Hang on, not yet,' says Gordo. 'That is a bloody spaghetti heap, Tabitha. Let me take a crack at it. Roddie was not Davey and Johnny's dad. We know that from the dates of their birth and death certificates. That's solid. If Watson was their dad, then he is not yours. We know that because Albie and Davey are not related. If Watson was your dad, then he's not theirs. Or at least he wasn't Davey's. But we have hearsay evidence from Rowan that Watson *was* Johnny's dad, and therefore Jo and Johnny should not marry.'

'Brilliant,' I say. 'Crystal clear.'

'And if you had to guess,' says Gordo, 'who gets the dad?'

'Not me. That's why he wanted to kill me. The cuckoo.'

Gordo grimaces. 'Deduction without corroborating evidence, but compelling. What else do we know?'

'When Watson killed himself – you're right; it's better to stick to names – Rowan knew the story of "reclusive husband alive and well" was done for.'

Gordo nods. 'And that's why she canned it. Deduction again, but it fits.'

'My mum— Sorry! Zelda, although it's different with mums, isn't it? – but Zelda was pregnant when Watson drove him and me on to the railway track. She saved me but she lost the new baby. And she buried it in Davey's garden.'

'*What?*' says Gordo.

'See, that's what I'm saying about there being so damn much of it. I never even *told* you that bit yet.'

'Bloody hell, Tab,' Gordo says.

'Do you need to stop?'

He gives a half-laugh as if to say if I can handle this he can too. 'Fast forward a few years,' he goes on, 'and Jo and Johnny fall in love. Which is not as weird as you think, you know.' He must have seen the shudder pass through me. 'Before they knew, I mean. What I'm saying is I loved Allison when I was that age. I would have married her.'

We both leave a beat for what might have been to rise and subside.

'Rowan freaks out when she hears the news of the wedding,' I say. 'This is a fact I know from being there and hearing the freaking. Even if I immediately buried the memory of it on account of some of the other stuff she covered. Anyway, she tells them they can't marry because they're half-siblings. But they go ahead.'

'Zelda also learns this sibling news but she does nothing to stop the wedding.'

'She said it was to pay Rowan back,' I tell him. 'But actually . . . When she came to visit me earlier today, I think she was trying to talk about it in a roundabout sort of way. Going on and on about the bond between a mother and child. I think she meant fathers don't matter.'

'Huh,' says Gordo. 'I'll be sure and show her my scar after the transplant. See what she makes of that.' Then he shakes the thought out of his head. 'What happened next?'

'I went off my rocker,' I say. 'No, it *is* relevant. Because that's how come I could be kicked out of my job all these years later. See?'

He stops objecting and nods again. 'And then we all jog along. Zelda paints a fake sunny village that never was and a flooded night village on the flip side. Jo and Johnny build a business.'

'What kind?'

'Dunno,' I say. 'I asked but I reckon it's something dull or hard to be proud of. She definitely didn't want to tell me. Meanwhile, I get married and have a baby. Davey starts building his empire.'

'Allison fakes a suicide,' says Gordo. 'I don't know if that's connected to much else but we know it's connected to Davey's wombling. He kept her coat.'

'The other thing is *definitely* related,' I say. 'Bess. The weekend of Bess . . .'

'. . . is the same weekend Davey murders his mother,' says Gordo. 'Per his confession. We think because he did a DNA thingy and found out all her lies about who was really his father.'

'Or because he was completely off his head,' I say. 'Like his dad – no matter which one of the brothers was his dad.'

'You're saying an insane person doesn't need a motive?'

'No,' I tell him. 'Every insane person I ever met – and some of my best friends, et cetera, et cetera – had reasons for everything they did. Just not sane ones. My best crazy friend ever used to eat her hair. When that stopped making sense to me, that's when I knew I was getting better.'

'But this isn't "an insane person",' Gordo says. 'This is Davey. My friend. Your friend. Yeah, he was a weirdo. Who isn't? But he was a good, kind, decent, normal weirdo. Like you and me.'

'Let's carry on with the chronology,' I say. 'We might see something if we set it all out plainly.' I have to wait for Gordo to catch up with his note-taking and it gives me a bit of thinking time.

'So Davey kills Rowan, by withholding her insulin and sedating her so she doesn't go after it. And Barrett's dog disappears and he gets an anonymous—'

'No,' says Gordo. 'Bess disappears that weekend, but it's a while afterwards that the photo and cartridge casing turn up. We spent a good week posting "Lost Dog" notices first.'

'Does that actually matter?' I begin, but he's holding up his hand and I see that something is – right now, right this minute – occurring to him.

'Yes! Oh, yes! Tabby, this is a breakthrough,' he says. 'I think it *does* matter. I think the photo and the cartridge came to make Barrett give up and take down all the notices. Because they – the notices, all over lampposts – were asking if people had been up Hiskith and saw anything!'

The truth of this sloshes over me like a bucket of ice water. I wipe my hands clean on a tea towel and abandon the bowl of flour. Albie's right. I wasn't ever going to make anything edible.

'Except what would there be to see?' I ask. 'Rowan was killed inside the house by someone who also lived here.'

He thinks hard but then shrugs. 'I don't know,' he says. 'What comes next then?'

'Nothing for ages.'

'Then Jo becomes Cassie, you leave Scott, Davey writes a will.'

'And instead of getting you and Barrett to witness it – which you would have, I'm assuming – he fakes your names.'

'Tries to blow up Hiskith Dam. Possibly. Or possibly not.'

'Fails. At least someone fails.'

'And kills himself with an overdose of insulin,' says Gordo, 'which he's presumably been keeping in the freezer for ten years. How long does insulin keep anyway?'

'No clue,' I say. 'But it's always bothered me. It's been bugging me since the start. Even those vet nurses at the funeral bugged me. They said they'd let Davey have old stuff when they upgraded and it stuck in my—'

Gordo looks up from his phone. 'Wait till you h—' He stops. 'What?'

'I've got it! All those ampoules and syringes in that wee room the day Davey died? That wasn't Auntie Rowan's leftover insulin! She upgraded bloody *years* before she died. She didn't use syringes and ampoules. She had a pen.'

Gordo nods and holds his phone out to me. 'Confirmed,' he says, 'It wasn't her insulin. It doesn't last anything like that long and it's useless once it's frozen.'

'Why would Davey score insulin to kill himself with?'

We stare at each other a while and then we both shrug in unison.

'And unfortunately that's it,' Gordo says. 'We're up to date. Aren't we?'

'Pretty much,' I say. 'Did we forget anything?'

'I hope so,' says Gordo. 'Because it still doesn't make any sense as it stands.' He starts shuffling all the scrap paper he didn't use.

'It did at the start when we – well, you – were being disciplined about types of evidence,' I say. I watch him try to make a neat stack of notes out of leaflets and envelopes. And suddenly I remember.

'Of course we forgot something!' I say, smacking myself in the head. 'Davey sent away to a family history service. Do we know when? That might be significant. And we've got documentary evidence too. If an envelope can be a document? Where did we put it anyway?'

Gordo is away ahead of me. 'I kept it with my one,' he says, rummaging in his jacket pockets. 'And I'll tell you something, Tabitha: if Davey can hear you questioning whether a franked envelope is a valuable document, he'll come back down and haunt you.'

'Down?' I say.

Gordo grimaces. 'I'm not a gambling man,' he says. 'But . . .' He pulls his hand out of his breast pocket. 'Here it is. Hand us the magnifier.' It should still be sitting on the kitchen table from when we used it on the photo of Bess, but it's been swept up somehow and I can't lay my hand on it. 'If the date stamp on this envelope is ten years ago, it pretty much clinches the theory that Davey killed Rowan because of what was inside it.'

He's holding the envelope close under the anglepoise lamp and squinting hard. I keep searching for the magnifier. It's not in any of the drawers, or in the bowl of keys and other junk.

'You know what though?' Gordo says, as I rummage. 'It's the wrong brother. Know what I mean?'

'You mean . . .' I say slowly, still rootling through the endless detritus. (How I ever thought I cleared this place! I suppose it's all relative.) 'If you've married someone who's either a cousin, or a sister, then *you're* the brother who cares about DNA. If you're a single man in your thirties and you find out your mum had a fling and you're the result, you might be angry, but why would you be murderously angry?'

'Exactly,' says Gordo. 'But like we keep saying, he confessed.'

'Eureka,' I say. I've opened the curtains and there's the magnifier on the windowsill. I hand it over and Gordo bends close.

'Huh,' he says. 'We're wrong anyway. This was sent less than a year ago.'

Then we both turn as headlights rake the room. It's got dark since we've been sitting here and Barrett's back. We hear his car door, his footsteps slapping on the wet gravel, then he's beside us in a flurry of cold air and flicked rain, his coat dripping as he hooks it over a chairback.

'Are you OK?' Gordo asks him. Of course, he knows Barrett better than I do. I've been fooled by the way the weather has pinked his cheeks. When I look closer there's obviously something *far* from OK. I rise and go to get the port and brandy, still sitting out from him dosing me.

He takes the glass and drops into a seat. 'Give me a minute,' he says. 'And then just listen. Hear me out.'

'Dad?' comes a voice from upstairs. I still can't tell those two girls apart.

'That's me back, So!' Barrett calls up, because of course *he* can. It's not true what Zelda said about mothers and children. Or no more true than for fathers anyway. 'You carry on, pet!'

When he's drained his glass and started on a strong cuppa, he tells us.

'Davey didn't kill himself.'

I want so much for it to be true that I say nothing.

'And he didn't kill his mother.'

'He confessed,' says Gordo again, like we've all been saying all this time, never quite convincing ourselves enough to stop assuming Davey's looking *down*.

'He might have tried to blow up the dam,' Barrett says. 'And I still don't know what happened to Bess. But he didn't kill his mum and he didn't kill himself. He was murdered.'

This is too much. I try to get him to climb back down to something easier. 'Did you find the plumber?' I ask. Gordo frowns and I realize that I never told him what Barrett was up to. 'We reckoned the guy who came to fix the washing machine must have been the last person to see Davey alive. Did you? Was he?'

'Not exactly,' Barrett says. 'Lorna couldn't remember the name of the company, so I asked round the rest of the farms and holdings. See if anyone else clocked the van. Now, you might not remember this, but something about it bothered me at the funeral. And I worked out what it was, about half an hour ago, while I was trundling about this bloody fell in the bloody rain trying to get round the last of them while it was light. The very last house up that long drive, just beyond the allotments? Know the one I mean? It's a blacksmith.'

'Right,' I say. 'C.C. Smith and Farrier.'

'C.C.,' says Barrett. 'Her name's Clarita.'

I know my eyebrows lift and I see Gordo's do the same.

'Exactly!' Barrett says. 'That's what switched the lightbulb on. She said sorry she couldn't help me, because she didn't see the van that day, away down a long drive like she is, and she fixes her own appliances, she told me. But she's no idea how *much* she helped me. Because *here's* what was bugging me. There were two of them in the van. And you don't get washing-machine repair people in twos, do you? Or even when you do, it's two blokes. A plumber and an apprentice lad. But the two folk in the repair van the day Davey died were a man and a woman. "Clarita, the blacksmith" jogged my memory. I saw a man and a *woman* in a repair van, headed up to Hiskith hours before Davey died.'

I can't breathe. It's such a habit, I suppose it would be unreasonable to expect it to let me go, just because I know now that I shouldn't drown every time I'm horrified.

'And remember, Tabby,' Barrett says. 'Also at the funeral, I was sure I knew your sister and she wasn't best pleased when I said so.'

If I don't inhale soon I'm going to faint. But it feels as if my throat has closed, just the same way it always did. Train tracks, I tell myself. No water anywhere. Breathe, Tabitha!

'You think Jo was in the repair van?' says Gordo. 'Fuck, she gets about, doesn't she?'

The plug of filthy water shoots out of my throat as I laugh. Gordo flushes and mumbles an apology. He doesn't know he's saved me from fainting. I'll tell him later.

'So . . .' I say instead. 'Was the man in the van Johnny?'

'I don't know,' Barrett says. 'I've never met him. He missed his own brother's funeral. What kind of man does that? I asked myself. And then I answered myself. The kind of man who killed him. The kind of man who killed his mother.'

'Barr,' says Gordo. 'Mate. Sorry to keep repeating it, but *Davey* confessed to killing his mother.'

'No,' says Barrett. 'No, he didn't.'

'He wrote a letter,' I say.

'He didn't.'

'He wrote a letter and it's the same handwriting as the note on the bottom of the will,' I say.

'The will he didn't get us to witness,' says Barrett. 'For some reason we've never been able to put our finger on.'

'The will,' says Gordo, 'that he handed over in person to Tim Hawes, remember? Man, Barrett, there's enough confusion in all of this without adding more.'

'You're wrong,' Barrett says. 'I've got three arguments in favour of what I'm saying. Besides the fact that I recognized Jo. If they convince you, then maybe you'll agree to help me prove it.'

'But what *is* it you're saying?' Gordo asks. My throat is closing again. I wish my ears would close too before he speaks.

'Jo and Johnny killed Rowan,' Barrett says. 'And they killed Davey too. If we start from there it makes sense of everything.' He takes a deep breath before he begins. 'Think about what was lying around in that wee room where Davey died.'

'Oh, Jesus,' I say. Because he's right. 'We just worked that out from the other end, didn't we, Gordo? Davey couldn't kill himself with Auntie Rowan's insulin because after ten years it would be useless. And he had no reason to get new insulin to make it look otherwise. If you're killing yourself, you don't care what it looks like. But . . .'

'But if you've killed a diabetic by withholding insulin,' says Gordo, 'and now you're trying to think how to kill someone else, using insulin again is a good way to suggest murder then suicide.'

'Exactly,' Barrett says.

I nod. 'OK, what's the second thing?'

'Jo dumped Scott when she had got you where she wanted you,' Barrett says. 'Which was here. In the house. You accepted the house even though you knew the will was a fraud. She never meant to ruin you. She just wanted you implicated so you'd keep quiet. She nearly managed it.'

'When I thought it was suicide,' I say. 'Not if it's murder.'

'Exactly,' says Barrett again. 'That's why I'm saying "nearly". And finally. This is the clincher, I hope. I'm pretty sure. But I need to check. Tabitha, have you got an order of service from Davey's funeral handy?'

'Why?' I ask.

'Just get me one if you saved any.'

Of course I have. I suppose I'll throw the spares out some day and keep just one tucked away with the rest of the family history. For now, there's a couple right there on the dresser shelf, peeping out from behind one of Auntie Rowan's willow pattern plates.

As I reach for it, I hear the kids thundering down the stairs and heading our way. I hesitate, but Barrett sees me and says, 'They're in on this too, Tab. I texted them. They're on the case.'

'Mum,' Albie says, 'did you know Uncle Johnny and Auntie Jo run an appliance servicing business?' I know my mouth has dropped open. 'Barrett told us to search for it. He knew!'

'Pretty cool, Dad,' says Sorrel.

'So they turned up . . .' I say. 'But how did they get in the door?'

'He must have been wearing some sort of disguise,' says Sorrel.

'But,' I say, 'surely his brother would still recognize him.' I'm holding the order of service, facedown. I don't want to see Davey right now. 'All of this is very . . . I mean, some of this seems quite likely . . . But Davey went in person to Tim Hawes, with the letter of confession, and the will, with the note along the bottom. Same handwriting. He went to Tim Hawes' office. Finally. After years of emailing. He drank a glass of—'

It hits me like a meteor.

'Johnny didn't go to the funeral,' Barrett says, 'because he knew Hawes would be there.' He nods at the paper that's now fluttering in my hand. 'You look at that,' he says.

I stare down at the photo on the front with his birth and death dates. Davey in his baseball cap and sunglasses, the newly dug haulm of spuds in perfect focus and him blurry as he grins in the background. I turn it over and there's the four of us kids in a row on the wall.

'Could you say for sure whose funeral that was?'

'No,' I tell him. 'It could easily be the man who went to Tim Hawes' office to drop off his will.' I rub my thumb over Johnny's smiling face as if I can obliterate him. 'Why?' I whisper.

'Now, listen to this,' Barrett says. 'And tell me I'm wrong. We know that Jo did her DNA because she pinged for Albie. We don't know *when* she did it. But let's assume she did it whenever Johnny did it. And let's assume that was ten years ago. Jo and

Johnny did their DNA and found out they weren't related. They killed Rowan to punish her for letting them believe they were siblings since they were sixteen.'

Gordo is nodding. 'It's what we said, Tab. It's the right brother.'

'And then what?' I say 'Davey got his done? And contacted them to tell them? Except they already knew?'

'That's not how it works,' says Sorrel. 'If Davey got his done he'd have found Johnny, if Johnny was in the system already. And he'd have found out that Jo was no relation. *And* he'd have known how long it was since *they'd* found out.'

'And then he put two and two together?' I say. 'The date they joined the database and the date his mother died? And he challenged them? Threatened them?'

'Not necessarily,' says Willow. 'Because he'd have pinged for them if he put *him*self into the database. They'd have found out he was on to them whether he told them or not.'

'Pinged?' I say. 'Like Jo pinged for you, Albie? So now they know *you're* on to them?' I stand and dart towards him, as if I can hide him from danger. As if he's a baby again.

'Never mind Albie,' says Barrett. '*I'm* on to them. They need to worry about me. He was my friend. I'm fucking well on to them.'

'That's right,' says Gordo. 'Me too.'

TWENTY-SEVEN

Tabitha

My mum spends all of pretty much every day in the studio, yards from me down here in the schoolhouse. So when she claims that the rest of this week is taken up with a Christmas shopping trip, a meeting with her agent, a festive lunch with the Historic Scotland buyer – 'he who leavens his gift shop tat with a soupçon of my work', as she puts it – and a hairdresser's appointment, I know she's avoiding me. She hasn't been to a hairdresser in my lifetime; she coats her mane in olive oil once a month and saws off the bottom few inches with kitchen scissors when it needs it. And she gave up buying Christmas presents when Jo left.

But she's definitely off somewhere.

'Just as well,' Barrett says. 'We can probably get them to the school easier than here.'

Which is exactly what we do. On the seventeenth of December, I phone Jo first thing in the morning. I don't have to fake the strain in my voice even though every word I say is a lie.

'I don't think it's her heart,' I say. 'And I don't think it's a stroke either. She's certainly not having any trouble talking.'

'What do you mean?'

'That's what makes me think she's really ill,' I say. 'Some of the stuff she's coming out with! Going back years.'

Gordo holds both thumbs up and I agree. I'm being so subtle.

'Are you taking her to the hospital?' Jo says. 'Which one?'

'She won't go,' I say. 'I've tried. She says she wants to die in her own bed but she needs to get it all off her chest before she goes.'

'Do you want me to come?' Jo says at last. Biting the fly I've tied and floated.

'Oh God, yes!' I say. The first true word of the call. 'That's why I'm phoning. Sorry. I mean, I should have . . . I would have phoned anyway, now that we're back in . . . Sorry! But yes, she's asking for you. Both of you. And she's quite distressed. Look, I'll go and see if she'll talk on the phone, will I?'

I start walking, hoping circuits of my kitchen will sound like a journey up the hard floor of the corridor towards the classrooms. Jo's on the move too, though.

'We'll come,' she says. 'What is it she's talking about? Johnny!'

'Week before Christmas, though,' I say. 'I know you must be busy. I'll hold the phone up to her mouth and—'

'Tab!' She says it so loud that I take my mobile away from my ear. 'We'll be there in an hour. Let her rest until then.' I can feel her thinking, down the line. 'Is it just you and her?'

That stops me walking. I put my finger to my lips to tell Gordo not to make a sound. Not that he has up till now. 'It's just the two of us,' I say. 'Albie's out for the day. He's not being heartless. He loves his granny, but he's just a kid and he's had a lot already, you know?'

'Right, right,' Jo says, the irritation in her voice telling me I've convinced her: she believes I'm prattling out of maternal guilt because my son's a jerk. 'An hour, Tabby. Let her rest, eh?'

Barrett arrives and assures me he has told all four kids to stay here in the house, doors locked, no matter what, until he, Gordo or me comes to tell them it's all over. 'I'm not sure they won't vaguebook,' he says. 'But I'm damn sure they won't come up and join in.'

We set off on foot to the school. It's what the old-timers in the valley used to call a wicked morning. The sky is low and black, like a headache on the hill, and the wind strikes like a vinegared tawse, making my hair sting my face. It's so cold there's not a whiff of life in the air, as if this umber grass and ochre bracken is a painting of nature, not nature itself. The old school sits in it like an etching, the playground, the stone walls, the blank glass, all leached of any colour by this pitiless day. Wicked indeed.

I let us all in, knowing she's gone yet still braced for her voice, confident and irritated, asking me what I'm doing here. But the house is empty, as dead as the world outside.

Then we wait. Gordo and me in the staffroom. Barrett in the head's office, a lamp on in the front classroom as if Zelda's in bed there, and every light in the studio off.

'Do you know you still call them classrooms and the staff-room?' Gordo says.

'And "girls" and "boys" instead of the front and back door,' I say. 'I know. And the playground and bike shelter instead of the garden and the shed. It started from the four of us playing at schools together – imagine how great it was! – and it stuck.'

'Except your mum's studio,' he points out.

'We never played in there.' I've had so much on my mind that I've barely thought about the Night Paintings since the news of how my dad actually died. Would I have been so frightened when I was tiny, if I hadn't believed she was painting a watery grave? If I hadn't assumed the diver eel was my daddy? There's no time to think about it now, because in spite of the wind howling in the flue and worrying at the window latches, we can both hear the car.

I don't go to the door and, believing there's an invalid inside, they don't clang the bell. They let themselves into the hallway and then into the staffroom.

Johnny frowns when he sees Gordo and turns to Jo as if there's something she can do about it.

'We've not met,' Gordo says, holding out his hand, 'but I've heard a lot about you.'

I can feel panic fermenting under my ribcage. But it works. Johnny comes right into the room, edging Jo aside, to share the handshake.

'How is she?' Jo asks, perching herself on the arm of the chair opposite me. She looks as if she's lost weight since the funeral. When she smiles, the lines bracketing her mouth make me think of piano strings and, by association, her voice sounds like a tuning fork.

'She's fine,' I say.

'Conscious?' says Jo. 'Talking?'

'Conscious,' I agree. 'Talking? Who knows. She's not here.'

'Hospital?' The tuning fork hums in a higher key.

'Change of plan,' I say. I lift the poker from beside my chair and thump it hard on the brass coal scuttle three times, as we agreed.

Through in the head's office, Barrett gets to his feet and opens the door. Before he's taken a step towards us, Johnny asks, 'Who's that?', as we hoped he would.

I bite my lip. If this doesn't work I don't know what our next move is. But I think it's going to work.

'Timothy Hawes,' I say. 'He wanted to meet—'

But Johnny's gone. He spins on the balls of his feet and flings himself out into the corridor and then out again.

'Hey!' Barrett's voice is loud and deep as he sets off in pursuit. Gordo's giving chase too. We can hear Johnny's boot soles ring out on the hard tarmac of the playground. Jo says nothing and neither do I until all three sets of footsteps have faded away.

'Idiot,' is what she chooses to break the silence. 'I've got the car keys. Where does he think he's going to go?' All I pray is that he goes straight past the schoolhouse or in the other direction entirely. Not that Barrett or Gordo would let him get inside. Should I dial 999? Will one of the men do it? '*You're* no fool, though,' Jo says next. 'I take it there's nothing wrong with Zelda after all?'

'What the hell happened, Jo?' I say to her. 'How did you end up here?'

'What do you already know?' she asks me.

'I know when Roddie died,' I tell her. 'How Rowan died. How Davey died.'

'But not why?' she says. As if it matters. As if there's any accounting for it.

'I know you ended my marriage,' I tell her.

'But not why,' she says again.

'Look,' I say. 'It's over. You must know th—'

'Don't!' she says. 'Don't you dare try to patronize me.' Then, as if someone's let her stopper out, she sinks back into the embrace of that same old armchair, like we're kids again. Like the dishes are done and we're waiting for the good telly to start after the news. She even tucks one foot up beside her, so her knee is next to her ear. 'Of course it's over,' she says to me. 'Do you know how "Dad" died?'

'Yes,' I say. 'But why's he in scare quotes? He's your dad even if he's not mine.'

She shakes her head and lets out a long, low, sarcastic chuckle, as if I've said I like a band I've never heard or I've said a rude word and pronounced it wrong.

'So you don't know at all.' She stares at me as if she's deciding whether to let me share a treat. Then she smacks her hands down on the arms of the chair and lifts herself up to let her get her feet more comfortable under her. 'Rowan killed him,' she says. 'Drugged him up and left him in the car on the railway line.'

'Left me too,' I say. 'If I was even . . . But how do you know?'

'She told us.'

'*What?* When?'

'After the wedding, when we came back for tea to try to calm things down. I think she told us to make us scared of her, so we'd annul, like she wanted us to.'

'Jesus Christ, it would have worked on me,' I say. 'How come it didn't work on you? If you knew she'd killed before.'

'Zelda told us not to worry,' says Jo. 'She said if we stayed away Rowan would leave us alone. She called it the magic of Hiskith. Said it worked both ways. If you stay up here other people forget how much they hate you. If you stay away people here forget you. She was right too.'

'But Rowan really killed Dad?' I say, when I can speak again.

'Oh definitely,' Jo says. 'Johnny thinks she killed Roddie too. Or drove him to it anyway. He always thought so. It's the main reason he wanted to get away as soon as possible. It's why we got married quite young.'

Quite? I must be showing my thoughts on my face, because she scowls.

'Can I remind you that we're still together, unlike you?' she snaps at me.

'Why didn't you just live together?' I ask her.

'Are you kidding? Rowan would have camped on our doorstep nagging us through the letterbox. Didn't you hear what I just told you? She tried to scare us into annulling a legal marriage, Tabitha. She'd have made our lives a misery if we were shacked up.'

'So . . . maybe she made up the story about killing people,' I say. 'To scare you.'

Jo shrugs. 'Davey knew she killed Dad,' she says. 'He never believed she killed Roddie, mind you. He always maintained that was men from the brickworks.'

'What? Why?' I say. 'I know the other men didn't think much of Dad and Roddie. Everyone says so. But why would they kill him? Or drive him to kill himself? That's insane.'

'That's miners for you,' says Jo. 'You remember '84?'

I stare at her a minute or two, half-bewildered but half-excited because I can feel understanding coming and I want to slow everything down to make sure and enjoy it. 'They weren't miners,' I say, rolling it round my mouth like a toffee. 'They were brickmakers.'

'For the colliery works,' says Jo. 'Big difference.'

And here it comes, crashing into my brain. There it is, taking up residence at last. In the winter of 1972, as in the discontented winter of 1978, and even more than those two put together, of course, in 1984, there was a coal strike. 'So . . . Dad and Roddie . . .?'

'Wouldn't picket,' says Jo. 'That's what Johnny tells me. Dad and Mum took off completely. They went on a trip to get away from all the aggro.'

Of course they did. I try not to react visibly, but inside I'm smacking my head with the heel of my hand. They went on a trip, and so they missed the aftermath of Roddie's death. 'Roddie just closed the curtains and pretended he wasn't in,' Jo goes on. 'It didn't go down too well with his old comrades, as you can imagine.'

'And Davey believed that one of them killed him for that?'

'Davey had some strange notions,' says Jo.

I find myself nodding. He not only thought a union man killed his father over a strike, he also believed the guy would come back one day. He saved DNA to try to catch him.

'Like I said,' she goes on, 'Johnny thinks it was Rowan. Not some angry miner from a too-thin picket line. And she definitely killed Dad. There's no denying that one.'

'And tried to kill me too?' I said. I can't get this new bombshell to stick. 'Why would she do that? Jo, was I really there? Or is that just another story?' Once again, I don't know anything. Even the new truth that I just got steady under me is rolling away. I press my back into the chair to keep myself from falling.

'Oh yes, you were there,' Jo says. 'Mum risked me being a full orphan to save you. That's true.'

'But why?' I ask her.

'Who knows,' says Jo. 'Because you look like her?'

'No, not that.' As if we need to ask why a mother would save her child! 'Why would Rowan try to kill us? Dad and me.'

'Because Mum was pregnant again. And Rowan had told him "no more". Ironic, eh?'

I try to echo the word, but I can't get enough breath together to make a sound. How could killing a man and attempting to kill a baby be 'ironic'? I always thought Jo was the balanced one, compared to me, but this conversation is unhinged. 'But that story isn't true,' I say. 'Rowan and Dad didn't make babies. The DNA proves it. If Albie's not related to Davey and you're not related to Johnny, then it's not true.'

'Oh come on!' Jo says, practically shouting. 'Catch up, Tabitha. Get a clue.'

But my brain feels like a snow globe, and I can only peer at her through the storm.

'It's true that we're not related,' she says. 'Johnny and me. Us and them. It was ten years ago we found out. When we did our DNA. But Rowan told us we were to stop the wedding.' She waits for a moment and then says, 'Come on, Tabitha!'

I can only shake my head. I'm completely bewildered.

Jo tuts and rolls her eyes. 'Rowan *thought* we were all siblings, because the man she *believed* was the father of the girls, she knew for a *fact* was the father of the boys. Zelda didn't disabuse her, although she knew better. That's why Zelda wasn't troubled by the thought of Johnny and me together.' She pauses and when she goes on her voice is light and chatty. 'We didn't work it all out until after Rowan had died, mind you.'

'Died,' I echo. I'm feeling stronger somehow. Maybe it's rage. '*Died?*'

'Nit-picker,' says Jo. 'OK, then. Until after we'd killed her. Simple mistake. Sort of thing that could happen to anyone.'

'Are you . . .?' I begin, but what would I even ask her. Insane? Drunk? Ill? High? 'You killed Rowan because she "lied to you",' I say, 'and then you found out she *wasn't* lying and that you'd killed her to pay her back for something she didn't actually do?'

'I'm not proud of it,' says Jo. 'But *c'est le mort.*'

I'm trying not to recoil from her, but her calm voice is making me feel dizzy. It's pitching me back to the days when everyone around me – even Elspeth sometimes – talked the wildest madness as if they were chatting about the weather.

'And yet you didn't kill Mum?' I say. You'd think I'd know better than to try to make sense of it. I was well-trained in nodding blandly, back on the ward. After the first time someone's come at you with a fork for not believing their claims, you pick it up quick enough.

'Zelda?' says Jo.

'She knew the truth and kept it from you.'

'She didn't try to stop us though,' Jo says. 'Zelda told us not to worry. Zelda told us to go and be happy. Zelda didn't bug us.'

Bug them. I'm trying to get my brain to open wide enough to swallow this horror the size of a house, this miserable impossible outrage the size of a mountain, the size of the moor.

'But you really did kill Rowan,' I say. 'You sedated her and took all her insulin away, just to be sure. In case she woke up.'

'She didn't.'

'And so ten years later when you wanted to kill Davey, you thought you'd tie the two together so that, if it started to unravel, his method of suicide would look like a confession.'

'Neat, eh?'

I can feel my stomach turn, taste bile in my throat. Neat. 'Why did you kill that poor dog?' I ask her.

'What poor dog?' says Jo. Then: 'Oh yeah! Christ, I'd forgotten about that bloody dog barking its head off.'

'Barrett thinks his wife shot her,' I say. 'He's been carrying that thought around for ten years, forced to be civil to her because of the shared custody. And it was you all along.'

'Jesus, Tabitha,' she says. 'What do you think I am?'

'I think you're the person who killed Auntie Rowan,' I say. 'Over a misunderstanding.'

'And it could have ended there if Davey hadn't started watching genealogy programmes on some budget streaming service. Or afternoon talk shows. Or whatever it was that got him off stamps and litter and on to his family tree.'

'*You* did it,' I remind her.

'Oh give me a break! I did it as an early warning system. A canary in the coalmine. So if Zelda or you or your kid or Davey ever took it into your head, we'd know. And of course it was bloody Davey.'

'Bloody Davey,' I say.

'Exactly,' says Jo. She either doesn't hear my heart breaking or she can't recognize the sounds of love and pain living where she lives now. 'He phoned up all excited, telling us we were free! Free at last!' Her face clouds briefly, remembering.

'But why didn't you just pretend it was an amazing surprise when he told you?'

'Too many loose ends. Couldn't be bothered dealing with any of them.'

'Loose ends?'

'Such as whatever havoc Zelda might wreak to stop her shabby little truths coming out.' She shakes her head briskly 'He had to go.'

'And if it *had* been Zelda?' I said. 'Or me, or "my kid"?'

But she's not listening. 'And that's where you came in. We had to get you willing to benefit and keep schtumm no matter what you found in this house as you cleared it.'

'Why couldn't *you* clear it?' I said. 'If Johnny hadn't written that fake will, he'd have inherited everything and I'd have lived my life.'

'Because Davey "confessing" to killing his mother and then "killing himself" is one thing if his heiress is as clean as a whistle. It's quite another thing if his heir is guilty of two murders. Tell the truth, Tabby; would you have kept quiet about any of this if you didn't need the house for Albie?'

I try to be honest with myself. Would I have accepted the story of suicide if Jo and Johnny had come out of the woodwork to scoop Davey's estate?

'Enter brilliant me and my brilliant scheme to make you so complicit that you'd tidy up after us and take it to your grave.'

Jo smiles at me. She's beyond calm now. She sounds happy. She sounds overjoyed. Tell the truth, Tabitha. She sounds crazy. As I'm trying to work out what to say to her, I hear the sound of the playground gate and heavy steps, as if someone's running but so slow and exhausted it's like a death knell.

'Here we go,' says Jo, standing up and shaking her legs to get rid of the pins and needles. She always sat curled up like that and her legs went numb every time. It never stopped her. She's so relaxed she barely flinches when Gordo bursts in, drenched from head to toe and panting so hard he can't catch his ragged breath to tell us what's wrong. He just stands there squeezing the chair back with one hand, pointing wildly behind him with his free arm as he hangs his head.

'Right,' says Jo, and walks steadily out into the hall.

'What is it?' I say. 'Are the kids OK?'

'He's in the loch,' Gordo manages to get out at last.

'Albie!' I yelp. 'Oliver?'

'Johnny. He ran down to the edge and kept going. He walked into the loch. I went after him. Barrett went in.'

'No!' I say. I'm running before I know I am, outside into the wind and the searing cold, out of the gate and galloping down the hill to the water. I overtake Jo almost immediately. She's making a steady pace, with her hands jammed in her pockets and her shoulders round her ears, but she's not racing like me.

'He's not . . .' Gordo pants at me as he catches up. But I've seen him. I've seen both of them. Barrett is knee-deep at the edge, just beyond the big boulders that mark off the car park. He's standing with a looped rope in his hands, watching Johnny.

Johnny is just a blob of dark, his head turned away from us, as he swims for the middle of the reservoir, the deep water. I clutch at Gordo's fingers and the chill of them shocks me. How can Johnny be swimming? How much longer can he keep going in that pitiless freezing black water?

'Barrett, come out!' I say, cupping my hands. 'There's no point. He's gone too far.'

When Jo catches up and walks right in, clambering over the rocks and ploughing ahead as the water rises to her knees, I think she's going to take the rope and try to shout to Johnny but she keeps on going, up to her thighs, then her waist, up to her chest, and then under. She comes up, slick and dark, her hair plastered over her shoulders, and strikes out, her arms in thick coat sleeves clumsy and useless, blatting the water up in spouts.

'Noooooo!' I scream. '*Joooooooo!*' But Gordo's got a tight hold round my waist in his shaking, soaking arms, his cold jelly fingers laced together. 'Barrett!' I wail. 'Stop her!'

For one moment, Jo turns back to face me. I don't know if the way her arm moves is just another stroke to get her out to where Johnny is waiting, or if she's saying goodbye. I pick uselessly at Gordo's hands, but he won't let go. Even when Barrett stumbles on the rocks as he's clambering out, Gordo keeps me locked in his arms instead of going to help his friend.

I look back at the water.

Johnny's head is no longer visible.

Jo keeps swimming.

And then she stops.

And then she's gone.

I turn away, dragging Gordo round with me, facing into the bite of the wind and the start of a squall of freezing hail and, over the sound of the gale rising and Gordo's teeth chattering and the unstoppable keening noise that's coming from me, I can still hear sirens. I look up and see the upstairs front windows of Davey's house, all four of them standing there, two boys and two girls, watching. Albie's got his phone at his ear and he's talking to someone; must be the cops or maybe the paramedics who're cresting the ridge right now. They look quite different, those four framed in the window, looking out at Hiskith Water. A mobile phone, blonde hair, a pale puffy face. They're completely different from the first four. I hold on hard to here and now, to real and true. Albie, Oliver, Sorrel and Willow. Barrett and Gordo. And me.

TWENTY-EIGHT

Tabitha

January

T he house is so drab now that we've taken down the
Christmas trees, the lights, the swags of holly, strings of
cards, velvet bows and glass icicles. God knows what
Gordo's place looks like. It hasn't got the glittering frosty loch
outside and the icy blue sky. But Gordo's not there to see it and
he won't care even when he gets out. I still can't believe they're
only keeping him in two nights. Oliver's recovery will be much
slower. But the procedure went smoothly and the signs are
hopeful. Barrett and I might even be able to suit up and see the
boy later today, take good news back to Gordo's bedside in a
different ward.

There's something I need to do first. I shouldn't have left it
this long. But there was Jo and Johnny, and keeping the press
away from this latest thrilling chapter in the saga of the Muirs
of Hiskith, making sure the kids had a good Christmas, especially
Oliver. And then there was making sure Oliver didn't feel us
making it especially for him. And a deluge of paperwork from
Scottish Water and the council, since they've definitely decided
to drain the loch and plant up amenity woodland, rushing it
through between Christmas and New Year, hoping no one would
notice until it was a fait accompli. There was even the first
Christmas managing to share custody with an ex-husband, which
wasn't nothing. Also, I've been grieving. She was my sister. He
was my cousin. I'm the only one left now.

But today's the day. My boot soles ring out on the iron ground
and my breath plumes and drifts in the creaking stillness of this
cruel frost, as I go to stand by the water for my morning . . . I
suppose prayer. There's a lacy edge to the loch as the ice creeps
inwards. It's never frozen over in my lifetime, but perhaps when

it's drained down to a little pond at the bottom of a wooded dell, we'll be able to skate there.

I turn away and start to climb the track past the old school-house and on towards the school itself. No child of Hiskith village trudging ever closer to a day of stifling boredom and sudden punishments can ever have felt more reluctance than I do now.

I don't know how I missed all the signs of her poverty: the heating turned down; the paint tubes squeezed dry; the empty shelves in the fridge. More than that, I should have seen the worry on her face, the way she gripped the arms of her chair and the way she clenched her jaw. I thought she was being bohemian. I thought she was striking poses at me.

I make for the studio and so I startle her, of course. She's used to a bit of shuffling and a tentative knock, not to me marching in as if I've every right to be there. But she doesn't try to chuck me out again. And she doesn't start throwing dust sheets over her paintings either. She stays behind the easel and waits to hear what I've got to say.

'Who's my biological father?' I ask her. 'Let's start there.'

'Ah,' she replies. 'I see. It's come to that, has it?' Of course, she's going to be drawling and lofty. Of course she is. As if I could be fooled that she's above all this when she's lived a lie for so long, to keep it secret. 'The thing is, Tabitha, I did love your father. Watson, I mean. I did love him. I appreciated his breadth of vision. I didn't hesitate when he and Roddie decided they wanted to move up here to Hiskith and have a different kind of life. It was glorious! I was his loudest advocate and cheerleader.'

She pauses. I wait.

'But,' she goes on, in the end, 'he wasn't good stock, you see. Neither of them was. Roddie started to unravel almost immediately under the bullying of those brickworks thugs, and your father became more and more peculiar. I didn't want to leave him. I couldn't have walked away from this studio once I'd found it. And I did so want a child. But, when I considered your dad's moods and dark times and imagined the possibility of children with the same affliction . . . Well. It seemed a far better idea to do what I did. I chose a man not dissimilar in appearance. But as steady as the Rock of Gibraltar. He was the stationmaster at

Sanquhar. Long gone now. He and his wife and their two children. He's probably a grandfather.'

'He's definitely a grandfather,' I say. 'Albie.' She inclines her head to acknowledge the point. 'And is he both our dads? Is that how you say that? It sounds weird.'

'Father of all three,' says Zelda. 'Most obliging. And as healthy as a horse. So,' she goes on, 'although I try to avoid motherly interfering, as you know, I will say this. Choose wisely, Tabitha. If you're thinking of it again.'

'Hang on,' I say. 'You think you're changing the subject to me re-marrying and having more babies? You think we're finished talking? Seriously?' I take a moment to gather myself. 'Mum, why didn't you tell Rowan, before the wedding? That there was no problem with Jo and Johnny getting married? That they were no relation?'

For the first time, she looks discomfited. 'Rowan would have been unbearable,' she says. 'Her bourgeois sensibilities would have been completely unable to cope with such news.'

'Rowan,' I remind her, 'knocked off her brother-in-law for years. And murdered him. Her bourgeois sensibilities were all smoke and mirrors. What was the real reason?'

'You're wrong,' she says. 'All Rowan ever cared about was the look of things. She hid the fact that Roddie was dead to avoid our pity. She got herself a pair of sons and didn't care how, as long as no one knew. She got over Jo and Johnny marrying as soon as they said they were moving away. Such a strange woman.'

I stare at her for a while, the bit of her that I can see over the top of the easel. She skirted the truth there. Rowan would have been beyond my *mum*'s capacity to bear, if she'd found out about the stationmaster. She'd have been on level-pegging after years of feeling second best. They'd have been in the same boat. A pair of slappers. I can see why it suited much better to raise an eyebrow at the shrieking and pretend to take the incest in her stride, making Rowan feel more 'bourgeois' than ever. But does she really think the hypocrisy is lost on me?

'Will you stay?' I ask her. It's what I wondered all the years I thought my dad drowned in the loch. How could she bear to be here? To paint it? Now that her daughter really has slipped under those freezing waters and died, can my mother stay on? I stare at the back of the canvas that's hiding her from me, feeling a worm of unease wriggling away deep down in my belly, not understanding why.

But now her head is round the side of the easel and she's staring at me with eyebrows raised so high it makes her spectacles fall from where they've been perched on top of her head. 'Stay?' she says. 'Of course I'll stay. This is my home and where I work. This studio is part of my body. And this place is my inspiration. How could I carry on if I didn't stay?'

'But will you paint the loch?' I say.

Her eyes flick to the canvas she's working on. 'Not any more,' she says. 'They're draining it. The explosion caused a structural shift. Didn't you get the letter?'

I did but it's not like Zelda to read junk mail. I must have been hoping it wasn't true, this thing I've worked out, because as she confirms it I feel sadness wash over me. 'It's to be woodland,' she's saying now. 'So I shall paint that. I've started already.' Then, unbelievably, she beckons me. To the other side of the easel, to look at what she's making.

It's a Night Painting. Gaunt, dead-looking trees tugging the black ground and the black sky together. Like Frankenstein stitches, I used to think. But they're more like giant staples.

'I've seen this already,' I say. 'Months ago. Before Davey's funeral. Before Albie came.'

'Nonsense,' she says. 'This is the start of a new series, for after the reservoir drains and the woods are planted.'

'I saw it before,' I tell her.

'I sometimes regret my single-mindedness,' she says. 'I devoted myself to my work and made sure domestic trivia didn't take over my life. Now I see that if I'd shared more with you, educated you, I wouldn't have a daughter who can't tell one painting from another. It's called an oeuvre, Tabitha. I do regret not imparting that.'

'Oh, that's what you regret, is it?' I say. 'From all that's on offer, *that*'s what's bothering you?' Then I walk away from her until the canvas is between us. I tap it on the blank side. 'You were upset,' I say. 'You were gesturing wildly. You dragged the ends of your hair in your paint and flicked it off when you turned your head away. It landed on the canvas. You started this painting months ago, Mum. I saw it through the window.'

'Rather a grubby thing to do, peeping in at windows.'

'No!' I say. 'You don't get to look down your nose at me anymore. You don't get to call me grubby. Not when you started your new woodland series of jigsaws and tea towels three months before they even decided to drain it, Mum.' She is so still that if I couldn't see her feet I'd imagine she'd been spirited away. 'Say it,' I tell her.

'I can't imagine what you're—'

'Say it,' I tell her again. 'Or I'll say it. Only *I'll* say it in Kirkconnel police station. And once I've said that I might carry on and say everything.'

She sighs and I can tell from the sound of it, the exaggeration, the groan at the back of it, that she's going to play this as a comedy. 'Oh very well!' she says. 'Yes, I helped things along a bit. How could I have known what else was happening?'

'You tried to blow up the dam, to force the decision to drain the loch, to help you market a new line of aprons and coasters?'

'Paintings,' she says, bitterly. 'I am an artist who makes paintings. The licensing of my art is another matter entirely.'

'Mum,' I say, and as the word comes out I realize it's probably the last time I'm ever going to call her that, 'they only chalked up Davey dying to suicide because there was a motive right outside his door. If you had come clean that morning, none of this . . . Jo might . . . Jo could—'

'Jo could be in prison. I could be in the next cell,' she says. 'What a marvellous chance to spend some time together after our estrangement.'

I wait to see if she's going to say any more but the next sound I hear is her brush dabbing at the palette and then dabbing at the canvas and so I leave her to it and walk away.

With the perfect timing that I am starting to believe is psychic, I see Barrett's car come over the tops as I let myself out of the playground gates. So, instead of trying to walk on my trembling legs, I wait for him to catch up to me.

He's grinning as if to make it meet round the back as he slows and slides the window down. 'You'll have to sit in the back, Tab!' he shouts to me. I see why as I get in. There's a dog sitting upright in the front passenger seat, turning now to regard me with mild interest. It's a Labrador, I think, or something like that. Mostly black but with a white muzzle and with that thick, barrelly body that meets most Labs in their middle age.

'This is your post-Christmas surprise?' I say. I knew the girls were planning something.

'This is her!' Barrett says, ruffling the old dog's ears so boisterously she has to brace herself.

'Why didn't they get you a pup?'

Barrett is almost at the car park now. I take it he's meaning to turn there and set straight off for the hospital. But he parks, puts the handbrake on and twists round until he's facing me.

'Tabitha,' he says. 'This is Bess.'

'How . . .?' I begin. But of course the answer is those girls. Those resourceful, irrepressible, unstoppable girls. I told them all every word Jo said to me on that last day, including when she chided me for accusing her of drowning a dog. Willow and Sorrel didn't need any more encouragement, Barrett tells me now. Armed with the date and an unshakable belief that life was going to be good to them, they pulled off a miracle.

'Bess!' I say and her tail thumps twice.

'Nearly thirteen but in fine fettle,' says Barrett. 'The people she's been with are going to keep in touch but they made no trouble. Not when they saw her greet me.'

He gets out and lets Bess out too, watching her climb down stiffly and shake herself before she goes for a sniff at the dead weeds edging the car park. It might be the bitter wind, but Barrett's eyes are streaming as he watches her squat to pee.

'My mum set the stuff to try and blow up the dam,' I say.

'I knew it wasn't Davey,' says Barrett. Then: 'What are you going to do?'

I don't answer because I don't know. She didn't succeed, after all. And she didn't kill anyone. She saved someone. She saved me. But can I live here with her so close and so unchanging? So untouched? Her lights shining in my windows and mine in hers?

I look out over the water, wondering. It doesn't look like a mirror today. I suppose it never did. And there's no one lost in it. They tried to bring Jo and Johnny up straight away, divers going down in pairs on short rotation, sitting wrapped in electric blankets in between times. But we had to wait until the bodies resurfaced on their own, days later. I managed not to see it and managed to keep Albie from seeing it. Now I wish I had. Surely the truth couldn't have been worse than what I'm imagining.

'How are you?' Barrett says.

'Confused,' I tell him. 'I still love it here and that makes me think I'm a monster.'

'Away!' Barrett says. 'You've deep ties. That's all. No such thing as a life that's all daisies and no dung.' I have no idea if that's a saying or just a Barrett saying but it makes me laugh. 'Besides,' he goes on, 'the girls love it too. So I'm biased.'

Something in his voice makes me look up at him. He grimaces. 'Portugal's beginning to look permanent, and I need all the help I can get to make that pair choose Kirkconnel instead.'

'Like Gordo and Oliver too,' I say. 'Have you heard anything? They can't just whisk him off again after this, can they?'

'Not if he's got anything to do with it,' Barrett says. 'Of course, it might be three ready-made pals and a dad fighting his corner that weighs heaviest with him, but I've seen the look in his eyes when he's up here. Puts me in mind of Davey. And you've got it too.'

'Not difficult on a day like this,' I say, letting my gaze roam over the far bank, the smudged purple and bruised blue of the hills and the sky, the water glittering like spangles. The hush of the cold, still morning

'Or a night like last night,' Barrett says. 'Beautiful clear night and that's my favourite face of the moon.'

I turn to him and whisper, 'What did you just say?'

'What?' he says, with half his attention on Bess lumbering back towards him, probably wanting into the warm car and off this cold ground. 'I like that new crescent moon best of all, even more than full.'

'You said the face of the moon? I thought it was just me who believed there was more than one face in the moon.'

He looks away from Bess at last. 'Phase, Tabitha,' he says. 'There's four phases. Crescent, half, gibbous and full.'

I laugh and laugh and laugh. I can't believe what I'm hearing. I can't believe how much I'm still capable of learning. Like: I didn't inherit mental illness from my father. Like: I didn't almost drown. And now this: I'm not the only one who doesn't get to meet the whole moon family.

'What?' Barrett asks me. 'What have I said? What's so funny?'

'You don't happen to know of a cartoon cat with an undecidable name, do you?' I ask him.

'That poem where they've all got three?'

'No, not them. This one's definitely a cartoon.'

He thinks about it quite seriously for a minute, which sets me off laughing all over again, and then he says, 'When we were wee there was a programme called *Boss Cat* about a cat called Top Cat. I never understood why. Did you?'

'No,' I say. 'But thinking about it saved me, plenty nights when I might have got lost forever if I hadn't had something to concentrate on.'

'Aye well,' says Barrett, opening the door and putting his forearm against Bess's backside to help shove her up and in. 'We all need a wee bit saving sometimes.' He grins at me. 'And there's no Jesus at the mo.'

FACTS AND FICTIONS

There is no such place as Hiskith Water in the hills between Kirkconnel and Muirkirk and, as far as I know, no Scottish reservoirs have whole villages at the bottom, although there's the odd submerged church. I used the public consultation documents about and press reporting upon the future of Roughrigg as a guide to what might happen when a disused reservoir needs expensive maintenance, but all the events in the book are fictional.

The police station in Kirkconnel is out of operation, as Gordo thought it would be, and none of the officers depicted here are based on Police Scotland personnel. Neither are the Muirs anything to do with the McPhersons, thankfully.